# Razarkha's Ruination
## Matthew J. Dave

# Table of Contents

| | |
|---|---:|
| Prologue | 3 |
| 1: Fears | 8 |
| 2: Arrangements | 19 |
| 3: Monsters | 32 |
| 4: Renewals | 49 |
| 5: Convergences | 66 |
| 6: Afflictions | 78 |
| 7: Outsiders | 98 |
| 8: Acquaintances | 114 |
| 9: Wanderers | 132 |
| 10: Siblings | 148 |
| 11: Destinations | 159 |
| 12: Secrets | 172 |
| 13: Invasions | 188 |
| 14: Follies | 205 |
| 15: Reflections | 219 |
| 16: Rebels | 231 |
| 17: Shadows | 243 |
| 18: Trails | 256 |
| 19: Murmurings | 270 |
| 20: Confrontations | 282 |
| 21: Severances | 298 |
| 22: Farewells | 311 |
| Epilogue | 323 |
| Afterword from the Sovereign | 331 |
| Appendix I: Map of the World | 338 |
| Appendix II: Races of the World | 339 |

# Special Thanks

Thank you to Jimi Simmonds, for making the map and creating this vast world alongside me, as well as pointing out worldbuilding issues when they come up.

Additional thanks to Milly, Sara and Nino for sticking with the series throughout its creation. A further thank-you as always to Nino for the fantastic covers.

# Prologue

Rakh Fel'thuz sat beside his sister-wife as she lay broken and bloodied in Wisdom Waldon's recovery bed. She was still breathing, but fortunately for him, wasn't awake. The infant that came out of her was blue-faced, and no matter what Waldon tried, it refused to cry, to move, to do anything but hang limply in the accoucheur's arms.

The wisdom had fled the room to try more desperate means of resuscitation, but Rakh knew it was another failed attempt at a legitimate child. He was only eighteen, and every day he cursed his father for leaving the family's headship to him at such a young age. Husband or not, Rakh didn't command the necessary respect to curb Razarkha's worst impulses.

It was his duty to at least try. The lifelessness of the baby's fuchsia eyes haunted him, pricking his anxiety-riddled brain while the anticipation of Razarkha's awakening swirled about like a melted daemon in a tar pit. All at once, the daemon reformed, tentacles spread and vicious, as Razarkha's voice tore him from his mind's hypothetical horrors.

"Why can't I hear crying? Where is he?" she said in a rare gentle, uncertain tone.

Rakh met his sister's eyes and took in her face. For a moment, she was just a mother filled with protective fear, not the image-obsessed, arrogant peacock he knew her as. He couldn't bring himself to tell her the truth, yet his sister pushed further.

"Where's our son, Rakh? *Where is he?*"

"He wasn't breathing," Rakh said, his voice giving way to tears. "I'm so sorry."

Rakh expected her to scream. Instead, she stared at the ceiling, her arms falling slack. Her pale face was expressionless, yet she filled the air with an inescapable dread.

"I wanted to call him Razander," she muttered.

"I know," Rakh said, offering a hand she was swift to pull away from.

"This isn't the time for empty comfort," Razarkha said, a familiar venom returning to her voice. "Razander was alive. He was healthy. Waldon killed him deliberately, this time I'm sure of it."

"I was there, he was trying everything to make him—"

"What would you know about medicine?" Razarkha asked. "For all you know, he could have been feigning the effort. You've seen Lord Nemeron and little Lady Kagura. What happens if we Fel'thuzes don't have an heir? The wisdom rules the city."

Rakh covered his face. He'd just lost a son, and without a minute's rest, Razarkha was back to her bitter paranoia, using her grief as an excuse to sow further discord. Father would have known what to do, but Rakh was practically a child in adult's clothing.

"Don't ignore me," Razarkha snapped. "Waldon's trying to cut the Fel'thuz family short, and now he's stooped to killing a child. *Our* child. If you, with your able body, won't take vengeance for Razander, I will."

Rakh stood. "I can't believe you. We've just lost a son, and instead of grieving, you just want more death. I know you're angry, but I'm grieving too. I'm not going to waste time listening to your poison."

As Rakh made his way to the room's exit, Razarkha raised her voice. "Where are you going? Don't you dare leave this castle! Don't leave me! You're going to a tavern, aren't you? *Aren't you?* If you leave me, you'll be the next to die at my hand! Do you hear me? *Rakh!*"

Count Fel'thuz left the room and wandered through the cold, ilmenite halls of Castle Selenia until Razarkha's screams became faint. He considered teaching himself sound-based illusionism; if there was anything that could help him get over another lost child, it'd be a way to deafen their venomous mother.

* * *

Two days had passed since Waldon had lost the latest Fel'thuz child. He hunched over his desk, staring at the piled-up, sealed letters cluttering it. A faint buzz in his head consumed every attempt to continue his duties. The window beckoned to him once again; he'd been a wisdom in his own right for over a decade, yet he still failed to save Razarkha's children. First, he failed her mother, then he failed her again and again.

The Selenias' and Fel'thuzes' insistence on maintaining 'pure' blood didn't help their fertility problems, but he could hardly blame the nobles without coming up a head short. Then again, when the window was so enticing, what threat did losing his head present? Without knocking, somebody barged into Wisdom Waldon's study, the pompous tone of his voice immediately recognisable.

"Waldon, have you caught up with the mail yet? If Moragar Foenaxas has made any more passive aggressive remarks, I want to know, and it's your duty to ensure every piece of information you can glean reaches me."

"You're literate, perhaps you can read the letters," Waldon mumbled, before his throat tightened at the realisation that he'd said his thoughts aloud.

*"What did you say?"* Lord Nemeron asked, his great strides impossible to ignore.

The high elf was a towering man with long, pale blonde hair and sapphire-blue eyes. What he lacked in musculature he made up for in sheer height, as well as a ridiculously expansive cape as dark blue as the night sky. Behind him was his favourite daughter, Kagura, a young rendition of the lord's late wife, black-haired and red-eyed. Waldon's words wedged in his throat, but after a few false starts, he managed to splutter something out.

"What I mean to say, my lord, is that I'm currently too emotionally compromised to perform my duties, and perhaps it would be better if, temporarily, you take over my duties of letter-reading and writing."

Nemeron snorted. "If a farmer asked the same of me, do you think I'd oblige?"

Waldon lowered his head. "No."

"I'm the lord, which means I delegate. You read and write in exchange for a privileged spot within this castle. Consider yourself lucky I didn't replace you the moment you lost my lady love. Razarkha Fel'thuz has had countless miscarriages, what's another dead infant? Get over yourself and *get back to work.*"

"I'm sorry," Waldon mumbled. "You're right, it's selfish of me."

"Open a letter, right now, prove that you can."

Waldon soullessly broke the white seal of a rolled-up letter, then after a quick scan, reported, "It's a letter from Lord Morris Gemfire, asking him if you can add pecan pies to the banquet in your upcoming naming-day celebration."

"See? That was easy. I'll leave you to write back telling him I'd be glad to, unless that's too difficult to perform without supervision."

Waldon stared through the paper. "I'll write it."

As the lord left, young Kagura approached his desk and patted Waldon's balding head.

"Don't worry, Wally. Even if the baby left for the moon, Countess Razarkha didn't leave too. She can try again and again until a baby stays here. Will mother ever come back down? I would like a brother soon, and Aunty Dina is married to that Boathis man."

"Leave me to my work, little lady," Waldon said, and the girl paused, then poked his sagging cheek.

"You'll be all right, Wally. When I'm lady, I'll make sure you have a clever novice to train before you have to go to the moon too."

With that, the little girl rushed out of the room, and Waldon shut the door behind her. Once it was closed, melancholy consumed the wisdom. Why had opening letters and writing responses become so hard? He knew the relevant political sensitivities, he was a handy diplomat when necessary, and he knew which of his lord's interests were worth upholding and which could be compromised on. His only obstacle was sheer, unending misery. He wandered to the ever-beckoning window and opened it. For a moment, he thought he heard the creaking of a doorframe, but when he checked, his door was still closed, albeit somewhat blurred.

Tears were in his eyes, Waldon realised. He lingered by the wide-open window, listened to the howling, high winds of Moonstone, letting the chill blister his ears and scalp. He leaned forward and beheld the courtyard beneath him. Servants moved to and fro, tending to the greenhouses while soldiers patrolled. His body would be discovered quickly.

As he moved his leg over the windowsill, the soft, youthful face of the little lady flickered before him. She would need advice, and he owed it to her to train a novice before he let himself die. He brought himself back into the room with a shiver, telling himself one word.

"No."

Away from the winds, Waldon was able to hear something quieter within his office. It resembled wet, ragged breathing, despite the room supposedly containing nothing but books, dust, and himself. Waldon made to close the window, before he noticed, in the corner of his eye, a glimmer. Before he could react, he was shoved backwards by an invisible assailant, and in moments, he was plummeting to the courtyard below.

# ears

To Razarkha's surprise, her influence still lingered in the ninth-hour outer city sector of Demidium. While she kept herself concealed due to only having the augmented Duncan Godswater to protect her, the scene was well worth the telekinesis sapping away her remaining days. A trio of augmentees protected a crowd of humans as they laid waste to the towers that once defined the coastal sector.

Ascendants were thinning their ranks from afar, as though Praetor Erre's massacres had reminded them that they too were mortal. If ascendants were living as though a soulstealer was around every corner, then she'd done something of worth. Pain shot through what remained of Razarkha's abdomen as the pair floated above the shattered streets, causing her cloaking to falter. She must have noticeably winced, as Duncan made a remark.

"Are you sure Demidium is the best place to escape Galdus from? Moneri has a western port too—"

"From here, we can restock at the Jaranese archipelago, instead of spending who knows how long on the sea before reaching Elarond," Razarkha replied. "Regardless, there's likely more ships to commandeer—"

"We're both levitating," Duncan pointed out. "We don't need a ship to cross the ocean, nor are we particularly hungry beings. There's no way you can eat with *that* for a stomach."

Razarkha touched the warm, glowing stone that kept her broken body together, and glimmers of a brown-haired spellbinder boy with orange eyes drifted beside her. It was just her illusionism slipping up again, but perhaps the bloody scene beneath her was equally illusory. Remembering that Ariel was unaffected by her abilities, she turned to Duncan, pushing down the lancing pain where her womb once was.

"Beneath us, there are humans fighting ascendants, aren't there?"

"Is this some sort of test?" Duncan asked.

"No. I just need confirmation."

Every time Razarkha had an exchange with Duncan, it felt distinctly wrong. For some reason, she should have been shifting her tongue constantly, not speaking in plain Common. A boyish, slurred Isleborn voice clouded her ears as her augmentee responded.

*"Sorry, could you say that again?"* Razarkha asked in Isleborn.

Instead of a face, Duncan had two glowing redstone orbs upon an obsidian shard, yet confusion was palpable in his rocky, scraping voice.

"Did you just speak Ilazari? I don't know what you just said."

"I told you to say what you said again, obviously," she snapped.

Duncan let silence linger before saying, "Obviously. I told you that yes, there are riots down there. It seems you've inspired quite the movement, though they're probably doomed."

Razarkha watched another tower collapse at the humans' hands, while the ascendants kept staying back. This couldn't have been her legacy. Despite all she'd built up, Darvith obliterated her true devotees, and after her miraculous escape, she killed the conglomerate ascendant alone. Images of purple-and-red portals and squatting Ilazari spellbinders plagued her peripheral vision, causing her cloaking to fail while her telekinesis held.

"You're not real, you're not real, you're not real," she babbled, and Duncan was quick to provide commentary.

"Who are you talking to? I'm grateful that you killed Argentus, but I'm starting to fear that—"

"Shut up, I'm stable, I'm perfectly stable!" Razarkha snapped, pointing her soulstealer at Duncan. "We're going to Arkhera together. We're going to take our vengeance, and you're going to enjoy it as much as I will. Just think of our traitorous brothers coughing up blood, begging for mercy that'll never come! You *need me.*"

"In that case, can you look down there for a moment?" Duncan asked, pointing his white-hot hand towards the western coastline of Demidium.

Almost none of the towers were standing anymore, and in the sea, metallic ships drifted towards Demidium's piers, bearing familiar orange flags with red insignias. From the closest of the invading hulks of steel and steam, swarms of men poured into the streets.

Razarkha's memories recobbled themselves. Though one name still evaded her, she remembered the mocking words of Hildegard Swan and her ascended pet, Anya Kasparov. She recalled the monstrous ship-mounted cannons that forced her surrender. For reasons she forgot, she had demanded the God of Chaos to serve her, but even they feared the Soltelle fleet.

"What are those? If they're ships, they're nothing like what I've seen before."

"It's the Soltelle Empire," Razarkha muttered. "We can't take a ship after all, I can't risk being spotted. We'll float above the battle and carry on to Jaranar."

"Why is that? Don't the Soltelles want the same thing as you?"

"It's a long story, let's stop dawdling and move west before they spot us!" Razarkha commanded.

The pair continued their flight above the ruined megalopolis, and though Razarkha had regained control of her cloaking, she felt the Yukishimans' eyes on her while mocking apparitions of Rakh appeared over the horizon. She could have sped up if she burnt more souls, but she knew she was simply paranoid; the Yookies couldn't see her, no more than any other army. Their hostility was likely as imagined as the miles-long, extremely distant Rakh, and she'd make it to the sea in no time.

"Razarkha, I don't mean to doubt that you're hiding us, but the Yookies down there are looking straight at us. I may be made of rock, but I don't fancy taking a volley from their fancy guns," Duncan remarked.

Razarkha's crystalline abdomen seared her extant flesh, causing her flight to falter.

*"You're lying, they can't see us, I know what I'm casting!"* she screamed in Isleborn, salving her agony with each strained vocal cord.

"I'm going to speed ahead, you just— catch up when you can."

"Oh no, you're not running away. Rowyn and Ariel abandoned me too— *Duncan!*"

The augmentee blasted ahead, leaving Razarkha no choice but to push ahead too. She could feel the souls within her withering away more viscerally now that she was powered by them, and maintaining this speed filled her with inescapable dread.

By the time the Yukishimans opened fire, they were long gone, soaring above the Jaranese Sea. As her view shifted from ruination to unspoilt tropical waters, Razarkha's shadow shuddered above the waves, and Darvith's green eyes shone from beneath the water.

*"You didn't think your legacy kept the ascendants afraid, did you?"* it asked in scornful Old Galdusian.

*"It was too good to be true,"* Razarkha admitted.

*"The Soltelles are more terrifying than you'll ever be. That's why you and Weil bowed to their whims."*

Razarkha's words halted in her mouth. Weil wasn't real. No matter how surreal her Galdusian campaign was, the notion that somebody loved her was too much to accept.

"Are you all right?" Duncan asked. "We made it past those imperialist scumbags, we're safe now. We can take whatever we need from Jaranar, then head back to Arkhera."

Razarkha lifted her gaze from the churning depths and smiled at Duncan. "Yes. First Petyr Godswater, then Rakh."

\* \* \*

Rowyn Khanas's legs were growing numb from standing around in blue and yellow Jaranese finery, but the day was still young. Surrounding him were the partially sheltered walls of a new shrine being built in honour of the whistling aeromantic augmentee beside him. Since settling on Jaranar and learning the language, Ariel had taken to draping herself in tassels that fluttered within her body's cyclones. Moss and lichens were growing on her shoulders, and though she'd attempted to grow a flower upon her head, her rocky, windy nature wasn't conducive to growing anything but the hardiest of plants.

Jaranese men would arrive with tributes, questions, or simple compliments for Ariel to address, and so it repeated until the sun set. While Rowyn had initially acted as an intermediary for her, the longer he stayed in Ma-Hith, the more he felt like a leech, accepting food and shelter from the generous people of Jaranar without offering anything of substance.

Occasionally he would assist in rigging a ship, and sometimes he operated on injured sailors, but oftentimes his calls to action would be silenced by a god-fearing human insisting that such 'busywork' was beneath Rowyn's station, as though they'd forgotten that Ariel had her own voice now. A wide-nosed, gamey-figured human in a midriff-exposing brown outfit entered the shrine and put his hands together in a Jaranese bow. Ariel, ever humble despite her local deification, returned the bow, and echoed a greeting.

*"A blessed day to you, friend. What brings you to the Shrine of the Storm's Saviour?"*

The man gave Ariel a wholehearted smile. *"I come seeking blessings for a trip to the northern fishing waters. Are you able to calm the winds this evening? I promise you half the catch as tribute!"*

"Make it a tenth and pledge it towards my fellow Galdusians in need of charity. If you do this, my help is assured," Ariel replied. *"You shall see me in the sky, watching the winds with my very body. If they step out of line, I shall calm them."*

*"I make this pledge in the eyes of the Storm above. You are generous and benevolent, Storm's Saviour. The tales told of you are true."*

*"I only hope to give you the respect that your people have given me. Thank you for your generous patronage."*

With that, the man bowed and left the shrine, prompting Ariel to bow back as he did. Rowyn, ever the spectator, whispered in Old Galdusian.

*"You'll be occupied all evening, then?"*

*"Of course! A promise is a promise. If the Jaranese eat well, then Ferrus eats well too. I see no reason not to work with them."*

Rowyn smiled widely. *"You've come into your own. You're no longer useful because you were made to be useful. You're simply kind. I'm proud of you."*

*"Thank you."*

There was a moment's hesitation before Rowyn broached his true concern. *"Ariel, I think I'm superfluous."*

*"What do you mean?"*

*"You're no longer reliant on me, and that's a good thing. You're your own woman, and I couldn't be happier for you. I can't in good conscience stand around, reaping the benefits of your hard work while contributing nothing. Additionally, I think Ma-Hith is too close to Demidium for my liking. What if Erre suspects I'm alive, and searches Jaranar?"*

"She will not hurt me, nor shall she hurt you. Erre is an honourable woman, even if she killed—"

The augmentee interrupted herself, and her redstone eyes dimmed a touch.

"She would kill you, wouldn't she?"

Rowyn nodded. *"I'm sorry to say it because I know she cared about you. As twisted as she might be, she's one of the reasons you're here now, happy and free from Lesteris. I don't think she'd kill you, but if she saw me, she'd kill me without hesitation."*

"Where would you go?" Ariel asked.

"I have somewhere in mind, but in case Razarkha arrives, I'm not going to say where," Rowyn said.

"You don't trust my discretion?"

While there were myriad compliments that applied to Ariel, she was not a master of deception. Rowyn wringed his hands within his loose, priestly sleeves, constructing what he hoped was a diplomatic sentence.

*"You're a truthful woman who doesn't have drop of hatred within her. The fact I'm withholding this information isn't an insult to you, it's an insult to the woman who'd use your honesty to harm me."*

*"It saddens me to think Praetor Erre could be hurting people that don't deserve it,"* Ariel remarked. *"I could watch Lesteris be humiliated again and again, but I remember Lestrio being sucked into her weapon, and how he'd pat my head when I still had hair."*

*"It's good to have complex feelings about her, and I don't think she's a simple monster. However, there are only two people in this world she'd hesitate to harm: You, and that Ilazari friend of hers."*

*"I never got to befriend Weil of Ilazar,"* Ariel said. *"His tongue was too strange, but seeing Erre repeat plans in his tongue made me think she was fond of him."*

"Unfortunately, she's not as fond of me as she is of him. I'm sorry I can't tell you the full truth, but I believe you'll prosper without me. These are your people now."

Ariel gave a single nod. "Let me know when you intend to leave. I want to give you a proper farewell. Lesteris would often gift his guests lavishly whenever they left."

"We deviated a touch with our own departure, I imagine," Rowyn said with a grin.

For the first time Rowyn had seen, Ariel laughed organically, free from the usual awkward confirmation that a joke had been told.

"A touch," she finally said.

"I'll miss you," Rowyn replied. "I hope you inspire Ma-Hith for the rest of your days."

\* \* \*

Godswater's sea air snaked through the Saltwater Temple's windows, and despite Rosaline Godswater's efforts, the incessant cawing of gulls woke her. She sat up in her silken bedsheets and rubbed her eyes, accepting that awakening was in her best interest. She was never good at telling the time from the sun but knew by instinct that in less than an hour, Uncle Petyr would enter her room if she wasn't awake.

She stayed wrapped in her sheets as she stood, wearing them like a sari, and gazed out the window. The gluttonous, screaming seabirds that circled the bustling markets of Godswater may not have been as dignified as the Eagle, but Rosaline envied them nonetheless.

A pair of statuettes lay upon her bedside table: The Moon Man, dark and mysterious, guarding Rosaline's secrets, and the Border, who reminded all within the room of right and wrong. Though she knew godly trinkets were nothing compared to their mortal mouthpiece, she still foolishly looked to them for protection. Her mirror had been turned to the wall for almost two years, and her underwear drawers made her shudder even in her peripheral vision. Still, she had to face her dresser if she was to avoid her uncle.

She took out some binding cloth and some bloomers, along with a red-white robe normally associated with male priests. Her bedroom door taunted her with hypothetical Petyrs lying beyond it. Rosaline winced and told herself that it didn't matter how long she waited. She clung to her bedding, then rushed into the halls of the Saltwater Temple's residential quarters.

Apostle Petyr wasn't there after all. There was nothing but an empty, elaborately decorated hall between her and the safety of the bathroom. She rushed atop the colourful tiles, pushed into the third door on the left, and locked it behind her. There was a basin in the centre of the room, a frosted window, and numerous fragrant oils. She ran a tap and wept for her younger, naïve self.

Once, she would have complained about the taps only having cold water, and demanded a basin of hot water be taken to her. As a woman of sixteen, she now knew that the fewer opportunities for men to see her naked, the better. A mirror to the far left of the room reminded her of the terrors a woman's body could provoke. The Border's Word said it true: A beautiful woman was the mother of all temptation. Men, in their infinite fallibility, were easily corrupted by the wiles of feminine curvaceousness, and long, teasing hair. Though the bath rumbled as water crashed into it, it couldn't deafen Rosaline to the truth.

No matter how she scarred herself, Petyr was always tempted. She bound her breasts until her chest resembled a boy's, she refused every sari gifted by well-meaning women who didn't understand, she hid her hair in veils, but nothing stopped it. She even tried to maim her face, but Shiloh Godspawn, her bastard cousin, stopped her before it could be done. If she made the truth known, the House of Godswater would be ruined, all because some stupid girl tempted the holiest priest in recent history. She was his one weakness, a rot that claimed the mightiest mangal tree, and she didn't know how to stop it.

She stopped the tap and sat in her cold bath, gingerly rubbing scented oils on herself, carefully avoiding her most recent scars. A sting rose from her chest, which went on to consume her throat and irritate her eyes. There was one solution that would save Uncle Petyr's soul at the cost of her own, along with the entire Godswater line. She lowered her mouth into the bathwater, then brought her nose in as well. She'd heard tales from resuscitated sailors; it started with holding one's breath, then, in desperation, breathing water in lieu of air.

At first, holding one's breath was easy. As Rosaline's lungs grew stiller, however, the anxiety rose. The instinct to breathe rushed through her, and though she begged her body to keep her head submerged, she flung her nose and mouth out of the water, gasping with horror. The Gods despised cowards that ran from their sins; this was how they let Rosaline know.

It didn't matter how long she stewed in her own sin, nor how she hid her base, womanly nature with robes and bindings. She was always going to be the Yukishiman bride of Grand Nzor Aturatzi the Wise; the final corruptor for a wise ruler the Gods saw fit to tempt and topple. Sin aside, leaving herself to be discovered naked would only prove her indecency to the world. She stepped out of the bath and towelled herself off, before a voice called through the door. It was Uncle Petyr's, thankfully in his gentler tone.

"Rosaline, are you in there? I checked your room, and you were gone, then I heard gasping. What's taking you so long?"

Rosaline clung to her towel as shame burned against her cheeks. "I was gasping because— because—"

Petyr's voice darkened. "Worry not, I'm aware of your sinful nature as a budding woman. You must learn to control your urges, and not use the moments where nudity is required to satisfy oneself wantonly."

"Of course, Uncle Petyr. I'm sorry."

"Don't apologise to me, apologise to the Border. His moral divisions are clearly drawn, yet your blind eyes refuse to see."

Rosaline couldn't drop her towel, even though she knew the door was opaque. Petyr's hungry eyes always found a way through it. It was a man's responsibility to resist sin, yet the holiest man in the known world couldn't resist her body. If the Gods didn't consider her death acceptable, what purpose could she serve?

She hid behind the bath, taking her clothes with her. After struggling her way into decency, she stood straight, hung her towel up, and left the bathroom, before realising her mistake; she hadn't taken a head covering in. When Petyr beheld her, he put his hands together and bowed.

"A tasteful expression of your femininity, allowing your hair to fall so freely. Be careful doing this when serving the commoners."

Despite his playful tone, Petyr Godswater's folded brown eyes had naught but disconcerting stillness. His shaved head and simple red-white robes contrasted with the long, lacelike moustache strands that hung from his upper lip, and it was impossible to tell whether he wanted deference or honesty.

"I was careless," Rosaline said in a hurried tone. "I'll put a veil on at once, I'm sorry, I'm so sorry, don't—"

She froze as Petyr put a soft hand on her cheek. "I only say what I do out of concern."

"I know," Rosaline replied, then broke from his touch and dashed to her room to retrieve a veil.

# Arrangements

Rakh Fel'thuz was once again trapped within Castle Selenia's council room, but his habit of allowing his mind to wander had died with his sense of relaxation. There wasn't time to fix what internal strife remained within the Forests of Winter. With Razarkha almost certainly charging for Arkhera, Baron Oswyk and Lady Gemfire's mutterings were irrelevant. All Moonstone could rely on was their own resources and, charitably, the loyalty of Ashglass.

Sat with him were Lady Selenia, whose pep still hadn't recovered, Wisdom Erwyn, whose cravat looked tight enough to choke him, the near-skeletal Minister of Criminal Affairs, Plutyn Khanas, and General Kareon Moonspawn, the only councillor who held some degree of professional stoicism.

"Shall we get started, then?" Erwyn asked. "Nobody wants to broach the topic, but before we discuss domestic matters, military threats should be discussed. Sir Khanas, have we received any word of Ashglass rallying its forces?"

Khanas responded with a level tone. "Lady Foenaxas is proving somewhat lax; her forces are, from what I can tell, on alert, but there's been no whispers of drills or preparations."

Rakh rubbed his forehead. "Then we can't expect them to aid us. If it's absolutely necessary, I'll visit Ashglass to remind Foenaxas of her duties."

General Kareon frowned. "Our latest report on Razarkha defines her as a powerful mage whose soulstealer powers her, rather than acting as a mass killing device. I think she'd be easily killed by Selenia men alone if her only goal is to take Moonstone."

Rakh shook his head. "That's not the primary concern. Anyone who's known Razarkha knows she's spiteful. Before our duel, she promised to humiliate me in front of the common people. Even if they don't love me, Razarkha understood that I loved them. Let me clarify something; her goals are apolitical. Her only goal is to hurt me, and she'll burn through everyone, civilian or soldier, if it means I suffer. One civilian dying is too many."

Plutyn's grim expression tightened. "Even now, you're self-absorbed. Razarkha Fel'thuz killed my cousin. She's not a danger to people *you* care about, she's a danger to everything she touches."

"Therefore we *must* consider the people's safety!" Rakh spluttered. "Regardless of if it's about me, Razarkha is not a typical warmonger. If civil war between the Verawors and the Crown broke out tomorrow, we could be assured that neither side would deliberately target civilians. They may non-lethally seize farms and hold out in enemy villages, but generally, Arkheran soldiers respect the sanctity of innocent life. Razarkha will not."

Erwyn sighed, his gaze drifting to his papers. "What are you suggesting, Rakh? Civilians will be targeted, I understand that, but what can we do about it?"

Lady Kag's posture straightened. "Oh, oh, I have an idea!"

The table hardened their faces and fell into bitter silence, yet Rakh had seen this look in Kag's eyes before. As foolish as she was, since Irikhos Foenaxas's kidnapping, she was determined to hear the truth from her underlings. This wasn't a token effort to appear ladylike; Kag'nemera Selenia was actually showing interest.

"What's your idea, my lady?" Rakh asked.

"You're not going to pretend it's good if it's stupid, are you?"

"No. If it's bad, I'll be the first to tell you," Rakh assured.

Lady Kag allowed herself a small smile, then spoke up. "Well, lots of Ashglass needs rebuilding, and we gave them a lot of ilmenite, but that still won't be enough. Also, lots of people in Ashglass died. Why don't we send some of the peasants to help mine the Ashpeaks and fill up all the empty districts in Ashglass?"

The table was silent, and Rakh's heart swelled. There was a first time for everything, and Lady Kagura had finally said something worthwhile in a council meeting. The count vanquished the quiet surrounding him and adopted a hopeful tone.

"That's brilliant, my lady. You've truly kept up with the situation, haven't you?"

"I don't know how long I have left as Lady of Moonstone, but I don't want to be the idiot people speak over when I have to leave," the high elf said.

"I'll inform Lady Foenaxas of this proposal, but if I'm honest, while this idea is mutually beneficial for Moonstone and Ashglass, it won't account for every peasant in the city," Rakh said.

Erwyn nodded. "Agreed. It'll at least solve part of the problem—"

Plutyn cleared his throat seemingly just to cut Erwyn off, then spoke slowly and quietly. "The rest of the people have another option. Those who are unwilling to leave their homes behind permanently can seek refuge through escape routes in the catacombs. While it is not officially maintained, my family and its rivals have ensured its functionality during their years of enterprise. I propose that through an Ashglass emigration and sheltering what remains via the catacombs, we can leave Moonstone to General Kareon's forces and my own."

Kareon's thin nose wrinkled. "You expect my soldiers to work with former thugs?"

The minister leaned over the table. "Never refuse free soldiers, friend. If you believe I'm preparing some sort of impossible betrayal against a vastly outnumbering force, so be it. I'll take my men underground with the civilians and leave yours to rot."

Erwyn tapped his pen hard enough that the nib fell off with an ear-splitting scrape. *"Enough,* both of you. Plutyn, your offer to augment our troops with your own is accepted, and once we've informed the other councillors, we can coordinate an evacuation effort. First, however, we must confirm that Lady Foenaxas will accept our builders and miners. Count Fel'thuz, I believe you're best suited to visit Ashglass and check up on our lady vassal."

While Rakh had already offered as much, returning to the ruined religious centre was hardly an attractive prospect. Still, if it preserved Moonstone's survival, Rakh would do it.

"As you say, Erwyn. I would have hoped that sending a letter would be enough, but given the complexities of our last visit, we can never be too careful. Make sure Rarakhi and Lady Selenia are safe while I'm gone."

Plutyn's thin face pursed up. "I'm insulted that you'd have to command such a thing. I'll protect young Rarakhi with my life."

Rakh doubted the specifics, yet the necromancer was certainly capable of throwing several of his underlings' lives away for the sake of his future son-by-law. Between him and Erwyn, the innocents of Moonstone were in good hands.

\* \* \*

The city of Napolli was not structured as a stereotypical Elarondian city. Irikhos expected curved spires and paths of pale tiles, yet the port was infused with Jaranese colours. Temples with stacks of curved roofing and symbology resembling Godswater's dotted the street corners where Eternalist churches would normally stand. According to Wisdom Khalver's visions, Napolli held the secrets to Yar and Tor's whereabouts, so despite the oddness of the apparently pantheistic city, fate decreed that he search the area.

Dark elves were as commonplace here as they were in Ashglass, with women covering their hair with Godswater veils while the men wore rugged sailor's garb that resembled his brother-in-law's tastes. As Irikhos walked further from the sea, he prayed to the God of Renewal that his Elarondian was as fluent as Mor'kha claimed it was. He approached an old woman whose garb was defiant compared to the younger generations, daring to show her ash-grey hair and sagging chest, a feathered tricorn resting askew upon her head. She was manning a stall with numerous baked goods, including puff pastry rolls and Passicaran-style flat pizza, small enough to be eaten with one hand.

"Hello there, Arkheran," the old woman said in Elarondian, and when Irikhos pondered over his words for more than a moment, she gave up and spoke Common. "You are Arkheran, yes? Would you like some traditional Elarondian food? The pizza here is richer than any Arkheran imitation, I assure you!"

*"I am Arkheran, but I do not know how far my time in Elarond is. I shall strive to speak the tongue of Elarond while here,"* Irikhos said, and judging from the crone's disapproving gaze, his Elarondian was utterly awful. *"I shall purchase a pizza for my travels."*

"I hope you take your time," the woman said as Soltelle Dollars exchanged hands. *"Your Elarondian is broken, but it'll get better after a few weeks. Most Arkherans who run here are the same."*

"You've seen Arkherans before?" Irikhos said as he took a passata-and-herb-filled bite.

*"Yes, they're quite common, though Virella is a much more popular destination."*

Irikhos rubbed his chin. *"Have you noticed a pair of high-class women, what is the word I'm looking for— n of the ruling class, from Arkhera?"*

*"Noblewomen?"*

*"Yes, that's the word."*

The exquisitely dressed baker chuckled to herself. *"It depends how long ago you're talking about. Years ago, there were these beggar nobles who claimed to be from some moon house in Arkhera. One of them, the younger one, was asking everywhere for where one could request the services of a militia, as if those are simply extant in Soltelle territory."*

Irikhos's heart wrenched as memories of Yarawyn flooded through his mind; the time they smeared Mor'kha's prayer beads with mashed garlic, making her smell for weeks, the time they sneaked a kiss behind the Renewalist Temple, and the time she asked Kagura to say the word 'anomaly' again and again to their hooting laughter.

"She was always a brash one," Irikhos remarked to himself, then continued in Elarondian. *"These beggar nobles, they were both white elven women, yes?"*

*"The typical entitled Arkheran sorts, yes. Blonde hair, one with blue eyes and the other red. They had all manner of moon-themed merchandise— oh, that reminds me, the fools tried to sell me some of it, as though I have any use for jewellery."*

*"You appear to have use for feathers,"* Irikhos remarked.

The old woman let out a throaty laugh. *"Oh, you're amusing for a foreigner speaking broken Virella Elarondian. I never found out what happened to them, but the red-eyed one was desperate for a militia."*

Irikhos finished off his pizza. *"Did anybody buy their lunar paraphernalia?"*

*"There's a jeweller just down the road who bought a set of opal moons from them, but the fool never managed to sell them for a profit. Your eyes grew misty from speaking about these women. Are they precious to you?"*

Irikhos's mind drifted to the pudgy young woman Torawyn Selenia once was, shrinking, quiet, afraid of her own shadow. She was originally supposed to be his betrothed, but she simply didn't leave an impression on him. Yarawyn, meanwhile, was boyish and unafraid to flirt with Irikhos, with looks that let his younger self ignore her cruel streak.

"One of them was precious to me," Irikhos said. "Now I'm tasked with finding both."

The old dark elf raised a white eyebrow. "Don't let old Armaxio see your attachment! He's still trying to sell those moons, and if he knows you've got a soft spot for them, he'll overcharge you, mark my words."

"Armaxio is the jewel man, I presume?"

"Yes. If you want to ask him a few questions, he's down the road, then you take the third right. He's got a sign boasting of the pantheistic figurines he creates; you can't miss it."

Irikhos nodded. "Good to know. Thank you, friend."

With that, he wandered through the bizarre mixture of Elarondian and Jaranese culture, the city's colourful tile paths winding towards a much more heavily guarded district. Tall, blonde-haired humans with rifled guns guarded prominent buildings, but *Il Emporio di joyas di Armaxio* was protected by more local-looking troops, dark-skinned and pointy-eared, though their arms cradled equally fearsome firearms.

Irikhos hefted his luggage past the heavily armed dark elves and entered the jewel emporium, where artful works of polished stone lay encased in reinforced glass. Past them all lay a counter staffed by a man so old he'd somehow managed to bald, an achievement on par with growing a beard to elves. The jeweller was inspecting a gem with a high-quality looking glass, but the moment Irikhos arrived at the counter, he put his lens down and spoke Common with poorly concealed enthusiasm.

"Hello, friend from across the sea! What brings you to Napolli?"

Irikhos frowned. "Is it really that obvious I'm from Arkhera?"

"No Elarondian wears phoenix paraphernalia! That symbol was adopted by our Arkheran cousins, the Foenaxases, was it not?" Armaxio correctly deduced.

Irikhos smiled. "Impressive. I hear a pair of Arkherans sold you some opal moons a while ago. Is that true?"

The old man's cheery demeanour flattened. "Who told you this? Was it Alteria?"

"The old baker who dresses like a noblewoman?"

"Yes, that's the one," he said, then abruptly shifted his tongue to Elarondian, gesticulating in a way only his countrymen would. *"Oh, she makes me furious! She married my brother knowing I loved her too, and then—"*

"I can understand Elarondian, even if spoken quickly," Irikhos interrupted. "I wouldn't want to be privy to your life's shames. I just want to know where the women who sold you the opal moons went."

"Those scammers are as good as dead!" the jeweller ranted, changing tongues once more. *"They're a priceless family heirloom, they said, they'll sell for twice the price we're asking for, they said."*

Irikhos's blood rushed to his extremities. "What do you mean, good as dead?"

"When I find them, they'll wish they got eaten by a wyvern!" the jeweller said. "Five years, and still, nobody wants to buy them for a profit! They shall buy the moons back and pay for the exacting care I gave them. Next time they're in Napolli, they'll pay, just you wait!"

Irikhos was beginning to see why so many beautiful works lay about unsold. He let the man wheeze his frustration away, then, in the calmest voice he could muster, tried to extract something meaningful from him.

"Did these women tell you where they were headed?"

"The one with red eyes, an impertinent minx it must be said, claimed they needed a train fare and a wyvern egg's worth for their moons, so I would wager they wanted to visit—"

"The Alaterran Mountains," Irikhos finished off. "Yarawyn's the same as ever."

"The further inland one goes in Elarond, the fierier the people," Armaxio claimed. "If they are lucky, those two Arkheran con artists got burned. Otherwise, they'll have to face the salt of a Napolli man!"

"Of course," Irikhos said, maintaining eye contact while backing from the dark elf.

"You're interested in buying the opal moons, are you not? These women are obviously something to you, surely you can part with—"

"I'd love to, but I have places to go, people to find, but thank you for the kind offer, may the Gods be with you!" Irikhos babbled, slipping out of the emporium and hoping that there'd still be a train running by the time he reached the station.

\* \* \*

The cold, salty air of Zemelnya was like the tang of one of Umbria's awful orange cheesecakes; hardly pleasant, but a reminder of safer times. Rowyn Khanas could see the bulbous domes of the Ilazari capital loom over the horizon, and patted Khun-Rax on the back as they shared the view from the bow of the *Xay-Haeng Phayu*.

*"We haven't known each other long, but it's been good knowing you and every god-fearing man of Ma-Hith. Ariel will keep you safe, I'm sure of it,"* he said in his strongly-accented Jaranese.

The fat man lacked his usual joviality. *"You fled from that horrific light of Demidium once before, and you're fleeing from it again. What makes you so faithless? Is the Storm's Saviour not enough?"*

"The light of Demidium has no quarrel with your people. Ariel will be able to defend you with her words alone. She won't be able to do the same for me. I abandoned the source of that destructive light, and I've worked with women scorned before."

Khun-Rax laughed. *"A treacherous wife in your Arkheran past?"*

"Not a wife, merely a lover. She was a beastmistress, a special kind of person only seen on the Arkheran Isles. Short, curvaceous, with pretty eyes none could match. She was such a change of pace from what my family made necromantic women seem like," Rowyn said, closing his eyes. "While my fellow necromancers seemed stoic and serious, she was like fire, wild, excitable, able to spread her warmth uncontrollably. I loved her more than anything."

*"What changed?"*

"It became clear that her pursuit of me was largely to upset her father, and when, as the Verawor spymaster, she proposed horrific war tactics like using crows to indiscriminately drop everflame onto hypothetical enemies, I realised the woman I loved was only partially real," Rowyn recounted. "Knowing how much ire my parents and miserly cousin had for my choice, I simply couldn't continue with her. Even now, I remember some parts of her fondly, but beauty doesn't counteract rot."

Khun-Rax laughed. *"For a foreigner, you have wisdom. The architects of Meung-Chaydan ought to learn from you; it matters not how beautifully paved your roads are if they're half your people's homes."*

"I'll admit, I'm glad I haven't seen the Jaranese capital. Homelessness, hunger, it appears there's nothing right with the city."

The sailor hit his belly. *"Those who do eat, eat well. It is said the finest culinary school in all the world resides there."*

*"It seems you'd go there if it wasn't for all the riots."*

Khun-Rax let a raucous laugh loose. *"You mock my belly, but this is my pride and joy. How many merchant sailors can boast such a satisfied appetite?"*

Rowyn rested his arms on the taffrail of the *Xay-Haeng Phayu*, the beaches of Zemelnya close enough to pick out individual pieces of shale. Ariel's final words to him echoed as a gentle whistle through a muted storm.

*"Have a safe and blessed life, Rowyn Khanas."*

Could it ever be safe again? Razarkha Fel'thuz would kill him on sight, the depraved Soltelle engineer would likely imprison him as some sort of amusing Arkheran novelty, and Zemelnya was a city torn apart by gang war. Rowyn shook his head and wryly chuckled. He was placing his happiness in the hands of a lover again.

He turned and headed towards the pinnaces. *"It's time, Khun-Rax. Anchor down and let me row away. I don't want you drifting too close to Zemelnya; Ilazar is dangerous at the best of times."*

*"And yet you flee towards it. You are an odd snake-man, Rowyn, but I'm glad to have known you,"* Khun-Rax said. *"Ma-Hith has a god's avatar protecting it, thanks to our fateful encounter. You will not be forgotten."*

*"Thank you for everything."*

Rowyn decided to let the departure be clean. He waved at the crew as he passed, then entered his pinnace, taking hold of the oars while the boat lowered. Without his armour, it was almost enjoyable to be swayed by the water's whims. Though he rowed against it, the gentle reminder of nature's inscrutable desires almost pushed the thought of his many enemies stumbling upon him out of his head.

The *Xay-Haeng Phayu* shrank and Zemelnya grew, reminding him of the day he met Vi'kara. When the pinnace ran aground, a pair of white-haired spellbinders spotted him. One was a boy and the other was a girl, both younger than thirteen with long faces similar to Rakh and Razarkha Fel'thuz. They were toying with a crab the size of a small cat, but upon seeing Rowyn arrive, they panicked and rushed towards a hauntingly tall, sharp-featured old spellbinder whose hair flowed long despite his icy armour. Occasionally, Rowyn swore he could see smoke spill from the man's mouth yet blinking corrected his faulty vision.

He knew how this worked; in Ilazar, there was no such thing as a forgotten grudge, so if he didn't address his spooking of the children, he was likely to find an icicle bayonet plunged between his scapulae. Approaching the man, he inclined his head low enough that he hopefully expressed contrition without excess.

*"Many apology,"* he said in broken Isleborn. *"Was no intention to fear the children."*

"Save your broken attempts to speak the language," the deep-voiced cryomancer said. "I speak Common perfectly well, not to mention— oh, is that Rowyn Khanas? Honestly, Niki, Vladlen, I expect better of you than to run from some short-tail."

Rowyn narrowed his eyes. "My apologies, do I know you?"

The cryomancer put his hand to his mouth in a gesture too spry and feminine for his apparent age and sex. "Perhaps you do, but then again, that'd require you to think. You were never one for figuring things out quickly, were you, Khanas?"

"I'm sorry, I don't understand. You're speaking like— oh, never mind. I need to find somebody. As long as you know I meant no harm to your children, that's all that matters."

"Of course," the old cryomancer said with a twitch. "Go on, be free, and do check the rebuilt library. They're selling many ideas for your lovers, male or female, young and old!"

Rowyn slipped away from the cryomantic family, and it was only after leaving their earshot that he realised the old man, save for his hair colour, looked nothing like his children.

# onsters

Yarawyn was a teenage girl again, standing on Moonstone's battlements, watching the sun set over the Forests of Winter. If she returned to Castle Selenia, her father would be waiting for her, rather than rotting in the ground. Moonrazer wasn't alive yet, this teenaged Yar knew, and for a moment, she doubted placing herself in the past.

The wyvern was an unfortunate sacrifice that needed to be made. In the past, she was still betrothed to Irikhos, she was still the heir to Moonstone, only this time, she knew who her saboteur would be ahead of time. She'd take the Razarkha Fel'thuz approach; while the countess claimed she was too weak to move following her stillbirth, everyone knew she solved the Wisdom Waldon issue by shoving him out of a window.

A younger Kag absent-mindedly ran along battlements, steadily nearing her doom. She wouldn't be a lady this time. The crows and shadowcats would appreciate her remains, at least. Yarawyn crouched, and as Kag passed her, she sprung towards her older sister. Kagura staggered sidewards, tripped over her own feet, then toppled over the battlement walls, falling head-first into the frost-encrusted ground beyond the city.

There were no guards to stop Yarawyn. She checked her handiwork, and though she couldn't see her eldest sister's stupid face due to her shattered skull, something wasn't right. Where long, raven hair should have been, blonde hair tangled with partially dried blood lay. Yar cautiously placed a hand on her head and withdrew it to find congealed ichor sticking to her fingers.

Yar jolted upright from her bed, and the dreambound Moonstone's chilliness was replaced by the sticky, sweltering air of Alaterra. She was often torn between going without bedsheets and having a single thin one, but neither was as comfortable as her bed in Moonstone; a thick duvet nestling her against the cold of Arkhera's northmost province.

Once, the warmth at least came with some comfort; when Moonrazer was the size of a large dog, he would sleep in her bed, curled by her bare legs as his inner flames dimmed for the night. His slow, content rattles lulled Yarawyn and quietened the voice in her head screaming about the hatred she felt for the condescending locals. Now the wyvern didn't fit in Torawyn's house, and he lay outside, his bellows rumbling through Yarawyn's open window. Though her hands were clean and her head intact, Yarawyn couldn't go back to sleep without tiring herself anew. She threw on a nightgown, picked up her housekey, and left her room.

As she passed Torawyn's room, she overheard her sister's snoring, and nearly kicked the door open out of spite. How was she content with this? Tor wasn't an Elarondian; she was Arkheran nobility. Yet she slept soundly as some glorified peasant, eking out a living healing loud, rude, gesticulating fops who mocked Yarawyn for adhering to their mother tongue. If she didn't need to curry favour with at least one Elarondian faction for her return to Arkhera, she'd have Moonrazer cook every last Alaterran alive.

She headed out of Torawyn's house and found Moonrazer sleeping beneath her window, his wings folded and his winding neck curled into his body. She patted the back of the wyvern's neck, then stroked along the grain of his scutes.

"Wake up, Moonrazer, there's a good boy."

The beast unwound his neck and made a slow, deep warble. He briefly fanned his crest-scutes and opened his beak, before noticing who had awakened him. Then he stood, stretching out his neck and wings alike. After a few tentative steps, he lowered his beak and made a demanding caw. Yarawyn scratched his wide, keratinous bill, before issuing more commands.

"Let's see if you remember this one. Time to saddle, Moonrazer!"

The wyvern folded his wings as low as was possible and crouched as though trying to make his belly touch the ground. Yarawyn couldn't help but smile at the awkward position her pet was willing to put himself in, but didn't waste time climbing onto his back. Gripping the beast's body was difficult without a harness, but until Torawyn saved enough for one, a short flight wouldn't hurt.

"Moonrazer, fly!"

The wyvern chattered in a low, distorted tone, then, following an awkward run-up, leapt into the air and flapped his massive, membranous wings, steadily gaining height despite the weight she encumbered him with. Yarawyn beheld the ground as it grew more distant; in the night, Alaterra glittered with golden streetlights, in keeping with the Soltelles' tendency to impose threadtech on every nation it touched.

When relatively close, one could see the tiles, terraces and spires flickering from the threadlamps' light, but as Yarawyn soared further from Alaterra, the more it became an amorphous spot of brightness upon a mountainside the moon didn't deign to illuminate. Though the night was unforgivingly dark, she could barely make out the ragged contours of the Alaterran Mountains, bumpy as a scab upon the ground, with a lake amidst the peaks reflecting the full moon as though the pooling blood of an exposed wound.

Yarawyn pressed Moonrazer's back, and the wyvern bore downwards. As his speed increased, she gripped the base of his neck for dear life, winds flinging her hair backwards and her key dropping into the unending blackness below. For a moment, she feared her legs would fly upwards, unable to grip Moonrazer's sides, but just as the air's upthrust became unbearable, the beast levelled his flight, likely due to the numerous crags beneath him. There was one cave she was looking for; it would be lit up, with slick slime adding to the effect. After commanding Moonrazer to veer about the shorter mountains, she found it amidst a group of stone pines, a tiny, distinct light nestled within nondescript jags of stone and foliage.

"Land, Moonrazer, there's a good wyvern!"

The creature bore backwards and flapped against his own flight path, slowing himself before latching onto the side of the mountain in front of him. Yarawyn struggled off the beast's back, tentatively ensuring the ground beneath her was stable before fully committing to it. She'd lost yet another key, but Torawyn would always let her back in. She would likely be asleep until the morning, so it was better to stay with Naas'khar until dawn.

She clambered over the shallow, rocky face of the mountain, towards a fire-lit cavern just above her. Moonrazer was right behind her, his sharp claws and low, quadrupedal gait perfect for such terrain. Once at the cave's mouth, she glanced at an oily spatter upon its closest wall, which provided a dim, warped reflection of what lay within.

"Naas'khar, are you there?" she called out, echoes acting as her only immediate reply.

Slowly, a brown-skinned, pointy-eared head edged from cover, squinting its two red eyes while a tentacle with a third red eye writhed about behind it. After a pause, the being slipped into view, revealing himself as a tall, dark elven-looking person in rags, with a combination of tentacles, leathern wings, and crablike ridges marring his emaciated body.

"Lady Yarawyn!" the pseudo-elf said, rushing up and hugging her with two arms, two tentacles, and a wing. "It's always a pleasure to see you."

"I'm sorry I don't visit you more often," Yarawyn replied, resisting the urge to squirm. "Is anything new?"

"I've claimed a new cave, as you can see," he said as he released her. "Come in, I've made it my own."

Moonrazer watched Yarawyn with slitted pupils, and it distressed the wyvern, she entered the cave with Naas'khar. The bones of what looked like a family of mountain goats dotted the lair, illuminated by a crackling fire that spat pine seeds out of it. Slathered upon the walls was black slime, some smears apparently growing tendrils and eyes.

"I think I might have *too much* food here," he remarked as he looked at one of the wall eyes. "While my daemonic half rejoices with every meal it indulges in, my elven half knows limitation, and sometimes, I cough up something strange."

"That's… interesting," Yarawyn stammered. "Do those eyes operate independently?"

"Yes, but sometimes I get a glimpse of what they see," Naas'khar explained. "Still, the best eyes for looking at you are the two on my head. You're beautiful as ever, Lady Yarawyn."

Though he was no Irikhos, a romantic compliment in plain Common was something Yarawyn would always accept. She knew that Naas'khar desired her, and if not for the deformities he was afflicted with, he'd be quite handsome, but she had her future to consider.

Naas'khar was a nephil, the unfortunate result of some female-presenting daemon wishing to experience the mortal 'joys' of pregnancy. His mother was apparently less interested child-*rearing,* as according to Naas'khar, he'd been hunting alone in the mountains since he could walk. The fact he spoke to those that didn't shun him on sight was a miracle unto itself. As miraculous as he was, he wasn't a fitting husband. He was a slime-spewing animal devourer; as friendly as he was, his place was far away from castles and courts.

"You're too kind," Yarawyn said, covering her chest with one hand. "I wish I had good news for you, but honestly, I came here because I can't sleep."

Naas'khar rested his back against the cave wall, forcing his tentacles and wings to unform, slip into his back, then burst out as writhing appendages by his torso. "You're not any closer to getting us to the land of the free?"

"Moonrazer's large enough for me to mount, and I think he could carry you too, so there's that."

"But you still have no army to take back your home," the daemonic hybrid muttered. "Just one wyvern."

Yarawyn sat beside him and opened her hands by the fire. "I'm afraid so. One day, I'll have the money, I promise you."

"Then I'll be free, able to face people of the city without fear of the cursed knotweed or mortals fleeing in terror?"

The eagerness in Naas'khar's voice forced Yarawyn to hesitate. "Yes. You'll be free. In Arkhera, there are daemonic musicians, and Ilazari daemonologists visit the City of False Faces to see the final stronghold of daemonkind in person."

"And they signify marriages with personally made pendants, unique to every couple," Naas'khar said, taking hold of Yar's hand.

Yarawyn faltered once again, then pulled her hand away. "They do. From peasants to nobility, love is considered free and worth signifying. When I was in Arkhera, I was going to marry a dark elf, that's how free I was."

"When you return, will you be free enough to marry a nephil?"

"I'm not sure," Yar said. "But you'll have a home in the City of False Faces and find peers of all natures. Daemons who look like mortals, daemons the size of houses, daemons who are small attachments upon animals, you'll have so many friends. You'll wonder why you ever limited yourself to me."

"Can full-blooded daemons love in the same way mortals can?"

"Of course!" Yarawyn bluffed. "the Riversong Sisters' most popular ballad is a love song about a lordling from some dead noble house. You'll be so happy when you get there, I promise."

"And I'll still be able to see you?"

"Of course," Yarawyn said, slumping back as her tiredness caught up to her. "You'll be friends with the most powerful woman in the Forests of Winter."

\* \* \*

The fine sands of the Jaranese Archipelago shifted against Razarkha's remaining foot, and though she wasn't wearing shoes, the sensation was indistinguishable from if she was. Every experience save pain was a fraction of its previous vividness. If the Sovereign's goal was to make her regret her brief escape from mortality, his efforts were in vain; no matter how her abdomen gnawed at her, looking into Rakh's eyes as he died would be worth it.

She limped towards a swampy inland forest while Duncan Godswater hovered silently by her side. He didn't excessively offer commentary, but never had anything kind to say when he did. She should have discarded him the moment he talked back to her in Demidium, but travelling alone was somehow a fate worse than the current situation.

"You were kidnapped from Jaranar by the breeders of Demidium, correct?" Razarkha asked, tossing her soulstealer upwards and swiping it from the air.

"That's right. I recognise this island. It's mostly jungle, but there should be a port city nearby called Ma-Hith.

It's a regular target of the Sulari," Duncan Godswater reported with a monotony matching his expressionless face.

"I shot down several ships departing north-west from Demidium. If there was any way for their crews to reach land, would they be here?"

"Well, we just travelled over the seas, north-west from Demidium, did we not? This was the first isle we came across. What do you think?"

Razarkha scowled. "I don't like your tone, Godswater. You're not right."

"Not right, Razarkha?" the augmentee asked, a scratching noise punctuating his voice.

"You lack the traits I seek in a travelling companion."

Duncan made an unusual rumbling noise. "Do you have any points of reference? I wouldn't count your revolution as analogous. If you don't value honesty or candid remarks, so be it. I can lie and say everything you do is brilliant—"

"*Shut up,* you waste of minerals!" Razarkha yelled, buckling over as she realised her crystalline leg had lodged itself within a boggy part of the jungle. "Wonderful, I'm stuck."

She telekinetically lifted herself from the mud and pointed to Duncan. "Finally, you can make yourself useful. I can't afford to cast spellwork unless it's necessary, but you're a well of geomantic power. Harden the mud before me and lead me to this 'Ma-Hith'. You can do that without sniping, I hope."

"Of course," Duncan said, his blank face only serving to taunt her more.

Rakh's laughter echoed from behind a cluster of trees, while multiple Teis could be seen in the canopy, dangling from branches like goblins. A hole in the air opened in front of her, revealing a red and purple realm with eyeballs that stared outwards. She attempted to climb into it, only to fall face-first onto the freshly hardened mud beneath her.

"Fel'thuz? Are you all right?" Duncan asked.

"I was just testing the mud's consistency," she snapped as she pushed herself up. "Good job, Godswater. Perhaps you'll be useful yet."

"As you say."

Duncan forged a path and Razarkha walked it, her false leg jutting into the flaky, dried sediment beneath her, all the way to the colourful gates that presumably belonged to Ma-Hith, flanked by the Jaranese's imaginary pantheon. Duncan emitted a wistful combination of a creak and a whistle, then spoke.

"Last time I was here, I had a body."

"I'm glad my body is no longer mortal," Razarkha claimed. "If I traversed that accursed jungle while attracting mosquitos, I would have likely burnt it to ashes."

"Destruction is your only solution, isn't it?"

Razarkha scoffed. "As though you're any different. What do you intend to do once you reunite with your brother? Lecture him on how immoral his actions are?"

"Admittedly, I intend to kill him. But not every problem is the same. Sometimes, we don't need conflict."

*"A naïve approach,"* the god within the soulstealer remarked. ***"Peaceful solutions leave neither opponent satisfied."***

"The god that forged my soulstealer thinks you're laughable," Razarkha relayed.

"Well, it's a good thing I don't worship that god, isn't it?"

Razarkha turned her nose up and walked into the Jaranese city, its architecture somewhere between artful and gaudy. The curved, often multi-layered roofs and god-specific colour combinations reminded her of the Saltwater Temple in Godswater. She'd only visited the monument to mass delusion once, and the brief memory she had of Petyr

Godswater's sermon caused her to eye Duncan. Snide as the augmentee was, his desires were valid; something about the holy city's apostle made her shudder.

The people of Ma-Hith were invariably short and brown-skinned humans. Galdus and Ilazar were refreshing, populated with people who were as tall, if not taller than her, but Jaranar was an even duller Arkhera; full of short, lesser people, but unlike her homeland they didn't even have the decency of being diverse. Rowyn and Ariel would be trivial to spot.

True enough, after less than an hour of drawing the eyes of every human they passed they noticed something out of place. A blue-and-yellow shrine that was still in construction stood at a street corner by the sea, lacking a roof or even a door. Its size was also laughable, barely capable of holding a congregation of ten. Within was an unmistakable set of floating rocks, their form defined by a perpetual storm raging around them, though it appeared since Razarkha last saw her, she'd acquired some tassels. Her redstone eyes glimmered from the doorway, and without warning, Razarkha stormed towards the unfinished building.

"You. I thought you would be here," Razarkha snapped in Nortezian. "Why are you wearing clothes? Why have you got the Storm's colours surrounding you?"

"Ah, Praetor Erre, good to see you!" Ariel said, seemingly oblivious to Razarkha's decrepit state. "My deepest apologies for abandoning you, but Rowyn said it would be for the best. Now I'm a religious figure, serving the community of Ma-Hith. I've become a servant by choice to the humans I likely hailed from. Isn't that good? I've finally become something I want to be, just like you wanted."

Razarkha's eyes twitched, and as her abdominal attachment braised her ruined flesh, Duncan caught up to her.

"What happened to make you veer off like this? Who's this augmentee, Fel'thuz?"

*"This is Ariel, Weil, you know her,"* she instinctively answered in Isleborn, before realising her error and responding in Common. "That is to say, this is Ariel. She was an ally before she and Rowyn abandoned me. Speaking of which, I'm going to interrogate her."

"Interrogate her? What for? We should just take what we need, arcane amplifiers, whatever you want, then—"

"If I can find out where Rowyn is, and he's on my path to Arkhera, I'm going to kill him. That is, if he's alive at all. Ariel is innocent, but that necromancer talked back to me, questioned my resolve, then abandoned me. The only person to betray me more is— is—"

Duncan let out a rocky groan. "Are you going to interrogate her or not?"

"Shut up!" Razarkha commanded, then switched her tongue to Nortezian. *"I'm happy for you, Ariel, but you mentioned Rowyn encouraging you to abandon me. Did he survive the ship sinking I caused?"*

Ariel paused. *"He did, and he helped me integrate with this community."*

Razarkha smiled, and her voice shifted up a semitone. *"You're as reliable as ever, Ariel. Not the most decisive or iron-willed, but you're cooperative and truthful. You should accompany me, not this seditious monster."*

*"Who is he?"* Ariel asked, cocking her head as Duncan lingered behind his insulter.

*"As an augmentee he was renamed to Brutus, but he's an Arkheran, just like me,"* Razarkha explained. *"So, will you accompany me?"*

*"I cannot. These are my people, and I serve them as I would hope a god would,"* Ariel said, her tassels whipping as her winds built.

Razarkha laughed. *"As naïve as ever. Gods don't serve people, they dominate them. Still, if you have your purpose here, I won't deny you. I'm proud of you."*

*"It means a lot to hear you say that, Erre."*

"If you won't accompany me, then can you at least tell me where Rowyn Khanas is?"

Ariel's winds reduced to a small eddy at her base. "I don't know where he is. He never told me his intended destination, aside from that he was heading north."

"North," Razarkha said, her tone sharpening. "As opposed to east, back to Demidium, or south, into a frozen wasteland? You know that's not an answer, Ariel. Are you lying to me?"

"No! He didn't tell me because he feared I would relay it to you!"

A lance of agony thrust out of her crystalline stomach, and her spine tugged on the insides of her ears, sending a sharp, ringing pain between the two. Though she no longer needed to breathe, she wheezed, hunched over, and pointed her soulstealer at Ariel's chest.

"You're lying," Razarkha stated. "You've turned against me, just like everyone else! Rakh, Rowyn, Adolita, and you. You're all traitors."

Ariel opened her rocky hands. "I assure you, I'm not, I wouldn't betray you. I owe you a debt of gratitude, and will help any way I can, just like your Isleborn friend, Weil. Where is Weil? Is he retrieving food somewhere else?"

Razarkha's eyes boiled within their sockets. Without hesitation, she blasted Ariel with a week's worth of lifespan concentrated into light, shattering the aeromancer. She straightened her back and laughed, but Duncan was quick to shout over her joy.

"What the fuck are you doing? She said she was a revered person here, we're going to— oh, forget it, people are coming!"

Razarkha noticed the Jaranese swarming in her peripheral vision and decided to recuperate her costs then abandon the city. She lifted her soulstealer and prompted it to consume the recently liberated Ariel, but it refused to glow.

"What's happening, Bold Individualist? Why isn't Ariel's soul being consumed?"

***"There's no loose soul to be consumed."***

"What do you *mean* there's no loose soul?"

Duncan Godswater put a hand on Razarkha's shoulder, burning off the tatters that clung to it. "Whatever you're talking about, we *need to go!*"

"Ariel's soul should be here. I'm not leaving unless she—"

"Oh, that? It's a new form of augmentation," Duncan claimed as Ariel's shards twitched. "Souls used to be a requirement to power an augmented body along with our brains' arcana node, but I'm pretty sure I'm soulless, same with most recent augmentees."

Razarkha huffed. "That would explain a lot. Let's go."

With that, the pair lifted themselves away from the surrounding angry citizens, leaving Ma-Hith behind.

\* \* \*

No matter how Weil's fantasies were fulfilled, his pleasure couldn't outweigh his guilt. A fuzzy rendition of Yukishiman jazz played from a hornlike contraption in the corner of the bedroom, and Hildegard Swan, curvaceous as humans tended to be, nudely sauntered towards Weil's restraining device, a metallic board with leather straps tying him down.

"The least you can do is look happy," Hildegard remarked as she loosened the straps. "For a moment you had this cute little grin, and I thought you'd finally let her go."

The Imperial Engineer's hands were gentle, despite the scars she'd inflicted on his body just minutes prior. Weil told himself it was penance, but *The Blinkered Stallion's* take on masochism easily refuted him. He was evading responsibility, nothing more. Even as Hildegard ran a finger along an unburnt part of his chest, Razarkha's wide, motionless eyes haunted him.

"I can't fuck you constantly, you know," Hilda said, turning around and slipping into her double bed. "If the only time you can forget about Razarkha is when your smaller tail's getting rubbed, I don't think I can help you."

"I apologise," Weil muttered, his Common just barely less accented than before. "I try to forget, but is— I can't— my vocabulary lacks the word."

"Last chance to join me in bed, otherwise I'll assume you're going to mope around acting like you're unworthy of aftercare," Hilda said.

"Can I speak my mother tongue to you?"

Hildegard rolled her eyes. "Fine, but only if you promise this isn't some twisted attempt to see me as Razarkha."

*"I don't love her anymore. I wouldn't insult you like that,"* he promised, getting off his metal slab and lying beside his human mistress. *"Can I hold you?"*

*"Just this once,"* Hilda replied in a strong Yukishiman accent.

Weil put his arm around the short woman's shoulder, the contact allowing for momentary distraction. Hildegard Swan was quite Ilazari in her sexuality; women and men were both acceptable to her, she was open about her tastes, yet she was utterly stingy when it came to kissing and holding. It was as though Yukishiman regimentation had snuck upon an Ilazari soul, imposing the unnecessary boundaries the Soltelles were famous for.

*"I liked what you did with your tail,"* Hildegard said, resting her head against his shoulder.

*"I love everything you do with your Yukishiman cigarettes,"* Weil replied, prodding the burns on his abdomen. *"Something about a woman seeing a man as an ashtray excites me."*

Hilda laughed. *"Take away the scared boy, and there's an extremely confident man. Half the men I fuck are ashamed of their masochism, as though it somehow makes them less masculine. Our little trysts will need to come to an end soon, but I think you'll be all right."*

"I'm glad you think that."

A loud knock on the bedroom's rusted metallic door ruined the moment, and Hilda hoisted her duvet over her chest. "What is this? I swear to the Mother if this is Ana letting her jealousy getting the better of her, I'll—"

"Imperial Engineer, it's important news from Demidium!" a man's voice responded.

"Come in, then."

A Yookie officer entered with a salute, his composure steady despite sharing a room with what Weil considered to be the most stereotypically human woman he'd ever seen naked. Keeping his eyes level, the officer began his report.

"Our forces have successfully taken the three western sectors of Demidium," he said, keeping his hands behind his back. "However, troops in the ninth-hour sector claim to have spotted a black-haired spellbinder with a tattered cloak, and intel suggests that—"

"Yes, yes, it's Razarkha Fel'thuz. Were there any other oddities in her appearance?" Hilda asked, not missing a beat as Weil shook with rage.

"Multiple soldiers said she had some kind of crystal in her stomach—"

*"Fucking dickshit train station whore!"* Weil interrupted, standing up without regard for his nudity. *"I killed that father-murdering bitch myself, I know what I saw!"*

"Calm down and cover yourself up, or I'll eject you from this ship," Hilda commanded, and like a whipped dog, Weil obeyed, picking up a dressing gown and falling silent.

The officer, unflappable as ever, stood steady and continued. "As I was saying, soldiers claimed to have seen a crystal in her stomach, and she was accompanied by an augmentee apparently unrelated to the riots we enabled."

"Interesting," Hilda said, rubbing her chin. "Well, I know for a fact Weil here killed Razarkha. He's been inconsolable over it, much to my chagrin."

"If I may, Imperial Engineer, perhaps he was mistaken?"

Hildegard Swan shook her head. "I don't think so. He ran her through the gut with a daemonic tentacle. Even an Arkheran orc wouldn't survive that, let alone a spellbinder. The reports of a crystalline structure suggests that somehow, her body is magically empowered. Perhaps she's a revenant, and some necromancer is raising her with the hopes of exploiting her spellwork. Was there anyone with her besides this augmentee?"

"Not from the reports, ma'am."

Hilda left her bed, forcing the officer to uncomfortably avert his eyes as she rummaged within a suitcase. Weil would have normally enjoyed the view, but the sheer possibility of Razarkha's survival filled the room with a red mist. She took out a blade whose metal was wavy, interspersing silvery grey with an unmistakeable golden tone.

"Do you know what this is, Weil?"

"It is knife with knotweed inside of it," he answered.

"What you call 'knotweed' we call 'the Thread', but yes, you're correct. I have a hunch as to what's happened," Hilda began. "I think that somehow, Razarkha used the souls she harvested to conduct some form of self-necromancy. If that's the case, the arcane within her wound is a life support system. If she's anything like a zombie or revenant, she'll be resistant to most attacks, but the Thread consumes arcana. One stab with this, and whatever magic she's using should fail. If not, may the Mother have mercy on us all."

Weil took the knife, not daring to test its sharpness. "I'll kill her again if I must. I know where she will go. She hates her brother, so she shall take revenge in Arkhera."

"Ah, excellent, just take one of your portals to Arkhera, intercept her, and this problem takes care of itself," Hildegard said with a dismissive wave.

"I can only visit places I remember at will," Weil explained. "Still, I should take portal to Zemelnya, for head-start—"

**"You may control how we open our paths to the mortal realm, but you shall never compel us to corrupt the very cosmos,"** the Rakh'vash echoed, refusing to open the portal Weil had mentally requested.

*"What are you talking about, it's just a portal to Zemelnya,"* Weil said in Chaostongue. *"You've opened a thousand portals there, even when you were unreceptive to my will."*

**"The knotweed has touched your mortal realm, and foolish mortals grow corrupt from its entropy-defying lustre. If the knotweed touches the chaotic realm, it would infest the very concept of entropy. Then, this pestilence would infest every object, every fraction of matter subject to the whims of chaos! Our cosmos would be choked with knotweed."**

Weil swallowed and accepted that this god likely knew what it was talking about. "Many apology, Imperial Engineer. I cannot open chaotic portal and hold this knotweed weapon at same time. I still intend to help, but—"

"Fine, I'll have some of the men take you to Zemelnya, but from there, you're on your own. Find your monster, put her down, and then maybe you'll be able to smile," the Imperial Engineer said. "Oh, and when you find her, tell her that Hildegard Swan said hello."

# Renewals

The screaming came as a pair; as Ascetic Montarys of the Moon Men held a wailing, black-haired infant, the boy's mother shrieked in agony, her flesh searing against wood. Apostle Petyr Godswater stood upon a platform, his eyes pitilessly watching the dying woman. Even as a spectre behind her uncle, Rosaline knew that if she looked away, he'd still find out.

Flanking her sides were two people she dared to trust. To her left was Shiloh Godspawn, her bastard cousin, his face hidden behind an ornate helmet replete with the red and white of the Border. To her right was her most feared attachment; High Ascetic Pleura, the leader of the Moon Men and the only female ascetic appointed within Petyr Godswater's rule.

She was only lightly armoured and wielded a holy staff of redstone and norvite. Most of her hair was the black one expected of a Godswater woman, but to her right, it was bleached a pale yellow, and her right eye had a patch over it. Rosaline often felt the urge to focus on her pretty face, her inspiring, flowing locks, and her poised, unflappable demeanour, but it was a trap. If Petyr noticed, he'd soon remind Rosaline of why such desires were inappropriate.

The dying woman's voice vanished into the aether, leaving the crackling of the pyre and the increasingly shrill cries of her orphaned son behind. Rosaline turned from the blackened body, and though Pleura opened her arms, she couldn't accept her offer. She instead sought the embrace of her metal-clad cousin, who held her as gently as a military man could.

"I know it's justice, Shiloh, but it still hurts to watch," Rosaline said in an undertone.

"It's hard for me too. If it was easy, it wouldn't be justice. I'm sure Uncle Petyr has a good reason for putting her to death. Once he's done with his speech, I'll ensure the woman's child is safe," the holy warrior promised.

Rosaline let Shiloh go. Affecting Petyr's will was futile. The apostle's reasoning was too elegant, his tongue too slick. His opponents always agreed with him in the end.

"And so, we must once again reflect on the wasted life before us," Uncle Petyr began, addressing the crowd of onlookers. "This woman, in a callous attempt to foist her natural duty of child-rearing onto the House of Godswater, accused me, the Voice of the Gods, of fathering her child. This child certainly is a bastard, but not mine.

"All women who seek carnal pleasures before marriage are pursuing folly; for if they fall with child, who shall protect them? The man whose clear willingness to indulge her sinfulness led to the conception in the first place? Her parents, whose failure to discipline their child led to such a wanton harlot? No, there is no recourse for such debauchery other than suffering for both mother and child.

"This woman's boldness and slander has yielded one good thing, however. Though her demands amounted to asking me, the Voice of the Gods, to accept a lie, I shall grant her child the Gods' protection. From here on, the Moon Men shall raise this boy as their own, an instrument of the Moon Man from his first steps!"

Shiloh cut into his uncle's speech and staggered forward. "Your Holiness, I volunteered to take the child, why are you—"

"Dearest Shiloh, you are the only good thing my wretched brother Duncan left behind. Your protectiveness and valour are encouraging signs to bastards everywhere, proof that their conception is no blockade to holiness. However, I cannot allow a bastard to raise a bastard. Luthor's care will fall to the Moon Men and the feminine nurturing of High Ascetic Pleura."

Pleura raised a hand. "I am honoured, Apostle Godswater, but I'm only seventeen—"

"My words are the words of the Gods, are they not?" Petyr Godswater asked, finally deigning to turn from the crowd.

Both ascetics quieted, while Ascetic Montarys, the Moon Man holding young Luthor, smirked beneath his crescent-moon half-mask. Rosaline trembled as Apostle Petyr went back to addressing the crowd, his words blurring into a slurry of pious declarations. Pleura's crestfallen expression forced Rosaline to break her discipline and take her hand.

"Don't worry," she whispered. "I think you'll make a wonderful mother."

Pleura paused. "The child won't be 'mine', it'll be the Moon Men's, but thank you for your kind words. We shouldn't be talking like this in public, though."

Rosaline knew she was right, yet she didn't want to let go. Pleura made the right decision for her, while Rosaline's whoredom consumed her once again.

"I'm sorry, I wasn't thinking."

"I'm not angry at you," Pleura assured her. "Just be mindful."

When Rosaline returned to reality, she found that Shiloh had already left the platform, while Montarys had taken his place by Rosaline's left. Terror shot through her, and though Petyr was still addressing his people, her face burned up. A flash of light danced between her and Pleura, causing both to jump, yet Ascetic Montarys acted as though he saw nothing.

"If you fear for the child, young Rosaline, you're mistaken," he said. "Luthor will be edified with the secrets of the Moon Man from an early age. He shall serve the Gods proudly, and keep a tight grip upon this city's secrets, never allowing them to spill into heathen hands."

Rosaline didn't respond; though Pleura strove to understand her and accepted her sinful attraction, this man served Petyr alone. Besieged by the black and blue of the

Moon Men, she pondered over what secrets the city could hold that weren't simple mysteries of the world. Watching Uncle Petyr's robes wave with every gesticulation, she accepted that one of them was likely what she'd done to the Voice of the Gods.

If she knew some of the Moon Men's secrets, who else was privy? Asking Pleura or Montarys was no good; Petyr would be informed immediately. There was somebody in her family who was always eager to talk about injustice but associating with him was similarly risky. She closed her eyes and winced. These thoughts were heresy, yet she knew Apostle Petyr wasn't the infallible man the city knew him as. She needed to speak to Uncle Gerold Applewood. When Petyr Godswater pulled himself from his podium and made his way towards the Saltwater Temple, Rosaline approached the apostle, adjusting her veil before she spoke.

"Uncle Petyr, may I visit the Shrine of the Storm before I head inside?"

Petyr stroked his moustache and frowned. "This is not some pretence, is it? What would you be praying to the Storm about?"

Rosaline's voice wavered; she couldn't lie to her uncle once he demanded the truth, but thankfully, she had every intent of visiting the shrine on the way home.

"For calm seas, so that our fishing fleets bring back a bountiful haul and our fishermen may return to their wives and children in peace," Rosaline said.

"How very generic," Petyr scoffed. "Every fishwife in this city prays for the same thing. Are you some fishwife?"

"No, I'm the heir to Godswater," Rosaline replied. "The city's people are my people. I pray for their wellbeing because I must."

Petyr shrugged. "So be it. Pleura, Montarys, take the child to the city nursery and find them a wetnurse. If Shiloh wasn't as sensitive as his feminine namesake implies, I'd have work for him too, but that shall wait. I look forward to your return, young Rosaline."

Rosaline put her hands together and gave him a Jaranese bow. "I know you do."

With that, she parted from Petyr and the Moon Man ascetics, rushing around the embers of the life her uncle snuffed out. The crowd who'd eagerly watched the woman perish were scattering. Rosaline wandered through the terraces of the holy city and considered the Gods. None were infallible or almighty, yet together, they were great, powerful beings whose combined facets made up the world. Each had their own morality and priorities, which led to different men having different patron gods. Rosaline, however, didn't have any. The Gods plainly favoured people like Petyr Godswater, and though she had a healthy fear of beings who would empower such a person, it didn't inspire genuine piety.

Where was the Border's justice when Uncle Petyr lost control of his urges? When the Eagle fought for every mortal's freedom, did he forget to fight for Rosaline's? If the Storm's role was to cast down arrogant mortals who built too high, too quickly, why was Petyr safe within the Saltwater Temple, weathering every controversy with contemptuous ease?

The Gods must have hated her. She wasn't free to die, she wasn't deserving of a better life, and whatever sins Petyr committed weren't considered heinous enough for him to be struck down. The sensation of Pleura's hand against her own reminded Rosaline of the issue. She desired wantonly. Men growing lecherous over women was a perversion of the natural urges that allowed mankind to persist. Women desiring their fellow woman was needless lust.

Yet Rosaline still had the gall to commit heresy despite her pre-existing sinfulness. The Gods were right to curse her, but if her suspicions were correct, perhaps the

Gods needed her to be a heretic; even Lara the Liberator was said to have spoken heresy in her youth before growing into the proud representative of the Eagle she was remembered as. She walked to the northern edge of the central district, towards a small cottage lying between a wine cellar and a smoke shop. Both wares were considered sinful excess by Uncle Petyr, yet many heroes of the Hexacron enjoyed both in moderation. Uncle Gerold, however, knew of no such concept.

Rosaline moved through the cottage's unlocked gate, and past a weed-strewn, overgrown garden. A dead peach tree stood defiantly amidst dandelions and nettles, gratefully unaware of the bracket fungi and ivies infesting its corpse. When Rosaline reached the door, it flew open, shocking her enough that, bizarrely, a nearby nettle blackened to a crisp. Within the entrance was a bearded fellow with great, flabby jowls and jaundiced eyes. He was dressed in full plate armour save for his helmet, and in his hand was a musket pistol.

"Who's there? Has Petyr finally decided I gotta go? Well, *come take me!*"

Rosaline opened her hands. "Uncle Gerold, it's me! Rosaline! Please tell me you're sober, I need to talk to you."

Gerold put his gun away and grunted. "Sorry for scaring you, Rosie. Come on in, before the Moon Men figure out where you are."

She followed her maternal uncle into his abode, and immediately regretted not taking a smelling sachet with her. The years-long rot of the cottage's wooden beams almost matched the horrors of a burning stake, the only difference being that one scent was associated with slow, agonising death, while the other was over within the day. He led her to a sitting room, where the floor teased at its presence beneath the countless flattened wine boxes. A moth-eaten settee and an armchair floated in the cardboard sea, the latter swiftly taken up by Uncle Gerold.

"Go on, Rosie, get comfortable, I don't mind if you don't want to take your shoes off."

"I won't be here long," she said, hoping this would allow her to avoid touching the mould-infested fabric before her.

"That so? I s'pose you ought to ask whatever you need to ask quickly," Gerold muttered, checking his musket pistol as he spoke.

Rosaline's chest tightened. What would be her first heretical question? It was unnerving to treat this shame to the House of Applewood as an oracle in the first place. She'd visited him as a child, but her father, Simeon Godswater, constantly argued with him. Now that father was dead and she was a woman grown, perhaps he would be willing to speak sincerely.

"Why do you drink so much?"

Gerold laughed, casually pointed his pistol at his own temple, then put the gun down. "You walk all the way to my house, risk being caught by your Uncle Petyr, just to ask why a daylight drinker drinks? I drink 'cause of your mother's death. 'cause of her life. If I tell you anything else, Petyr'll figure out where you got the information from. We both know what happens to people who inconvenience the good apostle."

Rosaline gazed at a wine box by her feet. Her mother, Lana Applewood, died soon after her birth, and while her father insisted it wasn't due to birthing complications, Rosaline hadn't stopped blaming herself. Gerold's gaze seared through her thoughts, forcing her to conceive another question.

"How did my mother die?"

Gerold sighed. "Officially, it's hysteria. I can't tell you what I think unless I fancy being tortured to death, but perhaps I can leave you with some questions. You remember your father a little, don't you?"

"I remember you and father always argued."

"Aye, and he was always drinking poppy milk," Gerold said. "Have you thought about why he did that?"

Rosaline flushed up. "Perhaps for the same reason you drink wine like most drink water? You lost a sister, he lost a wife, but everyone loses people. I don't understand what any of this cryptic allusion means."

"Fine, I'll ask something else. Say your mother died on purpose; why would she choose to die so soon after your birth? And why would Apostle Petyr want your Uncle Duncan exiled?"

"What in the world does my mother's death have to do with Duncan? He fathered Shiloh, brought shame to the House of Godswater, and was exiled long before I was born!"

Gerold sighed. "Fine, I'll be a little straighter with you, but know that if a Moon Man's listening, I'm probably going to die for this. Your mother and Shiloh's mother are connected. Lana, poor Lana, she— she couldn't cope with it. Gods, even now, I see her face, those sad, sad eyes. I remember what she was like before she married that coward, Simeon."

"My father was a brave man—"

"He was a coward, I was a coward, we both failed to do what was necessary!" Gerold spat, standing up and hobbling from the room. "Gods I need a drink. Look, Rosie, if all you want from me is information, then get out of my house. Don't worry, I'm sure your Uncle Petyr will clean up this loose end soon enough. Go on, out, you're not ready to hear what I know."

"I am! I'm a woman grown, and— and I'm a sinful heretic. Please, if you can't answer me properly, tell me where to look," Rosaline said, following him into a wine-filled kitchen.

"Ask why you've been made heir, despite being a woman. Ask why your mother chose to die. Then ask why me and your father numbed ourselves. Think of how it could go back to your Uncle Duncan."

Rosaline didn't understand. She hadn't even met her Uncle Duncan; he was simply a disgraceful third son according to Uncle Petyr. Suddenly, a heretical thought passed through her mind, a depraved notion that the Eagle within her wanted to explore.

"I think I understand. Thank you, Uncle Gerold."

The broken knight filled a fogged-up glass with boxed wine. "You wouldn't be thanking me if you knew the full truth, but you should get back to the Saltwater Temple. What's the old saying? Bad associations spoil useful habits?"

Rosaline put her hands together and bowed to Gerold. "Gods be with you, uncle."

* * *

While it was good that Rakh was able to take a train there at all, Ashglass's station did not fill him with hope. The locomotive he was on stopped with a hiss, and he left his carriage to see a building full of guards shivering in the cold, barely keeping an eye on the situation. He couldn't blame them; there were hardly any passengers to watch over. Though the station had reopened, Ashglass's status as a plagued city must have reached the ears of the kingdom.

On the way out, a guard turned to Rakh, muttering, "Tickets, please."

Rakh handed them over, and once the ticket was torn, he smiled. "Thank you. Keep fighting, all right?"

"The thought's nice, but if you knew what we've been fighting the past couple months you'd forgive me for giving up."

"I was there, albeit as a privileged nobleman," he said, fluffing his coat a little. "Don't you recognise me?"

"No, but you're a spellbinder noble, so you're probably that Fel'thuz guy. If you wanna fuck *our* commoners, don't bother. Most of 'em don't want to see a naked person again."

Rakh nodded. "I'm aware. Don't worry, I'm here for work, not pleasure."

He left the guardsman to it and walked through Ashglass's industrial district until Castle Foenaxas was in sight. The castle guards were barely more cognisant of their surroundings, but their shaking arms and overly straight stance told Rakh enough. Snow had long since covered the ashes upon the floor, yet the people couldn't cover the scars of their souls so easily. As he neared the building, a seer in mauve and gold left its grounds. It was Khalver Veritas, and considering his previous handling of the unpredictable, Rakh was surprised at how calm the wisdom was.

"I had a feeling I'd spot a visitor today. Don't worry, I told Lady Foenaxas to stay indoors, not that she needs much encouragement these days," Khalver remarked.

"What does that mean?" Rakh asked.

"Isn't it obvious?" the seer said. "The city's rebuilding, but she's lost her brother. Yes, I know what you're going to say, it could be worse, your lady is ever so magnanimous, but you'll forgive her some melancholy, I hope."

"I'd never begrudge that. I'm here to propose an arrangement and thought visiting her in person would be the best way to resolve the specifics quickly," Rakh said. "Would you be so kind as to lead me to her?"

"Of course, my count," the wisdom said with a bow.

Khalver was quick to scurry into Castle Foenaxas, Rakh's slow strides easily matching his feverish motions. For a moment, the difference between his and Khalver's heights became palpable, and he wondered if Razarkha would have grown up differently if she was raised in a country full of spellbinders, like Ilazar or Galdus.

Mor'kha was in a lounge with Lexana, Solyx, and a chestnut-brown girl with red-blonde hair who shared the lady's eyes, but little else. Lady Foenaxas was playing an organetto, Lexana was a lute, and the other girl a harp. The dark elven woman was so lost in her music that she only noticed Rakh was in the room when Lexana stopped playing her lute.

"What's stopped you, Lexie, we were— oh. Khalver was right," Mor'kha muttered. "Lexie, Mag, go to the dining room. It seems local politics has interrupted our quality time."

Lexana nodded and left, while 'Mag' was somewhat slower to follow. Khalver wringed his hands and his breathing grew shaky.

"My sincerest apologies, my lady, but as you know, you were—"

"I'm not angry. I'm just glad you informed me this time," Mor'kha said, putting her organetto on a now-empty sofa. "Sit, Count Fel'thuz. What seems to be the problem?"

Rakh inclined his head, first to Mor'kha, then to Lord Consort Solyx, then sat on what he hoped wasn't a precious armchair. Though Lady Foenaxas was technically loyal to her provincial liege, her narrowed golden eyes and slow, deep breaths spoke louder than any vow.

"We believe Razarkha could descend upon the Forests of Winter at any moment," Rakh said. "The good news is the artefact she's acquired isn't as powerful as we first assumed. We think Ashglass will be safe, as she probably won't start fights that aren't personal."

Solyx smirked. "I hope you don't intend to prolong your visit. We have our extended family over, and a monstrous spellbinder attack would ruin the mood."

Rakh shook his head. "By no means. I intend to be bait, but I believe Moonstone's citizens are in danger. Razarkha is aware of my fondness for peasants, so I believe she'll consider it worthwhile to target them. How are the reconstruction efforts going?"

Lady Foenaxas maintained her pitiless golden glare just long enough to run a chill through Rakh's spine, then answered. "While your wisdom's efforts have allowed us to rebuild, we're short of men, the ilmenite your lady has supplied us is running out, and businessmen are forever wittering in my ear about wanting to buy land to build establishments I'd hoped the renewed Ashglass would have grown beyond."

Solyx butted in. "I still believe that a casino could stimulate—"

"What the people need in these times are houses, godliness, and hope!" Mor'kha snapped. "The people of Ashglass are in pain, and you'd have me plunge them further into despair! Gambling was rightly considered a blight by Peregrine, and I would not be serving God *or* my people if I encouraged such vice!"

"The people need to find vice again too," Solyx said. "If you obstruct certain businesses for moral reasons, you're simply confirming the people's whisperings."

"I'm not having this conversation with you again, Solyx," Mor'kha said. "If you think bringing it up in front of Count Fel'thuz will somehow change my mind, you're mistaken."

Rakh scratched his false hand. "Should we discuss this later? Perhaps I could meet your relatives. I hear Solyx's sister-in-law Koaraxa is simply—"

"Not a chance," Mor'kha snapped. "I'm not housing the man who got my brother exiled for any longer than I need to."

There it was. If Kag was here, she would have grown defensive, and Plutyn would have made a scornful remark about how if life was fair, Irikhos would be executed. Rakh formulated what he prayed would be a diplomatic response, then spoke.

"As you say. Let's not waste any time," Rakh said. "The peasants of Moonstone are in danger as far as I'm concerned. I hope to send every builder and miner I can to Ashglass and the Ashpeaks respectively. This should help you rebuild, as well as offering my people refuge. I know you don't like me, but this arrangement should benefit us both—"

"The mercantile class is already assaulting the morals of Ashglass, why wouldn't the neighbouring nobility? Whenever Moonstone touches Ashglass, it withers," Mor'kha said.

Rakh faltered. "I don't understand. Wisdom Erwyn developed the cure to a plague that would have consumed this city, and I'm offering you skilled labourers that—"

"That I have to feed and shelter, who bring their own gods and a lack of precautions that the people of this city have had no choice but to develop," Mor'kha snapped. "I am grateful to your wisdom, and if you wanted me to be amenable, you should have sent him. But you and your lady have ruined my brother's life, and this 'offer' you propose is a poisoned chalice."

"I only want what's best for everyone!" Rakh said, his voice peaking before he recomposed himself. "I know that you're struggling, that your brother's gone, and that yes, you have every reason to hate Moonstone nobility, but these peasants are *innocent.*"

"They're Eternalists, and they'll corrupt my people when they need God the most."

Solyx Solerro stood and broke into the conversation. "Are you seriously suggesting leaving peasants to die for their faith? Is that what you're suggesting, Strakha? When we were in the middle of the rapeworm crisis, you showed a love for your people that truly inspired me. What makes our people worthy of this compassion and Moonstone Eternalists not? Their god? If that's the case, send me to Moonstone. Let me die with my fellow heathens."

Lady Mor'kha rose to meet her husband. "It's— it's not like that, you're different—"

"How am I different? Because you know me? Because I'm the father of your children?"

"No, because you— you understand me, you understand Renewalism, you can accept Ashglass's ways even if you're different," Mor'kha said, trembling with uncertainty.

"What's stopping them? I imagine peasants will be much more accepting than some half-Elarondian noble fop."

Mor'kha averted her husband's glare, inadvertently meeting Rakh's eyes. "Very well. I'll take your Moonstone men. I'm sorry for not putting our grudges aside."

"I'm sorry I had to ask so much of you," Rakh said, picking himself up. "Know that I wish for Irikhos's success. If all goes well, you'll see your brother again, and will likely attend his wedding."

"Don't salt a wounded woman," Mor'kha muttered. "You've got what you wanted."

Khalver Veritas spoke up. "Don't worry, Count Fel'thuz. I'll preserve what was agreed upon here in writing and negotiate the numbers in my office."

Rakh nodded. "Thank you, Wisdom Khalver. I hope that next time I visit Ashglass, it'll be under more joyous circumstances."

\* \* \*

Zemelnya's city square was more crowded than the last time Rowyn had visited, and where there was once a set of heads on spikes, there were now notices written in Isleborn and Plagueborn, with elaborately dressed spellbinders of both Ilazari peoples stopping to check them. Occasionally, fights broke out, but they seemed largely self-contained, and usually ended without collateral damage. A balalaika player sat and strummed upon a chest in the square's corner, singing in a rich Isleborn accent.

Rowyn couldn't help but consider the situation too idyllic, and true enough, once he drifted towards the Plagueborn side of town, a massive sign with jagged Isleborn runes loomed over the closest residential street. From what he could gauge, the sign read *'Plagueborn instigators, be warned: Breakers of the peace will be killed'*.

Ilazar and Arkhera were much the same; peace was not a natural facet of such internally divided nations, but something enforced by military might. Vi'kara and family were likely grateful for the truce, regardless of how it was enforced. As Rowyn approached a familiar ice-covered house, bittersweetness engulfed him. The sharpness of bergamot, the comfort of chamomile, it all flooded back to him in an overpoweringly pungent wave.

He got so lost in his wistfulness that he bumped forehead-first into a slab of ice that he could have sworn wasn't in his path before. He rubbed his head in pain, before noticing someone in his peripheral vision. It was her: Blonde-haired, clad in nought but a sewn-together seaweed dress and abalone bracers.

"*Vi'kara!*" Rowyn called out in terrible Isleborn. "*I sought you out, my travels grew hazardous!*"

The woman embraced Rowyn without hesitation, giving him a strong whiff of lavender oil. She stroked his hair, then let him go, speaking enthusiastic Old Galdusian.

"*Worry not, valiant Arkheran knight. I'll teach you the languages now that you've returned for good. You're staying, aren't you? After all, your colourful clothes and long hair make you look quite Ilazari.*"

Rowyn tapped the back of his hair. "*You're the first person to notice my hair's grown out. As for the robes, they're Jaranese. I've been on quite the adventure.*"

"*I wish I could say the same,*" Vi'kara remarked, taking Rowyn's hand and dragging him away from her house. *"I've been hiding out with the family, watching War'mal suddenly cease his hostilities with the Isleborn. I'm for it, but his behaviour is unusually overcorrecting."*

*"What do you mean?"* Rowyn asked. *"Where are you taking me?"*

Vi'kara smirked. *"I promised my mother that if you returned, I would take you to an inn. Apparently, my parents don't want to hear me while we—"*

*"I want you in that way, but I'd prefer to wait,"* Rowyn said. *"I'd like to adjust to Ilazar somewhat before we do anything irreversible. Though I'm glad to see you, Zemelnya is admittedly a last resort. I'm unable to return to Arkhera as long as Razarkha Fel'thuz lives."*

*"Ah, that reminds me!"* Vi'kara said, somehow undaunted by the mild rejection. *"As I was saying, War'mal is overcorrecting in bizarre ways. Not only has he put a one million credit bounty on his former ally, Razarkha Fel'thuz, he also commissioned the repair of Kasparov Manor, hired Isleborn servants to staff it, and has used it to home the remaining three Kasparov children, essentially ceding his leverage over the Isleborn."*

Rowyn squinted. *"Wait, is War'mal a cryomancer? Are the Kasparov children white-haired and blue-eyed by any chance?"*

*"That's correct,"* Vi'kara said. *"Why, have you seen them?"*

*"Yes, and they were together on a beach, as though they were family."*

Vi'kara rubbed her chin. *"That is unusual. This new War'mal is working to reduce tensions with the Isleborn. I cannot describe it as anything other than becoming a new man."*

Rowyn shrugged. *"I'm sure I'll have plenty of time to solve the mystery, if indeed one needs solving. For now, I need to seek out the ill and the injured."*

*"Why?"*

"I'm going to make my living as a medic," Rowyn declared. "When I save up enough money, I'll buy a house large enough for two. If you're interested, of course."

Vi'kara raised an eyebrow as they reached a row of taverns, one of which's windows blew out from a pyromantic blast. "So, having some enjoyable bedroom time is too much, but planning to buy a more expensive house just for my sake isn't?"

"By the time I'm buying a house, I'll know if you're the woman for me," Rowyn said.

"I like you, Sir Khanas, but you're ever so Arkheran. Come, let us drink some vodka, and then you'll see things the Plagueborn way."

Rowyn tightened his grip on Vi'kara's hand, and let her drag him into the nearest tavern *not* being ravaged by some manner of spellbinder scrap.

# Convergences

Far above Jaranar, Razarkha and Duncan drifted in silence. Ariel's words scratched at the calluses of her mind, and as though scissors snipping away dead flesh, they exposed something raw beneath. Weil was real after all, and so was her betrayal. She didn't know where he was, if he knew she was still alive after a fashion, or if he found new friends. She eyed her augmented accomplice and concluded that he couldn't have befriended new people when she'd claimed such a poor haul. He was a fool without her to guide him, a man unable to distinguish a ship with black fielded heraldry from a piratical vessel.

The salt of Zemelnya's waters coursed through her nostrils with a clarity no true sensation could currently achieve. Her eyes expelled similarly salty water, and her crystalline abdomen tugged against her non-functional innards. Weil was right to kill her, but if she saw him again, she would have to defend herself. Greatness had no room for sentimentality. Razarkha was weak, but Praetor Erre needed to be strong.

"Look down there, Fel'thuz," Duncan said while pointing downwards. "We're above Meung-Chaydan."

Razarkha checked to see smoke rising from numerous glowing spots within a city that was colourful even from the heavens. Descending to get a better view, she spotted a swarm of peasants burning numerous gated-off properties while human mages in yellow and blue attacked them from above. While the crowds won small victories, twenty of them died for each mage, and the most prominent property, a great fortress of jadeite and nephrite that lay behind three walls, was utterly untouched by the people's rampage. The magical enforcers continued to massacre the enraged peasants, and Razarkha, overcome by the craving of her soulstealer, descended to absorb some of the recently deceased.

"What are you doing?" Duncan asked.

"I'm restocking while I can," Razarkha said. "It's not as though these people weren't going to die anyway. Ariel being soulless was an unfortunate setback, but I won't go this entire journey without recuperation."

She briefly enjoyed the elation of the Jaranese humans' souls entering her body, and for a moment, she experienced the whip of the winds about her. The allure of playing the raven to each rioter's death overcame her, and she descended further, sweeping over the chaos like she was the Harvester herself.

"Watch out, you've been spotted!" Duncan called from above.

True to his word, a trio of human mages with fire dancing about their wrists were flying her way. Unlike ascendants, there was no radius of instant victory for Razarkha, but fortunately, she'd already confirmed that her lumomancy was powerful enough to sink fleets. Before they had a chance to coordinate an attack, she channelled a portion of her life force to her soulstealer and unleashed it in the form of a searing ray.

She swept the beam across the sky, scorching the mages' midsections and making them fall into the hungry crowd below. The Jaranese commoners cheered, then tore the enforcers apart, one particularly gaunt human going as far as to chew on a disembodied arm. Their role as food was not limited to the physical; Razarkha claimed their souls and grinned at Duncan.

"Let me show you how I permanently reshaped the Sulari power structure."

The augmentee lowered to Razarkha's level, then abruptly jutted a piece of ground upwards to impale a nearing aeromancer. "I understand you once ran a revolution, but we can't stay here too long. You said you wanted to attack Moonstone, and I just want Godswater out of Petyr's unworthy hands. We can't linger too long on the—"

"Look at these people," Razarkha said as she claimed the souls of a group blasted by a distant pyromancer. "They're ineffectual revolutionaries, and for all their destruction, they've failed to target what truly matters."

"With respect, Razarkha, your revolution also failed, as you yourself admitted. The rice riots have been happening since before I was augmented, and I don't think you can change that without significantly delaying our return—"

"Watch this," Razarkha said, telekinetically shoving the mass of volcanic sputa aside.

She focused her recently absorbed arcane power, directing it into the Soulstealer of Craving until the device was hot even to her numbed hands. The resultant beam was large and intense enough to bisect an unfortunate mage that happened to be in its way. Its intended destination, the walls of the jade palace, took it for mere moments before melting and cracking from the heat. A hole was made, and numerous palace guards were crushed.

Razarkha ascended once more, and beckoned Duncan to join her. "There, I've made an opening. Watch as the tide of battle shifts. I've significantly changed *spellbinder* nations, some backwards, island-dwelling humans don't need my full attention."

The rioters predictably surged towards the hole in the walls, and the mages were quick to flank them. A set of men in brown and green upon the battlements rushed into action, raising their hands and erecting rocky blockades to replace the shattered sections of the walls.

"They have geomancers," Duncan said. "Are you going to kill them too?"

Razarkha instinctively pointed her soulstealer at the palace's battlements before a twinge of lethargy struck her so palpably that her arms grew limp and her telekinesis faltered. She hurriedly regained control of her magic and caught her soulstealer before her grip failed too, then screamed into the artefact.

"What's the meaning of this? Why is your so-called boon failing me?"

*"You just spent a month of your remaining life focusing a beam while maintaining enough telekinesis to float in place. You are the only test case of this experimental form of undeath; a rational person wouldn't begrudge a few stutters."*

"A few stutters? You're a god, you should know the pitfalls of your handiwork!"

*"Wouldn't that be boring? No, I'm just as unsure of your form's limits as you are. After all, half the apparatus, that is to say, your body, doesn't belong to me."*

"Oh, you're so amusing, truly glib, you're Sir Sovereign of House Glib, do you realise this is a mortal body you're playing with?"

*"I'm quite aware, and I was under the impression you understood that too."*

"I hate you so much," Razarkha spat, then rose beyond the magical enforcers' attention. "Duncan, come. You were right, this fight isn't worth it."

The augmentee's scraping voice was somewhat high-pitched. "You're actually agreeing with me?"

Razarkha's vision blurred as the rioters rushed head-first into the temporary walls erected by Meung-Chaydan's geomancers, to get burnt alive by the remaining pyromancers.

"I'm not the woman I was when I was alive. The only thing left to do is kill Rakh," she said in a flat tone. "I'm sorry. I hoped to recapture the joy of fighting the Sons of Sula."

"Don't apologise to me," Duncan said. "Apologise to the folks you gave false hope to."

Razarkha could feel the souls in the air, and though her soulstealer begged to consume them, Duncan was right. They were dead because of her, like every insurrectionist scattered across Nova Tertia's inner city. Robbing them of an afterlife wasn't the same as denying a haughty Galdusian of one. After a brief dip, she ascended, then found the way north.

"Let's go," she muttered. "Petyr Godswater awaits."

"Of course," Duncan replied before trailing behind her.

* * *

The steam sloop Weil was napping in filled him with more nausea than any trip to the Chaotic Realm. He couldn't sleep deeply enough to dream, and had one hand on a sheath which contained the weapon Hildegard Swan insisted would put Razarkha down for good. Surrounded by Yukishimans with neither the heart nor body of the Imperial Engineer, all he wanted to do was cry.

He opened his eyes and sat up in his scratchy bunk, staring at the dull grey walls of his cabin. When he first heard Razarkha admit to killing his father, he was shocked, but when she attempted to excuse herself, the rift practically opened itself. Perhaps to her, his father was some whimpering animal in need of Ilazari mercy, but even Hilda knew he wasn't that to Weil.

He stared out of his small, circular window into the murky waters of the Accursed Sea and thought of his father's gentle voice. When his mother lost her life by being in the wrong place at the wrong time, Weil wanted nothing more than to wrap tentacles around every Muranov and squeeze them until they stopped squirming. When he tried to take his vengeance, Ivan forcefully took him into his arms and begged him to stay.

*"I've lost my wife, Weil,"* he'd said. *"Please don't make me lose my son too."*

*"I'm sorry, father,"* Weil told the memory. *"I'm choosing violence yet again."*

Perhaps Razarkha had a point. She didn't know the man Ivan once was, but if he'd have known what Weil did to preserve his life, perhaps he would have chosen to die. As the steam frigate bobbed, the sound of splintering wood filled his ears. Waters thoroughly chummed red and the writhing of a many-eyed, many-armed daemon covered the inner coating of his eyelids.

*"Would you be ashamed of me, father? Could you still love the man I've become?"*

Ivan was no ghost. Wherever he was, he couldn't hear his son. Weil shook his head and headed out of his cabin, skulking through the hull's dingy corridors then up to the deck, where a crew of freckled, broad-shouldered humans operated the frigate's weapons. One Yukishiman was cleaning the floor, but upon seeing Weil, stopped and rested against a guardrail.

"So, you ready to take a motorboat back to Illie city?" he asked in the lilting Common Yookies were wont to use.

"Motor boat? Is this variety of boat?" Weil asked.

"Yeah, you lesser naval nations have small oar boats called pinnaces for when you need to deploy a small set of people from a big ship. The motorboat's our version. Last I checked, the plan is for us to anchor far from Zemelnya, then you take a motorboat the rest of the way."

"I not understand much of what you say, but I take your Yukishiman motor boat to Zemelnya, yes?"

"Of course you don't speak Common like the rest of us," he said with a roll of his eyes. "I don't know what the Imperial Engineer is tryin' to say, sending us off on some stupid mission to bring an Illie moron home."

Weil snorted and muttered in Isleborn. *"To we Ilazari, Yukishiman pigs are stupid for not knowing our tongues."*

"What'd you say?"

"That Yukishiman are wondrous technology makers."

"Yeah, I don't believe that."

Weil laughed. "Much Yukishiman wisdom indeed."

The human scoffed and returned to cleaning. "Fucking snakes."

There was no point in picking a fight. This was one disgruntled Yukishiman, far from his cold northern home, likely missing his family for some snake's sake. He walked to the front of the ship, where the captain, a red-faced, watery-eyed human with a beard, stood with his arms behind his overly straight back. He barely moved when Weil approached, yet vocally acknowledged his presence.

"Look ahead, Ilazari. That rock over there resemble home?"

Weil gazed at the distant cliffs and shale beaches of Ilazar's southern coast, the Sudovykly jags piercing his heart anew. He nodded, then found the Common words.

"That is home. Coast of Zemelnya, Ilazar."

"Then my map's correct and my compass functional. With me, boy, I'll show you how our motorboats work," he said, before taking a strange, rectangular device out of his pocket. He pressed a button on it, then spoke into it. "All right, crew, to your stations, we're going to anchor as soon as possible, last thing we want is some Ilazari cliff monster taking this ship!"

Weil almost smiled at the thought that people had conjured legends of his desperate exploits but knew Razarkha would like that. She'd made him confuse evil for self-sufficiency, and abuse for well-meaning advice. He tapped the sheathe of his thread knife, then followed the captain to the starboard side of the ship, where a motorboat was ready for deployment.

"All right, to start the boat, turn this key that's stuck in this hole," the captain said, pointing to a small metallic protrusion by the front of the boat. "That'll ignite the engine, which you'll hear roar. Then there's this lever; push forward to go forward, pull back to go back. This wheel here is like any other rudder wheel, turns the boat. Push this kill-switch to stop the engine. Any questions?"

Weil blinked and attempted to repeat the instructions back in Common. "Turn little key to start boat roaring. Then use stick to move and wheel to turn. Switch of death stops engine."

The captain shrugged. "Good enough. All right, climb on in. When the ship stops, we'll lower you."

Weil did as commanded, and once he was comfortable, he turned the key to test the so-called roaring. The result was a loud, popping growl at the back of the boat, which almost made him jump clear off the side. He hit the kill-switch, and as the captain said, it stopped the engine. Once the captain left him, he muttered in Chaostongue.

*"You will correct my boat with tentacles if I am led astray by the waves, am I understood?"*

**"We understand, but We refuse to help. While you possess that abominable weapon, an opportunity for you to slip into our realm is an opportunity for the knotweed to infest the cosmos."**

*"Yes, yes!,"* Weil muttered.

With his god abandoning him, all Weil could ask for was that this motorboat wasn't as cursed as the *Dikamonstra* or *Maresancti*. The sloop to his left came to a halt, and a set of Yukishimans lowered his boat into the Accursed Sea. Black waters licked at the hull of the two-man boat, and as it bobbed, he turned the key once more.

It made a growl pleasing enough that it almost made him forgive the Yukishimans' disdain for his kind, and when the lever was pushed forward, it zipped through the water. There was something disturbing about the lack of sails upon the vessel, but the wind at his hair and the trail of churning waters behind him was confirmation enough that the vehicle worked.

As the Sudovykly cliffs grew closer, Weil noticed that the motorboat's lever was only partway pushed. His hand danced towards it, and the voice in his head that cooperated with the Rakh'vash told him what he needed to do. With a shove, he pushed it to its limit, and the engine's whirring became high-pitched. Something struck his feet quick enough that he was knocked upwards, only staying on the boat by the strength of his grip upon the steering wheel. He regained his balance and realised his boat was skimming atop the waves, making small leaps he'd never seen a larger vessel do.

*"Fool, fool, fool, fool, this isn't fucking happening, fool, fool, fool, no, this isn't happening, it isn't, why did I fucking push the lever, if I stop it it'll probably— oh shit."*

The sharp rocks that had gutted so many of Weil's victims were approaching him too quickly. Weil yanked the rudder wheel left and pulled the lever to a neutral position, but it was too sudden a change. The boat rotated, but refused to change direction, flinging Weil into its side and concussing him before he tipped into the water. Between blinding lights, he saw the shipbreaking cliffs of his past, shielded by a wobbling, liquid screen.

Though he could feel a coral-encrusted seabed beneath his feet, his lungs begged for breaths that would be fatal to take. The Rakh'vash wouldn't risk the cosmos for a mere follower, but even if it would, there were no words to be said beneath the waves. As much as Weil fought, his vision grew black.

\* \* \*

When Wisdom Khalver spoke of wyverns, Irikhos had assumed there was a figurative or measured manifestation of the seer's visions. Instead, as he clambered through the mountain paths between the train station at the foot of Monte Myrtilla and the city of Alaterra, wyverns filled the skies as gulls filled Winter Harbour's.

Dark elves in dull, hardy leathern garb walked past Irikhos, heading up and down the mountain alike. He puffed as his mountaineering betters overtook him, and regularly stopped to rest against the side of the mountain. If he'd have been a good nobleman, his legs would be comparable to any Alaterran's; the Ashpeaks were only a mile from his home city, after all.

Instead, like much of Arkhera's upper class, he'd neglected his people, visualised his lands as mere sections on a map, and assured himself that his skill in the increasingly irrelevant art of swordplay was the same as being a worthy ruler. His upper body was nimble, his feet swift, but he lacked the consistent power of a true mountain man. After half a dozen more repetitions of climbing and stopping, he reached the gates of Alaterra, which greeted him with an Elarondian sign boasting a population size. Beneath the sign was writing in the Common Tongue claiming it was a sister city to Midori Sora, presumably some Yukishiman region.

Beyond the gate were beautiful clean tiles of white, red, and blue, stretching across snaking streets flanked by lengthy terraces and boastful villas. Wyverns wandered the streets, often with their owners on their backs, though the smaller ones were generally tethered with leads. Irikhos reduced his silhouette in the hopes that it would make the beasts dismiss him. While the ploy mostly worked, a purple-and-red one noticed him, flared its neck scutes, and screeched. It didn't have an owner that Irikhos could see and waddled across the floor with deceptive speed towards him.

"Oh God, oh God, what do I— *what do I do?*" Irikhos screamed to a nearby Alaterran, who kept walking as though they'd heard nothing.

Iri had read that wild animals respected humanoids that stood their ground, but what if its respect morphed into fear? He slowly backed from the beaked lizard and maintained eye contact, but this didn't slow it. As it got close enough to smell, Irikhos's legs moved against his will. He staggered and dropped his luggage, yet every time he looked back, the beast was even closer. Eventually he felt the weight of the great creature knock him to the floor. Though he was face-down, he knew it was bearing over him, and it made a slow, unnerving rattle with its beak.

Irikhos wasn't going to die today. He rolled over, hitting the beast on its forelimb, then scrambled backwards as it snapped at his arm. He rushed to get up, but the wyvern tackled him again, this time screeching with a fully flared scute-crest. If it chose to snap at his face, there were only two easily eaten lines of defence before he was dead. Instead, the creature lifted its serpentine neck as a woman's voice called. It was familiar, yet unfamiliar, a few tones too deep. He attempted to discern her words, and realised she was speaking in the Common Tongue.

"Moonrazer! *Moonrazer!* Leave that man alone!"

The wyvern stepped off Irikhos with a defiant snap of the beak, and as he rose to his feet, he beheld its owner sprinting towards it. She was a blonde-haired, red-eyed high elf with the same features as Lady Kag. Her face was where the similarities ended, however. She was relatively wide-hipped, with strong legs that defined themselves through her trousers. He didn't dare believe it, she resembled Yarawyn as a woman grown.

"I'm ever so sorry," the woman said, putting her hands together. "He's friendly, I swear, but he's just a little unaware of his— *Iri?*"

Irikhos trembled until his lost love's name left his lips. "Yarawyn. It's really you, isn't it?"

"You looked for me after all this time, I just *knew* you would!" she shouted, hugging him with the strength of a Jaranese python.

"I can't believe it. I found you, I truly found you," Irikhos whispered as he returned the embrace.

After squeezing Irikhos's backside, Yarawyn let him go, then pointed down the street. "Come with me, I'll show you where I live now. Oh, Tor's going to be so shocked. She kept telling me to get over you, yet here you are. Before I forget, that beautiful wyvern is my baby, Moonrazer. Say hello, Moonrazer."

The wyvern opened its beak and made a distorted warble, then closed it to add a rattle. Irikhos was no less afraid of the beast, but he was too entranced by how Yarawyn had grown to pay his fears any heed.

# Afflictions

Yanked by the hand, Irikhos approached a two-floor house sitting detached from its neighbours. It lay within a street wide enough for the wyvern stalking behind him to spread his wings, and Yar was veering across its width from sheer excitement.

"Tor kept telling me I was needlessly holding on to the past," Yarawyn rambled. "I never forgot, though. I can still taste the kiss we shared all those years ago. You're the same, aren't you, Iri?"

Irikhos couldn't say his memories were quite so vivid, yet the warmth of her hand twisted his tongue until it formed platitudes.

"I never stopped thinking about you. Acting against your sister was what led me here."

Yarawyn's eyes lit up and she stopped, turning to face Irikhos while she took his other hand. "You fought Kag? Has Mor'kha readied her armies to take Moonstone?"

"Not quite, but there is good news," Irikhos promised. "I'd rather Torawyn heard it too, as it may be a tad unfortunate for her."

Yarawyn scoffed. "Anything doesn't involve giving up and hiding like a scared little girl is bad to Tor. I wouldn't worry about her feelings."

Irikhos released Yar's hands. "I was too harsh to her when we were young."

"You liked me better, that's not harsh, that's just liking the prettier sister," Yarawyn said with folded arms. "Don't indulge her self-pity, I get enough of it daily."

"If you say so," Irikhos muttered, trying to lose himself in Yarawyn's red eyes, only for the sting of her tone to render it impossible.

Moonrazer caught up to the pair, forcing Irikhos to jolt into motion. Yarawyn maintained her brisk pace, keeping her eyes averted from his. It was tempting to see her as a grown version of the girl he'd agreed to marry, but she lacked her former mischievousness. Her movements were as skulking as the wyvern she doted upon. No matter how much Irikhos told himself that she had a beautiful face and shapely rider's legs, this was a different Yarawyn.

They reached the house's door, and Yar led her wyvern around the building. "Just knock, Tor will answer. I just need to make sure Moonrazer stays."

Irikhos nodded. "All right, I'll see you soon."

She left him alone, and when Iri rapped his hands against the door, a shooting pain grasped his throat. He'd dreamt of the day he'd reunite with Yarawyn ever since her faux exile, but awakening from the fantasy stung. Part of him hoped that he was still on the train to Monte Myrtilla, fast asleep and simply suffering from doubts.

When the door opened, a high elven woman gaunt enough to pass as a short, pointy-eared, tailless spellbinder was on the other side, her eyes wide, watery, and blue. Irikhos's heart sank as he realised this person had the middle Selenia's nose and melancholic expression.

"Torawyn? Is that you?"

The woman shook in place. "Irikhos?"

"Yes, it's me, but— Torawyn, you look so thin," Irikhos blurted. "What happened? This isn't because of—"

"No, it's not your fault," she spluttered. "I just learned to measure my food intake, it's nothing to worry about."

"Yar and I were cruel to you, back when— you know. I just wanted to say I'm—"

Yarawyn shoved herself between the two and shouted over Irikhos. "Torawyn, you've *got* to let us in! Iri has brilliant news regarding our return to Arkhera, haven't you?"

Irikhos swallowed as he beheld Yar's wild eyes. "That's right. Can I come in?"

Torawyn moved inside without a word, and Irikhos followed her in. Yarawyn shut the door behind them, and practically raced them to a living room, dotted with a settee, a Yukishiman-style coffee table, and a large, fluffed cushion. Tor made to sit on the couch, but Yar beat her to it, then patted the spot beside her.

"Sit with me, Iri, it's been forever since we last held each other."

Torawyn's voice slipped into audibility seemingly against her own will. "Give him some time, Yar. It's been a decade, perhaps he's married someone else."

"So what? It's not as though any woman he'd settle for would compare to me. Who would he marry, his cousin Elrax? She was a spooky wench then and she's likely one now."

Irikhos had tolerated Yar's oddities, but this time his frustration boiled over.

"Complain about your kin as much as you like, but I won't let you insult mine. If you knew the half of how Elrax had to live, you'd reconsider your words," he said in a firm tone.

Yar's speech devolved into a sputtering fit, and Torawyn sat beside her, maintaining her silence throughout. Irikhos gave the middle sibling a nod and rested on the cushion.

"What's the good news, then?" Torawyn asked.

Irikhos waited for Yarawyn to stop muttering to herself, then spoke. "The reason I'm here is because your lady sister sent me. You see, she—"

*"Kag sent you?* Impossible! It must be a trick," Yarawyn spat. "What did she do to convince you? Don't you understand? Now that you're here, she'll just say you're unwelcome in Arkhera. She's— oh *no,* you didn't— she didn't— that conniving bitch plays the fool, but she's outsmarted us once again!"

Torawyn raised her voice to a dull roar. "Calm yourself, Yarawyn. Think about what you want to say, then say it."

"*Don't patronise me, Tor!* Can't you see? Irikhos has married Kag, she's probably pregnant, and now that she's got what she needs from him, she's sent him to rot in Elarond!"

Irikhos raised a hand. "That's not it at all—"

"Was she beautiful, Iri? Was she?"

All at once, Yarawyn's features became a meaningless collection of symmetrical shapes. Even Kag, with her imbecilic, wounded expression, came off as more appealing to him. Torawyn's stared at her coffee table, and Irikhos hardened his tone.

"I'm not married to Lady Kag," he stated. "She wants me to bring you both home. Once that happens, she'll abdicate, leaving Yar and I to rule as husband and wife."

Yarawyn shook in place. "She's just going to give up? Without protest?"

"Yes," Irikhos said. "I was conditionally exiled for kidnapping and assaulting her. She considered herself in the wrong and this is her attempt at atonement."

Torawyn hazarded a smile. "See, Yar? Holding onto hatred is foolish. Everyone, even Kag, can change. We don't need an army, all we need to do is make amends with Kag, you can marry Irikhos, and—"

"No," Yarawyn said.

Irikhos and Tor alike stared at the youngest Selenia. She stood, her hands tightly clenched and her eyes burning.

"No? What do you mean, no?" Irikhos said, standing to meet her height.

"I'm not going to let a decade of wandering around a country whose people despise me go. You know why Moonrazer is called Moonrazer? I fully intend to raze Moonstone with him and burn every traitor that supported Kag's ascension to death. He can burn fish on command, and

I assure you, he could do it to people if he needs to. Now Kag thinks because she went through some kidnapping that she can play the changed woman? It's ten years too late for that."

Tor rose too, her voice nearing a shout. "Yarawyn, you're rejecting an easy solution to all of this! I won't challenge your rule, I'm happy to stay here, with my patients! You'll have Moonstone all to yourself—"

"And what if it's a trap? What if Irikhos and I return without an army? Kag turns her armies on us or has her cabal of shifty illusionists stab us in the back, then poisons Moonrazer. What then?"

Irikhos opened his hands in front of him. "Trust me, I saw Lady Kag, she's genuinely intent on abdication. I'm telling you—"

"She's got to you somehow," Yarawyn said, stalking up to Irikhos and locking eyes with him. "How did she buy you? A kiss? Her maidenhood? Or perhaps that Sanguinasi opportunist, Erwyn, paid you in information. You've betrayed me, haven't you?"

"No, I swear to God, Yar, you're being paranoid—"

A sharp punch to his gut silenced him, and Yar stormed out of the room. Tor rushed after her, and the front door was heard opening.

"Yarawyn, stop! You're not listening to him! You've talked incessantly about how you've missed Irikhos, and he still wants to marry you! You're ruining this for yourself!"

"Shut up, Tor! If you're stupid enough to fall for Kag's tricks, *you* return to Arkhera without an army!"

*"Yarawyn Nemera Selenia,* return at— so be it."

The door shut, and Tor returned to the living room alone. Irikhos shook his head.

"I'm sorry I brought this turbulence to your home. You've done well for yourself."

"No thanks to Yarawyn, yes," Tor said in an unusually sharp tone.

"What happens now?" Irikhos asked. "If Yar refuses to leave with me, I can't return to Arkhera. Those were the terms of my exile."

Torawyn paused, looked Irikhos over, then sighed. "I'll prepare the spare room."

"Listen, Tor, about before, I wanted to apologise," he said. "You know, for calling you fat, saying I'd only marry a Selenia if it was Yar. I was only a boy, but you were a growing woman. I can't imagine how much I hurt you."

"It's fine," she mumbled. "Really, it is."

"No, it isn't," Irikhos said, taking one of her hands. "You're thin because of me and Yar, aren't you?"

Torawyn pulled her hand away. "You were a boy, you didn't know any better. It's my fault for taking a boy's words so seriously. Besides, I'm healthy now, so you did me a favour."

Irikhos's chest voided all hope in an outward tide. "As you say. Show me to your spare room, I'll set it up myself."

"As you wish. It's a shame we couldn't catch up under better circumstances."

* * *

Weil was breathing air again, fragranced with the oils he'd once had Vi'khash douse his father in. He wanted to open his eyes, but if he did, confirmation would follow. He didn't want to see the Bold Individualist just yet; he wasn't prepared for whatever mockery of his father's final moments the Underworld had to offer him.

His lungs' instinctive wrenching forced his eyes open, prompting him to sit up in whatever bed he was in, coughing up flecks of seawater and gasping between hacks. He looked around the room he was in, to find it was entirely average; various trinkets from the sea hung amidst regular items of carpentry. A window revealed a colourful terrace he'd seen on the Plagueborn side of Zemelnya, and he clambered out of his bed, coughing as he moved. He edged towards the room's exit in bedclothes he didn't recall changing into, only for it to open before he could mentally prepare. To his surprise, the Bold Individualist had taken the form of a strange version of Rowyn Khanas, with longer hair and a blue-yellow robe.

*"Ah, there you are,"* Weil said in his mother tongue. *"This is it. I died in a foolish accident I could have avoided, and you're going to admonish me for my inability to stand up for myself. I shall accept my sentence, Bold Individualist."*

"I'm sorry, I'm still terrible with Isleborn," the 'Bold Individualist' said in Common. "You said something about dying and punishment?"

"What? Bold Individualist only speak Common? But you are god, yes?" Weil asked.

"A god?" the necromancer asked. "No, I'm a healer who pushed the water out of your lungs. I also lent you some of my breaths, so—"

"I am alive? Then you are Rowyn Khanas!" Weil said with a wide smile.

"Shit," Rowyn muttered.

"Why are you fearing me?" Weil said as Rowyn began to fluster. "What is wrong? I am glad you live, after what Razarkha attempt."

Rowyn cocked his head. "Wait, you aren't with Razarkha anymore?"

Weil evaded his gaze. "I killed her."

The necromancer may not have spoken Weil's tongue, yet his suppressed smile transcended linguistic barriers. "Razarkha's dead?"

"She was, but is not. She... rise, become not-dead, like your kind create."

This caused the necromancer's joy to wither away. "She's a revenant? Do you know where she is? Who raised her?"

"I not know word 'revenant', but I have Yukishiman friend who give me special weapon to end her again," Weil said, patting his hips before bursting into Isleborn. *"Shit, where is it?"*

"What are you looking for? Sorry, I couldn't let you recover in those sodden clothes."

"Where is holder of knotweed knife? I need weapon, it is end of Razarkha! I cannot let her stay living!" Weil spluttered in his most desperate Common. "I have it on hip, it was covering blade."

Rowyn's verdant eyes widened. "Oh, that thing? Yes, I kept it safe for you, but I wouldn't recommend putting on your old clothes. They're not likely to dry for another few days, and that's assuming it doesn't rain."

"Yes, yes," Weil said. "Please take me to it."

The necromancer nodded, and led him into a dingy, salt-crusted hallway. After that, he headed down some stairs, where a blonde spellbinder with familiar looks lounged upon a decrepit, overpoweringly scented chair. Weil squinted, then turned to Rowyn.

"Are you certain we are not in after death world?" Weil asked. "That woman is Vi'khash, but beautiful and in seaweed."

Before Rowyn could answer, the woman approached Weil, speaking Isleborn in an exceedingly Plagueborn accent. *"Ah, you spoke of Vi'khash? Rowyn told me that you were friends with the ever-fearsome Razarkha Fel'thuz, but he never told me you know my sister! I'm Vi'kara, and I'm glad you're alive. When did you last see her?"*

"Last see whom? Razarkha?"

*"Vi'khash."*

Weil paused. *"I'm sorry. I believe Razarkha killed her, given recent revelations."*

The kelp-covered cryomancer paused. *"Yet you act as that woman's confidant?"*

"Not anymore. She is my enemy, and I must find a way to Arkhera, so I may ambush her," Weil explained. "Rowyn Khanas claims that my knotweed knife is here. May I have it?"

*"I wouldn't wield such a weapon. Even if used to defeat a murderer, the accursed Yukishiman parasite is never the answer."*

Weil backed off, unable to find a reply that wouldn't be shameful to his god and people alike. The knotweed was evidently ominous, yet he had no choice but to believe Hilda; after all, if Razarkha survived his tentacles, what else stood a chance at finishing her?

Rowyn edged between the two and spoke in Common. "I'm sorry, I don't know what you two are talking about, but your knife is here."

He rooted about in a closet, putting bottles of fragrant oils aside before retrieving the sheathe and the weapon. It stank of bladder wrack and rotting molluscs, but it was intact. Partially unsheathing it before putting it back, Weil nodded to Rowyn.

"Many apology," he said. "I must arrange my travel to Arkhera. Will I be welcome if I return later?"

Rowyn paused, then turned to Vi'kara, speaking in Old Galdusian for reasons unknown. Vi'kara replied in the same language, and between themselves, they agreed on something.

"Vi'kara says yes, but warns you that her heart belongs to me," Rowyn said in a stilted manner. "Her words, not mine."

"If you say," Weil said with a smile. "I shall speak later."

With that, the chaos-speaker left the house, undaunted by his relatively draughty clothing. Simply setting foot in Zemelnya felt like a return to his childhood.

There were no Razarkhas, no Anya Kasparovs, just the vibrant spires and onion domes of his home city.

He knew where he could acquire a ship with ease; the War'mal Group was excessively open-handed following Razarkha's humiliation of Elki Kasparov, and he was certain that if he returned to War'mal as the chaos-speaker who assisted in the Kasparovs' downfall, he would be given a skiff and a bottle of triple-distilled vodka for the trouble. It was the Ilazari way; one was merciless to their enemies, but forever warm to their friends.

The way to the Zemelnya Academy of Higher Learning sapped Weil of his nostalgia. He'd acted the Ilazari way to Razarkha, and she spat upon his efforts. He offered her his friendship, his unyielding support, the very roof over his head. Yet she'd murdered his father, and worse still, he'd gone along with her like an idiot. He thought he'd embodied Isleborn hospitality, but in truth he'd embodied Galdusian hubris.

Thankfully, he was merciless when the time came. Every fleck of pink upon the Academy's stained-glass windows resembled Razarkha's eyes, staring at Weil as a tentacle burst through her stomach. Somehow, knowing the woman he loved was like anyone else, filled with yellowed intestines and globs of viscera was enough to remind him how fallible she was.

Normally, the thought of guts would render Weil squeamish, yet he was exhilarated at the notion that Razarkha would go through that again. Hatred was easy to feed, but he didn't have enough hope to choose the harder path. When he arrived at the Academy, a familiar telekinete surrounded by floating blades hovered in place.

*"Ah, it's Weil, slayer of Kasparovs,"* the telekinete said in Plagueborn Ilazari. *"If you're after an audience with War'mal, you've picked a bad time. He's changed his ways, you see and is helping the remaining Kasparov children. I can't see him wanting to help—"*

As though summoned by the guard's words, a great slab of ice slammed onto the pavement, the cold crystal and ground alike veining with cracks from the impact. Atop the frozen chunk was War'mal himself, sitting cross-legged, his pale gaze occasionally flickering into an unusual malachite green.

"*Az'merath, don't presume to speak for me,*" the cryomancer chided in Plagueborn. "*It's good to see you again, Weil of Zemelnya. I hear that you've been adventuring in Sula as of late. Would you like to discuss matters in my office?*"

"*Yes, that would be good,*" Weil said, squinting as he tracked what may have been pipe smoke leaking from War'mal's nostrils.

"*With me, then.*"

The white-haired man put his hands behind his back and waited for his telekinetic doorman to let him into his academy. From there, he led Weil through the foyer, which had considerably more oil paintings than before. Accompanying the previously present picture of the Plague Emperor were works depicting the Isleborn's welcoming of the Plagueborn, along with Plagueborn-crafted depictions of the Isleborn and vice versa.

The oddities didn't end there; as he was led into War'mal's office, he was pleasantly surprised to find that the room was no longer chilled to the point of resembling an ice cellar, and the humanoid taxidermies of the past were thankfully absent. War'mal's desk remained, however, and the mob boss was quick to sit behind it.

"*Hello, Weil of Zemelnya,*" War'mal said in a playful tone that clashed with its depth. "*I must admit, I didn't expect you to return. Where's your friend? If I trusted you to properly observe your surroundings, I'd assume you knew that Razarkha is a wanted woman. One million credits are yours if you can tell me where she's hiding. I know you two. Never one without the other.*"

Weil swallowed. He recognised the Isleborn accent despite it being masked beneath War'mal's vocal cords. The green eyes weren't a hallucination, nor was the smoke. The dread he felt wasn't close to the time he visited the academy's office, but matched the monthly misery of collection day perfectly.

*"Speak Isleborn, I know it's your preferred tongue,"* Weil said, switching languages to prove the point.

*"Oh, you figured it out,"* War'mal said, pushing his chair back and putting his feet on the desk. *"Did you like 'the Blinkered Stallion'?"*

*"'Katina Anyanova' was an obvious penname, but yes, the story opened my eyes,"* Weil remarked. *"I owe you an apology. I confirmed the truth myself, Anya. Razarkha killed my father, so I killed her."*

Without warning, the mob boss slumped back against his chair, and out of his mouth slipped a magical cloud with glowing green embers for eyes.

*"You also owe me over ten thousand credits, but it's your lucky day. If you truly killed Razarkha, I'm obligated to give you a million credits!"* Anya Kasparov said. *"You know, after spending enough time possessing somebody, you start to miss being incorporeal. It's about balance. Anyway, do you have any proof that—"*

*"The death didn't stick."*

*"Ah, well, that's not called 'killing' a person, that's called 'injuring' them,"* Anya said in a sickly-sweet tone.

*"No, you don't understand. I killed her with my tentacles, just like I did with you, but she found a way to cheat death."*

*"Ah, so she shares more with me than her blood,"* Anya remarked. *"Accused of murdering your father, dead by tentacle, in a state of near immortality, heavens, I hope I don't become as miserable as Fel'thuz."*

Weil sighed. *"That's all very interesting, Anya, but I came here hoping that War'mal would supply me with means* to travel to Arkhera. Instead, I see that Anya Kasparov rules Zemelnya. I suppose given I intend to finish Razarkha off, you'd be willing to lend an ocean-capable skiff?"

"*Those tend to cost less than a million credits, so consider it done,*" Anya said, slipping back into War'mal's body. After some twitching, the mob boss straightened his back, and resumed Anya's words in a masculine voice. "*Return tomorrow, and I'll have everything set up for you. Don't get this one shot to pieces too.*"

Weil frowned. "*I can't guarantee that won't happen.*"

\* \* \*

Rosaline had lately been making a habit of leaving the Saltwater Temple. While Uncle Petyr always forced her to tell him what she'd been up to, with the exception of her visit to Uncle Gerold, she'd been truthful. She'd truly visited the rice kitchen for the hungry, she'd truly attended a barracks demonstration, and she'd truly tilled the outer lands with the Worm's Men. Petyr's words had power, but with every forced admission he induced, Rosaline could feel their grasp slipping. It was odd to wield virtue for heresy's sake, yet it was necessary. This was the night her work paid off. She ensured her robes were as chaste as mortally possible, then knocked on the door to Uncle Petyr's chamber.

"Who is it?"

"Rosaline," she said. "I wanted to visit Ascetic Pleura and see what her duties entail. May I?"

The door opened, and Petyr Godswater loomed over his niece, stroking his moustache while his eyes danced over her body. Rosaline almost dared to hope; there wasn't a hair out of place, nor an inch of inappropriately exposed skin. Eventually, the apostle scoffed.

"If you keep your clothes as modest as they are now, you're permitted. Don't think I'm unaware of your vile nature," Petyr remarked.

"I know you're aware," Rosaline mumbled. "You've fallen prey to it many times."

"Be quiet," Petyr commanded. "If you wish to visit the Moon Man's most devoted servant, you must understand discretion. Your greatest failure is a disgrace to the House of Godswater, and mustn't be said aloud to anyone, even me. What if a servant heard?"

"I'm sorry, Uncle Petyr, I won't speak of it again."

"Good," Petyr said. "Leave in peace and contain your desires."

"I pray for everyone in Godswater to do the same," Rosaline said with a Jaranese bow.

From there, she rushed downstairs and left the Saltwater Temple, moving past the twilit likenesses of the six gods. The way to the Moon Men's archives was almost natural to Rosaline, as Petyr had regularly visited the building during her childhood. It was a great six-sided tower, draping blue and black banners down its full height. Beneath the ground, the building stretched further, and merely approaching it without Petyr's supervision made Rosaline nauseous.

The guards lifted their pikes as she entered the tower, and she was met by the archives' reception. A spectacle-wearing ascetic with a crooked back and overgrown hair hunched over the only desk in the room, his queer blue stare acting as the guardian of the doors beyond him. He adjusted a book in his hands and spoke in a high-pitched tone only the aged could attain.

"Young Lady Rosaline. What brings you to the archives of the Moon Men?"

"I want to see Pleura," Rosaline stated. "She's here, isn't she?"

"She's guarding the restricted section," the ascetic reported. "I wouldn't approach her. Unlike some, she understands the meaning of godly devotion."

"I have no intention of distracting her from her duties," Rosaline insisted. "Please may I see her?"

"You'll have a better chance plucking a star from the sky."

"But— but—"

She couldn't afford to protest, but after going to the effort of convincing Petyr, giving up wasn't an option. She needed to know what the Moon Men knew. Rosaline put her hands together and prayed.

"Hallowed Moon Man, weaver of fate, painter of the cosmos and hider of secrets, shine your light upon me. Bless me this day and grant me insight."

"What are you doing?" the ascetic asked with a furrowed brow.

"Praying for assistance. If the Moon Man favours me, you must allow my passage."

"Prayer alone doesn't guarantee a god's blessing—"

The Moon Man worked swiftly; before the ascetic could finish, a door behind him swung open, revealing Pleura herself, her staff's light filling the room.

"Ascetic Osgrey, I'm thirsty, could you get me a drink— ah, Rosaline, wonderful to see you! Where's your uncle?"

"He's in the temple," Rosaline said, desperately pushing her joy down while she watched Osgrey cover his face. "I wanted to watch you work."

"That's a boring way to spend the night, but if that's what you want, who am I to refuse the heir to Godswater?" Pleura said with a more conventional Arkheran bow.

The receptionist left his desk and returned with a glass of water. "If I may, High Ascetic, I don't think Rosaline's presence is well-advised."

"Nonsense, Osgrey. She's the heir, and any knowledge she may overhear is simply being revealed to her a few years early. Petyr won't be the apostle forever, after all!"

"Such talk is dangerous, High Ascetic," Osgrey murmured.

"The truth is only dangerous to liars and the foolish," Pleura insisted. "My light shall illuminate all who seek it. Do you not believe I am the Moon Man's chosen?"

The receptionist unsuccessfully suppressed a scowl. "Of course I believe."

"Good. Come with me, Rosaline," she said, taking the glass of water and swigging it in one gulp, then putting it down on the desk.

Once through the door, Pleura led Rosaline down a spiralling staircase, lit by flickering braziers and her holy staff. The miraculous rock at its end was an unending source of illumination, lacking even a shadow. The staircase eventually ended, giving way to a sprawling network of walls inlaid with bookshelves. There didn't appear to be an ordering system to the books, but Rosaline could glance writings with Jaranese, Na'liman, and even Ikinamese characters upon their spines.

"Ikinamese heresies are stored here?" Rosaline whispered.

"Yes, tales of seventh and eighth gods whose roles are generally accepted to fall under the Moon Man's domain in truth," Pleura replied. "Don't ask too many questions while we're here; our words will carry."

"Is there somewhere we *can* speak?"

"Don't worry," Pleura said, taking Rosaline's hand. "We'll be there soon enough."

They continued down the winding subterranean path until they reached a rocky door that appeared impossible to open with strength alone. Flanking either side were two

Moon Men barely older than Pleura, standing with one hand on their heart and the other gripping a pike.

"Thank you for returning with your holy light, High Ascetic!" one blurted.

"No intruders passed in your absence, High Ascetic!" the other added.

"I'm glad to hear it," Pleura said, adjusting her eye patch. "Go back to the surface, men. I'll take it from here."

The pair eagerly obliged, and Rosaline wondered if Pleura noticed where the men were looking as they rushed past their superior. Once they were safely around the corner, the ascetic raised her staff.

"Watch this. I cannot tell you entirely how this works, but this door has been enchanted. While it's plausible some great, strong oaf could pry it open, the secret to an easy opening is in the holy staff entrusted to the High Ascetic of the Moon Man."

"Isn't that witchcraft?"

"Witchcraft and holy powers are the same things, manifested differently," Pleura claimed, and as the norvite in her staff glowed, so too did the calligraphy on the door.

It was plainly Jaranese, and from what Rosaline could read, it said *'The guardian of all the night sky cloaks.'* After a while of shared illumination, the wand and calligraphy dimmed. With a shuffle, the stone door parted in the middle, sliding open to reveal a dingy room within.

Rosaline edged in, and Pleura followed, closing the door and hitting her staff on the floor to resume its glowing. Scattered about tables and shelves were tomes as thick as alligators' jaws, and while Rosaline was quick to approach one of the already-removed books, Pleura seemed unperturbed.

"Finally, alone," the High Ascetic said with a deep breath. "Thank you for coming to see me. I imagine it was a great risk to you."

"Yes. I was hoping to—"

Pleura was right behind Rosaline, and her staff had been laid on the floor. This was all too familiar, but as Rosaline's body trembled, she realised this was a temptation she was dangerously close to reciprocating.

"I'm the same as you," she whispered to Rosaline, placing one hand on her waist. "I know it's hard to stay hidden, but we can do it if we keep each other secret."

Pleura kissed the back of Rosaline's neck, and tears came to her eyes. When she couldn't see Pleura's face, it was the same as when Petyr did it. Rosaline told herself it was different, that the woman she'd dreamt of for months was finally expressing her love, but her godliness shot through her body and jolted towards Pleura in a flash of light.

"What was that?" Pleura asked, jumping away from her.

Rosaline turned, the floodgates of her eyes fully breached. "I'm sorry, Pleura, I— I wish I was here to let our love be expressed. I *do* think of you that way, but I'm an— I'm an even worse than a mere invert. I'm here because…"

She'd already told Pleura about Petyr succumbing to her body's wiles, but when she confronted him about it, he'd talked her into forgetting about it. Then, with his rage and lust renewed, he reminded Rosaline of the futility of her actions.

"Pleura, you must promise not to confront Uncle Petyr about this. Last time it happened, you forgot, and— and—"

"I'd never forget something you told me. Never," Pleura said, taking both of her hands.

Rosaline stared at Pleura's single exposed eye in the dimming light of her holy staff. Sincerity radiated from it, but she'd forgotten before. Still, it was a prophet's duty to deliver a message, then deliver it again and again until all were converted.

"Uncle Petyr broke his apostolic vows with me. He considers me to be a temptress, and no matter how I cover myself, he still lusts for me. He's— he's been inside me. The first time was when I was thirteen, and—"

Rosaline couldn't continue. She gripped Pleura with all her strength, weeping into her shoulder.

"I'm sorry, Pleura. I'm so scared."

"I can only imagine how frightened you are," Pleura said, holding her in return.

"I've endured his lust for years. What scares me more is knowing he can make you forget. I'm sorry, Pleura, I'm so sorry."

"What for? I'm the one who should apologise, I kissed you not knowing what horrors you'd endured. So long as you love me back, we don't need to do anything with our bodies."

Rosaline shook her head. "You don't understand. I used you so I could access this room. I'm a heretic."

Pleura let Rosaline go and wiped her tears. "You're desperate. The thought that I'd forget you telling me this terrifies me. How could I ignore such a terrible thing?"

"You asked Petyr about it. His words compel people," Rosaline spluttered. "Surely you've noticed how the people respond to him."

"You want archives pertaining to him, don't you?" Pleura concluded.

"Yes."

The High Ascetic put a hand on Rosaline's shoulder. "I'm sorry I kissed you so hastily. I thought given how often you looked at me and how much you wanted to hold my hand that we were as together as inverts could be in Godswater, but that was my sin."

"We're already sinners for loving this way."

"Perhaps," she said, taking a tome from the shelf. "To read this in its entirety, we'd need to either regularly visit this room, which would be conspicuous, or take it. Thankfully, very few ascetics access this room, so it'll be unlikely somebody will notice it's missing."

"Are you suggesting I steal—"

"You're borrowing it with the High Ascetic of the Moon Man's blessing," Pleura said with a smile. "May I kiss your cheek?"

Rosaline blushed. "Thank you for asking. You may."

When she saw that it was Pleura leaning forward and pressing her lips against her face, the horror slipped away, if only for a moment. Heresy was terrifying, but if it came with moments like this, it was a worthy pursuit.

# Outsiders

"I don't understand," Yarawyn said, hitting Naas'khar's cave wall. "Irikhos finally returns, and he's some glorified messenger for my worthless sister."

Naas'khar lingered like a shadow, his spare eyeballs glinting from the cavern's fire. "Perhaps you built him up too much? I remember my mother telling me that I was born because she loved how mortals change over their short lifespans. Irikhos has probably—"

Yarawyn punched hard enough to make her knuckles bleed. "Curse it all! Yes, he was going to change, but I expected him to be *better,* not worse! It's as though Kag gelded him!"

Naas'khar paused. "Is that an Arkheran tradition?"

"I was being figurative," Yarawyn muttered, her momentum slowing as she registered the sting of her injury. "It's not fair. Kag tore me and Irikhos apart, and instead of avenging our relationship, he's her loyal toady."

The nephil slinked out from the darkness and opened his arms. "Would you like a hug? I know that hugging you makes me feel better about my situation."

Yarawyn became limp. "I don't want *you* to hold me, Naas'khar, I want *him* to, but it's over, isn't it?"

"I don't know," Naas'khar muttered as he turned away. "I'm not this Irikhos mortal, but if I was him, I'd want to marry you."

Yar stared at the night sky beyond the cave, then turned back to her friend. Her eyes began to well, but she blinked away her tears before they degraded into a stream.

"I'm sorry, Naas'khar. I'm thankful that you love me, but the only way I take over Moonstone with any legitimacy is through Irikhos," she said. "He's a spineless coward now, stupid enough to fall for Kag's tricks, but he's still the key to my return."

Naas'khar checked the rippling collection of slime coating the dimmer sections of his cavern. The eyeballs within the black, viscous pool beheld Yar from multiple angles, seemingly in his place. Yar untied her hair, then sat with her back against a cavern wall.

"He still looked at my body. He still wanted me. The only reason he'd come to hate me is because he has somebody better."

"That's not possible," Naas'khar said, approaching and crouching next to her. "You're the most beautiful woman in the world to me."

"I'm the *only* woman in the world to you, it's not the same," Yarawyn muttered. "Tor was never a threat, but *Kag*, Kag's different. Long black hair, pale skin, the sort of body that artists love. My father would draw her over and over, there are so many oil paintings in Castle Selenia that are just *her*. Irikhos must be in love with Kag, it's the only way this makes sense."

"But if he's happy and in love with her, why would he come here?" Naas'khar asked. "Why wouldn't he just stay home?"

"To hurt me. To spread more of Kag's lies."

Naas'khar pondered over this, then edged closer, scraping the floor with his tentacles until he was directly in front of Yarawyn.

"If he travelled all this way to hurt you, he's not worth worrying about," Naas'khar said. "You spent years appreciating a man that didn't exist, but I'm right in front of you."

"Thank you," Yarawyn replied, unable to meet the nephil's eyes.

It was an obvious, socially stunted attempt at manipulation, but Yarawyn couldn't begrudge the hybrid's attempts at romance. She'd insulted Irikhos's cousin for no reason other than her being his hypothetical wife. She'd tried to silence her naysaying sister, yet repeatedly insulted

Irikhos in the process. His golden eyes lost their lustre within minutes of sharing a house with her.

He was supposed to hold her on the settee, they were supposed to touch each other in ways neither of their parents would have allowed a decade ago. Instead, she'd frightened him away. Even if she accepted the marriage, it would be like the Fel'thuzes'; miserable and politically convenient. He was so toned, his face pretty in a way only dark-skinned elves could be, and his ashen hair would stay the same regardless of age. If he could love her, he would be the perfect husband.

"What does he look like?" Naas'khar asked, a mild distortion in his voice.

"Why do you want to know?"

"You obviously hate him, but enjoy his looks," Naas'khar claimed. "Why else would you be conflicted?"

"It's not just his looks, it's his— if I return to Arkhera with just an army, I'll need to find a different noble husband to come off as more legitimate than my older sisters."

"So he *isn't* attractive to you?"

Yarawyn finally managed to face Naas'khar, and her voice grew nippy. "Of course he's attractive, but I don't want to go on about that because I know it'd hurt you. Why are you asking for something that you know will put you through pain?"

"Because you're my only friend, and I want to know what you enjoy."

The high elven woman groaned. "If you want to suffer, so be it. He's got a muscular bottom, and it's brilliant to squeeze. His ashen hair excites me, because even when he's fifty, it'll be the same. His golden eyes and straight-bridged nose are pretty, and under his clothes, I could make out *wonderful* toning. I like the man he's grown into, but only in body, not spirit."

Naas'khar took this in, trembling with every word. Abruptly, he rushed into the shadowy depths of the cavern, and grunted to the sound of wet, writhing meat.

"What are you doing?" Yarawyn stood and started to stammer. "Nassy! You *asked me to tell you,* why are you running away?"

Hacking and spluttering echoed through the cavern, along with guttural noises that almost constituted a language. Yarawyn almost dared to travel into the darkness, but by the time she committed to it, the nephil stepped into his fire's illumination.

His red eyes had shifted into a bloodshot attempt at gold, while his head was covered by grey tentacles thin enough to poorly imitate hair. The daemonic hybrid's back no longer possessed tendrils or wings, while his once-emaciated figure was a trembling, obviously hollow rendition of a toned dark elven figure. He shook on his feet and opened his arms.

"Here you are, Yarawyn," he said, twitching as a pectoral muscle threatened to unravel. "I look like him, but I'm still as devoted to you as ever. We can go back to Arkhera without this Moonstone nonsense, and I'll be free to be with you!"

Yarawyn covered her mouth as vomit rushed into it. Thoughts of Irikhos stroking Kag's hair while sharing her bed, laughing at the manipulations he'd visit upon his hapless former betrothed clouded her mind. This daemonspawn couldn't understand her, but mortals despised her too. There was only one creature she could trust. She backed off until she could safely turn her back on the nephil, then sprinted from the cave, where Moonrazer was snoozing. She climbed onto her pet's back and tapped the back of his neck.

"Moonrazer! Wake up, wake up, there's a good wyvern!" she babbled, and thankfully, he was quick to shake off his slumber.

"What's wrong?" Naas'khar called from his cavern. "Did I frighten you? I thought that if I lost the tentacles, I'd be *less* scary! Yarawyn, what's—"

"I can't do this anymore. I'm sorry, Nassy. Moonrazer, fly."

Her wyvern took off, and while she had nowhere to go but Tor's house, she knew better than to place faith in her, Irikhos, or even Naas'khar. She needed someone who wanted what she wanted, who couldn't be seduced by Kag. More than anything, she needed an army as eager to raze Moonstone as herself.

* * *

The southern coast of Elarond was in sight, and though Razarkha had a vague notion of the nations of Passicare and Amocare, separated by a mountain range but united by Soltelle control, she didn't know the name of the city she and Duncan were drifting towards. It had a bustling harbour with ships of varying designs; wooden Jaranese merchant ships with bright sails, steam chugging Soltelle freighters, and curvaceous Elarondian pleasure yachts.

As they approached, multiple flags could be discerned; yellow starbursts on red represented the Passicaran royal family, red and yellow stripes the United Kingdom of Elarond, red suns upon orange the Soltelle Empire, and orange, curved-rayed suns on yellow the Solerros, of all families.

"Interesting," Razarkha muttered. "I think I know the city we're approaching."

"That's good, because if I'm honest, I never liked Elarond. The elves don't like people with Jaranese looks unless you're in Napolli. Then they treat you like a god," Duncan remarked.

"It's a good thing you don't look Jaranese anymore, eh?" Razarkha said with a smirk.

"Coming from the woman with a geode for a stomach," Duncan retorted.

Razarkha closed her eyes and chuckled. Even if this augmentee was a poor substitute for the asset she could never reclaim, she'd at least come to enjoy his remarks. When they weren't a direct attempt to undermine her, they proved somewhat witty, even insightful.

"I believe this city is Sulaporta," Razarkha guessed. "The yellow flags with orange suns are for the House of Solerro. I presume you remember them?"

"Weren't they some new-rich Elarondian immigrants?" Duncan said. "Last I heard they were granted the Yagaskas' old lands."

"That's correct, but if I recall, they're not-so-new rich in Elarond, and have held Sulaporta for centuries," she explained. "Still, that Soltelle flag isn't good for us."

"What now, then? Are the souls you've absorbed from the Meung-Chaydan incident enough? You killed a lot of people—"

"I didn't absorb the ones that died from my false hope," she interrupted. "Overall, my attack was low-yield for the costs. Am I right in thinking that I need a rest, Bold Individualist?"

**"You didn't take what you could,"** the Sovereign remarked. **"I'm glad you didn't, however; those souls are in my custody due to your restraint. Despite this, you ought to rest your telekinesis. Maintaining a journey from Jaranar to Elarond without stopping at Malassai isn't recommended even for mages without your limitations."**

Visions of brown-skinned, almond-eyed humans uttering incomprehensible words of gratitude haunted Razarkha. She clenched her fist around her soulstealer and shook her head.

"I couldn't stay there. Not with those tribal people."

*"I'm not fond of them myself. Too directly connected to my divine enemy for my liking. Their pacifism renders them weak and vulnerable to pirates, and this failure to protect themselves validates my thoughts on mortals."*

"If the incompetents of Winter Harbour give them trouble, they're a weak culture."

*"I'm glad we agree on so much. If you seek my advice regarding this city, I'd recommend resting in an area away from the Soltelles. You could buy some time by using a train rather than your magic reserves."*

"A train, with Soltelle Dollars I don't have?" Razarkha snapped.

Duncan broke into the conversation. "The voice in your stone is suggesting we take a train? Is it aware of what I look like?"

"Almost certainly. It isn't always sensible for all its supposed divinity."

*"Unless you're ashamed of the people you've become, what's stopping you stealing some dollars and boarding a train?"*

Razarkha's abdomen flared up, and she gave her soulstealer a withering glare. "You were the one who did this to me. You knew this form would be abominable, painful, and cause for mockery in every nation of the world. Now you lecture me about shame? You *wanted* me to be ashamed!"

*"A truly great person is never **consumed** by shame. Shame may change one's trajectory when done for one's own sake, but it should never paralyse one with fear. The crowd is a great, indecisive imbecile; a great man takes action."*

"How inspiring and utterly impractical. I hope the Plague Emperor despised you."

*"Andros and I differed in many ways, but we never lost our respect for one another."*

"Profound. Duncan, we're going to ignore the idiotic voice claiming to be a god."

Duncan shrugged. "I'm glad to hear that, but what's the alternative? Is your telekinesis going to hold out?"

Razarkha's abdomen cooled off, and she rose to gain a better vantage point. Beneath them was the squared off, urban tiling of Sulaporta, then acres upon acres of forest, with a small line's worth of clearing connecting it to other settlements. Just north of this was a gash of rocky jags across the country, moving from the south east to the north west.

"See those mountains? They separate the Elarondian states of Passicare and Amocare. There are numerous smaller ranges within this set, and they're sparsely populated, meaning we can rest our magic without attracting attention. From there, we seek the Alaterran Mountains."

Duncan stopped drifting. "The Alaterran Mountains? Don't they have wyverns?"

Razarkha grinned. "Exactly. With a wyvern, we can fly without exhausting my arcane resources, and given neither of us eat, they'll carry us as far as they can before they themselves get hungry."

The augmentee continued to hover in place. "Razarkha, if I may—"

"Oh, of course you have naysaying to do. Go on, out with it."

"If the plan works, I'll agree it's a good way to save arcana. However, you're making a large assumption."

"And that assumption is?"

Duncan's blank expression was paired with a rub of his 'face'. "Taming a wyvern isn't easy. The Alaterrans make it look easy, but they're elves who live on a mountain face, interacting with them every day. I haven't seen many wyverns, but those I have tried to kill me when I got too close, and only listened to their masters."

Razarkha paused. "Very well, Duncan. You're right, this plan is risky, and who knows what wyvern fire could do to my body. Perhaps it'll stop functioning altogether."

"You're agreeing with me? Again? Is there a catch?" Duncan asked.

"Yes, but it's nothing a genius like you can't handle. Just devise a better plan that will reduce my need for telekinesis and get us to Arkhera in a timely manner. No, you can't leave me to rot, if your plan involves that, well, you've seen what I did to Ariel."

Duncan paused. "Duly noted."

The pair hovered together, swaying from the whipping air currents. Godswater flexed his magmalike fingers, tapped his hairless head, then answered.

"We could land somewhere unpopulated, then walk through wild areas until we reach north-west Elarond. From there, we can telekinetically fly a short distance to Godswater."

"Ah, yes, walk across the most jagged, difficult-to-traverse, unpopulated places in Elarond. In those months, how many people do you think your older brother will have victimised?" Razarkha asked.

Duncan's veins glowed white-hot. "You have a point."

"So, we take the risk for a fast and efficient solution in the Alaterran Mountains?"

"As you wish, Fel'thuz."

It wasn't the same as an Isleborn boy whose planning skills were as non-existent as Rakh's fidelity, but the submission allowed a rare warmth to wash over Razarkha. Taming a wyvern or stealing a domesticated animal was no mean feat, but as immortals, they had a better chance than any warm-blooded humanoid.

\* \* \*

Though Rakh had returned to Moonstone, rest wasn't an option. As his train came to a stop, he tapped his feet against the carriage floor, drummed his fingers against the table, and muttered to himself while the conductors delayed opening the doors. He glanced out of the window while he waited and noticed a boy at the platform.

His messy black hair, teal eyes and knitted woollen coat were unmistakeable; the true mystery was why he was here in the first place. Rarakhi may have been Rakh's son, but the boy's love was likely unattainable. He was likely there on the urging of one of the Khanases. The conductor finally announced the carriage doors' opening, and Count Fel'thuz joined the deluge of people pouring onto the platform, approaching Rarakhi once he found his bearings.

"Hey, dad," Rarakhi muttered, bunching himself up in his coat. "How was Ashglass?"

"As good as it could have been," Rakh replied, leading the boy towards the station's exit. "I anticipated resentment from Lady Foenaxas, but she's taken Irikhos's absence terribly."

"Guess some noble folks actually love their families, huh?"

Rakh laughed in a way that couldn't even convince himself. "I should assume given everything's intact that Razarkha didn't visit while I was gone."

"Nah, she did, she's just been really nice to the buildings."

Terror shot through Rakh, and he fumbled for a throwing knife. "Is she occupying the castle? Does she know about you? Is that why you've been waiting for me?"

The boy's serious expression melted, and he burst into hooting laughter. "Shit, you should have seen your face, dad! I don't think I've ever seen you that scared, and I was watching when the Boss wanted to ice you!"

Rakh's face burnt against the chill of Moonstone's air. "That wasn't funny, Rarakhi."

"Was to me."

"Being truthful this time, has anything of note happened in my absence?"

Rarakhi shrugged. "The Boss had a couple of marriage pendants produced ahead of time, but he's kept them hidden even though it's me and Plutera getting married. If you want to know anything political, I've haven't been paying attention. I've got a plan for fighting that bitch, though. You know me existing would piss her off? I say let her know about me, but I stay hidden and leave lots of clues, occupy her while everyone else is safe, then I lure her to a flammable building and throw everflame all over her!"

"No," Rakh snapped. "We're not doing this again, Rara, you're not going to—"

"I'm not gonna be the guy to deny my girl her vengeance!"

"If Razarkha dies, does it matter who kills her? The vengeance will be taken," Rakh said. "I'm an adult, you're a child, and I'll hear nothing more of this."

"You're an adult who spent his life as some prissy nobleman. I've been icing fools since I was twelve!"

"I won't allow my son to die before he's twenty," Rakh affirmed. "I'll hear no more of this. No schemes, no plots, you're going to be evacuated like everyone else."

"The Boss's men are gonna be working with the soldiers to protect the city. I'm a Khanas man. You can't stop me from serving the Boss," Rarakhi stated.

Rakh covered his face with his remaining hand. An adage he'd once scoffed at was that vigour was wasted on the young and conviction on the foolhardy. Rarakhi, however, proved both with contemptuous ease. As the illusionists walked into the snowy streets of Moonstone, the count pondered over his son. Appeals to reason were futile, and while it was a shot in the dark, it was the only approach remaining to him.

"How do you think I feel about this suicidal need to kill Razarkha? As a father?"

Rarakhi scoffed. "I don't think you do anything 'as a father'. You're just Count Fel'thuz getting frightened over the former Countess Fel'thuz, wanting all the vengeance for yourself."

"How can you accuse me of that, after everything?" Rakh blurted, his voice tightening. "Rarakhi, I'm— I know I was absent most of your life. Do you think I'm happy with that?"

The boy's voice lowered to a mumble. "No."

"Good. Therefore, do you think it's so much of a stretch that I don't want to lose the son I've only just started to know?"

Rarakhi stopped walking. "How are you gonna get to know me if you're dead?"

The frigid air seemed to mute all ambient noise. Rakh kept his back facing Rarakhi, hiding his hands within his sleeves. A slush of words flowed through his mind, but nothing of value came to his mouth. No matter what happened, he would never relate to his boy.

"It's better for me to die than you," Rakh muttered before he continued walking.

Rarakhi's hurried footsteps pattered behind him. "You don't know that. You're a nobleman, raised to rule an' all that shit, you're smarter than that Kag idiot, Erwyn seems—"

Rakh turned, then used his illusionism to accentuate his voice. "The commoners I champion despise my noble upbringing. I'm a failed husband, a failed father, I took advantage of my little sister when we were desperate, I treated commoner women as novelties to enjoy, and the one time I lived by my principles I spared a madwoman who's coming to destroy this city and all the lives within it.

"You, meanwhile, have a betrothal partner with whom you share mutual adoration. You have genuine rapport with the men of the lower class. If I die, who will grieve me? Erwyn, perhaps. If you die, I'll grieve you, Tei, Plutyn, Plutera, Erwyn, every single Khanas man you fought alongside will grieve too. You're more beloved than you think, but me? I'm not worth the purple in my hair."

Rarakhi's eyes met his father's, and after allowing silence to stew, he spoke. "I'd grieve if you died."

Rakh continued moving forward. "That's kind of you to say."

The pair walked towards the castle in silence, until Rarakhi made a sharp turn towards Plutyn Khanas's manor.

"You know what, fuck this. If you're not gonna believe me, fine. Just get killed by your mad bitch sister, after all you don't think I care, right? Be a fucking martyr or whatever you think you're doing. I'm done trying to be a Fel'thuz."

Rakh watched the boy leave, and while his heart begged him to intervene, his mind counselled against it. If Rarakhi didn't care about his father, then he'd be more likely to show self-preservation. Still, his foolish notion of avenging Rowyn for Plutera's sake needed to be quashed. There was only one person who could do that, and it was a coin's toss whether he was in the castle.

Without Rarakhi to selfishly focus on, every peasant of Moonstone was highlighted as they slipped in and out of the fog surrounding Rakh. A wine merchant closing shop for the night, a pregnant dark elven woman linking arms with her high elven husband, a goblinese street urchin scaling a library without heed for the icy heights he clambered upon. Each of them was unique, yet he couldn't truly know them.

Playing the humble count was foolish, just as Razarkha claimed. Her conclusion that oppression and dominance was the best alternative was equally foolish, but his dear sister had a talent for connecting legitimate points to deranged conclusions. As each commoner passed him, he couldn't help but wonder if any of his virtues were more than illusory.

Selenia guardsmen greeted Rakh at the castle gates, but he forgot his response mere moments after the interaction. His legs mindlessly dragged him through the courtyard, and into the castle. He'd barely brushed the snow off his coat before something was touching his upper body, and he looked down to see Lady Selenia gripping him with all her strength.

"Count Fel'thuz! Lady Foenaxas didn't burn you on a stake! Thank you for visiting Ashglass in my stead, I know I'd be too stupid to help with that," she said.

Rakh's eyes welled, and he held the elf close. "Stop calling yourself stupid. You're not made to be a lady, but you'll find your place in the world, I promise."

"Will you find your place too?"

"I don't know if I have one."

Kag let him go and looked up to her count. "If I have one, you have one too. Erwyn's been so worried, he kept telling saying that he should have come with you."

"I need to work on a speech with him; we have some builders and miners to talk into moving cities."

Kag's face stretched into a smile. "You made Lady Mor'kha agree to it? I'm so impressed. I'm sure if I went, I'd just get kidnapped again."

Rakh mussed his lady's hair. "Where's Sir Plutyn? Before I start work on this speech, I need to ask a personal favour of him."

"Oh, he's filling one of my lounges with bhang smoke, but he's too scary to tell off."

"Thank you," Rakh said, finding his will to smile once again.

True enough, Plutyn Khanas was playing *Wraiths and Wyverns* with Plutera in the downstairs lounge closest to the dining hall. Without breaking concentration, the Lost

Lord removed his pipe from his mouth, exhaled sideways to avoid fumigating his daughter's face, and spoke to Rakh.

"Count Fel'thuz. It's good to see our bait still lives."

Rakh laughed, which somehow dislodged a tear from his eye. "At least you don't hide your distaste for almost every living thing that isn't you."

While Plutyn said nothing, his daughter wore a defiant expression. "My father isn't a monster. He cares for a lot of people. Me, Rowyn, mother, Uncle Mortyn, he's just selective."

Rakh swallowed as he realised most of these people were dead. Unwilling to tolerate another argument with a child, he cleared his throat and addressed her father.

"Plutyn, I wouldn't approach you for idle chatter. I need your help."

The necromancer took his eyes off the game table. "As Minister of Criminal Affairs, I live to assist my count. Though something tells me that this isn't a matter pertaining to my official expertise."

"Don't twist the knife," Rakh muttered. "I'll be honest, Plutyn. You understand Rarakhi more than I ever will. He respects you, he looks up to you, and most importantly, he follows your orders. Can you convince him to leave for Deathsport with Plutera? I don't trust him to obey my word alone."

Plutera's face flushed. "Deathsport? But father, I need to be here! I need to watch Rowyn's killer die!"

Plutyn took his daughter's spellbinder with a diagonal stride of a wyvern. "No, you'll content yourself with word of Razarkha's death. Count Fel'thuz speaks sense. Once, Rarakhi was a mere soldier, an efficient assassin for my enterprises. Now he's your betrothed, my son by law, and the heir to Moonstone's advisory branch. Both of you are too important for me— and this city— to lose."

"But father, what about you?"

"I shall stay with my men. They've been ordered to give their lives for this city along with the Selenia army. If I refused to stay with them, what kind of lord would I be?"

Plutera's mint-green eyes grew misty. "What kind of heiress would I be if I abandoned the men while you didn't?"

"The sort who has a caring father," Plutyn said. "You will go to Deathsport, and Rarakhi will go with you. If you don't relay this command to him, then I shall. Am I understood?"

"Yes, father," Plutera said, hanging her head and knocking over her necromancer.

Rakh folded his arms and exhaled. "Thank you, Lord Khanas."

"This isn't a favour to you," the necromancer said with a sharp inhale from his pipe. "I just want to protect the ones I love."

# Acquaintances

Uncle Petyr had never been less composed. Ascetics Pleura and Montarys stood before him as he paced, and Rosaline was behind him, unable to meet the apostle's eyes. The Saltwater Temple's dining hall filled with his wooden sandals' clacking, and once he stopped moving, he replaced the noise with his voice.

"So, the only book missing is the Apostolic Chronicle? Nothing else?"

Montarys straightened his back. "That's correct. I've already taken the liberty of asking the ascetics who were guarding the restricted section what happened."

Petyr raised his eyebrow and turned to Pleura. "Rosaline visited you on the night it vanished, didn't she?"

Rosaline trembled and stared at the high ascetic, but she didn't return the look. Instead, the lumomancer lowered her head.

"She did," Pleura said. "As the keeper of the Holy Staff of the Moon Man, I'm the only one who can reliably access the restricted section, however, there is another way to open it."

Montarys nodded. "Indeed. With a crowbar and some determination, a sufficiently strong man could pry the entrance open. Two ascetics overheard Pleura mentioning as much."

The back of Petyr's hairless head tied Rosaline's tongue, but she would need to take over the conversation if this continued. While her uncle could drag the truth from everyone else, Rosaline's mind had seemingly formed a resistance to his convincing ways. Pleura would betray her with the right question, but thankfully, only Rosie knew where the Chronicle resided.

"Uncle Petyr, is it possible one of the Moon Men did this?" Rosaline asked.

Petyr frowned. "All Moon Men are proven loyalists. None of them would betray me. High Ascetic Pleura, when did your guard duty end?"

"Around the third hour past midnight," Pleura said. "There wasn't a guard at the post until the fifth hour. Ascetic Osgrey would have noticed somebody entering the tower."

Apostle Petyr turned to his Arkheran-styled long table and pushed his weight onto it. "Those who have the opportunity lack the motive, and those who have the motive lack the opportunity. All save for— Rosaline, did you steal the Chronicle?"

Rosaline was almost relieved to be directly asked; if the same question was asked of Pleura, the ruse would have fallen apart. Though a whisper snaked through her mind, snapping at the truth she concealed, she'd grown numb to Petyr's hands and words alike.

"I didn't," she said, looking her uncle in the eye. "Pleura *did* take me into the restricted section, and I saw the chronicle on the shelf, but it never left the room."

"It must have been stolen between the final night shift and the first day shift," Montarys concluded. "The thief must have unusual sleeping hours and decent strength for this theft to have happened at all."

Petyr narrowed his eyes at Rosaline. "You're not lying to me, are you?"

"I could never lie to you," Rosaline said. "You are the Voice of the Gods, and I do everything you want."

The apostle gritted his teeth and scratched the table. "Watch what you imply, Rosaline."

"I'm not implying anything. What are you referring to, uncle?" Rosaline said, her heart fluttering with a feeling she didn't have a word for.

Despite the eyes of Montarys and Pleura upon him, Petyr stalked up to Rosaline and took hold of her veil, almost pulling it off before he released it.

"You're still allowing your hair to peek through your coverings. You should be grateful you have such a holy guardian watching over you."

The fluttering gave way to pain, and Rosaline couldn't even bring herself to see if Pleura was upset. In her meekest voice, she mumbled, "I am grateful, Uncle Petyr."

The High Ascetic broke in shortly after. "If I may, apostle, reprimanding an innocent girl when there's a worrisome heresy afoot is unproductive—"

"Enough of this nonsense. I know of a man that sleeps through the day and despises all that's holy," Petyr concluded. "Pleura, Montarys, gather some Moon Men and some Border's Men, then raid the house of Sir Gerold Applewood. He may have drunk his life away, but if anybody can find the strength to force his way into the restricted section, it's him."

Rosaline's head flared, and a light jumped from her hand to Petyr's. The apostle turned, raising a thin eyebrow.

"What did you just do, Rosaline?"

"I don't know, it's just something that's been happening lately!"

Montarys rubbed his chin. "Perhaps she's a budding Stormcaller. It wouldn't be the first time a Godswater's been blessed with godly favour."

"You shall be quiet, and you shall arrest Sir Applewood," Petyr snapped. "Am I understood?"

"Of course, Your Holiness."

Montarys left the dining hall first, and Pleura, after a nod in Rosaline's direction, followed. Rosaline was alone with Uncle Petyr, and he didn't look ready to accept platitudes.

"You're a whore," Petyr snapped without a hint of his apostolic tone.

"I know," Rosaline said, hanging her head.

"You visited your worthless uncle the other day," Petyr stated. "Didn't you?"

The shock of the statement negated Rosaline's attempts to resist. "I did, but I don't think he's responsible for—"

Petyr took Rosaline by the hips and lowered his voice. "If you acted as his accomplice, I'm not sure what I can do to punish you. Gerold would be burnt for corrupting such an impressionable youth, but you're my only heir, and because of your parents' cowardice, there aren't any other options. I suppose I'll have to devise a punishment worse than death."

"Please, Uncle Petyr, I'm not his accomplice, I promise, I swear to the Border, and if I lie the Harvester will take me away—"

"You'd like that, wouldn't you?" Petyr said, putting a hand on Rosaline's neck. "You're just like your parents, too *weak* to continue living."

"I'm not like them," Rosaline croaked as he squeezed out half her voice.

"Then how would you suggest I punish you?"

"I could fast, I could flog myself, I could—"

"I asked how *I* could punish you," Petyr reiterated. "Wash yourself and enter my bedroom."

Rosaline's head was overcome by a fizzing sensation, and her temples shot sparks of heat through the resultant numbness. She could have resisted, but if she did, she'd reveal that his voice no longer affected her. There was one way she could delay the inevitable, but it didn't leave Uncle Gerold in a good position, seeing as he'd bear the brunt of Petyr's frustration.

She headed upstairs, and with as much leisure as she could muster, laboured over her change of clothes, which towel she'd use, and so on; if it was something that could be artificially prolonged, she prolonged it. Once she was done selecting her redundant clothes, she moseyed to the bathroom, shut the door, and ran the tap at a slow, but still audible rate.

The most slowly prepared bath of all time commenced a good hour after it had been requested, and Rosaline wasn't brisk in washing herself. She wallowed in half a day's worth of filth mixed with every fragrant oil she could conceivably need, staying in place until the skin at her extremities resembled olive-coloured raisins. She almost tricked herself into hoping that her prune-like feet would be unappealing to Petyr, but she killed her foolishness in the womb. Her body was only part of why Petyr desired her; somehow, her whoredom was innate, whether she was a child or a disgusting, oversoaked woman. Eventually a knocking was heard at the door, and Petyr spoke before Rosaline could acknowledge it.

"Rosaline, are you all right? You've been in the bathroom for four hours," he said in his apostolic tone.

"I'm fine," Rosaline mumbled.

"Well, you ought to leave soon, lest your vanity overcome you."

"Of course."

Further delaying was futile. She stood and let the water drip from her; while she stretched each moment she could, Petyr's breathing beyond the bathroom urged her forward. She dressed herself, then headed out to see her uncle's hungry eyes fixating upon her.

"I hope your hair was adequately dried before you put that veil on," he said. "Quickly, to my room, we must undertake our purification ritual—"

A servant rushed upstairs and cut his master off, albeit with a bowed head and pressed-together hands. "Your Holiness, Ascetic Shiloh Godspawn has successfully arrested Gerold Applewood. They're waiting for you in the worship hall."

Petyr clenched his fists and roared to the roof. "Must *everything* go wrong today? With me, Rosaline, I'm not letting you leave my sight."

"You rarely do," Rosaline mumbled.

This only angered her apostolic uncle further, and he wrenched her wrist before dragging her downstairs. Gerold Applewood was far from alone; along with Ascetic Shiloh, who was keeping him restrained, a small crowd of worshippers had gathered, murmuring amongst themselves. Petyr released Rosaline the moment he saw the peasants and put on a warm smile as he approached Shiloh.

"Good work, nephew," he said. "Behold, people of Godswater, the true face of heresy; gluttonous, red-faced, besotted with hedonism and wretchedness."

Gerold spat at Petyr's feet. "You arresting people for being wretched now? I thought I was safe seeing as you hadn't fucked me before."

Petyr bit his lip, and he squeezed Gerold's cheeks in his hand. "Only the truly perverse would imagine a holy apostle indulging in wanton inversion with such a pathetic specimen."

"Of course, I'm too disgusting," Gerold said with a grin Rosaline didn't consider him capable of. "You like 'em young and girly."

Rosaline's hands began to shake, as did Petyr's, who made a theatrical laugh for the crowd. "People of Godswater, behold the folly of excessive drinking. This man is unaware of the very words he speaks. Thankfully, I'm a merciful man, and this creature's existence is punishment enough."

Gerold scoffed. "You brought me all the way here, and you aren't gonna kill me? That's your mistake, Godswater. Though I have a few better noble names for you. How 'bout Horngiver? Bastardsower? Virtuekiller?"

"Consider yourself lucky that I had such... fondness for your sister," Petyr said with unmoving, contemptuous eyes. "Take him to the dungeons, Shiloh. I must pray regarding this wretched soul's fate."

Shiloh began to drag the fat knight away, but Applewood pushed forward with all his weight, temporarily breaking free. Despite being cuffed, he rushed Petyr swiftly enough to headbutt him.

The thin apostle fell backwards and rubbed his forehead. "My mercy is infinite towards former kin."

"Fuck yourself," Gerold sneered as Shiloh grabbed him. "You're showin' mercy 'cause if I die, people will think you fear my words. You made a mistake arresting me, Petyr. I ain't got nothing to lose now."

"How quaint," Petyr said, standing while Applewood was dragged away. "It's a shame you have nothing to accuse me of."

"Really? 'cause I know you raped my sister, and for all I know, Rosie over there is just another one of your bastards, like Shiloh, an' that other girl, they're all yours!"

Shiloh froze up before continuing his efforts while Petyr glanced at Rosaline. She couldn't fully believe what she'd just heard, and the crowd appeared to be similarly stunned. Petyr's lips began moving, but it was a while before coherent words were formed.

"Can you believe this heretic? What form of evil desperation drives a man to besmirch the honour of his late sister? This heretic only lives because of that very woman, and yet he slanders her anyway. You mustn't take heed of his words. He's a monster and a fool."

Rosaline had worked so hard numbing her mind to Petyr's words, but the fear of being a Godspawn overtook her. Within moments of hearing the apostle speak, all notions of bastardy vanished from her memory.

* * *

The Deathsport line was coming to an end. Though Rarakhi was sorely tempted to use his illusionism to sneak himself and Plutera out of the train before it left Moonstone, two people sat in their way; the undead orcs, Bloodmetal and

Notongue. Plutera was slumped against the carriage window, her normally bright eyes as lifeless as the mute orc beside her.

"It doesn't make sense," Plutera mumbled as the train entered Deathsport's station. "Father always went on about the value of growing cold to suit the world, yet now that I want to watch somebody suffer, he's trying to protect my innocence."

Rarakhi's upper lip trembled as his final words to his father tugged on his eardrums. The count hadn't even bothered to make up with him, he just sent Plutyn to do his job for him. Perhaps he'd finally given up on being a father.

"The Boss loves you, that's all," Rarakhi said. "He wants you out of a war zone. You ain't a soldier like me, so it makes sense. It's not like my dad. He didn't even see us off."

"Isn't that what you wanted?" Plutera asked.

"I don't know," Rarakhi replied. "He doesn't understand me like your dad understands you. He underestimates me when I would beat him in a fight without trying."

"Don't you think you're expecting too much? How could he possibly know you as my father knows me? When he asked father to command you on his behalf, he seemed upset about the situation. It's not as though he doesn't *want* to understand you."

Rarakhi vented air in time with the steam engine and played with his hands. "It's too late to make amends."

Bloodmetal put a hand on Rarakhi's shoulder. "Don't you worry about that, lad. Your father killed a daemon the size of a house and only lost a hand. Your Aunt Razarkha's nothing compared to a daemon. You'll see, this'll be a short stay with your mam, then you'll go home, say sorry, and it'll be back to arguing and making up like the angry kid you are."

"I guess," Rarakhi muttered.

When he thought of the warm, ghastly winds that once haunted the catacombs, and how, of all people, Rakh put an end to it, he almost believed Bloodmetal's attempt at comfort. His Aunt Razarkha, however, was even more amorphous than a daemon. Though he'd listened to laughter-laden tales of her humiliation at his father's hands, all that meant was that his aunt returned, it would be with the means to guarantee his father's death. The train doors opened, and their orcish bodyguards rose, wobbling the carriage before heading through the aisle. Plutera stood soon after and offered her hand to Rarakhi.

"This won't be completely terrible," the necromantic girl said, before lowering her voice to a whisper. "Your mother doesn't seem like the most hands-on parent. Perhaps we could have enough privacy to sneak something in before our official consummation."

Rarakhi was swift to take his betrothed's hand, whispering back. "I hadn't even thought of that. Shit, now I'm excited."

"Are you feeling better than you were after Ashglass?"

"Still have nightmares about it, but I'm dreaming of you more often."

They caught up to their bodyguards, and Notongue was hissing with a smirk, while Bloodmetal had his arms folded.

"What were you two talking about? If you're thinking of doing some spooky illusion magic to escape, don't bother. Your mam's expecting you, the Boss and Count Fel'thuz will be keeping a close eye, and I have your return tickets. You ain't going anywhere without us founding out."

Rarakhi grinned. "Nah, we're just plotting how much we're gonna kiss, ain't that right, Petal?"

"Yes, and it's going to be positively beautiful!"

"To you two, maybe," Bloodmetal remarked. "To me it's like watching two baby snakes coiling around each other."

"If love isn't beautiful to you, what is?" Plutera asked.

The orc sighed. "To me, there's somethin' beautiful about watching the snow fall. You and the Boss's gardens are pretty as well. As for romance, my perfect woman's a big lass, with thin body hair I can stroke, tits I can bury my face in, and an arse the size of a—"

"I'm starting to wish Bloodmetal also lost his tongue," Rarakhi cut off.

"Now, now, all it shows is we got different ideas for what's good-looking," Bloodmetal said. "I'm glad you two look at each other like you're the most beautiful things in the world, an' I assure you, you'll be glad others don't think the same. If they did, your marriage would be constantly interrupted."

"You won't interrupt us if we do anything, will you, Bloodmetal?" Plutera asked with a coy cock of her head. "Notongue obviously knows how to keep a secret, but you aren't a loose end, I hope."

"Quit talking like your father, I ain't gonna stop owt unless there's a direct order from the Boss. Go wild, you dumb kids," Bloodmetal said, then glanced at Notongue. "Meaning no offence to dumb folks."

Notongue made a brusque huff and left it at that. Together, the four wandered from the crowded station to the even more crowded streets of Deathsport. Gnomes that barely reached Rarakhi's hips vied for a way through humans, elves, and orcs, while the Moonstone four exuded enough of a presence to part the sea of men passively. The alternative explanation was that Rarakhi was overly used to whatever stench the two revenants guarding them had.

The walk to Tei's house was short, and though Rarakhi was the only one who knew its location, he didn't have the spirit to give the orcs the run-around. Plutera's joy had returned, so it was better to make the most of their time cowering on the other side of the kingdom while Moonstone was ravaged. When he knocked on the house's door, a tiny old woman opened the door, seemingly a crooked-backed seer. Once the pseudo-crone recognised her visitor, she dropped her illusionism and revealed her true, heterochromatic form.

"Ah, you actually arrived. I'm glad you listened to reason in the end," Tei said. "Sometimes the best thing to do regarding a family fight is stay out of it."

"You'd know all about that, huh?" Rarakhi snapped.

"Merciless as ever, I see. Come in. Your lover is tall, but a tad broad for a necromancer," Tei replied, winking at Notongue. "That young girl isn't bad-looking either."

Notongue made a chuckling hiss while Rarakhi face flared up. Plutera, however, was undaunted, and offered Tei a curtsey.

"It's a pleasure to finally meet my mother by law."

"I hope that once this Razarkha nonsense is dead and buried, we can meet more often," she said, ushering them into her house. "The bodyguards will have to sleep in the halls, but I have a spare room with two single beds."

"Actually, sleep won't be a problem, milady," Bloodmetal said. "We're both undead, if my caved-in chest wasn't an indication."

"Ah, excellent," Tei said. "I've tried to spruce up the living room, so go ahead and make yourselves at home. I've still got work to do, so occupy yourselves. You two aren't exactly here for my wonderful hosting."

Plutera stooped to put a hand on Tei's shoulder. "I would like to spend some time with you when I can."

"You say that now, but my job greys my hair, and the worst part is, half of the matters I handle are confidential, so I can't even tell you about them," she said. "Is there anything you want to ask me before I head back to my office?"

Rarakhi folded his arms and looked away. Plutera shouldn't have humoured his mother's self-pity. Just as he thought Tei would waddle back to her usual parental neglect, Bloodmetal opened his big orcish mouth.

"Hold on, I almost forgot. I have a message from the Boss," he said, opening a satchel and pulling out a wax-sealed roll of parchment.

Tei retrieved the letter and unrolled it. Her eyes scanned the paper, occasionally flitting towards Plutera and Rarakhi. By the end, she was laughing to herself.

"Bad news, you two. It appears this so-called Lord Khanas is part seerish."

Plutera began to splutter. "What do you mean? Our blood hails from the purest of old necromantic nobility, we aren't diluted in any way!"

"That doesn't explain his apparent prescience. If you were intent on sharing a bed with each other, I'm afraid Lord Khanas has commanded me, and these orcish bodyguards, not to allow this under any circumstances."

Rarakhi slumped his back. "Fuck's sake."

Plutera didn't say anything, but her eyes had dimmed once more. There was no making the most of this cowardice; they were trapped with his worst parent, a whole kingdom away from where their vengeance lay.

\* \* \*

Razarkha would have considered it good to have her feet on the ground if she had both of them. Her crystal leg was a glorified crutch, but this lugging was at least less draining on her 'lifespan'. She and Duncan had landed just north of a town by the Alaterran Mountains and as neither of them required sleep, they'd been walking non-stop.

They reached a lush lake surrounded by pine-covered mountains and wyvern-filled skies. Occasionally one dove towards the water, snatched a fish with its beak, then landed on a bank, charring their catch before swallowing it. Duncan gazed at the creatures with his typical dispassion, but Razarkha couldn't help but rejoice at the beasts' raw power.

Such creatures were only rivalled by krakens and sea giants, though naturally dragons dominated them and all other magical beasts. Dragons were much like men in how they thought, so enslaving them was no different to treating an augmentee as a pet, but wyverns, for all their gifts, were as intelligent as dogs. An image of Ariel shattering projected itself above the lake, and a nearby wyvern noticed it, then flew away.

"Wait, come back you stupid animal, that was an arcane slip-up!" Razarkha stammered as she charged towards the spot where it was cooking its fish.

It was long gone by the time she reached its landing spot, and Duncan caught up to her, then picked up the half-charred fish. "Would you like to see if you can still taste? I would do the same, but I have no mouth."

"Shut up, Godswater."

Duncan shrugged and threw the blackened carp into the water. "Well, we're here. While I agreed to this plan, you need to prove capable of taming a wyvern. I don't need to ride one, you do. If you're going to spook them with your illusionism, they're never going to obey you."

Razarkha raised her hand and considered recalling her rarely used geomantic incantations to turn Duncan into a modern-day Conditor, but lowered her hand when a notion struck her.

*"That's it,* Duncan!"

"What's it?"

"My illusionism just spooked that wyvern, didn't it?"

"Yes, and if I'm honest, your arcane incontinence is somewhat disconcerting."

"Oh, shut up and listen to what I have to say," Razarkha said with a fan of her hands. "There are wyvern riders throughout this range, and that means there are wyverns that trust people. Therefore, if I use my illusionism to imitate a wyvern's rider, they'll let me handle them as though they've trusted me their entire life!"

Duncan stared through her. "It's as good a plan as any. We'll need to find a mountain settlement for the best chance of finding a tamed wyvern."

"I know that," Razarkha snapped.

"I can never be sure, because you just needed to be informed about the difficulty of taming a wyvern."

Razarkha's abdomen seared her skin. She approached the glorified golem, made herself tall, and pointed her soulstealer.

"One more clever comment and I'll kill you, then find a way to use your remains as magical fuel. Am I clear?"

"As clear as this lake," Duncan unwaveringly droned.

"Weil was never like this," Razarkha said. "He adored me."

"You're finally willing to talk about this 'Weil'? I was afraid to bring him up after what you did to that poor augmentee."

"You don't need to know about him," Razarkha insisted. "All you need to know is that he was better than you."

"If you say so."

Razarkha refused to give the snide igneous slab further ammunition and continued walking around the lake, towards a road that stretched along a mountain with a large town upon its face. She cast illusionism to magnify her view, and saw that, as expected, there were countless humanoids walking alongside wyverns along the path.

"We have our target."

As a pleasant surprise, Duncan stayed silent, and so they stalked through pine forests, using the brush as well as a floating fire hazard and a half-living abomination could.

They reached small clearing where a rider sat alone, patting a lanky, purple-and-red wyvern on its beak. She was a high elf with tied-back blonde hair, and as Razarkha magnified her view of her, something struck her. The rider's eyes were the same pale red as Lady Selenia's, and her nose, small and button-like, reminded Razarkha of Moonstone. Duncan broke in with a remark.

"Well? She's vulnerable, if there's a time to replace her, it's now."

"One moment, I think— by the Gods, that's little Yar," Razarkha muttered, returning her view to normal.

"Little Yar?"

"Yarawyn Selenia, you idiot, don't you know anything about Arkheran politics?"

"I've been away from Arkhera for over twenty years," Duncan pointed out.

"She was a toddler when you left, that's no excuse."

Duncan made a grinding noise. "Forgive me for not keeping track of obscure northern politics, I was busy having my life ruined by my older brother."

"I think I have a way to get a wyvern back to Arkhera without a fight. In fact, I think she'd be willing to become a military asset," Razarkha replied. "You stay close, keep your mouth shut, and leave everything to me."

Duncan pointed to his own face. "No mouth."

"You know what I mean. With me."

Razarkha burst into the clearing and walked towards the woman, surging as much energy into her motions as possible without casting magic.

"If it isn't baby Yar in the flesh," Razarkha said, opening her arms. "I've been looking for you."

The woman scrambled to her feet, and her wyvern wound its neck around her, rumbling in a low tone while it fanned its neck-scutes.

"What in the world are you?" the high elf spluttered.

Razarkha forced a chuckle even as her abdomen cooked her from within. "Silly girl. Don't you remember Countess Razarkha Fel'thuz? The better half of the Fel'thuz family?"

"I remember you used to call me an impudent child and mocked me for liking a dark elf," the girl spat.

"Oh, good, so you *are* Yarawyn," she said, catching herself as her crystal leg wobbled. "It seems you've been busy since your unjust exile."

Yarawyn came out from behind her beastly protector's neck and puffed her chest up. "I see how it is. *Now* you consider my exile unjust. What happened to you, anyway? It seems I did better in my ten years of exile than however long you spent yours."

"It depends. I'm not as beautiful as I once was, but how many continents can *you* boast of destabilising?" Razarkha asked, putting her hand on her chest.

Her crystalline life support system cooled, and surprisingly, positive memories of her campaign rushed through her. Despite this, Yarawyn's stance was still confrontational.

"You've destabilised a continent? Which one?"

"Sula," she answered. "I don't know how fast news has travelled, but I'm sure historians will consider Erre's Insurrection crucial to the reformation of contemporary Sula."

"Haven't heard of it," Yarawyn said. "Looks to me like you're some sort of undead abomination exaggerating her achievements."

The joys of humiliating Consigliere Lesteris vanished, and Razarkha lifted a half-clenched fist, channelling a telekinetic spell through her motions. She lifted Yarawyn, then dragged her close, meeting her fiery eyes while her wyvern screeched.

"Listen, girl. I sought you out hoping to give you an opportunity. You can mock me, or you can listen to me. One of these options comes with the bonus of your survival."

"All right, I'm listening, I'm listening!" Yar stammered.

Razarkha flung Yar away, allowing her beast to sniff her as she got to her feet. Allowing a moment for the humiliation to set in, she concocted a small speech.

"Still as impudent as ever," she said. "If you've grown up at all over the decade you've wasted here, you've likely debated your options for retaking Moonstone. You were going to marry Irikhos Foenaxas after all, and an impure heir is better than no heir at all. The Gods know Rakh was an ever-present reminder of that fact with all his potential bastards. My point is, Kag knew you were a threat and threw you away, didn't she?"

"And you, like every other Moonstone snake, were complicit," Yarawyn snapped.

"Shush, baby Yar, and let the grown-up finish," Razarkha said with a tut. "I'll admit, I saw your worthless drama as little more than proof that the Selenia family were unworthy of governing a restaurant, let alone a province. I wouldn't have intervened then, but here, now? We're natural allies. You wish to retake Moonstone, yes? Perhaps you hope to visit Ashglass again, and visit your beautiful Irikhos? He still ties his hair back, you know."

"I know," Yarawyn said. "He's here."

"*More* Arkheran exiles? Oh, this is wonderful, we'll have a whole gaggle of vengeance seekers," Razarkha said, her abdomen once again running cool. "This silent augmentee beside me is Duncan Godswater. He was being betrayed by treacherous siblings while you were in your swaddling clothes."

"Hello," Duncan echoed.

"Hello," Yarawyn repeated. "So, you're willing to help me take Moonstone?"

"If Kagura and Rakh are the unworthy siblings who exiled us, we're the true leaders who'll reclaim our rightful places as Lady Selenia and her loyal advisor," Razarkha said with a deep bow. "With your wyvern, my experience bringing entire megalopolises to the ground, and Duncan's... geomancy, I suppose, we can overwhelm any paltry Arkheran army. Come, I want to see Irikhos Foenaxas again. Time is dead siblings, and it waits for no-one."

Yarawyn stared at Razarkha, fixating on the replacement for her mangled midsection. Eventually, the elf nodded.

"Very well," she said. "Let's head home. Tor managed to ruin my reunion with Irikhos, but there'll be little love lost between all of us."

"I'm not here to befriend you. I live only to serve," Razarkha said with a hollow smile.

# Wanderers

Irikhos sat in Torawyn's living room while she and a patient chatted in swift, fluent Elarondian on the other side of a wall. Yarawyn still hadn't returned, having fallen off her wyvern for all he knew. He'd despised Kagura for sending her impetuous younger sister away, yet as he dwelled upon Yar's behaviour, he couldn't help but think like the overlady.

Perhaps in her simple idiocy, Kag saw something that Irikhos's desire-fogged eyes couldn't. He'd kidnapped an overlady, accepted an exile and crossed a foreign nation for her sake, yet she was a disappointment. Iri shook his head. It wasn't his place to expect desirability from a woman he hadn't seen in a decade, but decency shouldn't have been too much to ask. An obese dark elf waddled out of the side room, shaking all three of his chins as he laughed at something Torawyn said. While he walked past the living room, Tor called out.

*"Remember, stick to fish and greens. If you eat pasta, ensure it fits into a serving bowl, not a mixing bowl,"* she said.

*"Yes, yes, foreign doctor,"* the patient replied as he opened the door. *"It is a miserable thing to give up on, but for my daughter's sake, I shall heed your advice."*

*"I'm glad,"* Torawyn said, and with that, the door creaked, then slammed.

A few disembodied stepping sounds later, and Tor joined Irikhos. She threw herself onto the couch and slumped her twiglike body.

"I wish I didn't have to work like this."

"I'm worried about her too," Irikhos was quick to say, meeting her eyes. "I can't imagine patients with dietary issues are easy for you even without this nonsense."

"At least I have experience in losing weight," Torawyn said with a soft, defeated laugh. "It's not much, but you being here at least proves that I'm not mad."

"Why would you think you're mad?"

"Yarawyn constantly doubts my decision to embrace life in Elarond," she explained. "She's forever calling me spineless, weak, without conviction. I just want to survive, and at least you don't seem to begrudge me that."

"Any reasonable person wouldn't."

Torawyn looked away from him. "Am I evil for smiling about you thinking Yarawyn is unreasonable?"

"There's no question about it; she's unreasonable," Irikhos stated. "I arrived with an opportunity for her to gain power without a fight, yet she's driving conflict for its own sake. I know I shouldn't tell you this, but the way we met, she way she treated you when I first came here, it destroyed my attraction to her in hours. I'd spent years dreaming of the woman Yarawyn could become, and the Yar I found was some vengeance-obsessed lunatic."

"Didn't you attempt to take vengeance on Kagura too?" Torawyn pointed out.

"I— I didn't actively stew upon it," Irikhos claimed. "I hated Lady Selenia, but I stayed quiet. Mor'kha and Cousin Gelth made suggestions for alternative marriage prospects, and I heard them. But when the rapeworm epidemic hit Ashglass, and *her* of all people visited, my rage frothed up. I told myself I could reconcile with her, but when I invited her to dinner, I knew deep down I'd end up hurting her. What I did was wrong, but it also led to Kag accepting her wrongdoing. I should have got through to her in almost any other way, but I'm grateful some good came of it. I don't think Yar and I's situations are comparable."

"You got to stay home, while she's been stuck in a foreign nation for years," Tor said. "You may not know this, and Yar hates it when I tell people, but... she has difficulty with letters. They shift about and tangle together in her head.

She has a hard enough time reading Common, let alone Elarondian, and that naturally limits the methods one uses to learn language. Yarawyn so often considers herself helpless, and I want to sympathise with her rage, but when she turns it on me, I resent her."

Irikhos's face burned up, and he clenched his hands. "Even if I convince Yar to return in peace, I'll need to marry her to stay true to the overlady's conditions. I'll be honest, being bound to someone like her sounds like a miserable existence. As perverse as it might sound, I envy my brother-in-law."

Tor's sorrowful expression briefly lightened. "My parents were siblings, I'm not going to judge you for being attracted to your sister—"

*"That's not what I meant!"* Irikhos stammered. "Mor'kha isn't a woman I consider attractive and being candid I don't believe Solyx thinks so either. Despite this, they understand each other, work together, and take their duties as politicians and parents seriously. I can't see myself doing that with Yarawyn."

Torawyn paused, then shuffled closer to Irikhos. "Do you think Kag would be willing to loosen the conditions for your return?"

"What do you mean?" Irikhos said, then upon seeing the glint in Torawyn's eyes, quickly figured it out. "I'm not sure, perhaps if Yarawyn doesn't return, but if we let things happen too quickly, we'd—"

A loud banging at the door cut him off, and Torawyn stood, her milky-white face flushing. "Oh, it's probably a patient. I thought I didn't have appointments for at least another hour, but perhaps they're early."

Irikhos stayed on the couch, trying to blink away the image of Tor's hungry eyes, then overheard Yarawyn's voice.

"Look who I found, Tor! Please, you must let her in!"

"Let her in? She's a *ghoul,* Yar!" Torawyn exploded.

"Well, yes, she's undead, but that's not the point! She's here to bolster our return!"

A Moonstone-accented, deeper feminine voice made itself heard. "It's all right, Yarawyn. If I don't have her permission, I'll just take the house myself. I highly doubt she could stop me."

Irikhos rushed to the door, to find Yarawyn flanked by a strange collection of levitating lava chunks and the most abominable excuse for a spellbinder he'd seen. She had Rakh Fel'thuz's black hair, where it hadn't faded to grey, and was skeletally thin. Her midsection was replaced by a great, arcane geode, and her left leg was an articulated crystalline tower. Her clothes barely hung onto her, and around her neck were the tattered remains of a cape.

Irikhos backed off and shook his head. "No, no, that can't be—"

"If it isn't Irikhos Foenaxas in the flesh!" Razarkha Fel'thuz said with a wide gesture. "I heard all about your unjust exile. Lady Kag and my terrible brother are quite drunk on their unearned power. It's about time we did something about them, wouldn't you agree?"

"With respect, Countess Fel'thuz, whatever Yar relayed to you can't have been the full story," Irikhos said, standing by Torawyn's side. "I came here with the intent of peacefully returning to Arkhera, and if you'll have me start my reign of Moonstone with blood on my hands, then I'd rather stay in Elarond."

"So disappointing," Razarkha snapped, lifting her hand.

Without warning, a thousand tiny, invisible hands lifted him by the chest, pressing against his muscles and ribs alike, tightening their grip as the spellbinder clenched her fist.

"Let's not fight amongst ourselves," Razarkha said in a tone as snakelike as her face. "We have common enemies, and we can't return to Arkhera hoping to coexist with those who've wronged us. If they exist, we cannot. Torawyn, show us some hospitality, seeing as this foolish Foenaxas is being so rude. I wouldn't want my telekinesis to slip."

Tor stared at Irikhos, who tried and failed to form words in his throat. Without his voice, he resorted to a desperate nod, which she was quick to act upon.

"Come in. Please note this house is also a medical practice, so there will be members of the Alaterran public coming through," Torawyn said in a tone battling between trembling terror and unwavering professionalism.

Razarkha released Irikhos, and he fell to the floor, leaving Yar and the spellbinder to step over him as they entered. The rocky construct waited for him to stand but said nothing. Torawyn helped him up and whispered to him in Elarondian.

*"What in the world do we do?"*

*"I don't know, but that thing could be hearing us,"* Irikhos hissed in a broken rendition of the language.

Torawyn nodded, and they walked to the living room with the arcane construct lingering behind them. Yarawyn and the walking corpse had already taken up the settee, the former's eyes as wild as an out-of-control bonfire.

"Look, Irikhos! This is our answer! Razarkha Fel'thuz has been on all kinds of adventures, and now she's an undead, illusion-casting, telekinetic, lumomantic, geomantic one-woman army!" the youngest Selenia sister ranted. "With Moonrazer and that— apparently that thing is Duncan Godswater— the point is, we have the power to take Moonstone by force."

Irikhos and Torawyn looked to each other. The woman was a healer; she may have been thoughtful, but she took her time to reach decisions that weren't over a bleeding patient, no doubt. He knew he wouldn't want a healer who rushed to decisive conclusions. Here, they needed a knight who could think on his feet. Irikhos prayed he lived up to his qualifications.

"I'm happy for you, Yarawyn."

"That's good," she said, slouching as though she hadn't stood by while her pet revenant nearly crushed his ribcage. "I know you said you'd rather stay in Elarond than have blood on your hands, but thankfully for me, father's will is moot. I'll take Moonstone by force, and if King Silas has an issue, I dare him to take his southern soldiers to the snowy north. You're ultimately irrelevant to the equation, Iri, but I'll still make you the offer. Stay here, away from your sister, your cousins, all your friends in Ashglass, feeling sorry for yourself with my spineless sister until the day you die, or be my husband, and make love to a beautiful woman for the rest of your life as a lord consort all will envy."

Torawyn stared at Irikhos, pleading with her eyes. She mouthed to him in Elarondian, but he couldn't make out the words. It didn't matter; survival came first, then principles could be worked into the mix.

"I'll admit, Yarawyn, you're not as beautiful to me as you once were," Irikhos stated, adding the tartness of truth to disguise his forthcoming sweet lie. "However, I do wish to see my sister again. If you'll have me, I'll accompany you to Arkhera."

Torawyn slumped. "Irikhos, *no...*"

Yarawyn let a scornful laugh loose, then squared up to her sister. "Looks like you lost again, dear sister. Don't think I was blind to what you were considering. If there's one thing Razarkha and I have learned, it's that kin have no inherent claim to our trust. I'll leave you behind to die an irrelevant Elarondian wretch, while I'll rule supreme as Overlady of the Forests of Winter!"

Tears flooded down Torawyn's face. "You're a monster. I should have left you to go homeless."

"That was your mistake," Yarawyn said with a smirk, and turned to Razarkha. "All right, I need to make up with a friend that I think you'd like a lot. He has tentacles, just like that fellow you talked about."

Strangely, this attempt at flattery made the undead spellbinder's eye twitch. "He sounds enchanting. Let us meet him, now that Irikhos's cooperation is assured."

This was Irikhos's time to strike. He broke in with a few fractured syllables before finally making coherent words.

"I'm unsure Moonrazer could carry all of us, and besides, I fear the beast. You lot visit this friend without me, I'll start packing our things."

Yarawyn took Irikhos by the shoulders and planted a kiss on his forced-shut lips. "That's the spirit. You'll come to enjoy being my husband, even if you hate me now."

Razarkha chuckled. "And if it goes wrong, you could always end things as Rakh and I did. Show me the way, Lady Selenia."

Yar made to lead Fel'thuz out, but before they left, the latter stopped and pointed at the augmentee in the corner. "Duncan, you keep an eye on Irikhos. Make sure he doesn't betray his lady love."

"Of course," Duncan replied.

The door opened and slammed shut once again. Despite Duncan Godswater's glowing redstone eyes, Irikhos wasted no time shouting to Torawyn.

"We need to pack our bags and leave, *now!*"

Torawyn started to splutter. "But my patients— the— that augmentee's watching us!"

"I don't care, if we don't leave now, they're going to kill everyone I know and care about. I know you don't have anyone, but if I leave and you don't, do you think Yar's going to be merciful? Your life here is over, and we need to warn Moonstone!" Irikhos yelled.

Torawyn nodded, then rushed upstairs. Irikhos eyed the arcane construct in the corner.

"You'll stay quiet about this, won't you?"

Duncan paused. "I'm with Razarkha so I have assistance killing my brother, Petyr Godswater. I have nothing against you running away. I'll claim you exhibited unpredictable antimagical prowess and temporarily disincorporated me."

Irikhos let his tension vent. "Thank you so much. I passed Godswater to reach here, and it looks like Petyr is still in power, using stake-burning as a deterrent against dissent."

"He's not changed for over two decades," Duncan remarked. "Does he have an heir or was Simeon too much for him to handle?"

"As far as I know, Simeon Godswater is dead, but I don't know the details. He did have a daughter, though. Rosaline, I believe her name is."

Duncan made a scraping sound. "I doubt Rosaline was his. Any wife Simeon took, Petyr would eye. If that girl's started to bleed, she's probably a target too. By every god there is, I'll kill that monster. As for you, you'd best get packing."

"Thank you once again," Irikhos said with a nod.

The augmentee fell apart, leaving charred spots upon the floorboards. "Don't worry about it. I was defeated by a clever antimage, after all."

\* \* \*

The people of Moonstone were as turbulent as seawater, and despite Rakh's greatest efforts, he couldn't blur them together. There were mothers with babes in their arms, scuffed-up scoundrels being dragged off by guards, tall spellbinders and diminutive goblins, elves with light and dark skin alike. They roiled about, subject to whatever tides swayed the common man, and as he stood on a platform guarded by several waves of soldiers, he internally reiterated that Moonstone's lives rested upon his words. Lady Kag and

Erwyn flanked him, while Plutyn's men were perched upon buildings in his peripheral vision, magitech coil guns at the ready.

Kagura put a hand on Rakh's shoulder. "Are you ready, Count Fel'thuz? I can make a speech up really quickly if you need me to."

"No. I must be the one to do this," Rakh whispered back.

"Don't worry," Erwyn assured him. "I've proofread the speech, it'll rein in all but the most seditious of peasants. Before long Moonstone will be evacuated."

Rakh shook his head. "We can't know that until we see their reaction. This is it. Unless either of you have something to say, I'm going to amplify myself."

Erwyn and Kag alike shook their heads, so Rakh cast the appropriate auditory illusionism. He cleared his throat, and it echoed throughout the city, just as he'd hoped.

"People of Moonstone. I cannot know for certain, but you have likely noticed the increased deployment of soldiers and rapid construction of blockades. The brave men of the military and the builders of the city are working hard in preparation for an invasion that could come at any moment. A threat looms over Moonstone, and all non-combatants must relocate as swiftly as possible. I know that not all who stand before me can afford to take the train to the Rainbow Fort and stay at an inn, however for some, there is a free home awaiting you.

"Any builders or miners are being homed for free in Ashglass and the Ashpeaks respectively, courtesy of our faithful friend and vassal, Lady Mor'kha Foenaxas. They require you for their rebuilding efforts following the rapeworm epidemic, and your dedication shall be rewarded. For those who cannot relocate and aren't of the professions stated—"

"What's the threat?" one dark elf called.

"Yeah, you're gonna tell us to drop everything we've worked for and pull gold out our arses?" a goblin perched upon a sign said. "We ain't rich fuckheads like you, we got real jobs."

"Yeah, what's so scary that you'll empty a bloody city? You may think stubbing a toe's a big danger, but unlike you scumbags in the castle, we can take hardship!" a hairy orc added.

Rakh looked over the rumbling commoners, noting the overlap with the people who rioted in response to his foolish attempt at mercy. They would be furious, and rightly so, but the people deserved the truth. He'd once deluded himself into thinking nobles could be loved by the common man, but he had to cast his childish fantasies aside.

"My sister and former wife, Razarkha Fel'thuz, is predicted to return with magical abilities she lacked before. She could be a threat akin to the Parakosi masters of ice and fire. Making matters worse, there's no guarantee she'll show mercy simply because you aren't me."

The people were roaring before Rakh's could finish, and the soldiers tightened their formation, pointing guns and spears as the peasants charged and backed off in a tidal motion. Sentences reared from the churning pool of discontent, each as pitiless as the other.

"You let that bitch go for something we'd have died for!"

"You let that Irikhos twat go too, what if he also returns to Moonstone?"

"One rule for us, another for the noblewoman who'd kill us by the thousand!"

"You did this!"

"You can't protect us at all!"

Rakh shook as the people's anger washed through him. This was the true face of nobility: Impotent failures who at best ruined their subjects' lives, and at worst killed them in droves. He couldn't pretend he wasn't one of them.

He'd grown up in a castle, his father had groomed him to see rulership as a right, and no matter how much he professed his regret, he spared his sister from the death sentence any regular peasant would have received. The crowd kept crashing against the soldiers' shields, and the back line raised their guns. Rakh's tail whipped beneath his coat and his back straightened as his voice returned to him.

"Men, *stop!* Lower your guns, don't escalate this. The people are right to hate my decision," Rakh stated, and this appeared to quieten the commoners, albeit with a small contingent of murmurers remaining. "I regret sparing Razarkha every day of my life. Firstly, I will address Irikhos Foenaxas. His crime was against our lady, and she, the one wronged, opted to show mercy. It was no act of nepotism, but a reflection of Irikhos's otherwise good character.

"Razarkha, however, was a monster that I spared in the hopes of overcoming her murderousness with mercy. Sometimes, like now, with the people who just attempted to break our soldiers' lines and kill me, mercy can overcome violence. However, I was wrong about my sister. My greatest hope was that she'd find purpose far away from the innocents of Moonstone. My naivety has led to the disruption of so many of your lives, and for that I wholeheartedly apologise. I cannot expect you to forgive me, but I pray that you at least heed my words and survive the consequences of my failure."

The people quietened so much that Rakh could hear the wind again, and he turned around for a brief reprieve, removing his illusory amplification. Without thought, he clutched Erwyn and held the wisdom to his chest, then wept into his shoulders.

"I'm sorry, Erwyn. I can't stay strong for the people. If you'd have just poisoned Razarkha while she was recovering, if I'd have just put a blade in her spine, we'd all be safe," he cried. "I should be thrown to them."

"Save that for after we've killed Razarkha," Erwyn said, his voice calm and resolute as ever. "Once we're out of danger, punish yourself however you like, but for now, we have a population to save. Are you going to finish this speech, or shall I?"

Rakh let Erwyn go. "Thank you for being hard on me. I'll finish this myself."

The count returned to his podium and, after steadying his shaking breaths, cast illusions to amplify his voice and hide the tears running down his face.

"There are numerous entrances to a catacomb network beneath the city. These were normally used by members of the clergy and organised criminals, but thanks to the Minister of Criminal Affairs' efforts, they shall be safe to use as a temporary shelter. While relocation is preferred to minimise the amount of people we need to feed, there are exits to the catacombs that lie beyond the city, in villages that may appreciate the commerce your arrival will bring. We shall work tirelessly to ensure you survive this, but Moonstone must be left to those who have already pledged their lives to protect it."

One young woman called out from the front. "How long do you expect us to hide underground?"

"Until Razarkha is dead. When I see my sister's corpse bloodied and broken before me," Rakh said, his tone hardening. "I hoped to extend mercy to every enemy I faced, but with her, mercy has put innocents in danger. If your thirst for blood demands it, I shall host a festival parading her corpse through the streets. Then, and only then, will Moonstone be safe."

Dishearteningly, it was Rakh's slip into sadism that caused the crowd to erupt into applause. Talk of self-preservation, mercy, and collaboration meant nothing to them, but the notion of a mad noblewoman dragged around like the world's least meaty carvery roast was what apparently spoke to the common man. He stared into the distance, his back threatening to give way and instinctively muted whatever Erwyn and Kag were saying behind him.

"Thank you so much for listening to me. Guards will assist in the evacuation shortly," Rakh concluded, and with that, he turned his back on the people he once professed to love.

Though Erwyn appeared happy, Rakh still couldn't hear him. Lady Kag attempted to stand in his way, but he pushed her aside as he strode towards the castle he'd spent his privileged upbringing in.

\* \* \*

As his skiff carved through the Accursed Sea, Weil kept its sail aligned to take advantage of the westbound tailwind. There were no landmarks fore or aft, no sign that he was nearing Arkhera other than the map Anya Kasparov had provided and the compass's assurance that he was, in fact, travelling west. There was enough food, and, more importantly, water stored in the back to last him a month, but he had high hopes that most would be surplus.

According to the map, the closest Arkheran port was Winter Harbour, which from his estimations was a few degrees south of west from his current location. He took a bite of an arcana-enhanced cracker from his ration packet, swallowed, then used his mouth for something much less dry: Song.

*"Yes, yes, yes, I am an Ilazari, I fight all day and I sleep all night, the children hide and the magic's bright, anyone I hate goes to Azraiyen, 'cause when they go there, they don't come back again."*

He continued, running out of verses and eventually making them up as he went. The rhythm was off and the lyrics were cringeworthy, but who was there to critique him? His next verse's words caught in his throat as Razarkha's snide remarks nipped at his mind. How Weil had ever mistaken her attitude for anything other than thinly veiled contempt was beyond him.

He ceased his melodic attempts and spoke in Chaostongue. *"Great Living Entropy, did you approve of my connection to Razarkha?"*

**"We presumed you intended to do what all mortals crave instinctively."**

Weil scowled. *"I was attracted to her, but my relationship with her was so much more. I saw her as a saviour. I worshipped the ground she walked upon."*

**"Such was your folly. Mortals should never worship other mortals, nor should they worship us. Any god that craves tribute from mere mortals is a weak god."**

*"The Rakh'norv, the Eternal Order, once controlled the Galdusian Empire, did it not?"*

The Rakh'vash made an odd noise. **"Before the Sovereign struck a deal with us to grant chaos-speech to a wrath-invoking soul. Andros, Albedo, the Plague Emperor, no matter his name, his role proved that the Rakh'norv fundamentally misunderstood mortals."**

*"You fundamentally misunderstand them too, Great Rakh'vash."*

**"Mortals are decaying, self-operating meat whose goal is to replicate. They strive to be orderly, but their entropic nature consumes their very life."**

*"And yet you consider some of this self-operating meat worthy of your services and communication, as do your immortal representatives,"* Weil pointed out.

**"We do not force our daemons to mirror our philosophy. We are not the Rakh'norv; deviation is its own end."**

Weil sighed. *"Father wrote of daemons who grew interested enough in mortals that they fell in love with them, and in some cases formed the necessary parts to have children. I hope to meet a daemon such as this one day."*

*"You wish to mimic Andros, as Razarkha Fel'thuz would have you do?"*

*"Razarkha would not want me to marry a daemon,"* Weil said with a laugh. *"Even if she mocked me for my desires and never reciprocated my love, she would hate me for desiring a woman that wasn't her."*

*"You're still sentimental for the one you hope to kill. Remember that you hinder your chaos-speech with that abominable knife, all to kill the woman you fondly laugh over."*

*"She didn't deserve my love, but memories of her are fond as often as they are painful."*

Weil unsheathed his thread knife and checked the shimmering, gold-waved metal. Even looking at it made him uneasy; somehow, he knew the material craved his very brain. This was Razarkha's end, but it wasn't enough to deliver the knife to Arkhera. He'd have to plunge the blade into the woman who'd built him up and torn him down like some mad architect. A strong wind forced him out of his contemplation, and he sheathed the unnerving blade as his skiff tilted northwards. The sail tugged its mast, dragging him further and further off course.

*"No, no, no, a thousand times, no!"* Weil ranted as he took the sail down, only for the boat to bob high enough to trip him over. *"Seven stone cock, get up you worthless idiot!"*

Every moment was another yard in the wrong direction, and after a few false starts at getting to his feet, Weil finally took the sail down, then span his rudder wheel in the hopes that the remaining momentum could be used to correct himself. Instead, the boat drifted to a stop midturn, and the wind continued to blow northwards. Weil checked his map, and then westward, where nothing lay over the horizon. He paused, then looked south, where a coastline was spotted as a distant smudge. He checked his map again, then screamed to the heavens.

*"Fuck my bald skull, I overshot Arkhera's east coast ages ago!"*

# Siblings

Rosaline knew the sensation all too well but couldn't accept that it had happened. Half a day had vanished, which meant only one thing: She'd forgotten something on Petyr's command. She'd grown resilient enough to remember when he touched her, yet somehow his words had torn memories out through her brain's folds. Rosaline sat up in bed and squeezed her pillow, begging her mind for a clue. She couldn't even remember what she'd done with Pleura on the night they spent together. A sinking sensation spread through her chest as she realised they'd probably engaged in sinful, aimless lust together. Rosaline breathed heavily, memories of Pleura's kisses filling her with terror.

Perhaps Petyr wasn't the cause of these lapses. Perhaps every person ordained by the Gods could induce it, and for some reason, Pleura wanted Rosaline to forget too. Tears were wringed from her eyes, and a refracted glint reminded her that morning had arrived. It was safest to get ready before Petyr awakened. While her recollection was spotty, she knew that visiting Uncle Gerold had angered him to the point that he had the knight arrested. Anger and lust were often bedfellows and the last thing Rosaline wanted was to tempt her apostolic uncle.

After bathing and putting on a chaste, androgynous outfit, she headed into the Saltwater Temple's worship hall, where shrines to the six gods stood proudly. She couldn't bring herself to face the Moon Man, the secret-keeper who saw fit to rob her of her own sights, nor the Eagle, who cared for everyone's freedom but hers.

She instead turned to the Border, a statuette of jet and opal, with a batlike daemonic wing on one side and an angular, angelic wing opposing it. Surrounding the figure were offerings Uncle Petyr took for himself or burnt in service of the god. This morning's haul included coins, paired sticks of dark and light-coloured incense, and stale bread. Rosaline knelt, closed her eyes and put her hands together before speaking in an undertone.

"Hallowed Border, keeper of all balance, line between good and evil, please guide me. I don't know who to turn to, and I cannot trust my own memories. Am I mad? Have Petyr and Pleura deceived me, or have I deceived myself? Surely you, arbiter of right and wrong, know the truth. I beg of you, illuminate my mind in a way the Moon Man refuses to."

Initially, the only voice that answered was her own echo. Before she opened her eyes, however, a man's voice softly spoke to her.

"Rosie? Are you all right?"

Rosaline's elation at a living god presenting himself was all-consuming, but the truth was soon revealed. Beside her was her ever-armoured cousin, Shiloh Godspawn. A tugging sensation gripped her brain, and she couldn't form a coherent sentence before the ascetic spoke.

"I'm sorry. You're probably shaken up about what happened."

"Uncle Gerold was arrested because of me," Rosaline muttered. "I bring misfortune to everyone I speak to."

Shiloh's brow flexed beneath his helmet's visor. "Aren't you worried about how the city will view your succession?"

Rosaline squinted. "What do you mean? I don't follow."

Shiloh knelt and lowered his voice to a whisper. "Don't you remember? Your Uncle Gerold accused Petyr of fathering me, you, and who knows how many other bastards. If he's right, we'd be half-siblings, and you'd be a—"

"Bastard," Rosaline said. The tugging dislodged a mental dam, unleashing a torrent of information that made her voice grow frenzied. "That was it, Shiloh! That's what I forgot!"

"Not so loud, Petyr could be up at any time," Shiloh hissed. "Do you believe it?"

Rosaline hesitated. If Gerold was right, then her status was a lie. His father's poppy-milk addiction would have made sense, as would her mother choosing to die. She expected to break from the shock, but Petyr's robbery of her revelation had numbed the punch.

"It makes sense," Rosaline admitted. "I've been cursed my entire life, just like you. The way my parents died, the reason Uncle Duncan was sent away, it all makes sense. Don't let Petyr know I believe Uncle Gerold."

Shiloh shook his head. "I'd never. If he's capable of fathering so many bastards, I can't imagine what living with him is like."

"You don't want to know," Rosaline bluntly confirmed. "Keep Petyr in the temple if you can. I've remembered something else, and I need confirmation."

The ascetic stood. "I can't believe I'm turning heretic, but all right. Let's serve the Gods our own way."

Rosaline wanted to hold him, but now was not the time for hesitation. She rushed into the dawn-lit streets of Godswater, then south, towards the white-sand beaches of Storm's Respite Bay. The sandy flats directly accessible from the paths weren't the only part of the coastal area; beyond, bluffs transitioned into cliff faces and caves carved by the very waves.

Rosaline had ran to the western side of the beach following her heist of the Moon Men's archives, and as she retraced her steps, her mind cleared itself. Pleura never hoped to erase her memories; she'd overstepped briefly, before asking if she could kiss her on the cheek. The blood she felt rushing to her face wasn't humiliation, but unmitigated, sinful joy. If she was a bastard, why fear heresy? She was abandoned by the Gods, a broken being from birth. If the Gods created her this way, they couldn't feign surprise at her rebellion.

She found her way to a jagged cavern whose mouth regularly filled with, then emptied itself of seawater. She confirmed that her only stalker was her shadow, then slipped into the cave, lifting her robe as she hopped between semi-submerged rocks. Finally, she reached an elevated crag with naught but a ledge and a wall with numerous chunks taken out of it. She approached one of the holes and reached inside, dragging out the Apostolic Chronicle. As the rising sun illuminated the cavern, she knew her time had come. She sat against the rocky wall and flitted through the book, skipping to the latest apostle on the record: Petyr, son of Sampson.

The records' handwriting regularly changed, and the first sections were dull remarks on him being a studious, savvy, young man who had a way with convincing his parents and siblings alike of his blamelessness. Footnotes from various authors began to outweigh the text body as various controversies and narratives contradicted each other. Finally, she reached a section titled *'Regarding Prior Discrepancies'*, authored by Ascetic Montarys himself. Rosaline stopped scanning and took in every word. The section read as such:

*The Apostolic Chronicle has fallen into historic levels of unreliability regarding the nature of Petyr Godswater. Some authors tout him as a genuinely pious restorer of old Jaranese values, while others have noted his suspicious behaviour regarding his younger brothers. I have come to believe that Petyr Godswater possesses the magical ability known to Imperial Na'limans as 'the Grand Nzor's will', and to the Ikinamese as 'the Serpent's Tongue'.*

*This ability enables one to convince a person of almost anything through words alone. Simply put, if Petyr speaks to people who want to believe his words, his speech is the truth, and prior memories will be altered to suit such a narrative. In addition, other restricted documents confirm that most, if not all of his controversies are true.*

*Shiloh Godspawn is Petyr Godswater's first bastard, a child named Dolora his second, Rosaline Godswater his third, passed off as the legitimate child of his brother. Hale, a boy killed in a Moon Man raid upon a heretical household, may be the fourth, while Luthor, an infant in the custody of the Moon Men following his mother's execution, is a likely fifth.*

Rosaline closed the book. Gerold was right about everything. Montarys knew, but did nothing. Was he concealing his authorship from Pleura, or did she know? Why weren't the Moon Men exposing Petyr? Rosaline trembled and put the Apostolic Chronicle back into its crag, when she felt a presence looming behind her.

She turned to see Montarys, partially risen from her shadow, a dagger in hand. "I should have known you were the thief. I'm sorry, Rosaline, but Godswater's stability rests on—"

Rosaline yanked the umbromancer out of her shadow, causing him to stumble off the ledge. He cracked his back against the bumpy rocks below, his airy robes covered in saltwater. The visible half of the ascetic's face was twisted with rage, and he made to slip into another umbra, but the Storm rushed through Rosaline's body, then surged out of her hands.

Lightning arced towards the sodden ascetic and seared his skin in a continuous barrage. He convulsed, he screamed, he twisted and turned, then fell silent. Once the Storm ceased his blessing, a ringing sensation filled Rosaline's ears. Montarys wasn't moving and smelled just like one of Petyr's stakes. Returning home was no longer an option.

If heresy was her goal, she was certainly an overachiever.

\* \* \*

The thrill of flying above the Alaterran Mountains was somewhat dampened by the lump of cold flesh and rock clinging to Yarawyn's back. The snake she'd once only known as the bullying wife of Count Fel'thuz claimed to be able to fly, yet she weighed Moonrazer down and made wet, rhythmic gurgling noises in the back of Yar's ear instead.

"Can you stop that?"

"Stop what?" Razarkha asked.

"That *noise,*" Yarawyn said. "It's like you're exhaling constantly."

"Oh," Razarkha muttered. "Duncan never mentioned it, but I suppose he hasn't dealt with breathing people for a while. I only need air to speak these days."

"You seem perky enough about it," Yarawyn remarked. "Did you do this to yourself?"

"My god did this to me," Razarkha explained. "I'd triumphed over Darvith, a corrupting influence on Sula, then Weil— Weil—"

Yarawyn paused. "Are you sure you want to meet Naas'khar? I didn't realise Weil was the one to kill you. He seemed like a friend the last time you mentioned him."

"He was a friend, but he also killed me," Razarkha said, her tone softening. "I'm not so weak as to overreact to every tentacle before me."

"If you say so," Yarawyn replied. "Once we collect Naas'khar, we'll pick up Irikhos and your pet augmentee, then head home as conquerors."

Yar suddenly felt a sidewards jolt, followed by invisible hands pushing her back into a balanced position. Razarkha's arms were no longer around her, and the illusionist sounded further away when she spoke.

"Compare me to some augmentee-keeping Sulari ascendant again, and I'll throw you off your unruly beast. Am I clear?"

Though she maintained outward composure for Moonrazer's sake, Yarawyn's heart was pounding against her ribcage. This was the third time Razarkha had casually threatened her life, and while she was likely an effective ally, it appeared that a light breeze would turn her into an even deadlier enemy.

"You're clear," Yarawyn said in a shaking voice, darting her eyes about. "Oh, look, we're almost there, why don't you get back on Moonrazer and we'll forget I said anything."

Razarkha's arms wrapped around Yarawyn's waist, and the spellbinder spoke in a sickening purr. "Of course, my lady."

Yarawyn prayed to every god there was that Naas'khar hadn't relocated, not only because she owed him an apology, but also due to the undead homicidal snake clinging to her. If her tentacle friend was her undoing, Naas'khar was probably the backup she needed.

Landing Moonrazer by the nephil's latest cavern, she clambered upwards, exhaling her tension and inhaling fresh relief. Naas'khar's signature black slime was still slathered across the cavern walls, possessing more eyeballs than ever. Yarawyn froze under their collective gaze, then put on a lighter voice for the Fel'thuz levitating behind her.

"Good news, he's here!"

"Really? I thought slime with randomly assorted body parts was *angelic,*" Razarkha snapped as she floated into the cave without hesitation.

"Wait, no, don't!" Yarawyn spluttered.

"Why not? There isn't going to be *another* daemonic being this deep in Soltelle territory," Razarkha replied.

"No, I just need to talk to him," Yarawyn explained. "One moment."

"Fine," Razarkha scoffed. "As though your illogical need for Irikhos wasn't enough, it seems you have drama with *every* man in your life."

"You tried to kill your husband, I don't think you're in a position to lecture me," Yar replied, then called into the cave's depths. "Naas'khar, are you there? It's me, Yarawyn. I'm sorry about running away from you, I was just overwhelmed. I know you didn't mean anything malicious, you just misread the situation. I'm not angry with you, I promise."

A familiar, oddly accented voice echoed from within. "Who's with you? Are you luring me out so she can kill me? She stinks of a young god. She has darkness akin to my own."

"You smell the Bold Individualist upon me," Razarkha boasted. "I'm your natural ally, half-breed. I'm a wretched hybrid myself, and Yarawyn took me all the way here so I could help you reach Arkhera with her."

A humanoid silhouette poked himself out of the shadows, tentacles spread and crimson eyes glinting. Razarkha stopped floating, while Yarawyn frowned.

"I didn't realise you were a half-breed. Did your father have an affair?"

"No, but a pure Fel'thuz is by definition a half-breed. It's a long story, but there's a reason illusionism is a rare magic," Razarkha replied, then continued calling to Naas'khar. "Come out, nephil. I won't hurt you."

Naas'khar stepped into the light properly, and eyed Yarawyn over before hazarding a smile. "Does this decayed mortal speak truly? Is she how we return to your land of the free?"

Yarawyn nodded. "She is. She has an augmentee travelling with her, that is, a nigh-indestructible rocky mage, and has all manner of powers. Along with my wyvern, we're going to take my home back by force."

"And will you still crave the love of your betrothed? The person I..." Naas'khar trailed off, then slunk back into the shadows, "...I'm sorry I did that."

"It doesn't matter," Yarawyn said. "Unfortunately, you *will* have to coexist with Irikhos. He's agreed to return to Arkhera with me."

"But he doesn't love you anymore," Naas'khar pointed out.

Yar folded her arms. "Love isn't a necessary factor in a noble marriage. What matters is who it connects you to and how functional it is. He'll be a serviceable Foenaxas trophy."

Naas'khar's voice tightened. "Could I be the man you seek out for love aside from your political marriage, then?"

Razarkha covered her mouth, then burst into a hacking cross between a laugh and a mucus-lined cough. While there was obvious danger in doing so, Yarawyn needed to rein in her countess's behaviour swiftly.

"Stop mocking this situation."

"You misapprehend me," Razarkha said, spitting out a fleck of long-blackened blood. "His behaviour reminds me of Weil's. It's uncanny, actually. Be mindful not to get a tentacle in your gut."

Naas'khar absorbed some slime from his wall, bulking up considerably. "I would never hurt Yarawyn."

"Don't make promises you can't keep, boy," Razarkha said. "Weil adored me, yet he found a reason to kill me nonetheless."

Yarawyn broke in once more. "Countess Fel'thuz, if you slander—"

"I'm not saying we should abandon him," Razarkha interrupted. "After all, you haven't wronged Naas'khar as I wronged Weil, at least, as far as you've told me. Come, let's return to Alaterra. I'm sure he'd *love* to meet Irikhos."

The now nine-foot-tall nephil looked down on Yar, who shared his sheepish expression. She glanced to Razarkha, who was already taking to the air, then sighed.

"All right, I suppose we're walking home, seeing as Nassy is too big to ride Moonrazer. I'm sure we'll figure out a means of transport that works out for everyone once the time comes."

Razarkha shrugged. "Provided Duncan's done his job, there's nothing to fear. Irikhos and Torawyn are waiting for us, they'll have the Soltelle Dollars to transport everyone."

\* \* \*

The train from Monte Myrtilla to Napolli, despite being faster than any Arkheran locomotive, was still too slow for Irikhos. All he could do was sit, praying a wyvern wouldn't burn his carriage from above. Tor was resting against his shoulder, her eyes red from weeping.

"What if Kag doesn't let me return in Yarawyn's stead?"

"I don't care. I'll make her," Irikhos assured her.

"You can't," Torawyn said. "She'll have the Crown on her side if your exile is legal, and then you'll be a criminal all over again. This journey will be for nothing."

"I hated Kag, but I still held back. If she throws me to the dogs after I've warned her, I'll kill her long before Yar gets the chance," Irikhos snapped.

Torawyn straightened her back and stopped leaning on Irikhos. For a moment that resembled an eternity, the two stayed silent, forcing Irikhos to seek solace in the rapidly flitting pieces of scenery beyond the carriage. Just as he lost himself in the thought of seeing Morganix again, the middle Selenia spoke.

"Everything's gone."

"I know," Irikhos mumbled.

"There were people who had appointments for tomorrow."

"I know, I'm sorry," Irikhos repeated, his voice cracking.

"I should have left Yarawyn to die. I should have known she'd ruin my life."

Irikhos met her eyes. "You've been unlucky regarding your family. I can't say I know what you're going through; I love my family, even Cousin Gelth. When we reach Moonstone, you can talk to Count Rakh, he knows all about horrible sisters."

"I don't need you to know what it's like, I just need you to care."

Irikhos put his arm around her and let her nestle into him. "I promise I'll do what I can to make your life in Arkhera as meaningful as your life in Alaterra was."

"Don't make a promise you can't keep."

"If Arkhera returns to normalcy, and we're both alive, there's nothing that'll stop me," Irikhos insisted. "I've kidnapped one Selenia and broken the heart of another. Please let me do right by you."

Torawyn smiled shyly. "Yarawyn complained about how you've changed, but I love the man you've grown into. Women who dislike kindness have the tastes of immature girls."

Irikhos cocked his head. "And what do mature women like yourself enjoy?"

Torawyn laughed. "You'd consider me mad if you found out."

"Perhaps one day you'll trust me enough to sate my curiosity."

# Destinations

The Selenia sisters' street was considerably more crowded than before, but thankfully for Razarkha, the pointy-eared, stunted residents of Alaterra weren't focused on her, nor the daemonic monster wandering beside her and Yarawyn. Uniformed elves in red and blue were rushing towards a smoking area. While Razarkha was more than accustomed to infernos, her Selenia meal ticket's brow was furrowed.

"Those are members of the Alaterran Fire Department. They're often seen around, what with all the wyvern tamers," Yarawyn explained. "The fact they're headed the same way as our house is worrying."

Razarkha snorted. "Duncan is loyal. He wouldn't have started any fires."

"Are you sure?" Yarawyn asked. "If our house *is* burning, I'd recommend you revise your trust in that mockery of life."

The urge to throttle Yarawyn steadily wormed its way deeper into Razarkha's mind. As a Selenia she could provide some semblance of legitimacy once they took over Moonstone, but ultimately, Razarkha needed her no more than she needed to breathe. She slowed her pace until she was out of Yarawyn's peripheral vision, then pointed her soulstealer at her. Naas'khar jutted a tentacle from his back, and swiftly, she withdrew her weapon. Her crystalline leg gave way, and she caught herself with her arms.

"Fel'thuz? What's wrong?" Yarawyn asked while her wyvern warbled.

"It's nothing," Razarkha muttered, looking up at the vaguely elven monstrosity Naas'khar had become.

The nephil nodded. "I was simply watching her too closely."

Yarawyn scoffed. "I thought you said you were strong enough to tolerate tentacles. Like it or not, Naas'khar is coming to Arkhera with us."

Razarkha shot the abomination a scowl, then picked herself up and hastily limped towards the fruits of Torawyn Selenia's passiveness. Yarawyn and her pets weren't far behind, so when the former countess beheld what remained of the house, she felt Moonrazer's beak push against her back. The Alaterran Fire Department were throwing bucket after bucket upon the smouldering remains of Torawyn's house. Though the stony support beams mostly remained upright, the wooden sections had collapsed, and there was no sign of Torawyn, Irikhos, or Duncan. Razarkha trembled, then charged towards the firemen guarding the site.

"You! You lot, let me through!" she demanded.

A dark elven fireman replied in broken Common. "You stay back, it's dangerous, no? Especially for a non-dead such as yourself."

*"I'm not some zombie who'll collapse on immolation!"* she said in hastily constructed Elarondian. *"Behind me is one of this house's permanent residents, we need to check the remains, now!"*

*"We're working, sorry,"* the fireman said. *"When it ceases to be dangerous, we—"*

The crunch of snapping wood interrupted him, and Duncan Godswater rose from the ashes, his floating, disconnected form assembling piece by piece. Yarawyn's unwelcome auditory torment made itself heard once more.

"It looks like your so-called friend burnt our house down after all. I *knew* trusting him was a bad idea, now Irikhos is gone, and—"

Razarkha back-handed Yarawyn to the floor, causing her wyvern and nephil to fan their respective silhouette enhancers. Undaunted, she continued to loom over Selenia.

"There's no way what happened was intentional. If it was, why would he stay?"

"Godswater betrayed us, just like Iri and Tor," Yar spat, squaring up to Razarkha as she stood. "Just accept it, when you commanded your pet to guard Irikhos, he released him!"

"Shut up," Razarkha snapped. "Irikhos is irrelevant, my command was a courtesy to you and your irrational attachment. Even if Duncan intentionally released him, his decision was better than anything you could have made regarding that imbecile."

"So, because I want a husband, I'm irrational, is that it?"

"Have you seen what marriage earned me? You're better off without the fool."

"Duncan worked to undermine the future lady of Moonstone," Yar said, emboldened by the beasts backing her. "He ought to be executed for his incompetence."

Razarkha recalled every time a subordinate failed her during her insurrection, and how despite it all, she worked to preserve their lives. Her memories mocked the notion in good time, the wet thud of Adolita breaking against the ground and the glint of a knife lingering by Lesteris's crotch consuming her perception.

"If he was insubordinate, he'll be treated as such, but we do not kill loyal subordinates for honest mistakes," Razarkha commanded, spotting Duncan floating past the wall of firemen. "Ah, there he is, we'll soon figure out what transpired."

"My sincerest apologies, Razarkha," Duncan said, his voice making up for the non-existent contrition upon his 'face'. "It was Foenaxas. We underestimated him."

Yarawyn shoved Razarkha out of the way and strode up to the augmentee. "You *burned down my house!*"

"*Torawyn's* house, as she was wont to mention," the augmentee said with a familiar defiance. "If you're angry, go ahead and have your wyvern burn me. Perhaps it'll make me feel something again."

Naas'khar stooped over. "I'm not fond of this undead woman, but he mentioned your Irikhos was somehow underestimated. I think we should listen to him."

Duncan put his rocky fingers together. "The daemon speaks sense. You can choose to hurt me or choose to go without crucial information."

Razarkha rolled her eyes. "Enough of this nonsense. What happened?"

"Irikhos Foenaxas was, unbeknownst to me, an antimage. He disincorporated me, at least temporarily, and when I fell to the floor, I set the house on fire. My deepest apologies."

"It's fine," Razarkha muttered. "See, Yarawyn? Duncan was taken by surprise."

Yarawyn narrowed her eyes. "Did you see where Irikhos and Torawyn were headed? Did they leave together?"

"They left together, but their destination is unknown. I would presume Arkhera," Godswater reported.

Yar scowled. "Knowing Tor, she's probably attempting to replace me as the Selenia to reclaim Moonstone through marriage. I suggest we rush to Moonstone as quickly as possible. Godswater can wait; catching Irikhos is what matters most."

Razarkha shook her head. "Lady Selenia, with due deference, you're being an idiot. We're not claiming Moonstone as part of some dead madman's will, we're claiming it by conquest. As such, Irikhos is irrelevant. Duncan's loyalty, however, is paramount. We'll attack Godswater, then Moonstone, just as we originally planned."

Yarawyn stammered. "But Irikhos will—"

"I think the undead one is correct," the daemonic hybrid interjected. "We shouldn't think about Irikhos. He is a betrayer, a coward, and half the man I am."

Razarkha chuckled. "How adorable. Well, with Duncan, Naas'khar and myself against you, the group's decision is Godswater first. Unless you can train that wyvern to speak it's three against one."

"This isn't a Parakosi democracy, it's a feudal autocracy and *I'm* in charge!" Yarawyn protested.

Razarkha straightened her back. "Are you sure?"

"I— I— well, I suppose Irikhos is lost. We can find him later, but he *will* be my husband. For now, we travel to Godswater."

"What a kind concession," Razarkha remarked. "A good lady takes the will of her council into account. I'm glad you saw sense."

Yarawyn made a few false starts, then pointed away from her former house. "Between Duncan and Moonrazer, we can fly to Napolli. Let's waste no time. To Godswater!"

* * *

Weil had absolutely no idea where he was. He'd attempted to turn south a while ago, only to nearly veer into an uninhabited icy coast, presumably the very north of Arkhera. His second noteworthy spot was a set of buildings along a coastline he had already long since overshot, and his third was his realisation that he'd passed Arkhera's western coast some time overnight. Since then, he'd drifted southwards, passing various fleets and praying he'd remain beneath their notice, occasionally risking an eastwards veer in the hopes that there was a port he'd land at before his rations were depleted.

He awoke in his skiff and began his morning routine of checking leftwards to see if Arkhera's west coast had anything to offer. At first, the view was blurry, but after a moment of rubbing the sleep from his eyes it refined into a city skyline, such as they were in Arkhera. The port was filled with warships, sloops and caravels with all manner of heraldry upon their sails. The most common sigil was a black and white sword on blue, which was the symbol of Arkhera as a whole, though most depictions he'd seen had its field as purple.

Weil released a thirst-weakened laugh; it was likely they couldn't afford to dye a whole sail purple for multiple ships. Razarkha, however, had little regard for money; when she took the *Dikamonstra,* her sail had a purple rabbit's head, front and centre. It was likely the sea addling his mind, but there was a twisted joy in remembering Razarkha's little quirks.

He veered the ship eastwards and opened the sail, for once experiencing a perfect tailwind. This relative lack of worries allowed his mind to wander. She was his father's killer. He'd killed her so quickly when she admitted it, yet doubts had fermented within his skull. She was once a pathetic, unwashed woman deliriously demanding a bath from a stranger. Her excitement at being taken to a library and her joy whenever they reunited weren't false. She needed to die, if only because of her destructive nature, but she wasn't a monster. She was a friend. If she had to die, it was best for a friend to make it happen.

The harbour had consumed the horizon, and though there were ports for medium-to-large ships, there didn't appear to be designated areas for skiffs. It wasn't as though Weil could land legally; not only was he ignorant of which city he was landing in, but also lacked the king-stamped circles he'd no doubt need to tribute. As such, he used his rudder to weave between the larger ships and drift to a rocky beach at the northern end of the harbour.

As he ran aground, he patted his hips, confirming he still had his knotweed knife, and checked his surroundings. He was resting by an anemone-covered rockpool, and much of the ground was either barnacle-encrusted rock or worm-infested bladder wrack. Beyond the beach was an abandoned shack, along with a path towards what he presumed was the city proper.

Weil swallowed his scepticism and desperately hoped that he'd made it to Arkhera without being forced to pay a toll or register as some king-fellating citizen. He hoisted a package of arcane ration crackers out of his skiff, then edged towards the path, only to look back at the water. There were already boats heading towards the beach, and upon their masts, cabin boys were using some manner of lighting to signal to people on the coast.

*"Shit."*

He rushed along the beach, hoping to find some crags to take refuge in, but only hermit crabs stood a chance at finding suitable refuge on this coast. Soon enough, gun-wielding men were on the rocks with him, calling in an unfamiliar accent of the Common Tongue.

"You, there! Stop! You've illegally landed in Deathsport. Put your hands up or we'll assume your intentions are hostile!" one said, pointing his weapon towards Weil.

*"I don't suppose you'll open a portal for me?"* Weil whispered in Chaostongue.

***"Never."***

*"Thanks for nothing."*

Weil's ingenious scheme of hoping everyone in Arkhera was blind had failed, and so he stopped running, put his hands up, and got on his knees. "I surrender. No hurting you."

The armoured men drew closer until Weil was surrounded. Most were around Hildegard Swan's height, but one was some great, hairy creature whose monstrousness couldn't be disguised by the metal encasing it. Unfortunately for Weil, it was the beast who spoke.

"Before we take you in, we gotta ask you some questions. Where you from?"

Weil paused. "I am from Ilazar. You know of it, yes? Land of vodka, spellbinder freedom, and squat dance."

The tusked monster scowled beneath his half-helm and lifted his gun. "Harbourmaster Cordelia says we gotta take any undocumented Ilazari to the holding cells."

"Got it, Commander Backbreaker," a smaller soldier said, opening a set of handcuffs that appeared to be made of redstone.

Weil attempted to protest, but the panic mixed with the need to translate his thoughts led to naught but incoherency. In moments, he was pushed against algae-covered rocks and cuffed, his connection to the Rakh'vash severed the moment they were secured around his wrists. The soldiers patted his body over and retrieved the thread knife.

"No! You must not take that, is important item—"

The fellow who confiscated it passed it to the tall, beastly commander, who inspected it with an unnerving calm.

"Nice-looking blade. Getting those golden waves into the metal like that really is something. Almost like one of those Yookie blades that go for millions of gold. Well, I'm sure you'll have plenty of time to tell the higher-ups how you made this thing. If you want it, you'd best hope you can weave silver into your tongue," he said, laughing to himself. "All right, boys, let's get him locked up—"

"Excuse me," a woman's voice behind the gaggle of metal and gunpowder broke in.

It was an unusual tone, its dialect a fusion of the Common these soldiers spoke and Razarkha's. When the men cleared, the child-sized being before Weil had distortions about her face that he'd experienced before. Somehow, despite the ability being limited to the Fel'thuzes and Kasparovs, this adult-voiced little girl was an illusionist.

"Who the fuck are you?" the orcish commander asked.

The girl handed him a piece of paper, and the man's indignancy sloughed off to reveal panicked deference. He waved to his men and spoke in a shaky voice.

"Do whatever this woman asks, boys, she's got a royal seal of command."

Once the men were done murmuring amongst themselves, the hooded halfling gestured towards the streets beyond the beach. "Thank you, Commander Backbreaker. Take this man to the Royal Interrogation Cells and leave the rest with me. Your cooperation is appreciated."

"You may want to look at this, milady," the commander added, passing the thread knife to her.

"Do not take it!" Weil spluttered. "It is special weapon. Needed to kill dangerous woman. Razarkha Fel'thuz is notable in Arkhera, yes?"

The name caused the woman to pause, yet she still pocketed the knife. "This shall remain in my custody. I'll speak to you soon, self-proclaimed hunter of Razarkha Fel'thuz. Take him away."

Weil was dragged to his feet, and though he was deficient in chaos-speech and Common speech alike, he protested.

"You are mistaken! You must free me, so that Razarkha may die! She returns to Arkhera, she kill everyone, perhaps. Her home, Moonstone, will suffer!"

The illusionist was unmoved and watched pitilessly as her men dragged him away.

\* \* \*

Irikhos was a watcher of a watcher, staring as Torawyn witnessed the last of her Soltelle Dollars get converted to cumbersome Arkheran coins. It was a fair amount to lug, but they didn't have time to set up a bank account that would only be helpful in Havenport, an obscure and mostly subterranean port town just south of the Sanguinas Territories.

The teller was a gnomish fellow with dark-tinted goggles that protected him from the sun, and though the town was mostly made for his kind, the counter and chair were altered to accommodate for elven heights. This was typical of gnomish settlements; if it was above ground, it was either by necessity or made for taller visitors.

One last copper was dropped into a large sack of coins, and the round-faced halfling smiled warmly. "There you are, friend. Must say, Yookie currency is always intimidating. Don't get me wrong, it's great to have, the Soltelle Empire's always on the rise, but whenever someone exchanges it, I know I'm bleeding Landons."

"Of course," Torawyn mumbled, taking the pouch and quickly getting dragged down by its weight. "Angels, this is heavier than I thought."

Irikhos offered his hand. "I'll carry it if you want."

Torawyn handed it over with a smile. "Thank you. Do you think that Godswater fellow is safe?"

"If Razarkha believes his excuse, he has a chance. If we make it through this, we ought to keep an eye on the city of Godswater. If Duncan takes over, it could be a key southern ally."

"We shouldn't talk of the future so casually," Tor said. "If the loss of everything I've built up is proof of anything, it's that the greatest-laid plans are made for fate to unravel."

Irikhos swallowed, tugged at his collar, and exited the currency exchange. Before them lay rolling hills with the occasional jutting tower or sunken building. Torawyn was swift to follow him outside, but unable to accept a perfectly good silence.

"Am I making you uncomfortable?" she asked.

"No, I just don't know what else I can say regarding your old life."

Torawyn sighed. "There was a little, foolish part of me that blamed you, but you didn't cause Yarawyn to grow monstrous. Even if you didn't arrive, she'd have met Fel'thuz and become power-hungry all the same."

"I still gave her false hope," Irikhos pointed out.

"The hope wasn't false; she chose to ignore it in favour of war," Torawyn rebutted. "Trust me, I hate my sisters much more than I hate you. Despite the tensions, one of my sisters at least deserves to be warned of the storm coming."

Irikhos nodded. "Indeed. Let's find the station."

Owing to most of its complexities residing underground, Havenport's train station was easily spotted. It jutted from the ground, likely catering for multiple entrances, and Irikhos was glad to see that at above ground, the doors were tall enough to accommodate his height. There were only two platforms within the station, and a single ticket booth manned by a grim-faced orc and a gnomish woman a third of his size. The latter leaned over the counter from a highchair and spoke in a squeaking tone.

"Hey there, you two! Where you headed?"

Irikhos cleared his throat and made to speak, only for Torawyn to get there first.

"Moonstone, two single tickets."

"Moonstone? *Single* tickets? You mad?" the gnome asked. "You realise there's some real suspicious activity up there, right?"

Irikhos found his voice again. "Suspicious activity? Like what?"

The gnomish woman prodded her chubby cheek. "Well, I ain't been there personally, but conductors and drivers who've been up there say there's nobody around. A whole bunch of working men took singles to Ashglass, then after that, nothing. Strange for a provincial capital to have no-one around. I wonder if they've got a tapeworm problem like Ashglass did."

"Rapeworm," the orc corrected.

"No, no, it's tapeworm, it's named because it's long and tapelike."

"Tapeworms don't fuck over an entire city, idiot," the orc muttered. "Rapeworm's different, it makes people mad, spreads real fast."

"It seems like you're an *expert,* Trainspotter. Let me know when you become a wisdom," the gnome sniped.

"Actually, Trainspotter's right," Irikhos said. "I was there. Ashglass is likely still recovering, but the brave work of a Moonstone wisdom saved the city. I need to save him, and anyone else still in the city. Are trains still running to Moonstone, at least?"

"Well, yeah, but nobody's getting off there," the gnome said, tinkering with a machine which printed two ink-stamped slips of paper. "All right, that's two silver and two coppers."

Irikhos fished through Torawyn's small fortune and found the appropriate coinage, then handed it over. "There we are."

"Enjoy your time in a ghost city, I s'pose," the gnome said.

"Best o' luck saving your wisdom friend," the orc added.

With an incline of his head, Irikhos headed to the platform for northbound trains, with Torawyn trailing behind him. After taking up the one bench in the area, Tor spoke.

"You must have been terrified, being trapped in a city overrun by rapeworm."

Irikhos shook his head. "As afraid as I was, the infectees had it worse. Perhaps you can help the Forests of Winter with your medical knowledge. Presumably training in a Soltelle nation has given you access to some Yookie secrets."

"You'd think, but the Yookies hide their sharpest knowledge behind linguistic barriers. Unless approved for translation, academic texts made in Wrenfall are written in Yukishiman, even though everyone that way speaks Common."

"They're the biggest empire in the world for a reason," Irikhos remarked. "Don't worry, I'll pay you back for my half of the fare."

Torawyn's blue eyes lit up. "Only half? How cruel."

"Well, you're capable of paying your own way, aren't you—"

"I was only joking," Torawyn said, forcing a smile. "Kag would always talk about how when our brother arrived, she'd make him spend lavish amounts of money on her, seemingly forgetting that she already had access to the coffers any hypothetical brother would have. I've wanted to scream at Kag's bottomless stupidity many times, but sometimes remembering her slower moments makes me smile."

"My past self would hate me for saying this, but I hope she's still alive," Irikhos remarked. "If not for her endearing idiocy, then for the fact she's the only shield between me and a royal execution for prematurely returning from exile."

# Secrets

Peasants were pouring out of Moonstone at an acceptable rate. While Rakh had hoped there'd be more skilled labourers to send to Ashglass, the catacombs were a decent enough refuge for the time being. There were subterranean routes to villages that Razarkha would likely take no interest in, so if food was impossible to deliver, there would still be means for the people to survive.

The issue was always going to be timing. Rakh stood in his room, staring over the deserted city of his own making, praying that if his accursed sister descended upon Moonstone, it'd be soon. The longer a predicted catastrophe took to unfold, the more impatient heeders of the warnings would become. He remembered mocking overzealous Eternalists who'd made spurious claims about the world's final days, and if he proved to be a similarly false prophet, his adherents would endure much worse than jeering bystanders.

Sharing the castle with him were Erwyn Yagaska, Plutyn Khanas, and of course, Lady Kag, while General Kareon Moonspawn kept control of the barracks. Ruminating in his bedclothes wouldn't help anything, so after washing and putting on some clothes, he moved about the castle, seeking out Plutyn in the hopes of getting a smoke. As he headed towards the lounge, a high elven guard rushed into the foyer and stopped him.

"Count Fel'thuz, thank goodness you're awake," the man said, his hands shaking as much as his voice. "There's someone outside the castle gates, and you're not gonna believe it, they claiming to be Torawyn Selenia. She's—she's Lord Nemeron's late wife, right?"

"And his second daughter," Rakh said, before blood rushed to his brain. "Wait, *Torawyn Selenia* is outside the castle?"

"Yeah, along with someone claiming to be Irikhos Foenaxas. I can tell he at least has Foenaxas looks, but I'll admit, I have no idea if they're telling the truth," the guard answered.

"I can confirm Irikhos, but I haven't seen young Torawyn in a decade," Rakh remarked, pausing before raising another question. "Were they with another woman? One that looks like 'Torawyn', but with Kag's red eyes?"

"No second woman, sorry."

"Thank you," Rakh said, then moved out of the castle's front door.

The castle courtyard appeared three times longer than usual, and though Rakh didn't have a headache, he couldn't dismiss the possibility that his powers were acting up. Erwyn and Kag had both attempted to calm him, but lately, his existence resembled a sick joke. He protected people who despised him, while shooing away his loved ones.

A flicker of Tei danced through a greenhouse, refracting with each new angle he beheld her at. Rakh covered his face, shielding himself from his visions and the gardeners from his tears. He wandered blindly for a short while, and by the time he let Moonstone's dim sunrise in again, he was at the castle gates. The dark elf before Rakh was indeed Irikhos Foenaxas, but the woman beside him didn't resemble the Torawyn he remembered. The shy, chubby elven teenager had grown willowy, her eyes watery to the point of leakiness. She didn't quite match his estranged wife in terms of boniness, but elves weren't supposed to be this thin.

"By God, it really is you," Rakh said to Irikhos, then turned to his female companion. "I presume you're Torawyn Selenia."

"Yes," she said with an averted gaze. "You haven't aged a day, Count Fel'thuz."

Rakh tried to bask in the warmth of her compliment, but the hearth within his soul refused to ignite.

"The will had Irikhos's inheritance of Moonstone be contingent on him marrying Yarawyn," Rakh reminded them. "I'm sure Lady Kag will welcome you back, but I must ask; what happened to Yarawyn? Is she— well—"

"She's not dead, it's worse than that," Irikhos said. "I was hoping to save this for when we got indoors, but I met your sister in Elarond."

Torawyn nodded. "She took over my home, and seduced Yarawyn with promises of power and military might. She's got some geomantic rock-man with her too, though his loyalty is questionable. I know it doesn't sound like a lot, but combined with Yar's wyvern, Moonrazer, they're intent on taking Moonstone by force."

Rakh stared through Torawyn. For a moment, her shaky, yet coherent explanation of horrible matters reminded him of Erwyn. He rubbed his left temple and gestured to the pair.

"Come with me. I'm sure Lady Kag will be overjoyed to see you, Torawyn," the count said, moving back through the courtyard.

"Did you not hear me?" Torawyn said, hurriedly following him. "Your sister is backed by some geomantic monster and a wyvern! That's not to mention Yarawyn's cave friend, some daemonic abomination. Moonstone is under serious threat!"

Rakh let his numbness bleed outwards. "I'm already operating under the assumption that Razarkha has an extremely powerful weapon. A wyvern is immaterial to the equation. Were either of you able to confirm that Razarkha had an artefact known as a soulstealer?"

Torawyn was quick to respond. "She didn't just have an artefact in her hands, Count Fel'thuz, she was half an artefact herself!"

This tugged Rakh from his melancholy. "What do you mean?"

Irikhos gesticulated around his belly. "Her clothes were completely tattered; she had some rags around her top and her stomach wasn't made of flesh at all. It was some sort of magical crystal, glowing and whatnot. Also, I know you spellbinder folks are pale, but she was corpse-white. I don't think she's an ordinary mage anymore."

Rakh frowned. "Do you think she's undead? Was she accompanied by a necromancer?"

"Not that I could see," Foenaxas replied.

Despite breaking bread with necromancers for the better part of a year, Rakh hadn't once heard of self-necromancy. There'd been cases of partial ascension during the death throes of particularly determined spellbinders, even without magical conduits, but from Iri's remarks, Razarkha was very much solid. Somehow, she'd transformed herself into her own revenant.

"I'll ask our resident necromancer if he's heard of such phenomena," Rakh promised. "While this is troubling, don't worry; you two will be safe."

Torawyn trembled. "You won't sell us to Yarawyn if she threatens you?"

Rakh stared at the castle entrance as an apparition of Rarakhi moved through it. He scratched the top of his wooden hand, then adjusted his hair.

"I'm prepared to die to distract Razarkha long enough to save everyone else. Plutyn and Erwyn are similarly devoted. We all have loved ones, but our duty is to preserve the Moonstone of the present, so it stands a chance at fostering a better Moonstone in the future."

Irikhos raised an eyebrow. "You didn't include Lady Kag in that declaration."

"She'll soon be irrelevant to Moonstone," Rakh admitted, before noticing Torawyn's horrified expression. "I mean that in the best possible way."

Torawyn exhaled. "I was worried you intended to use her as bait."

"I meant nothing of the sort," Rakh said, entering the castle with the pair. "You'll see what I mean when you reunite."

Rakh looked to Tor, expecting a response, only to see her taking in the foyer. It was the usual ilmenite expanse filled with banners and tapestries, yet she was struggling to find words.

"It's strange, I expected more to change," she finally said. "I'm sorry, it's been a while. I just lost a home, so seeing this one— it's emotional."

Irikhos put a hand on her shoulder. "It's all right, Tor. I'd get like this over Castle Foenaxas, and I wasn't gone long. You shouldn't apologise for being an ordinary woman."

"Living with Yar conditions one to apologise," she replied.

"I know," the dark elf said. "Would you like a hug?"

"I would."

Rakh watched the two elves embrace, and their heights along with their demeanour reminded him of a tailless rendition of his son and daughter by law. For a moment, he doubted where his discomfort came from; were Rarakhi's affectionate displays the source, or was it his own inability to accept loving relationships?

"Move on when you wish," Rakh muttered, heading towards the dining room. "Hopefully, the lady is breaking her fast."

When he reached the room, he found Erwyn and Plutyn filling the surroundings with bhang smoke, the latter nursing an almost-full bowl of porridge. Fittingly, the seldom-necessary Kag was missing the one time she was needed. Rakh sat by Erwyn and got chatting.

"Irikhos has already returned, and he has Torawyn with him," he said, surprising even himself with the dullness of the announcement.

Erwyn squinted. "What the— when did you find that out? I checked my letters, and there's been no indication of that. Speaking of which, Rakh, Tei recently wrote, she says a suspicious Ilazari has been—"

The wisdom cut himself off when he saw the two enter the room, and Rakh chuckled. "That's how I found out."

Erwyn barely had the chance to stand before Torawyn hugged him.

"It's wonderful to see you again," Tor said, constricting him a tad. "I wish we were reunited under better circumstances. The only reason I survived was because of you."

"Because of me? I don't understand," Erwyn replied, his arms limp by.

"The books you let me borrow, the terms you explained to me," she elaborated. "I was a healer in Elarond, all thanks to you."

The wisdom returned the embrace, and he replied in an undertone. "I'd forgotten I'd done that. I'm glad I did something to help you given how I betrayed you and Yarawyn."

This inconvenient truth unleashed a silence that devoured the room, and the tension apparently entertained Plutyn enough that he started to eat his breakfast. Torawyn released Erwyn and hardened her expression.

"It doesn't matter anymore. Yarawyn is returning with Razarkha Fel'thuz by her side."

Plutyn stopped eating, and Erwyn paused. "Her intentions are hostile?"

"No, she's sided with an undead madwoman who wants to raze the city for bargaining power," Irikhos snapped. *"Of course her intentions are hostile!"*

Erwyn sighed. "All right, you made your point. I presume you met Razarkha?"

Rakh spoke up. "He's already told me everything, Erwyn. We'll go over it later, once Lady Kag is safely on her way to Gods' Peak. Where is she?"

As though summoned by his words, the soon-to-be-former Lady of Moonstone entered the dining hall and stopped as she beheld her replacement. Torawyn met her eyes, and during the pause, Rakh assessed the table, ensuring no knives had been redundantly set out.

Finally, Kag dashed to Torawyn, almost tripping up as she took her into her arms, swaying her side to side like she was a stick-thin plush toy. She pushed her face against Tor's, and though the middle Selenia appeared fearful for her life, she didn't push her away.

*"Torawyn, Torawyn, it's really you!"* Kag babbled. "You're so *light* now, you really worked hard to not be fat, didn't you?"

Torawyn's tone dulled a touch. "Thank you for noticing, Kag."

"I'm so glad you're home and safe! Where's Yar?"

Rakh tugged on his collar. "There's a lot to discuss. Once we've all eaten, we should convene in the council room with General Kareon. I'm sorry, Kag, but Yarawyn isn't with us. She's an enemy."

Kag released her sister, then squinted at Irikhos. "But he's here. Did he get Yar and Tor confused, because there's an easy way to tell them apart. Yarawyn has red eyes and sounds like she's going to punch you."

Irikhos groaned, and Rakh shook his head. "Just trust that everything will make sense once it's explained. For now, I need some porridge. Erwyn, arrange Lady Kagura's official letter of abdication and her passage to Gods' Peak."

"At once, Count Fel'thuz," Erwyn said with a sad smile. "Even if everything's mounting against us, it's good to see you animated again."

\* \* \*

Rosaline had no choice but to tolerate the dank scent of mould and rotted wood that pervaded Uncle Gerold's home. The door was broken from Shiloh and the Border Men's arrest of the knight; as a murderer on the run, it had become her hideout. She did her best to slink through the city undetected and had shed her robes in an effort to be less recognisable.

Now she was in her maternal uncle's kitchen, eating hardtack and jellied pork from the mostly bare cupboards. Montarys's screams rang in her ears, and as she listened to the wittering of commoners beyond the house, a spark dashed from her free hand to the floor. She hadn't understood the strange light that appeared whenever she fretted; while she'd craved answers, she wished they could have come in any form but the one they did.

Montarys tried to kill her, but no man deserved to die as he did. Shiloh would have honourably cut his enemies down; Pleura would have blasted their heads with holy light. Their enemies would die quickly. Visions of the ascetic's wide-eyed expression, his writhing body steadily cooking, and his wordless begging for the ordeal to end plagued her.

Petyr burned all dissidents despite being overcome by magic-assisted sinfulness. He'd put countless women through what she'd done to Montarys, yet he never meditated on the horrors he perpetrated. Rosaline shook her head; not being as evil as her uncle wasn't good enough. She finished her hardtack and winced.

He wasn't her uncle. He was her father, and she was some vile mage's spawn, a consequence of the greatest evil imaginable. She wasn't an accomplished temptress who'd snared a virtuous man; she was one item in a long list. Sparks danced between her hands as she remembered his touch, his ragged breath as he called his own daughter a harlot.

Against all self-preservation, she screamed, unleashing a bolt upon a nearby, grime-infested window. It shattered, its shards mostly flying outwards. It took a moment of her magic buzzing along her wrists for her to panic. Commoners babbled outside, and soon enough, the metallic tromp of guardsmen, or worse, ascetics, followed.

Rosaline wanted to wail, but there was no time. She rushed through the house, knowing that given how many empty wine boxes lay about, there had to be a room that stored *full* boxes. She found a back room with relatively little dust, sparsely furnished with a trap door entrance at its centre. She almost thanked the Gods for her uncle's alcoholism; Gerold hadn't bothered to lock it. She opened it and charged down the stairs beneath, shutting the entrance behind her and using her sparks to find her way through the otherwise unlit cellar.

From what Rosaline could piece together, there were shelves lined with boxes of wine, enough for a regular man to drink over a lifetime. There were a couple of casks too, which she quickly identified as cover. She hid behind one and stared at her hands while willing the sparks to stop. They refused to be suppressed, and one jumped to her underdress, setting it alight. She yelled, threw her burning top off, then stamped until it stopped glowing. Allowing herself to whimper calmed her hands and ceased the fizzing. She slunk back into her hiding spot and regulated her breathing.

Slowly, she unravelled her binding bands, and for the first time since she was twelve, let her chest go unbound. She may have been a heretic, a murderer, and a fugitive, but she would never deny her womanhood again. Even if she was found, she would scream Petyr's sins to the city, loud enough that his powers couldn't counteract her.

The thought of martyring herself for the truth almost made Rosaline smile. As she heard feet rumbling on the floor above her, serenity overtook her; perhaps the Border was finally assuring her of her justice, or the Harvester was comforting her before her imminent death. It was over, but it wasn't for nothing. If she had one regret, it was not returning Pleura's kiss.

Eventually, the trap door opened, and illumination poured into the cellar. A surprisingly slender silhouette descended to her level, and even after the trap door was shut, light continued to spill through the room. Rosaline wanted to peek, but the figure was too close to risk it. The sound of slow footsteps and fingers brushing against wood was heard, until eventually, Pleura was seen, staring at Rosaline from above her poorly conceived hiding spot.

"Rosie," Pleura whispered. "I'm sorry, I had to participate in this search. The apostle thinks you're linked to Montarys's death. He was found in a sea cavern with the Apostolic Chronicle. You didn't do it, did you?"

Rosaline paused. "Does it matter? Once you tell your fellow ascetics I'm here, they'll have me burned no matter what."

Pleura furrowed her brow. She made to speak, but the trap door opened once more, forcing her to cover the area previously exposing Rosaline. A voice called from above.

"Is she down there, High Ascetic?"

The young lumomancer rested her staff on her shoulder. "Nothing but boxes of cheap wine. Gerold Applewood is truly wretched."

"A man controlled by his desires is no true man at all. Come, let's investigate the shattered window," the unseen ascetic replied.

"Agreed. See you at the top."

With that, the high ascetic walked away from Rosaline, not once turning back. It was enough to make her smile; somehow, she'd trumped the very Gods in Pleura's eyes.

\* \* \*

While Rarakhi could appreciate that his mother had at least tried to make her home more entertaining, the board games she'd left behind were mostly unengaging, save *World Conquest*. It was a long-form game in which the board was a slightly modified world map, with territories forming continents that provided its owner's army with a small bonus.

The goal was to conquer the world, and so far, Rarakhi was losing, holding onto the 'continent' known as the 'Northern Isles', which consisted of Arkhera, Wor'ghan, Ilazar, and the Serenity Isles. Meanwhile, Plutera had held Northern and Southern Amerist for most of the game, Notongue had a tenuous grasp on Nortez and Sula, and Bloodmetal controlled Yukishima and the 'Southern Isles', consisting of both sides of Elarond, Malassai, and Jaranar. His empire's continuity was disrupted by Rarakhi's mere existence.

"I guess you'll be invading Ilazar any moment now," Rarakhi remarked to Bloodmetal as he placed three armies on the Isle of Dreams. "Just know I'm prepared."

"What if I attacked the Serenity Isles first?" Bloodmetal asked.

"And don't forget I could attack Wor'ghan or Arkhera any time!" Plutera pointed out.

"You wouldn't do that to me, would you?" Rarakhi asked, trying to give Petal a disarming smile. She was unmoved.

"If I showed favouritism I'd be cheating. If we formed a two-person team, then what's stopping Notongue and Bloodmetal doing the same? They'd easily overwhelm us, too."

Rarakhi groaned. "You saying I'm a liability?"

Plutera kissed his cheek. "Sorry, Rara. It looks like once we take our turns, me or Bloodmetal will wipe you out."

Rarakhi still had four armies to place. Ilazar had five armies to Amocare's ten, so there was no defending it once Bloodmetal placed his starting armies. Instead, he placed them on the Serenity Isles, which was able to attack Passicare. Even though it was defending with a respectable three armies, he had to take the chance, or he'd be out of the game.

"I attack Passicare."

Bloodmetal laughed. "I was wondering why you were watering down your Ilazari front, but that's a bold move. Probably won't pay off, though."

The orc threw his defending dice, and amusingly enough, rolled two ones. Rarakhi rolled his attacking dice, winning on both, and so Passicare was worn down to one army. The next set of rolls had Rarakhi claim Passicare, denying Bloodmetal of the Southern Isles. He moved all four armies into the territory, and the orc laughed.

"Well done, little ghost, I didn't expect that. You've earned your bonus card—"

"I want to attack Malassai next."

*"What?"*

The island, much like its real-life counterpart, was laughably underdefended, with Bloodmetal clearly having hoped that Elarond and Jaranar would shield it. As such, Rarakhi stamped through it, and though Bloodmetal rolled a lucky six, he claimed Malassai with two armies remaining. The next territory, Jaranar, was too well-reinforced to conquer, but if Bloodmetal used its armies to reclaim the Southern Isles, he'd be open on the Sulari front, allowing Notongue to devour him from the east. Rarakhi passed his dice to Plutera with a smirk.

"I end my turn."

"Looks like you live to fight another day," Plutera said. "Well played, my big, scary ghost."

Seeing Plutera's eyes light up was enough to make Rarakhi accept his in-game demise. Yes, he was likely going to meet his end, but if he had to go out, he preferred going out with her appreciating him. He watched Petal place her myriad armies on Na'lima and Na'dya, expecting to be stormed from the west by the world's prettiest Ameristian despot.

"I attack Midori Sora," Plutera said to Bloodmetal.

"Wait, what the fuck is this? Collusion?" Bloodmetal asked as Notongue hiss-laughed.

"You're weak on your southern front, thanks to Rara," Plutera explained. "You're also my biggest northern threat, so I may as well deal with you while you're weak."

"But that's— you're a sneaky young woman, Plutera," Bloodmetal remarked.

"I'm my father's daughter," she claimed. "One day, you'll call me Boss."

"If your father lets you take over my revenancy," Bloodmetal qualified. "I don't even know if it's possible to transfer that sort of stuff."

Plutera smiled. "I won't let you die so easily. When the time comes, I'll preserve you."

Rarakhi had almost lost himself in Plutera's face when the door opened. Seeing as he wasn't under attack, he left the living room to meet Tei, whose illusory disguise was body-encompassing this time around. She looked like a human preteen and was hiding something shiny in her hand.

"Hey, mum," Rarakhi muttered. "What's in your hand?"

"A royal secret," she claimed, then moved towards the stairs, her glamour sloughing off her as she passed her son.

As she waddled upstairs, Rarakhi peeked at her hand, noticing a peculiar golden glow emanating from a blade. He'd seen the colour before, but he couldn't recall when. It was something to do with his father and the Boss, but the connection was unclear. He headed back to the *World Conquest* game, to find that Plutera had carved a path through half of Yukishima. She consolidated units at Wrenfall, then ended her turn. When Rarakhi sat down, she passed Notongue the attacking dice and spoke to him.

"What happened? What was the 'royal secret'?"

"Some sort of golden blade. I swear I've seen dad use something like it—"

"It's the Yukishiman thread, isn't it?" Plutera said. "I didn't realise it was possible to imbue a blade with it, it seemed quite insistent on occupying organic hosts."

Rarakhi's chest fluttered. "That's it, it's the Yookie thread! I know mum has a job that requires her to know things, but I wonder if she knows what the Thread is."

Notongue pointed to Jaranar, separating a set of armies from Demidium, making a dry laughing noise. Petal stood, and patted Rarakhi's shoulder.

"It looks like Notongue also smells blood on Bloodmetal, so we should be relatively unoccupied. Let's tell her, just to be sure."

Rarakhi took her hand, and they walked up to Tei's office together. He knocked on her door, only to receive a dismissive response.

"Sorry, Rarakhi, I'm busy. I'll play *World Conquest* later, I've got a report to write."

"Yeah, it's about the report," Rarakhi said. "Plutera's got some useful information."

After a pause, the door opened, and for a moment Rarakhi forgot that his mother was shorter than him. Tei waddled back to her desk and hoisted herself onto her chair.

"All right, Plutera, what is it?"

"May I see the blade you were carrying?" Plutera asked.

Tei opened a drawer, revealing a knife with steel that waved between silvery white and queerly luminous gold. Plutera tapped her lips and nodded.

"That's almost certainly the Yukishiman thread. It's a magical parasite Yukishimans possess. It introduces numerous problems; for example, thread-infested hosts cannot be resurrected, nor can—"

"I know what the Thread is, but I've never seen it in person," Tei said, and held up the blade. "The man who I confiscated this from called it a 'knotweed blade', but his Common was *extremely* spotty. I suppose he must have meant a thread knife, but I was hesitant to label it as such. Threadsteel is near-legendary, only produced by highly skilled thread mages. The fact some Ilazari nobody has a genuine article is— I'm sorry, Rarakhi, I won't be able to play *World Conquest* tonight."

"That's fine—"

"Get out of my office. I'm sorry, there are too many secrets here," Tei interrupted, herding her son and daughter by law out of the room, before locking the door with a key produced from her sleeve.

Without a word, she charged downstairs, leaving Rarakhi and Plutera glancing at each other. Once the front door opened, creaked, and slammed shut, Plutera's face curled upwards.

"Would you like to see her notes?"

Rarakhi spluttered. "What do you mean?"

From behind her back, Plutera produced the same key Tei had used moments ago.

"But— what— how'd you outsmart an illusionist like ma?"

"She was flustered, so I took a chance," Plutera said with a shrug. "If I got caught, all it would cost is an apology."

Rarakhi wanted to kiss her, but there was no telling when Tei would be back. Together, they ventured into her office and looked over the most recent report. Its ink was still wet, and it ended mid-sentence, yet the message was clear: The man Tei had confiscated the knife from was convinced that it was the only way to kill an imminently arriving Razarkha Fel'thuz.

"So, mum's captured some guy who claims to know Aunt Razarkha," Rarakhi said.

"It seems so," Plutera replied. "The claim that only the knife can kill her is worrying. It means Razarkha must be stronger, or at least more durable, than most spellbinders. Perhaps she's undead, or magically protected."

Rarakhi remembered leaving Moonstone, staring at the absence where his father should have been. His hand danced towards the drawer the knife was in, but Plutera placed her own hand in its way.

"No, Rara."

"But dad's in danger!"

"That's why he sent you here. Both of our fathers wanted us to be safe while they faced peril on our behalf. Your mother will act," Plutera shakily promised. "She's probably asking that knife wielder more questions as we speak, then the royals will step in."

Rarakhi swallowed. "You're right, Petal. Come on, let's get back to *World Conquest.*"

# Invasions

The interior of a cell was almost comforting to Weil at this point. He'd seen Yukishiman cells and Nortezian cells; Arkheran cells were simply an addition to his world-travelling experiences. Sinking boats and imprisonment were the only constants the young man knew since he'd let Razarkha into his life.

It appeared Arkherans had a degree of respect for their prisoners; while it wasn't as spacious as the *Celestia's* cells, it wasn't a restrictive Nortezian slot either. Still, it was dull, subterranean, and dank, with a pail of water lying on the floor, which Weil had deigned to lap from numerous times. He rested against a wall and pondered; the diminutive illusionist he'd met was almost certainly a Fel'thuz, but aside from Razarkha's brother-husband, he couldn't recall the family's members. He sighed, then cleared his throat in preparation for a song.

"*Oh, great Ilazar, island of dreams, your emperor calls upon—*"

"You have a nice voice," a strangely artificial contralto said, cutting him off.

Weil turned to see the same short woman as before beyond his bars, her form barely more than a cloak-shaped silhouette against the surrounding braziers' light. Her voice and posture proved feminine through the obfuscation, and she put her stunted arms on her hips.

"You return quickly," Weil remarked.

"I have more questions for you. I had my doubts before, but I'm willing to believe you about that blade," the questioner said. "It's the genuine article, isn't it? A true thread blade made by a Yukishiman. Do you know who produced it?"

"I was given knife by Hildegard Swan. She is big imperial device fashioner, but she is not blade maker. She is... I lack the vocabulary."

The dark shape shifted. "When you say 'Hildegard Swan', are you referring to the Imperial Engineer of the entire Soltelle Empire?"

"Yes, yes, engineer, that is term! She is great engineer, also fashioner of great delights with whip and chain."

The shadow's voice deepened. "I seek information, but not of that nature. How did an Ilazari like yourself come to be allied with the Soltelles?"

"It is long story," Weil began. "When I meet Razarkha, she was without home, she— do you know of Kasparov Family? It is long tale; I must relay all context."

The questioner allowed silence to stew, then raised a darkened hand. "One moment. I'm aware that your Common is less than ideal. You told me that you were a chaos-speaker. Can you still make the noises that form Chaostongue without the magic that allows it to summon daemons?"

Weil shifted his shoulders and tested this notion. *"Great Rakh'vash, hear my words."*

The sounds were indeed correct, yet the Living Entropy didn't hear him. He prepared to translate his thoughts into Common, then answered his interrogator.

"I can make Chaostongue sounds, yes."

"Please wait here," the shrouded woman said before vanishing.

If Weil hadn't been overexposed to Razarkha's own illusory antics, he may have been intimidated, but as it was, he just wanted the woman to release him so he could reach Moonstone. He moved along the floor and lapped from his water pail, then lay on his back, staring at the ceiling until the illusionist returned with four other women.

One nearly matched his height, and while she had a necromantic nose, her figure was akin to a human's; wide-hipped, with a bosom Razarkha would have deemed disgustingly large. She had blonde hair and lilac eyes, confirming that she at least had spellbinder or necromantic blood, yet something about her unnerved Weil on a primal level. He quickly realised it was her lower half; she completely lacked a tail.

Accompanying her were three beings that resembled humans, yet the slickness of their 'hair', along with their glassy eyes and familiar aura made it clear they were daemons. He'd never summoned a humanoid daemon but knew of their existence; the Plague Emperor married one, after all.

"These three are known as the Riversong Sisters," the interrogator explained, gesturing to the daemons. "Accompanying them is Royal Advisor Quira Abraxas. I want you to explain your story, in Chaostongue, to the Riversongs, who shall *hopefully* relay it to us in plain Common. Isn't that right, Riversongs?"

A daemon with head-tentacles a yellow that imitated blonde, walked towards the cell, then seamlessly disrupted her form to slip through its bars. She knelt beside Weil and smiled.

*"I'm Luna Riversong,"* the daemon said in Chaostongue. *"No need for the honorific. What's your name, mortal?"*

*"I'm Weil of Zemelnya,"* he answered, sitting up and meeting her blue, square-pupiled eyes. *"Should I start my story from the beginning?"*

*"Quira told me not to ask for anything overly literal, such as your tale from birth. Apparently, we must focus on this exceedingly dull mortal, Razarkha Fel'thuz, along with your blasphemous blade. Are you aware the knotweed shall consume all if unimpeded?"*

*"I am aware, but I believe the blade is necessary to kill Razarkha Fel'thuz."*

"*I know that,*" the daemon said, sitting down and propping herself up with an ejected set of tentacles. "*Tell me how you met Razarkha Fel'thuz, and how it led to you associating with the knotweed's puppet empire.*"

"*You're referring to the Soltelle Empire, correct?*"

"*There are no other empires so married to that accursed parasite. My apologies, the knotweed is a horror for all daemonkind, something you should know as a chaos-speaker.*"

Weil nodded. "*Indeed. Shall I begin?*"

"*Go ahead, Weil of Zemelnya.*"

When it was told in a language he could instinctively attach ideas to, his story flowed with unexpected vigour. If not for the cuffs, he would have gesticulated as the last year of his life made itself audible for the first time. He recounted the unwashed, desperate woman he took in, the bath that lured him in physically, the tours through Zemelnya he'd given to impress the beautiful older woman, and the toppling of the Kasparovs prompted by his father's death.

Luna Riversong was mostly silent, occasionally interjecting with a remark or question. As the tale continued, she leaned closer and closer. Weil was unsure if she wanted his words or his flesh, but with her apparent mistress keeping watch, he was certain he'd escape mortal injury. He went on to explain the nature of the soulstealer Razarkha claimed after killing Elki Kasparov, her decision to harvest souls in Nortez, and the resultant capture by Soltelle ships, which suddenly spurred the daemon to speak.

"*And when you were a prisoner of this Hildegard Swan, you betrayed your Razarkha friend and took the engineer's knife, only for her to have already escaped, yes?*"

"No," Weil said. "Give me some credit. I was loyal to the bitter end with Razarkha. She was my love, and when we reunited, the only thing to distract me from my joy was finding out Anya Kasparov was alive and aboard the ship."

"*Oh, the loan collector you killed, who transformed into an ascendant?*"

"*Yes.*"

From there, the next part of the tale unfurled. He waxed as poetically as Chaostongue allowed for, recounting the joy and purpose he found in dismantling the Galdusian megalopolises' stagnation. Together, he and Razarkha were unstoppable; reliving it stung Weil more than he cared to admit. It was easy to claim that his joy was a lie, but it simply wasn't true. As they tore up the streets, rooting out Sons of Sula cells, he fell more and more in love with Razarkha's carnage.

He elaborated on mysteriously gifted Isleborn erotica known as *the Blinkered Stallion,* and how the characters were clear allegories of himself, his father, Razarkha, and Anya Kasparov. He had his suspicions about the author, Katina Anyanova's identity, but kept quiet for the sake of their fledgling insurrection. Once Demidium's liberation operation failed, and Darvith's massacre snuffed out his hope, there was less to lose.

"*Even with no rebellion to protect, there were still reasons to keep quiet,*" Weil said.

"*What were they?*" Luna said, now close enough to touch shoulders with Weil.

"*Love and the knowledge that, with my poorly controlled chaos-speech, I would never be able to return home,*" Weil said. "*Suspicion had gnawed at my adoration for her, but it wasn't completely extinguished. Razarkha's boldness and audacity had freed me from debt. She'd unleashed an intense part of me that I didn't know existed. I didn't want to believe the woman I loved was my father's killer.*"

Luna paused. "*I once loved a serial murderer. It's strange, most daemons kill mortals to grow. Verasmus killed for pleasure. I didn't fully understand him, and this intrigued me. Better still, even as he strangled mortal after mortal with his telekinesis, he spoke to me as an equal, and kept me well fed on his victims. Later, I realised he was kind because I was a convenient means to dispose of bodies. I understand what it means to have one's heart broken, even if I lack a conventional vascular system."*

Weil wished he could hold the daemon's hand. Though he knew she was nought but processed flesh temporarily adopting the form of a human, her words seemed genuine. If the Plague Emperor could marry Rakh'dor ge Luzma, he could take this daemon's talk of love at face value. He continued his tale, explaining how the Prospector stabilised his portal formation magic and how Razarkha learned antimagic, then the resultant fight between them and Darvith. After relaying the chaotic corruption of Darvith's singular ascendant form, his voice wavered.

*"Then I asked her, and true to my assumptions that she'd be too lost in the moment to formulate a lie, she didn't even try to hide the truth,"* Weil said, tears flowing without the expected sobs. *"She tried to excuse herself, as though she hadn't betrayed me. The man who took her in, who loved her. The nobility I saw in her vanished, and in moments, I'd impaled her with summoned tentacles."*

*"Yet she is still alive,"* Luna Riversong said, her eyes slick with her own tears.

Weil swallowed his bitterness as it crept up his throat. *"I used my newfound control to return to Hildegard Swan and seek solace in her body. When I was her prisoner, she identified me as a masochist, and expressed interest in having me. Razarkha had never shown such blatant desire for me, and in my grief I needed a swift, easy means of taking the pain away."*

*"Then your lover gifted you this knotweed blade?"*

*"No. The news of Razarkha's survival prompted her to gift me the blade, then send me to Arkhera to ambush her,"* Weil explained. *"She believed that if Razarkha survived my attack, she was likely magically empowered to*

the point that only the arcana-consuming knotweed could ensure her death."

Luna stood. *"Now you hope end this death-evading killer?"*

"That's right," Weil said. *"I believe she could arrive at Arkhera soon if she hasn't already arrived. Her target will be Moonstone, her home city, but beyond that, I know nothing about her nature, only that the knotweed blade is the best chance of ending her."*

Luna Riversong gave a glassy-eyed smile, then backed through the cell bars, disrupting her own form once again. She then turned to her mortal mistress and whispered in the Common Tongue. After a period of muttering between the Arkherans, the short silhouette spoke.

"We're going to translate and write up your story. From there, I'll inform the King so we can weigh our options. He may trust your words enough to authorise your release. For now, wait patiently; your cooperation is appreciated."

Weil made to reply, but the five figures of varying heights were already leaving the prison. Before she left his view, however, Luna Riversong waved at him. Without thinking, Weil tried, and failed, to wave back.

\* \* \*

Dangling from Duncan Godswater's lower half was a great fusion of daemonic and mortal matter, and beside him was Razarkha, holding onto her mad beast atop a wyvern. They were high enough to view the mangal forests of Southern Arkhera as a cohesive whole, but low enough that it was possible to gauge Godswater's coastal defences.

Strangely enough, the soldiers were most present in the city centre. Duncan wished he could smile; it seemed that even Petyr couldn't maintain his power with words alone.

Soldiers belonged on the outer edges; if all a city's threats came from within, then the lord was to blame.

"Their soldiers appear to be occupied," Razarkha remarked. "All right, Duncan, you know Godswater's stupid six god culture better than me, what should we expect from this?"

"I've been away for twenty years, but assuming Petyr's never needed to experiment with his methods, I'd assume he's weaponised piety. Ironically, this will backfire; each of the Gods have their own associated colours, so if most of the warriors in the city are ascetics, we should understand their priorities well."

Yarawyn scoffed. "We had holy men in Moonstone too, they just got fat off peasants' generosity. You can't use a person's patron god to predict military tactics."

To Duncan's relief, Razarkha was firmly on his side lately, and turned her spiteful tone towards the high elf she was holding.

"If you have a better means to infer military information beyond the generic, tell us."

"If I had my way, we wouldn't be bothering with this glorified cult commune," Yarawyn snapped.

Razarkha spat a black glob of an unknown substance, then dismounted Moonrazer, catching herself with her own telekinesis. "Brilliant insight, Yarawyn. Duncan, please continue with what few predictions you can make."

"The men in red and white are the Border's Men. Their primary concern is order, resilience and justice, and thus will be most concerned with defending the people and the temple. While I can't see combatant ascetics being common in either, if brown-white or brown-green men are seen, they're with the Eagle and the Worm, both of which are protective gods. They'll be even less aggressive than the Border's Men."

"That leaves the Storm, the Harvester, and the Moon, correct?" Razarkha asked.

"The Moon *Man,* but yes, those are the groups. The Storm is associated with holy magic, so if we must prioritise threats, Stormcallers in blue and yellow are the ones to look for. The Ascetics of the Harvester always unnerved me, but those I've seen deal primarily with burials and cremation. I imagine those who *are* fighters will be deadly, so watch for black and white. Finally, the Moon Men, blue and black; I'll be honest, I don't know what to expect from them. As the keepers of secrets, they're likely to be protective of their apostle; if Petyr hasn't already died by their hand, it's because they're with him."

"So, yellow-blue Stormcallers are the threats," Razarkha said. "It reminds me of Meung-Chaydan. There's a reason Godswater's called 'Little Jaranar', it appears. Where would we find the Saltwater Temple?"

Duncan surveyed the city, descending a touch to clarify his view. From the sky, the terraces resembled blood vessels, carrying people to and from Godswater's stony, colourful heart, the Saltwater Temple. He pointed at the monument to holy vanity and spoke.

"There it is," he said. "If Petyr realises there's unrest that poses a risk to him, he'll hide in the temple behind numerous ascetics. If the Gods are on our side, he'll be giving one of his speeches, which will allow us to cut him off. Nobody gets to kill him but me; is that clear?"

Once again, the pointy-eared creature Duncan tolerated for her wyvern's sake found her voice. "Perhaps we should hold a vote."

"You'll have Kag and Tor all to yourself, my lady," Razarkha said. "Let Duncan have his fun."

"This isn't 'fun'. Justice is coming for my brother, decades late," Duncan claimed.

"Vengeance, justice, it's all the same," Razarkha said. "Come, let's descend upon the Saltwater Temple. Yarawyn, set all escape routes aflame, then have your wyvern roost atop the temple roof to remind the people it's no safe haven. Naas'khar, do what your nature does best and wreak havoc upon all armoured targets until we tell you to stop. I'll shoot down any Stormcallers that fly above our blockades, which leaves Duncan to have his family reunion."

For once, Yarawyn had nothing to say, and pushed on her wyvern's back, causing it to dive at a shocking speed. Duncan lowered and checked the nephil gripping his levitating form.

"Tell me when you can let go safely," Duncan said.

"I shall," Naas'khar responded.

Razarkha dashed downwards, claiming a lookout spot directly above the Saltwater Temple, and within moments, she was sweeping great, devastating rays across swathes of ascetics, collapsing the buildings behind them. Moonrazer torched those Razarkha missed, showing none of the discretion between ascetics her countess was at least attempting to.

Duncan neared the ground and Naas'khar released himself, charging through the streets as some irrepressible force of nature. As the augmentee beheld the antics of his miserly bedfellows, his rocky body churned, and for a moment, he remembered what nausea felt like. The ascetics deserved their fates; they were enablers of a plainly evil man. Those who stood duty at the Saltwater Temple knew the monstrosity they perpetuated.

The screams that filled the air weren't from soldiers alone, however. Between wyvern flames, lumomantic demolishment, and a nephil who only saw mortals in terms of 'food' and 'not food', the innocents of Godswater were dying in terror. Duncan knew these streets, joked with Simeon and Uncle Gregor at the inns, prayed at the shrines that were collapsing under the strain of a completely unpredictable attack. A set of Eagle's Men herded peasants away from the central plaza, and Yarawyn was quick to notice. Razarkha remained above the temple, but Selenia was even madder than the self-raised undead abomination. She reared her wyvern up, got a good angle, then pointed.

"Moonrazer, cook your dinner!"

Searching for Petyr could wait. Duncan dashed into the wyvern's stream of fire and lifted his hands, prompting his geomancy to make the nearby street jut up, acting as a rocky shield for he and the innocents both. Moonrazer screeched, then winged over the upturned road.

"What do you think you're doing, Godswater?" Yarawyn asked. "You're supposed to be at the temple, finding your brother!"

"And you're *not* supposed to be targeting non-combatant ascetics. If Razarkha can show restraint, why can't you?"

"Unlike her, I'm not limited to however many souls I've eaten. Leave this to me."

"Prioritise soldiers, or I'll skewer your wyvern here and now."

Yarawyn's smirk was just barely readable. "I knew you were a traitor. I'll let Razarkha know ahead of time. She's told me about how easy it is to kill your kind."

"Razarkha is not the reliable source you believe her to be," Duncan replied.

Ultimately, his words were superfluous; Yarawyn had already given up and brought her wyvern around, flying towards the Saltwater Temple. The peasants and ascetics beheld him, one of the latter daring to call out.

"Thank you, whoever you are. We'll find shelter, you keep doing what you can."

Duncan was glad he didn't have a face. He drifted over Godswater's central plaza, lifting tiles and chunks of ground whenever Naas'khar happened to threaten unarmed peasants, which, due to his half-bestial nature, was remarkably common. Eventually, it got to the point that Duncan decided to get in his way.

The half-mortal had shortened considerably, but was flanked by quasi-autonomous blobs of black slime that possessed their own eyes and tendrils. He was in an alleyway, closing in on a young woman wearing a man's tunic that was much too big for her. Despite his splitting, he still dwarfed Duncan, and puffed out his bony chest when the augmentee blocked his way.

"I saw you obstructing Yarawyn, and now you hope to obstruct me? We're only attacking this city because of you, and now you hope to sabotage us?"

"You're supposed to be targeting soldiers. Yarawyn didn't respect the distinction, but she's a mortal who should know the difference. I'm willing to assume you're ignorant to the concept of uniform, but now that the plaza is sealed off, I'm asking you to stand down."

"And what if more arrive?"

"We'll deal with them as they come. For now, the fight is over. Join your lady love, such as she is, and leave the rest to me."

The nephil hacked, then ejected a set of tentacles from his back, and Duncan got to work. With a swift clap of his hands, he dragged the stony walls of the surrounding buildings together, crushing the nephil's shoulders and reducing him to a mixture of bones, organs, and inky daemonic slurry. His head and spine remained intact, albeit unconscious, which left his liquid form to slide away from danger, carrying its mortal components in tow.

Duncan watched him get away, then turned to the girl. She had Petyr's folded, dark brown eyes and small, soft features, along with the wavy black hair of Lana Applewood, Simeon's wife. He took her bizarre clothing in, then asked a burning question.

"Are you Rosaline Godswater?"

"How— how did you know? I normally wear a veil, I—"

"You look like your mother," Duncan stated. "I no longer resemble my kin, but I'm your uncle. I'm Duncan Godswater."

Silence permeated the air, allowing Duncan time to push the buildings apart and allow his niece a way out. Finally, Rosaline spoke.

"Apostle Petyr blamed you for fathering Shiloh, didn't he?"

"Yes."

"You're supposed to be in Jaranar. Don't tell me you're the one who's brought these horrible people to Godswater."

Duncan's voice scraped. "I'm sorry, Rosaline. We need to bring Petyr to justice."

"Killing all these people *isn't justice.*"

"You're right," Duncan admitted. "That's why I need to reach the Saltwater Temple. Stay safe, Rosaline. I'm sorry I did this to your home."

He couldn't bear to look at his niece a moment longer. This invasion was a mistake. He could have approached this any number of ways; Razarkha could have used her illusionism to facilitate an assassination, Duncan could have protested deploying Naas'khar, he could have killed Yarawyn along with her beast the moment he saw her getting indiscriminate.

He flew as fast as his geomancy allowed for, darting towards the Saltwater Temple's entrance. Sat upon the roof were Razarkha, Yarawyn, and Moonrazer, the former giving him a mocking salute. He hadn't seen Fel'thuz wear such a content expression before; it appeared the chaos of war was where she belonged.

"Welcome home, Duncan Godswater. Now that you're done bickering with Lady Selenia, why don't you do what you came here for? Don't worry, your brother is untouched, as far as I know. Have fun crushing the ascetics within."

Yarawyn began to splutter. "Wait, before you just let him through, where's Naas'khar? I saw you heading his way, Godswater."

"You're correct, but at some point, I lost sight of him. I'm sure he'll show himself," Duncan said with a level tone.

Lying came as easily as levitation now that Duncan had no expressions to give himself away. Still, he didn't have the option to rewrite others' memories like Petyr. When Naas'khar reformed, he'd be exposed. Duncan moved into the Saltwater Temple and cursed himself for not finishing the half-breed when he had the chance. A paltry guard force stood at the end of the worship hall, blocking the door to the temple's residential section, where his brother was no doubt cowering. One particularly bold ascetic in red and white pointed a spear his way.

"I heard what those monsters beyond the temple called you. 'Duncan Godswater', my supposed father," the man said. "If you truly are Duncan, you'll know not to defile this holy ground with bloodshed."

"If I have my way, only one man's blood will be shed. Petyr Godswater, your true father," Duncan stated. "Shiloh, isn't it? I'm sorry you were lied to. It seems you even devoted yourself to the gods my brother corrupted."

The ascetic lowered his spear. "No matter how corrupt Apostle Petyr may be, he will never be powerful enough to corrupt the Border."

Duncan's eyes glowed. "If that's true, then you know that justice is greater than blind loyalty to your apostle. Let me through."

Withering under the augmentee's unblinking gaze, Shiloh Godspawn stood down, then gestured to his men.

"If we want to live, we should do as he says."

"But he'll take the apostle! We swore to defend him to the death!" one of his subordinates protested.

Shiloh raised his voice. "We also swore to uphold the Border's justice, and I'll admit it, I don't think Apostle Petyr stands for that!"

"Heresy—"

Duncan geomantically slung a tile into the man's helmet, denting it and knocking him unconscious. He was quick to subdue the rest, leaving his bastard nephew untouched.

"Thank you for believing in the Border when the rest only believed in enabling a monster," Duncan stated, moving into the residential area before Shiloh could respond.

Seeing the old foyer, along with the colourful, geometric rugs and well-sewn tapestries embittered what joyous memories remained in Duncan. Servants cowered in the kitchens, but they were the only other occupants save his target. He found Apostle Petyr Godswater within a girl's room, the floor strewn with binding bands and hair veils. Aside from his ridiculously long, tapering moustache, he'd barely aged, the only sign of time's ravages being small, dark bags beneath his eyes.

"What are you? Are you sentient, or some automaton those mad mages have sent?"

Duncan gripped Petyr by the neck and slammed him against the wall, cooking his skin with his magmalike hands.

"Don't you recognise me, brother? Surely you expected my time in exile to change me," Duncan said, venom bleeding from his inorganic husk.

*"Duncan?* Impossible—"

The augmentee used his free hand to cover his brother's mouth, then increased his body's heat, just enough to light his laughable facial hair at its source. Singed at the root, the lip-worms fell to the floor, crisp and glowing at the edges. Petyr screamed beneath Duncan's rocky hand, and for curiosity's sake, he lifted it, taking much of the apostle's skin with it. His jaw and lips were raw, burnt flesh, yet beneath it, his tongue was still intact. The apostle wheezed, but still found the arrogance to unleash a distorted, lipless slur.

"Ehen now, you are hy hroher. You will leah he hoo lih ah neher rehurn."

Duncan scraped up a noise resembling laughter. "Even if what you said made a lick of sense, I'm not a susceptible victim anymore. See this body? I don't have a brain to influence."

Petyr's composure evaporated, and he began struggling under Duncan's increasingly intense heat. He screamed, he wriggled, he pissed himself, but it was a feminine voice that loosened Duncan's grip.

"Uncle, stop."

Duncan turned to see Rosaline, breathing heavily with a set of magic-dampening handcuffs. His eyes dimmed, but despite his faceless stare, she stood resolute.

"Torturing Petyr to death isn't justice."

Duncan's voice malfunctioned, revealing a range he forgot he had. "Putting the peasants through Razarkha and Yarawyn isn't justice either, but that's what happened! If they suffered as a side-effect, why shouldn't the person who actually deserves it?"

Despite her small figure, Rosaline stood tall. "This isn't right."

Petyr weakly hissed. "You're righ, Rohaline. Hay your ahohle lie a hood hurl."

Duncan's heat became volcanic. "You've seen what I did to this city! What's happened to the ascetics! Just because most of them swore to put their lives on the line is no excuse. They died protecting a *monster!* A monster I need to put down! Are you going to claim killing him will make me the same as him? Our crimes are nothing alike!"

"Are you hure?" Petyr mockingly said between groans.

Rosaline shook her head. "I never said that. I don't want you to kill Petyr. I want him to be executed, with his crimes exposed to the Royal Court, instead of dying a martyr."

Petyr's smugness vanished, and he stood with the last of his strength. "Rohaline, you *whore!* You *hare* hend your lie henhinh he wih your huddinh hody and your henhinh hair—"

Duncan geomantically pulled a tile from behind Petyr, smacking the back of his head and knocking him unconscious. He turned around and cooled his temperature.

"Go ahead, put the cuffs on him," he said.

Rosaline took a moment to process this. "You're listening to me?"

"I misinterpreted your intent. I thought you were a victim, standing up for a man who, from the sound of it has abused you your entire life. So many claim fighting monsters is tantamount to becoming one, but tolerating people like Petyr is little more than cowardice."

Rosaline knelt by the apostle and cuffed his wrists. "I used to be a coward. I used to accept everything that happened. If you'd have arrived a month earlier, I would have defended Petyr for very different motives. Don't worry; we're going to see his destruction first-hand. But more importantly, the notion that he was wrongly usurped will die too. Only when my father's legacy is destroyed will I sleep easy."

Duncan wanted to hug his niece. He settled for an approximation of a warm tone.

"I think you and I could get on with each other, though I fear I'm not long for this world. Stay in the temple, Rosaline. I need to face the terrible allies I brought with me."

# Follies

Outside the Saltwater Temple, Razarkha stood, a hand on her hip while she casually threw and caught her soulstealer. Yarawyn remained on the roof with her wyvern, likely assuming her simulated height would translate into power. Duncan was taking his time, but it was only fair; when Razarkha reunited with Rakh, she intended to savour the moment.

Seeing Arkheran heraldry again was enough to make her giddy, and while it wasn't a sustainable takeover, they'd done exceptionally well. The red-whites and blue-yellows had died in droves, but the most amusing group were the blue-blacks serving the Moon Man. Contrary to Duncan's assessment, they didn't fight back at all. Instead, they arranged themselves, took a single lumomantic blast, then scattered like roaches. The only surprise was the lumomancer in their ranks; they'd unleashed a blinding flare that ruined Razarkha's subsequent shots, but given the souls she'd harvested, she wasn't too bothered about wasted magic.

There was one troubling facet of the battle, however; Yarawyn's talking pet was missing. The elf maintained her distance, yet the way her wyvern milled about was enough to convey her vulnerability. Razarkha telekinetically raised herself to Yarawyn's level and scanned the plaza's surrounding streets.

"Are you still worried about him?"

"Of course I am!" Yarawyn snapped. "I promised him a better life in Arkhera. If he's died for me, then— are you mocking me?"

Without thinking, Razarkha had covered her mouth, and abruptly, something shot up her ravaged throat. She hacked hard enough to destabilise her hovering, then spat out scraps of blackened, congealed blood. She thumped her chest, and coughed up more dark red slime, mixed with pale blue flesh.

Wheezing, she forced out an explanation. "My apologies. I didn't mean to cut you off."

"An apology from the great Razarkha," Yarawyn scoffed. "I ought to be honoured."

"Shut up," Razarkha muttered. "If Naas'khar has died, he at least died fighting for the woman he loved."

"I don't want him to be a martyr, I want him to find his place in the City of False Faces and move on," Yarawyn said. "He's not like us, he can't live with mortals, but at least in Arkhera, he'll be with people who can understand him."

"Are you sure you're all that different?" Razarkha asked. "You chased after ascetics that had no intention of fighting us for what, exactly? Sport? You don't need to feast on flesh like a daemon does. Not even your wyvern needs that degree of sustenance."

Yarawyn narrowed her eyes. "What's the point in riding a wyvern into battle unless you can have fun with it?"

"Fun? What's fun about putting down innocents? If you're congratulating yourself over burning people that can't fight back, you're pathetic," Razarkha said. "Let me tell you about the worst moment of my life. Weil had transported me and my revolutionaries into the Demidium Breeding Facility, a farm that bred humans for augmentation similar to Duncan's.

"As a group, we decided to free the humans and escape. However, everything went awry. The humans panicked, refused to listen to us, and rampaged suicidally once released, getting themselves killed in swathes when I'd hoped to liberate them. I lost a loyal man who housed us in our early days and my only fellow Arkheran, all due to our recklessness."

"What's your point? You hoped to save those humans, and instead got them killed, but these Godswater peasants are nothing to me."

Razarkha scowled. "If you intend to be the Forests of Winter's overlady, they need to be. Unless you *want* war with the south."

Yarawyn patted her wyvern and looked past Razarkha. "Moonrazer can stand against any— by God, it's *Naas'khar!*"

This outburst caused Razarkha to glance along Yarawyn's line of sight, to see a sloppily constructed rendition of the cave nephil they'd taken across the sea. His arms were limp, with tentacles sprouting from his torso in their place. His spine was more visible than ever, and his legs were skinny by spellbinder standards. Yarawyn was quick to have Moonrazer glide to the ground, dismounting to embrace the monstrous half-breed.

Razarkha descended and got to work. "What happened to you?"

Naas'khar was too busy wrapping his tentacles around Yarawyn to listen, but thankfully for Razarkha, Selenia was thinking similarly.

"Nassy, I'm sorry I wasn't there to protect you. Who did this?"

The nephil's grip tightened. "It was that construct of Razarkha's. Duncan Godswater."

Yarawyn wriggled from her servant's grip and quickly shifted her tone. "See, Razarkha? That *thing* is a liability! He let Irikhos and Torawyn get away, then he tried to kill Naas'khar. He used us to subdue Godswater, and he intends to dispose of us. He threatened to kill me, you know."

"Yes, yes, he didn't let you waste time hunting people who weren't threats, woe is you," Razarkha snapped, then turned to Naas'khar. "Explain the situation fully."

"I hunted mortals, just as I was commanded to."

"You were commanded to hunt *armoured* mortals."

"The girl he protected was a threat. As she ran through the streets, *lightning* arced from her fingers. She could have shot Yarawyn from the sky."

This didn't appear to be an exaggeration. While Duncan betraying Razarkha at Alaterra made no sense, this was disloyal at the very least. He also attempted to hide this act when he entered the Saltwater Temple, so his intent was indeed mutinous. Suddenly, it came together; when she was blinded by the Moon Man lumomancer, she saw a silhouette enter the Saltwater Temple. She was ready to attribute it to her illusionism acting up from the recently devoured souls, but if it was the electromantic girl, then she was almost certainly something to Duncan.

Yarawyn shoved Razarkha from the side. "Well? Will you admit your augmentee was a traitor all along?"

"It's plausible that he's changed his loyalties," Razarkha said. "While he despised his brother, it could well be he has family he's fond of. We'll wait to see if he leaves the temple with anyone. If he's with the girl Naas'khar attacked, we'll know he's turned on us."

Selenia clambered onto Moonrazer's back. "It's more than you'll normally grant me. Let's wait and see."

True enough, Duncan left the Saltwater Temple with two people by his side; an armoured man in red and white, and a young woman in a man's tunic, both of which had the stereotypical Godswater looks. Slung over the former's shoulder was a bald, unconscious man in simple robes, his hands cuffed behind him. Razarkha was quick to point her soulstealer at yet another traitor.

"Stop right there, Duncan."

Duncan raised his hands. "Calm down, these are family. Save for Petyr, they're— oh."

The augmentee had spotted Naas'khar, and before the nephil started his nonsense, Razarkha spoke up. "You got in the way, Duncan. You put your family ahead of *me,* your liberator. You didn't even know that girl before today, yet you have the gall to nearly kill your ally over her."

"He was menacing an innocent girl!" Duncan shouted, moving in front of his kin.

"She was an electromantic threat! Not to mention, it looks like there's an armed ascetic you missed. More kin, I presume?"

"I only have ill will against Petyr," Duncan stated. "What was I to do, kill what remains of my family? Unlike you two, I don't *need* to be the only Godswater."

Razarkha's abdomen lit up and burnt so hot that her remaining clothing became singed. As she desperately contained her rage, her illusionism ran roughshod, with Rakhs, Teis, Razanders, Ranis and Terrezas flitting in and out of existence around her. Razander was grown, but blue-skinned, his decayed stomach steadily flaking into crystal. Something in her chest cavity fell out of place, which unleashed the scream building within her.

"Pick a relative, now!" she yelled, swiftly switching her aim between the tunicked girl and the armoured man.

"What are you—"

*"Now!"*

Suddenly, Razarkha's sides were pressed by rocky walls, and her arm was forced to point forward. The shock of the assault made her drop her soulstealer, leaving her wriggling like a rat in a vice, stretching for an artefact just beyond her reach.

"No, no, stop, please, I *need it!*" she babbled.

"That's too bad," Duncan stated.

Razarkha's confidence reignited for a moment when, just beyond her crushers, she saw Yarawyn wing upwards, only for a burning beam much like her own to hit the beast in its scaled chest, downing the beast. Yar fell off Moonrazer's side and hit her head, presumably rendering her useless. While Naas'khar's signature hacking and cracking was heard, the sound of another blast came not long after, followed by a wet, fleshy thud.

"What's happening? Who's that?" Razarkha asked.

Her answer was quickly answered as a young woman in blue-black light armour ran into view, hugging the Godswater girl, then, peculiarly, kissing her on the mouth.

"Pleura! I was afraid you'd died in the skirmishes," the girl that was presumably Rosaline said. "I'm so glad to see you."

"I managed to buy my men some time with a flare, but I had no choice but to retreat. Their geomancer's defection allowed for a counterattack," the human lumomancer said.

"This is my Uncle Duncan," Rosaline explained. "He looks a little different, but now that Petyr's under arrest, we can start making reforms to how we view non-holy mages."

Razarkha watched Duncan hover while his family celebrated their safety, and against all expectations, her eyes began to leak.

"Is this how you repay your saviour?" Razarkha spat. "If it wasn't for me, you'd still be serving that foreman ascendant in Moneri!"

Duncan approached her and lowered his grinding tones to a rumble. "You're right. I owe you a lot. I don't owe you enough to let that monster and her pet kill the Godswaters who deserve to live. I don't want us to be enemies, Razarkha."

"You have an odd way of showing it. You spent every moment with me voicing your doubts, and now you're apprehending me."

Duncan's eyes glowed up. "Rosaline, Shiloh, and… I presume your name is Pleura? Take shelter, and if Petyr wakes up, knock him out again."

The man responded. "Right away, Uncle Duncan."

With that, the flesh-and-blood Godswaters, along with their inverted compatriot, ran off to somewhere beyond

Razarkha's view. Duncan stared at Razarkha while he waited, knowing that all she could do was seethe. Eventually, he spoke again.

"I'll give you a chance to get away unscathed. Before you say yes, shatter me, and then rampage around the city, know that I've kept something secret from you."

Razarkha mouth slackened. "Ariel wasn't dead, was she?"

"You're quick when you want to be," Duncan said. "Best of luck attempting to disconnect my soul from this body. It won't work. With that in mind, I'll make you an offer. I release you, and in exchange, you telekinetically pick up the refuse you consider to be allies and never set foot in Godswater again."

Razarkha closed her eyes. "I was wrong to see you as another Weil."

"You were. So, what will it be? Do you die here, without your precious vengeance, or can you leave like a civilised spellbinder? After living in Galdus, I doubt they exist, but perhaps you can prove me wrong."

It pained her to admit it, but Duncan had bested her. Better still, he was merciful enough to spare her. It was Rakh all over again, but without the mockery of her stillbirths. Her pride battled with her self-preservation, but what good was pride without the ability to experience it?

She hung her head and swallowed a thick liquid. "I'll leave in peace. Even if you rebelled against me, I'm proud. This is the boldness I wanted all augmentees to have, back when I was Erre."

"Back when you stood for something," Duncan said, releasing her. "Leave, and never return."

Razarkha didn't waste time. She picked up her soulstealer, leveraged as much telekinetic force as she could, then lugged the unconscious elf, the wounded wyvern, and the pile of broken bones mixed with black, daemonic slime upwards. After taking a moment to get her bearings, she dashed north, as far from Godswater as her magic would allow.

* * *

Tei had left Luna Riversong to write up her report on Weil's interrogation, and prayed Quira could force her daemons not to skew their story. She'd seen the look Luna had given the Ilazari before, though she was amazed daemons were capable of such emotions. As much as biased reporting was a risk, she'd secured an ally who could consistently loosen Weil's tongue.

She reached her house, unlocked the front door, then checked through her sleeve pockets for her office key. Her chest tightened, she checked her alternative pockets, then groaned. Slamming the door upon entry and tromping through the hallway as much as her short legs could allow, she called to her son.

"Rarakhi, get here, *now!*"

The boy was quick to leave the living room, but upon meeting Tei's eyes, he was quick to vanish. She counteracted his predictable illusionism and caught him heading upstairs.

"Not so fast," she snapped. "You're not getting away with what you did."

"I don't know what you're talking about," Rarakhi said.

"Then explain how I lost a key that I keep in my sleeves. Now, if I think of a skilled pickpocket, I'd assume somebody with a criminal background, and if they were an illusionist I'd almost take it as a given. Hand it over."

"I haven't got it," the boy claimed. "Have you looked around the house?"

Tei's tone hardened. "Don't feign idiocy, Rarakhi. Only cowards dodge responsibility."

"You'd know all about that, wouldn't you?"

Blood rushed to Tei's cheeks, and she marched up the stairs, shoving her son aside. As she reached her landing, she found the key on the floor, by a pot containing the wilted remains of a house plant. She checked its grooves and stuck it in her office door; true enough, it opened. She grumbled to herself, until, as she placed her notes on her desk, an idea came to her.

"Rarakhi, Plutera, come here!"

She lingered beyond her office, leaning on the doorframe and projecting a piercing gaze. The adolescents arrived at the landing, and while Rarakhi's line of sight shifted every few moments, Plutera had an assurance only spoilt noblewomen could achieve.

"Some clever youth stole my key and then put it by my house plant," Tei began. "Rarakhi has the criminal versatility and illusionism to pull it off, but don't think you're above suspicion, Plutera. Rara is a follower, not a planner, and you seem the sort to come up with the 'dropped in the landing' decoy, while also giving yourself away with a subconscious tell."

"What do you mean?" Plutera stammered.

"You planted the key by a plant," Tei said, a smile forming beneath her facial veil. "Perhaps I'm reading too much into it, but the key wasn't quite in a position that fits with a simple slip from my pocket. Well, which of you is responsible?"

Plutera remained resolute, but Rarakhi's forehead was slick with sweat. Tei needed to apply one last piece of pressure.

"I'll be writing a letter to Rakh and Plutyn Khanas today regarding information I've gathered. I wouldn't want to inform Sir Plutyn that his daughter's been misbehaving—"

"Fine, I did it!" Rarakhi spluttered. "I used my illusionism to nick your key, just like you said."

Tei folded her arms. "You know better than this, Rarakhi. My office contains some of the kingdom's darkest secrets. Access to this room falling into the hands of a child is possibly the worst thing that could happen to Arkhera, yet you helped it happen. To say I'm angry is an understatement. Off with you."

"Sorry, mum," Rarakhi said, hanging his head in dramatic contrition.

Both made to leave, but Tei raised her arm. "Plutera, stay with me a moment."

"As you wish, mother," Plutera said, keeping her hands clasped.

Once Rarakhi was safely downstairs, Tei lowered her voice. "The fact you stayed quiet and let Rarakhi take the fall disappoints me. What did you find out?"

"That your sister is likely immune to everything but the Thread," the girl reported.

"You're clever for your age, but not nearly clever enough for me. Go downstairs and consider yourself lucky I've let Rarakhi believe he took the blame on your behalf."

Plutera left without another word, and Tei locked herself within her office. From there, she composed a letter containing an abridged version of Weil's story according to Luna Riversong: Razarkha overthrew an Ilazari crime lord to claim a soulstealer, rampaged through Galdus, died at Weil's hand, then was spotted in Demidium. She added notes regarding the thread weapon, and the possibility of releasing Weil to augment troops in Moonstone.

Once the letter was written, she rolled it, sealed it with purple wax and the Royal Electorate's stamp, then checked the thread knife in her drawer. Fortunately, it appeared the children had the sense not to steal it. She would need to present this to the men of the Royal Armoury. With any luck, there'd be a way to mass produce this threaded steel without the costly assistance of Yukishimans.

* * *

The snow had subsided into slush by Moonstone's train station. While sharing a roof with Kagura Selenia was as irritating as Irikhos expected, it was good to see Torawyn smiling in her presence. Whenever he and Tor were alone, she had some hidden irritation she would vent, but to Kag's credit, she had been careful to ensure her words were complimentary as of late. Lingering by the three elves were Kag's security detail and Plutyn Khanas, the ever-ghoulish 'Minister of Criminal Affairs', though if half the tales Count Fel'thuz told were true, he was closer to a criminal minister. Tor took Kag's hands and met her eyes.

"This is it, Kag. The King will soon acknowledge your abdication, and you'll be free in the Vale. I almost envy the life you have ahead of you."

"I'm not weak for running away from ladyship, am I?" Kag asked.

"No," Tor assured her sister as she let go of her hands. "You're strong for acknowledging your weaknesses."

Irikhos shakily reinforced his almost-betrothed's point. "The only thing I don't regret about my kidnapping is the realisation it sparked within you. I wish you every happiness with the Yookie artist. Eika Hijibaru, is it?"

"Eiji Hibari," Kag corrected. "He's actually an impressionist, much like the art you said you preferred when we went to dinner."

Irikhos paused. "You actually remembered that?"

"Of course," Kag said with a beaming smile. "I remember everything to do with art."

Irikhos put a hand on her shoulder, causing her to jump. He softened his voice to make up for the shock.

"You'll be where you belong. Mor'kha believes that even the tick has a divinely orchestrated purpose. Modelling is yours."

Kag gave Irikhos a quick hug, her sister an extended hug, and finally, patted Plutyn on the head. "Well, I'll see you all later, after Razarkha stops being mean forever. You'll visit me in the Vale, won't you?"

Torawyn's expression warmed. "Of course we will."

With that, Kag entered the train station, her silent guards following her. Plutyn was quick to break his silence.

"I am glad that the sentimentality ended before it made Lady Selenia late."

Irikhos chuckled. "I know necromancers are fond of the cold, but you *do* have blood in your veins, right?"

"Ah, insulting your guide's race, always a good idea," Plutyn remarked. "Come, lady and lord presumptive. We have a catacomb route to traverse."

The necromancer seemingly glided across the partially melted snows towards the southern walls. Upon the battlements, men in the blue and silver of the Selenias and the black and green of Plutyn marched about. Some were disassembling and cleaning their rifles, while those with magitech firearms played with their scopes.

"Just beneath a section of walling is a subterranean route to the village of Snowy Bank," Plutyn explained. "With me."

He walked to a part of the southern wall supported by scaffolding, with orcish builders hard at work restoring its strength. Plutyn then moved towards a pile of snow, which, to Irikhos's surprise, was completely incorporeal. Tor unsurely joined him in walking through the visibly solid, leaving Iri no choice but to at least attempt it. When he walked into the illusion, a sudden change in elevation made him lose his footing, and soon he was falling down some rocky stairs. At the bottom, he landed on something soft; the fact it wriggled and spoke in a feminine tone quickly revealed its identity.

"While I'm not averse to this, perhaps we should wait until after we're securely ruling Moonstone," Torawyn said from beneath him.

Irikhos allowed a moment's laughter. "When we have some time to ourselves, perhaps."

"Stand," Plutyn commanded, drifting past them. "I expect this behaviour from my daughter and her lover, not two adults."

Tor and Iri stood, both opting against speech. Instead, they followed the near-skeletal minister through the dank, brazier-lit way. Dripping and distant murmuring filled their ears, the situation painful enough that Minister Khanas took it upon himself to fill the void.

"After this right, keep heading forward. You'll soon catch up to a group of peasants. They already have a guide; be sure to listen to them."

Irikhos made a few linguistic fumbles before he replied. "You're turning back, aren't you? Facing the danger like Count Fel'thuz. I know he's busy cloaking the catacombs entrances and the troops, and Erwyn's keeping the Crown informed, but what are *you* staying for?"

"I'm staying because I know there's a future beyond this travesty," Plutyn said. "When we return to relative peace, will the men respect a leader who offered their lives on their behalf then scrambled to safety? Unlike lords and their peasants, when the rulers of *my* system lose the admiration of their subjects, they don't last long, regardless of their good intentions."

The necromancer's normally unchanging voice briefly grew wistful, and Torawyn gave him a small curtsy. "I'm grateful for your help, Sir Khanas. May you stay safe in Moonstone."

"I don't need your gratitude, just the knowledge that you won't get yourself killed despite my efforts," Khanas replied, turning his back on his lady and lord presumptive.

As Minister Plutyn walked back the way he came, his dark clothing amidst the dim lighting made him look like half an illusionist himself.

# Reflections

Royal Armourer Metalshaper took the thread knife into his massive hand and squinted his deep brown eyes. After a moment's contemplation, the orc put the dagger on his desk and pushed it back to Tei.

"Sorry, Royal Looking Glass," he said, sitting back so far his chair rested against his office wall. "That sort of work is exclusive property of the Soltelle Empire."

Tei rolled her eyes behind an illusorily neutral expression. "I don't care about the legality of it in the Soltelles' eyes, if they catch us and get angry, so be it, we'll work something out, what matters is the ability to put my rabid sister down."

"Look, crafting a blade like that requires thread mages," Metalshaper said. "Now admittedly, they ain't as rare as those folks who can turn into monsters, co-gains or somethin', but if you searched the entire bloody kingdom for a Yookie thread mage who can specifically craft threadsteel, you'd be searchin' for years. Factor in that perhaps they wouldn't want to give away one of their home nation's biggest secrets and you'll be searchin' forever. Sorry, Royal Looking Glass. It ain't possible."

Pushing back a second time was pointless. Tei slumped within her orc-sized chair, then took the thread blade back. After allowing the moment to simmer, she hopped onto the floor, reminding herself that she didn't even measure to the height of Metalshaper's desk.

"Thank you for your honesty," she finally said. "Looks like I'll be finishing my day writing a formal pardon request."

The orc chuckled. "Best of luck, milady. Convincing Landon to release a prisoner sounds harder than squeezing blood from a stone."

"Something like that," Tei said. "Though as far as I know, the man I hope to release isn't a daylight drinker. If he was, then Landon would have already told me to toss his cell key into the ocean."

"Keep safe, Royal Looking Glass," Metalshaper said. "Hope you get to do somethin' nice along with all the boring writing."

"I hope so too," Tei replied before heading out of the Royal Armourer's office.

From there, she cloaked herself, walking down through a complex of smithies housing some of the greatest blacksmiths in the kingdom. Madaki and Elarondian elves, orcs with great muscular arms shaved to prevent fires, and pyromantic goblins all worked in concert for the mass production of swords, yet none of them were fit for her purpose.

She left the Royal Armoury no closer to a solution to Moonstone's impending doom than before, and even the night sky couldn't provide the comfort she needed. Deathsport's streetlamps were dim and red-tinged, so while the glittering stars told Tei it was night, the city was perpetually twilit from the ground. She invisibly left a silver by a blind, homeless goblin she passed, briefly visited the Cheegal Incident Memorial, and returned home. Her house was dark, and the lack of light seeping from any of the rooms suggested that Rarakhi and Plutera had gone to sleep.

She clambered up the stairs, entered her office, lit her lantern, and opened her ink pot. She fumbled for a blank piece of paper, then dipped a nib in the ink. The formalities flowed as naturally as breathing, and from there, she extolled Weil of Zemelnya's virtues, despite not knowing the man in the slightest. Luna Riversong would have no doubt served as a glowing endorsement if not for the fact she was a living embodiment of chaos.

After half-heartedly mentioning a bold, warrior's spirit and a sympathetic reason for breaking Arkheran docking law, she signed, sanded, rolled and sealed the letter. She groaned, put the thread knife back in its drawer, and slumped her head against her desk. A creeping drowsiness invited by the ink fumes and wasted day snaked through her body. Soon enough, her eyes were shut, and illusions that were thankfully sealed in her head flitted about. A knock on the door snatched her from slumber before it could take her for the night.

Tei lifted her head and mumbled in response. "Who's there?"

"Hey, mum, it's me, Rarakhi," a boyish voice answered.

"Oh, I thought you were asleep. One moment."

Tei almost collapsed off her chair, grumbling all the way to the door. When she opened it, she looked upwards to see her son's features were tightened.

"What's troubling you?" Tei asked.

"I just wanted to say sorry for getting in your way," Rarakhi replied. "Are you all right? I know you work for the royals an' everything, but you've been running around a lot lately."

Tei backed from the doorway. "If you want to talk, you may as well come in."

"Thanks," Rarakhi said, entering the office and shutting the door behind him. "So, I was thinking about how I'm staying here, how you're just letting me and Plutera do our own thing while you work, and I've realised you have every reason to hate me."

Tei blinked, then realised what was just said. "What are you talking about? Has Plutera talked you into thinking I resent you?"

"It's nothing Petal said," Rarakhi replied, folding his legs on the floor. "Remember when we first met? I threatened you like a fucking thug. I was so angry at you for leaving me behind, but you've got your life together. Having some kid weighing you down would just get in the way, right?"

Tei sat by her tall, thin son. "I'll admit I'm still afraid of you. I'm short compared to all my kin, I've always been physically threatened by them. Even when your father embraced me, I knew I was the size of a child to him. Even if you didn't threaten me, I'd be—"

"But I *did* threaten you. Now me and Plutera are doing stupid shit like stealing your keys an' fucking up your work, and you'd be right to be upset with us."

Tei averted her eyes. "I hate Rakh for dragging me back into he and Razarkha's dysfunction after all these years. I've forged a new life, and yes, parenthood is incompatible with it, but that doesn't mean you, the innocent child that sprouted from all the horrible things Rakh and I did, deserves to be abandoned."

"I'm hardly innocent, though," Rarakhi said with a laugh.

"Innocent's the wrong word," Tei admitted. "Regardless, nobody deserves what you've been through. Even though I resent Rakh for getting me involved in his drama, I don't blame you for existing. I'm trying to help his situation as best I can, despite everything. I'm going to abuse my authority to release a prisoner I *hope* has a fighting chance against Razarkha.

"Your father lured me with sweet words and we took solace in each other in a way that I'll never stop regretting. I can't look at myself in the mirror and see a loveable woman thanks to your father, yet I still want to help him. The only thing you've done is loom over me and say a few mean words. Why wouldn't I want to stand by you?"

"But you ran from me all my life," Rarakhi mumbled. "What changed?"

"I'd become so lost in my own life that I'd convinced myself I had no family," Tei explained. "Rakh, as intrusive and stupid as he was, reminded me of the kin I have.

Razarkha's absence was the catalyst, but in truth, I should have been there from the start. I wandered the kingdom when I first left Moonstone. I could have raised you on the move."

"Nah," Rarakhi cut in. "If Aunt Razarkha spotted you, she'd want to know who the Fel'thuz-looking kid was, and then I'd get myself killed by calling you ma or something."

Tei sighed. "I was going to chase up Quira Abraxas's interrogation transcript, but I'm about to collapse. Would you like to share some wine with me? It's good, I promise you, it was expensive."

"You don't think I'm too young?"

"You're bigger than me, you'll probably handle it well," Tei said, standing up. "Just put the cap on my ink pot, won't you?"

The boy did so, saving her an unnecessary clamber. "You know, mum, my dad's tried so hard to understand me, but it feels like you see something he doesn't."

Tei laughed sadly. "Your father projects illusions onto his loved ones. Sometimes, they magnify them, other times they transform them into monstrous caricatures, but the result is the same; he connects to their shadows, not the person behind the glamour."

"How can I make him look past that?"

"I wish I knew," Tei said. "Once all this Razarkha nonsense is over, we'll figure out a way together, how does that sound?"

"It sounds good, ma."

With a soft smile, Tei led her son downstairs, where a bottle of Sanguinas Isle Ghostwood Vintage was waiting in the kitchen.

\* \* \*

Castle Selenia's halls were abandoned, every servant and soul vacated save for Erwyn, the carrier pigeons, and

Rakh Fel'thuz. Even Plutyn Khanas had steered clear lately, presumably spending time with his underground compatriots. This didn't free Rakh of the scent of bhang weed, however; Erwyn had taken to smoking it heavily, and much like Khanas, its intended effects weren't evident.

The pair were sat together in a lounge, tending to letters in partial states of writing. Erwyn had already written two, and had a third on the way, while Rakh was stuck on his first. Together, they'd decided to leave notes for their loved ones. Erwyn had chosen to write for Lady Kag, his younger brother, and his niece, while Rakh was trying to find the words for Rarakhi before moving on to Tei.

His pain had subsided since his final argument with the boy, but regret squatted in the emptiness left behind, and as ink puddled on the upper corner of his page, all he could think of was the loneliness his son must have felt taking the train to Deathsport. To this day, Rakh didn't know if Rara wanted his love, but if he was dead, it did no good to leave anything unsaid.

He began to write how he would regret not being able to see Rarakhi grow up, and that he accepted that there would be mixed feelings regarding his death. He went on to explain that he watched Rarakhi leave at the train station, but stayed invisible to avoid upsetting him. Finally, he urged his son to accept the Fel'thuz name, but also let him know that if he chose not to, he would still be proud of him. Even now, writing with his left hand was a task unto itself, and the context of the letters only worsened the affair. Rakh stared at his paper, but inspiration vanished when a sob drew his gaze away.

Erwyn had stubbed his smoke out on his desk, and was facing away from his letter. Despite the softness of his armchair, he was hunched over, weeping into his hands. Rakh put his nib in his ink pot and spoke softly.

"It's all right, Erwyn."

"I don't want to say goodbye," Erwyn muttered. "I hate my brother so much that I never visit him, yet as I wrote his letter, I realised I should have said more to him. I want to see him again, but I'm here."

"If you like, I could—"

"No," Erwyn said, uncovering his face and sniffling. "If I let you control the messaging during these trying times, the Royal Wisdom would need a translator."

"I never realised how much I'd miss writing effortlessly," Rakh remarked.

Erwyn smiled through his tears. "The fact you're going to this effort is a testament to your love for him. If you don't make it, I still believe Rarakhi will forgive you."

"It doesn't matter," Rakh claimed. "If I'm dead, he'd only be forgiving a corpse."

"He'd be choosing to make your legacy a positive one," Erwyn insisted. "You're an illusionist, Rakh, surely you know the power of perception. Even beyond the grave."

Rakh looked at his letter. "Still, I won't ask for forgiveness. I just want him to grow into a kind, thoughtful man. I don't want him twisted by my accursed generation."

"Leave the forgiveness in his hands," Erwyn suggested. "Don't ask for it, but don't tell him not to forgive you either. Just tell him your thoughts and let him choose what he will."

Count Fel'thuz pondered over this, and then glanced at Erwyn's current letter. "What's got to you?"

"It's my niece," Erwyn explained. "I've only really kept touch by letter, but she's the only part of Ellaria I still have. She's a girl who needs friends."

"Lady Strakha Safiros, correct?"

Erwyn nodded. "She's a lot like me, but didn't stand up for herself before it was too late. Chiefly when it comes to marriage. Father wanted me to be a bold, married count with three children by my mid-twenties, but of course, that was never going to happen."

Rakh cocked his head. "Why 'of course'? I know you wanted to be a wisdom instead, but there's nothing stopping you getting married."

The wisdom stared at Rakh with welling eyes. "Don't— don't make me say it out loud."

"If there's something on your mind, there's no better time than now," Rakh replied.

The high elven scholar stood, milled about the lounge, then supported himself on a game table. "You never suspected I was inverted?"

Blood drained from Rakh's face, and his heart felt like it was constricting itself. He stood up and approached Erwyn.

"Does that mean what I think it means?"

Erwyn mixed laughter with sobbing, his lungs playing havoc with his attempts to communicate. "It does. I'm sorry if that changes how you see me."

Rakh opened his arms. "Come here, Erwyn."

Without words, the wisdom brought himself into Rakh's embrace, and for a while, the two simply held each other. Rakh tightened his grip and smiled over Erwyn's shoulder.

"You know, you really have bad taste."

"I suppose I so," Erwyn said with a laugh.

"I'm sorry I can't return your feelings, but that's a blessing of sorts," Rakh claimed. "You could do much better than me."

Erwyn let Rakh go. "Don't say that. You've made terrible mistakes, but I see a compassionate, convicted man who stands by his beliefs no matter what."

"Standing by my convictions led to this crisis in the first place," Rakh pointed out. "If I'd have stuck with *King Landon's* convictions, or yours, then we wouldn't be crying over our imminent deaths, would we?"

Erwyn looked out of a window. "I suppose. Still, it's a little late for me to find love. I'm in my forties."

"If I could find women—"

"You're an illusionist, don't talk to me about how easy seduction is for you," the wisdom replied with a wry edge.

Rakh picked a crust of dried tears from his eye. "I believe you can find someone. If you and your niece are both inverted, then there's enough men like you out there. I know it's not as simple as just, be an invert, find an invert, they need to be someone you admire, but—"

"It's all right, Rakh," Erwyn said, still averting his eyes. "I know you mean well. If we survive, I'm going to take a break. Ghosts know I've earned one. Perhaps I could travel to the Isolas Sereni, I hear the people there are beautiful to every race."

Rakh took his seat back, returning to his letter. "Is that so? I wouldn't mind visiting them myself. I'm sure Rara wouldn't mind being acting count for a few weeks."

\* \* \*

By Sanguinas Lagoon, Razarkha sat amidst a trio of unconscious beings she despised. She stared over the brackish waters, squinted to find the speck on the horizon where Sanguinas Isle resided, then adjusted her hands, reminding herself of the silt she sat upon. She'd flown northwards hoping that they would awaken on the way to Moonstone, but their continued unresponsiveness concerned her. Moonrazer's breaths were deep and wheezing, Yarawyn's were shallow, and given his nature, Razarkha couldn't fathom if Naas'khar was even alive.

Even if they woke up, what was left for her? As Praetor Erre, she was glorious, accentuated by a beautiful cape sewn by an augmentee who admired her. Her companions idolised her, and one outright loved her. She'd resented Weil's fawning once, but now she'd give anything to hear his Isleborn ramblings. He could have babbled about stupid poetry or all-black piratical sails, anything to hear his joyful tones.

"Are those dancing spellbinders in the distance your magic?" a familiar voice asked.

"Oh. You're awake," Razarkha muttered, not bothering to face Yarawyn.

Predictably, the elf's tone grew snappy. "Unfortunately for you, yes."

"I can make you fall asleep permanently if you want," Razarkha said with an unexpected flatness. It appeared even insulting Yarawyn had lost its lustre.

Despite the lack of punch, Yarawyn still hesitated before she spoke. "Where are we?"

"Somewhere between Crabber's Mouth and Moonrock," Razarkha answered.

"Why are we this far north? Did Duncan properly subdue you?" Yarawyn spluttered, then moved into view. "Don't tell me you ran away."

Razarkha stood. "Would you rather be dead?"

"If you got free enough to run away, you should have been free enough to kill him!" Yarawyn said. "You introduced yourself boasting about your time as some revolutionary in Galdus. How did you topple multiple ascendant megalopolises if you can't stand against a single augmentee?"

Razarkha's body became limp save for her soulstealer's arm, which she used to point at her lady. "Perhaps you could do better in my position. Worry not, you can become this artefact's wielder. All it'd take is a duel to the death."

"Oh, so because I'm not you, you're exempt from criticism?" Yarawyn said, starting to pace along the muddy bank. "You trusted that faceless, lying pile of rocks for far longer than you should have. From the moment he let Irikhos and Tor go, you should have killed him. Instead, you stood by his side. Well, guess who was right? Me. Then we wasted time on his stupid city full of religious idiots, and now Naas'khar's injured, as is Moonrazer."

Rakh superimposed his smug face onto Yarawyn. Razarkha's hand trembled, the request to the arcane god was on the verge of being sent, yet somehow, her anger morphed into misery. The undead illusionist slumped, and she was soon coughing up more discoloured flesh.

Yarawyn folded her arms. "Pitiful. I thought you weren't the sort to accept losses, yet you ran away from Godswater without even attempting to take Duncan with you."

Without thinking, Razarkha lunged towards her high elven charge, then grabbed her by the collar. She tossed Yarawyn into the silt, then stepped on her chest with her crystalline leg.

"Do you think I don't ponder over my life now that I'm beyond it?" Razarkha yelled. "You may think it's strong to ignore every loss, to fight to the bitter end every time. That's because even when you had everything taken away from you, you had some idiot kind enough to give you everything back! *I* had to live another day, I had no-one to rely on but myself!"

Yarawyn struggled to breathe, but still found her words. "Do you think I was happy just because Tor kept me alive?"

"If you *weren't* happy with your pretty little life in Elarond, then you were ungrateful!"

Somehow, Razarkha surprised herself with the outburst. She lifted her artificial leg and backed away from Yarawyn.

"I should have been happy with Weil."

For once, Yarawyn kept her tone amicable. "What do you mean?"

"You should have accepted the life Tor gifted you. I was in a similar situation. It wasn't quite as comfortable, my benefactor was in debt in a crime ridden Ilazari city, but I still could have accepted it. Yet his quack doctor and his suffering father forced me into action, and from there, I couldn't stop. Each taste of power pushed me to seek more. First, I controlled Weil's life, then the fate of the Kasparov Family, more and more, never enough. I died at the very top, but perhaps even that would have left me wanting."

For a while, the only sounds in earshot were the gentle waves of Sanguinas Lagoon and the screaming of gulls. Yarawyn moseyed past Razarkha and knelt by Moonrazer.

"Thank you for dragging us out of Godswater."

"Thank Duncan's infinite mercy," Razarkha muttered.

The high elf quietened. "Will killing your brother put an end to your craving?"

"It has to," Razarkha replied, staring at the scrap of lung by her feet. "What else is left?"

Moonrazer woke up, and as the beast stretched his wings, Yarawyn shot her countess a bold grin. "Moonstone."

# Rebels

Though the attack on Godswater had topped Razarkha's magical reserves up, it was still a burden to drag the freshly reformed Naas'khar through the air along with herself. If Duncan was with them, it would be different, but as it was, she floated towards Moonstone with an ever-renewing dread.

"There it is," Yarawyn said from her wyvern. "Moonstone, after all these years. It looks different from the sky."

Razarkha glanced downwards at the great walled settlement. There didn't appear to be peasants or guards moving through the streets or battlements. Tattered flags rippled in the wind, and the castle stood undefended.

"Something's wrong," Razarkha muttered. "Either we're higher than I anticipated and Moonstone's grown, or the city's empty."

Yarawyn paused. "I hoped you'd know something about that. What could it mean?"

"It means they know we're coming."

"Could Duncan Godswater have warned them?" Yarawyn asked.

"No. Even if he did, they'd still be evacuating. Somehow they predicted my return *much* earlier—"

"It's Irikhos," Yarawyn claimed. "Iri and Tor, they have to be here!"

"Yarawyn, don't you dare—"

The elf and her wyvern had already started their dive. Razarkha was tempted to leave them to die, but Naas'khar started babbling within her telekinetic grasp.

"Well? If there's nobody here, this Arkheran city is ours for the taking!"

"Surely as a goat hunter you understand the notion of an ambush," Razarkha remarked. "If she's too stupid to avoid an obvious trap, then—"

The daemonic hybrid unveiled his tentacles and stretched them around Razarkha. In her panic, her telekinesis failed, and together, the pair plummeted.

*"What are you doing?"*

"Forcing you to save her," Naas'khar stated.

"Are *all* submissive men traitors in disguise? *Fine,* but you're taking the brunt of this."

Naas'khar released Razarkha, and the pair continued their fall. She applied some telekinesis to slow their descent as they reached Yarawyn, then called to her idiotic companion.

"Watch out, you imbecile!"

"For what?" Yarawyn replied, levelling her flight and pointing to the surrounding battlements. "There's nobody here!"

Razarkha stabilised Naas'khar and herself into a hover while Yarawyn circled. "Even if we can't see anybody, remember my brother's an *illusionist*. Unlike me, he hasn't discovered any new tricks, so he's more likely to use the ones he was born with—"

Something fast-moving pierced her arm, causing black fluid to ooze out. Razarkha applied some counter-illusory refraction to find that the battlements were teeming with gunners, some of which possessed magitech rifles she hadn't seen before.

"Keep your blasted wyvern steady so I can cover you!" Razarkha screamed, then brought her arms inwards, shouting an Old Galdusian incantation for focus. *"Nolite en aere!"*

Sections of the battlements split from the city walls, flinging riflemen and musketeers to their deaths, then floated towards Razarkha and her cohorts, forming a cobbled-together shield. Once the pattering of musket balls against her airborne wall ceased, Razarkha spoke.

"Are you suicidal, or mentally deficient?" Razarkha asked Yarawyn, whose wyvern had dug its claws into a floating fragment of city wall.

"I'm sorry, the knowledge that Irikhos is close enticed me," the elf spluttered.

"Apologies don't fix my arm!" Razarkha spat. "Now that we know the battlements are manned, I want you to lay a stream of fire along them. I'll cast a wide illusion in the sky, cloaking your flight patterns. They'll be able to see your flames, but by then it'll be too late. Do you have any questions?"

"Are you sure we'll stay unseen? If Moonrazer's wings get shot, we'll be quick to fall."

Razarkha scowled. "Oh, *now* you're concerned about getting yourself shot. I'll keep a personal cloak over you when you rise, then make everything above a certain point appear as clear sky. If you still get shot despite that, it's your own fault."

Yarawyn swallowed, then patted her wyvern. "Moonrazer, *fly!*"

As the pair ascended beyond her barrier, Razarkha obfuscated their form, and once they was in position to begin their attack flight, she applied the generic cloak, as promised. She turned to Naas'khar and folded her arms.

"Happy?"

"Very."

"I don't know what you see in her," Razarkha muttered. "Horrible taste aside, you'll accompany me. While Yarawyn kills the elevated troops, you and I shall subdue any ground forces in our way. We're headed there."

Razarkha pointed towards Castle Selenia. It was technically still standing, yet the flags looked like they hadn't been switched out in a while, as they were too sodden to wave in the wind. She descended with her chunks of battlement, crushing an empty cottage as she landed. She stretched her pain-stricken arm and shoved a piece of battlement forward, then poked her head out. Almost immediately, a musket ball whizzed past her head.

"You said you'd take the brunt of the battle," Razarkha said. "Time to make good on your promise."

"Actually, you just told me I would, I never promised—"

"I just saved Yarawyn's life, if you don't want to be a black stain against this ilmenite I suggest you stop speaking and start collaborating," Razarkha commanded. "Weil's tentacles were regularly used as shields, and I can't see how yours wouldn't be similarly tough."

"I am not my mother's god," Naas'khar protested. "I'm but a half-breed—"

*"I'm a half-breed, and I'm perfectly strong!"* Razarkha yelled, pointing her soulstealer at the abomination. "Figure out a way to protect me, even if it risks your life, or I'll do away with the preamble and kill you myself!"

"I'll figure something out," Naas'khar said, raising his tentacles while his arms remained limp.

Abruptly, he fell to his knees, coughing up enough black liquid to render his elf-shaped body a set of upright bones and organs. This gooey pile reared up to form a pair of fleshy walls with creeping, millipede-like limbs. Naas'khar stood between them, breathing heavily.

"I don't know how long I can stay like this, but this should block what they sling at us."

Razarkha joined the nephil. "Good. To the castle!"

The journey was a test of endurance rather than skill. Naas'khar's walking daemonic walls crawled rather than walked through the city, and occasionally, the inky substance would take too many bullets at once, forcing Razarkha to quickly snag a piece of the city to act as a temporary shield. When she couldn't do this, she swept a lumomantic beam in the general direction of her assailants, which generally put an end to the gunfire.

Eventually, the castle was close enough to tell that its guard force was conspicuously absent. Naas'khar took the opportunity to reabsorb his daemonic matter, collapsing and ejecting musket balls and shredded bones from his body.

"Good work," Razarkha said, pointing her soulstealer at the castle gates. "Can I trust you to distract any soldiers that close in on the castle?"

Naas'khar got up by bending over backwards. His arms remained limp, and his tentacles were partially melted, but despite this, the nephil nodded. Razarkha smiled, then caught the glow of fire upon the distant battlements.

"Good man. It looks like whatever trap these idiots set up failed. Now that I know illusionism is in play, finding my brother will be easy. Occupy them as long as you can."

With that, she blasted the gates open and charged through the courtyard. Numerous sharpshooters' towers had been erected, only to be telekinetically pulled to the ground. She levitated just above the ground to keep her pace brisk, practically dancing past the greenhouses she'd once beheld daily, blasting every armed fool in her way. So many castle guards resented their duty of protecting her; now that they were her enemies, she could demonstrate why shutting up and obeying their countess was always the superior option. As she neared the entrance proper, she put down two more guards, drank their souls, and spoke to her god.

"You'll be able to tell me if Rakh's here, won't you?"

***"Rakh Fel'thuz is definitely here,"*** the Bold Individualist answered. ***"Along with a couple of non-combatants. It appears your rampage was quite effective."***

"My brother was a fool to have most of his troops guarding an empty city. I suppose he hoped to gun me down before I reached the castle," Razarkha remarked. "Unfortunate for him."

***"Indeed. I hope this makes you happy."***

Razarkha's voice wavered. "Of course it will."

When she entered the castle, signs of activity were scant. The foyer was dusty, and though the scent of porridge wafted from the dining room, checking it revealed naught but three empty bowls. There were no servants throughout the castle, though scraps of the remaining residents' presence made themselves known.

Stubs from bhang weed smokes were scattered throughout a lounge, along with ink stains. Droppings from a hastily retrieved carrier pigeon could be seen along a hallway on the first floor, and one of the rugs was ruffled from what was likely an overly forceful step. When she reached Rakh's bedroom door, she found a sloppily written note pinned to it.

*Dearest Razarkha: Fuck you.*

The audacity almost amused her. She tore the paper from the door, scrunched it up, and threw it behind her, continuing up the castle until she reached Erwyn's spire. Shadows crept into her peripheral vision as she climbed the final staircase, to the point where she turned and shot a beam mild enough to blacken the walls rather than demolish them. When the shadows subsided, she edged back down and checked for a corpse at the staircase's foot.

Sadly, there was nothing, and so she finished her ascent without apparitions tugging against her paranoia. She took her crystalline leg and kicked in the door to Erwyn's study, finding the wisdom by an open window, gasping heavily. Beside him was a necromancer she'd never seen before, a beautiful older man with blacks and greens associated with the criminal side of the Khanas family.

"Good to see you again, Yagaska. What were you sending in such a hurry?" Razarkha asked, picking both up with her telekinesis.

Erwyn spat in Razarkha's face. "A letter informing the Crown you've arrived. How long do you hope to hold Moonstone?"

"Long enough to kill Rakh. Where is that coward?"

The necromancer chuckled. "He chose to stay in this city. The fact he's using the powers afforded to him is hardly dishonourable."

"If you had any sense, you would have abandoned Moonstone along with your peasants," Razarkha said, pushing both men against a wall while she searched Erwyn's desks.

For the most part, his drawers were stuffed with worthless medicinal projects gone awry, however, one locked section of the desk, easily picked with telekinesis, revealed a peculiar document. It was a confirmation of legitimisation, signed by Erwyn, the King, and the Royal Wisdom, regarding some boy named 'Rarakhi'. What little blood she had surged towards her face, and she pointed her soulstealer at Erwyn, telekinetically locking him in place.

"Who is this 'Rarakhi'?" Razarkha asked.

Erwyn narrowed his red eyes. "If you kill me, you'll never find out."

"Oh, I don't need you to confirm it. They're one of Rakh's bastards, legitimised into an heir," Razarkha stated. "Who's the mother? Some tavern wench he liked the look of? I know better than most that the Fel'thuz bloodline is a delicate balancing act. It'll be better for the line if I prune him from the family bush along with his father. Is he here?"

"No," Erwyn said with a laugh.

Razarkha's soulstealer glimmered with an instinctive transfer of arcane energy. "I don't know what's so amusing. If you want to kiss your beloved Rakh one last time, you'll tell me where this Rarakhi boy is."

"I'd never put him in danger."

A dry, wheezing sigh escaped Razarkha's body, and she turned to the necromancer. "Who are you, then? Some Khanas? Would you like to know how Rowyn Khanas died?"

The green-black shadow raised an eyebrow. "I always considered myself to be awful at rapport-building, but it's good to remember there's somebody worse."

"Oh, I simply can't help it," Razarkha said, tilting her soulstealer towards his arm. "He tried to escape me on a boat, so I blasted its hull apart like this."

She shot a lumomantic beam through his upper arm, causing his disconnected forearm to drop to the floor with a wet thud. Khanas was, amazingly, still conscious, albeit with a few bouts of vomiting following the impromptu amputation.

"What do you need to know?" the man asked, his voice low and bitter.

"Who are you, and do you know where Rarakhi Fel'thuz is?"

"I'm Plutyn Khanas, and the first place I'd suggest you seek Rarakhi is the Eternal Hellfire," the necromancer scoffed.

"How discouraging," Razarkha said with a small smile. "What exactly do you hope to achieve by insulting me? Are you trying to buy time? Erwyn has an excuse, what with his irrational attachment to my brother, but you're some crime lord, last I heard. Some Fel'thuz bastard is nothing to you."

"That boy is like a son to me," Plutyn declared. "You'll choke on your own decaying lungs before you learn where Rarakhi is."

Razarkha felt a wet chunk hit her crystalline abdomen, and sucked air in through her teeth. "Oh, *I* see. You're both attached to this Fel'thuz offshoot to the point that you'd die for him. What, do you expect me to kill everyone in this castle, then let the child return to Moonstone some boy hero ready to slay his evil aunt?"

Plutyn smirked. "Actually, I was stating a fact. Whoever worked on your necromancy did an awful job.

Perhaps if you didn't kill my cousin, you'd have a decently maintained body."

Razarkha's midsection heated up, sizzling whatever scraps of viscera lay atop it, and her hands shook. "I'm not falling for this. Dying or distracting, neither plan will work. You heard me casting magic at the bottom of the spire. Rakh's *dead.*"

"You're a terrible bluffer," Plutyn said. "Then again, your brain has likely deteriorated throughout your revenancy. If you had a hint of necromantic sense, you'd have worked harder to preserve yourself, but Rakh never gave me the impression you worked hard on anything."

"*I've been through more than he ever has!*" Razarkha snapped, her soulstealer glowing. "You can't trick me. I know you're trying to provoke me—"

"You disappoint me," Plutyn interrupted. "Rakh Fel'thuz built you up as some grand monster. Even if I *did* give you Rarakhi's location, you'd fail to kill him. The boy's a far greater person than this husk his father fears. Perhaps I'm giving you too many excuses with all this talk of undeath. I can tell from your face that even *before* you died, you were an ugly halfwit."

"*Shut up!*"

Without her will, a searing beam shot through the necromancer's chest. As she stepped back in shock, she tripped over a chair and lost control of her telekinesis, dropping Plutyn's body and Erwyn alike. She scrambled to her feet, tripping over her crystalline leg and yelping from overreliance on her recently shot arm, only to find that the wisdom had fled the room.

Razarkha grunted and charged out the study, rushing down the spire's staircase, only to trip and tumble down the stairs. When she reached the bottom, she could feel ooze seeping from her head, and her vision blurred. She lay on the cold ilmenite floor, hacking as her lungs expelled more of themselves.

Once her vision refined itself, she found one more terribly written note.

*Dearest Razarkha: Fuck you again.*

All she could do was scream her brother's name.

\* \* \*

Rarakhi was hunched over his game of *World Conquest,* having expanded from the Northern Isles to the Southern Isles, which he shared with Notongue. Bloodmetal was contained to Yukishima, which Plutera was steadily encroaching upon. His mother was out, petitioning the King about releasing the Ilazari prisoner she'd been obsessed with as of late, so the most he could do was kill time with Plutera and the orcs.

It was Bloodmetal's turn, and he picked up his attack dice. "Right, I'm going to take Midori Sora back."

Plutera smirked. "Are you sure about that?"

Given she had five defenders against his pitiful three attackers, it was near impossible to reclaim, yet the undead orc had little to lose. Despite the odds, his first roll took two from Plutera, his second led to one off each, leaving the last roll to be an even, two on two fight.

He rolled a pair of sixes, and Plutera's eyes widened. "Heavens, it looks like you *are* retaking Midori Sora after all."

"Still a chance you match it," Bloodmetal said. "Go on, Lady Plutera."

She rolled her defending dice, getting a three and a five. She removed her defenders and started arranging her unused armies.

"Well done, Bloodmetal. You took a chance, and it worked out," she said, and Rarakhi looked to the orc, expecting him to move his armies into the territory.

Instead, the orc sat with unusual stiffness. He made a creaking noise, then slumped, and Notongue wasn't long after him.

"Shit, what's going on?" Rarakhi asked, shoving the board aside to prop Notongue up.

Plutera put a hand on Bloodmetal's forehead and hyperventilated. "No, no, that can't be right, my father wouldn't—"

"What is it?"

"My father's magic has left them," Plutera stammered. "One moment, I can fix this, I'll fix it right now, don't worry."

She extended her arms over the limp pair of orcs, regulating her breathing while an unnerving miasma filled the room. Soon, Bloodmetal and Notongue were twitching. Plutera closed her eyes and breathed exclusively through her nose, then lifted her hands. To Rarakhi's shock, the orcs stood, however their wobbly gaits worried him. Plutera took Bloodmetal's shoulders and gave him a desperate smile.

"You're back, don't worry, I saved you. You're safe, it's all right."

Bloodmetal only responded with a dull, unintelligible groan, which made Plutera pace about. Bumps spread along Rarakhi's skin, and he turned to his betrothed.

"Something's the matter with 'em, Petal—"

"I *know that,* they're zombies now, not revenants! I don't know what's going on, but it's as though father's magic just vanished— no. No, no, this can't be happening."

Plutera covered her face and began to wail while Rarakhi edged towards her.

"Does this mean what I think it does?"

"Father's dead," Petal sobbed, falling to her knees.

"We don't know that, he may have needed to drop his magic for…"

Rarakhi couldn't continue pretending, even for his love's sake. He stood by her and lowered his voice.

"It's going to be all right—"

"We're taking that thread knife and killing her ourselves," Plutera snapped, marching upstairs with the mindless husks of her bodyguards.

Rarakhi scrambled after her, desperately trying to cobble a sentence together. "Wait, Plutera, before you do anything, my mum's going to set something up so—"

"Why do you think you never see royal troops in Moonstone?" Plutera asked. "The royals don't *care* what happens beyond the Plains of Death! It doesn't matter how hard your mother tries, the King will settle on what he always does: Nothing!"

Plutera pointed at Tei's office door, and Notongue tackled it, breaking it down with ease. She walked into the room and retrieved the thread knife while Rarakhi stood behind her.

"Petal, please just wait 'til mum gets back!"

Plutera turned to Rarakhi, her pale green eyes as shiny as her late father's. "Why do you care about what your mother has to say? I've loved you through the hardest times of your life, while your mother only started to care when your father forced her to. If you aren't coming with me, I'll take my vengeance alone. Your aunt killed Rowyn, and now she's killed my father. I'm not going to wait for royal intervention that'll never come."

Rarakhi remembered everything he'd shared with Tei the night before, only for the memories to be swept away by a typhoon of shared experiences with his love. He glanced at the floor, then met Petal's eyes again.

"All right. I'll help you avenge the Boss."

# Shadows

The moment Tei opened her house door, a sickening stench wafted towards her. She looked along her hall, to the top of her stairs, and her momentary questions were answered. Rarakhi and Plutera's bodyguards had been rendered motionless, and when Tei checked on them, it was obvious they weren't about to move again.

The Royal Looking Glass swallowed the burning liquid creeping up her throat, stepping over the laid-to-rest revenants to discover further horrors. Her office door had been smashed open, and cursory examination of Notongue's armour revealed he was the culprit. While the office appeared to be ransacked, there was only one item out of place: The thread knife.

This was no break-in. Any enemy of Arkhera's would have stolen much more and wouldn't have used someone who was ostensibly a protector of the house. The suspects were obvious, but Tei didn't want to rush to conclusions. She scurried through her house, checking Rarakhi's room, then her own, then edged around the bodies and checked downstairs.

"Rarakhi? Plutera? Are you there?"

Once the last room was checked, she accepted the truth. Oftentimes, the simplest solution was the correct one. Her maternal fears combined with other stressors, and she hit her head against a wall.

*"I knew I should have taken the thread blade with me!"* Tei ranted. "That sneaky little necromancer already proved how insecure my office was, then I trust her not to—oh, this is worse than I—"

This was no time to soliloquise. She hurriedly cast a cloak upon herself, rushed through her passageways, and marched towards the Royal Palace's throne room. There, Landon Shearwater slouched upon his throne, his crown heavy upon his grey-blonde hair. In a twist of good fortune amidst the disasters, Royal Advisor Quira Abraxas and her daemonic bards were beside the monarch, the former swaying to the latter's music in a display of idleness.

Tei revealed herself and raised her voice. "Your Majesty, if you have the time to lounge about enjoying the Riversongs' music, you should have approved my pardon request!"

Landon stared through her with his jaundiced, iron-blue eyes, his expression unmoving. "You have written convincing pardon requests in the past, Royal Looking Glass, but your latest was notably vague—"

"Plutyn Khanas is likely dead, Your Majesty. His revenants have fallen, my son and his betrothed are missing, as is the thread blade. You know what this means, don't you?"

The King faltered. "Razarkha Fel'thuz has truly returned. Your prisoner intends putting this returning exile to death, yes?"

Suddenly, Luna Riversong, the blonde member of Quira's troupe, spoke up. "Oh, he most certainly does. He's not doing it because of some Arkheran law she violated, more several tenets of mortal decency. For example, if a mortal shows another mortal hospitality, it's considered poor form for the guest to murder the host's father."

"The motive doesn't matter if the law is upheld," Landon said. "Your concern for your child and the urgency of the situation justifies immediate action. You are hereby permitted to release Weil of Zemelnya, and he is in turn granted clemency from any charges of vigilantism for upholding the law Rakh Fel'thuz should have."

Tei nodded. "Thank you, Your Majesty. Quira, may I have the Riversongs as backup? Now that the thread blade is gone, I believe Weil would benefit from their presence."

Quira nodded. "Of course. Go on, retrieve that Ilazari. I'll make sure Landon's words get put down in writing."

For a moment, Tei gazed at her employer and co-worker. They had frustrated and inspired her over the years, yet in the worst-case scenario, this was the last time she'd see them. She couldn't find the appropriate parting words.

"I'll be back once Razarkha's dead," she finally said, then beckoned the Riversongs to follow her to the interrogation cells.

It was a short walk from the palace; once past the gates they travelled down a twisting road which contained the barracks, towards a small building whose subterranean levels were deceptively large. The four descended past empty cells until they reached their target. Normally, Tei would have looked for the gaoler, but the King had given her permission to release the man; he never specified how.

The Ilazari was thin, his clothes ragged and stinking. "Are you here to ask question?"

Tei ignored him. "Riversongs, break the cell open."

The daemons spoke in unison. "Oh, how we love to break things!"

"*Without* breaking the prisoner."

Luna desynchronised from her so-called siblings. "I would never."

"Good," Tei said. "All right, do what you daemons do best."

With frightening speed, the Riversong sisters collapsed into three globs of black fluid that lunged at the bars of his cell, tearing through them like locusts tore through wheat fields. Throughout the ordeal, Weil curled up, whimpering and whispering in his mother tongue. Tei removed her usual illusory intimidation tool and approached as herself once it was over.

"Don't worry. You're not going to die. From this day forth, you're a free citizen of Arkhera with royal permission to travel to Moonstone and kill my sister."

The long-tailed Ilazari backed away. "This is trick, no? Wait, *sister?*"

Tei removed his arcane cuffs. "Yes. I'm Tei Fel'thuz, the forgotten Fel'thuz sibling. It's what happens when you're born deformed. What's your countly father to do, scream to the world that he has a broken daughter?"

"His first was broken too," Weil remarked.

"That's the spirit, keep that humour!" Tei babbled while the Riversongs reformed and spat out chunks of metal. "Firstly, you stink, we need to get you washed and into a change of clothes. I hope Rarakhi's left some behind; he's a little smaller than you but his clothes will do. Then it's to the train station before it closes for the night. By the Gods, by the Gods—"

Weil turned to Luna Riversong. "Is small Fel'thuz well?"

"No, I believe her son is missing."

"Razarkha has *nephew?*"

"Yes, and he's put himself in grave danger! The thread knife is missing, and I need your help finding Rarakhi, retrieving that knife, and putting an end to Razarkha!" Tei ranted. "Now let's get going before I breathe myself into a stupor."

"As little Fel'thuz says."

\* \* \*

Rakh and Erwyn invisibly ran through the halls of Castle Selenia, their footsteps muted. The wisdom had been gasping for as long as Rakh had cloaked him, and once they reached a suitably obscure corner, they sat down to get a grip on the situation.

"What happened up there?" Rakh asked. "I presume Plutyn not descending with you is a bad sign."

After another bout of hyperventilation, Erwyn finally found his words. "He didn't fall prisoner. We can be thankful for that."

"He was more loyal than I expected. He goaded her into killing him, correct?"

"She shot off his arm with lumomancy and from there it was as though he was possessed by the world's most tone-deaf jester. Whatever sanity Razarkha had before her exile is gone. She's more than undead, like Irikhos said, she's got some bizarre crystal in her abdomen."

"Did you notice anything unusual about it when she cast her magic?"

Erwyn stared at the floor. "It was— it glowed whenever her soulstealer did, and it appeared to be linked to her mental state."

Rakh nodded. "I know it may be hard to think about, but when Razarkha killed Plutyn, did it appear to be a case of arcane incontinence?"

"Most certainly," Erwyn answered.

"Then I have a plan," Rakh said, folding his legs and double-checking his words were silenced to ears beyond Erwyn's. "Please critique as I go if it seems infeasible."

Erwyn cracked a shaky smile. "That's my job."

"I believe that whatever this abdominal crystal is, it's linked to her soulstealer, and acts as the means for her to be her own necromancer," Rakh said. "As such, whenever she uses magic beyond her illusionism, she's not just burning through her captured souls, but her lifespan too. Would this be jumping to a conclusion?"

The wisdom rubbed his chin. "It's a worthy hypothesis. It's a shame the only way to test it would be to bait out her magic and hope it's true."

"At any rate, seeing as she blew right through our trap, it's fair to assume giving her more souls to consume is a bad call. I think we should signal to General Kareon that the garrison we hoped to surround the castle with should stay hidden."

Erwyn sighed. "All right. Let's check the pigeons if we can. If I can send a message explaining that Plutyn Khanas is dead to Tei, perhaps she can control how that information reaches Rarakhi and Plutera."

Rakh stood. "All right. Following that, your work in the castle is complete. I'll escort you through the Snowy Bank catacombs path and give General Kareon the signal."

"What will you do after that? Without the ambush, is Moonstone lost to Razarkha?" Erwyn asked, rising to match his count.

"No," Rakh said. "You heard her reaction to a simple note. I intend to haunt the castle and torment her until she has enough bouts of arcane incontinence to exhaust her soul supply."

Erwyn's voice dulled. "Rakh, we don't know how many souls she absorbed in Galdus. Who knows how many she absorbed on her way to Arkhera? We don't even know the rate at which her magic burns through these souls."

"It's a better plan than giving her even more, is it not?"

"It is," Erwyn admitted. "All right, let's get a pencil and paper, then grab a pigeon."

Together, they snuck back to Erwyn's spire, now that Razarkha was audibly yelling through the lower floors. Occasionally, the sound of something being blasted apart rumbled up the castle, and Rakh almost laughed at his sister's charge towards her own demise. His internal humour died as they reached Erwyn's study.

Lying with a crisp, blackened maw for a chest was Plutyn Khanas, his green eyes wide open. One of his forearms lay detached by his side and he lay in a puddle of his own vomit, yet his mouth was turned up in a manner he never allowed for in life. Rakh had never seen someone so happy to be dead. Erwyn swiftly retrieved writing materials without facing the dead minister, and practically pushed past Rakh to leave the study. The count closed Plutyn's eyes then followed his wisdom back down the spire. They descended through the castle, and Razarkha's incomprehensible screeching grew louder with every step.

Once Rakh neared the foyer, he was quick retreat around the corner, as several beings, humanoid and less humanoid, walked through the castle entrance. One was a high elven woman with Kag's eyes, Tor's hair, and her father's nose, another was a wyvern large enough to seat one and a half people, and the third was some dark elven-looking person who looked like he needed two baths and five times as many meals.

Yarawyn span on her feet, making the most of the floor's slipperiness. "Look at this, Moonrazer! *This* is a home worth staying in. No more sleeping out in the rain for you!"

The elf cuddled up to her wyvern's beak and stroked along its length while the beast made presumably contented warbles. The dark elven-looking man ejected daemonic tentacles that briefly made Rakh's magic falter, and from the kitchen, Razarkha's shrill voice echoed.

*"Stop projecting copies and show yourself!* You can't cast illusions forever," she claimed. "I've surpassed the need to sleep, but unless that pet necromancer I just snuffed out had a friend raise you, you're still mortal. You will lower your illusions eventually."

Yarawyn moved towards Razarkha's voice. "Fel'thuz? What are you shouting about? My work in the battlements was a success, and Naas'khar is in one piece. Don't tell me you somehow failed to kill the count—"

"*Shut up!*"

A blast followed this declaration, and a hole was formed in some distant wall. Yarawyn started to pace, and when Razarkha marched into the foyer, the wyvern rider shakily spoke.

"Don't worry, Razarkha, I'm sure we'll find him!"

His sister looked utterly dreadful. Her makeup had long since faded, revealing a sickly blue tone beneath, her hair dye had become lifeless and grey, her clothing was a set of disconnected tatters that barely covered her bruised, pale body, and even her fuchsia eyes had lost their lustre. True to Erwyn's assessment, her abdominal crystal glowed brightly enough from her rage that he wondered if she could feel the heat it plainly produced.

"He's using illusionism to hide, but he'll grow tired eventually," Razarkha snapped.

Yarawyn sidled behind her wyvern's wing, then edged out a question. "Did you see any signs of Tor and Iri—"

*"Who cares about them?"* Razarkha yelled. "I found Erwyn, he'd just sent a pigeon to Deathsport, along with some Khanas. I killed the Khanas, but Yagaska is somewhere in this castle, cloaked by my coward brother."

"How do you know Rakh's here at all?"

"He left notes that only he would write."

The bizarre tentacled dark elf looked side to side. "I could track him by scent if you like. Do you still have that note?"

Razarkha pointed to Naas'khar. "Brilliant idea, half-breed. I knew there was a reason I didn't kill you. Yarawyn, find where Erwyn's keeping the pigeons and have Moonrazer eat them. Naas'khar, follow me, I'll show you that accursed note."

Rakh froze; they would likely pass him in the process. If this ambiguously mortal being could track people by scent, he'd need a distraction. He dragged Erwyn across the foyer, past Yarawyn and her pet wyvern, just as Razarkha walked by his previous hiding spot. Erwyn didn't speak, but his expression begged for an explanation. Rakh pointed to the exit, and once Yarawyn left with her pet, he left the castle with his wisdom in tow.

"What are you doing?" Erwyn asked. "I thought we were to—"

"We can't risk attempting to save the pigeons. I have another use for the paper," Rakh claimed. "May I?"

Defeated, Erwyn handed the pencil and paper over, then Rakh leaned it against the side of the castle to scrawl another note. This time, it read *'You look terrible, Razarkha. I hope you enjoy ruling over an empty castle for the rest of your life.'* From there, he put it in his coat's inner pocket, moved through the courtyard, and threw it off by an abandoned greenhouse.

Erwyn nodded. "I see. You intend to throw that thing off the scent for a while?"

"Hopefully," he said. "Do you have any idea what he might be? I first thought he was a daemon, yet he seemed afflicted by his very being."

"I wouldn't want to conclude right away, but there's a possibility he's a daemonic hybrid. Razarkha *did* call him a half-breed, after all. They're exceedingly rare, especially beyond Arkhera."

"Whatever it is, if it has eyes, it can be fooled. Let's get you to Snowy Bank."

Erwyn took Rakh's hands. "Even with that thing tracking you, will you still return to the castle to continue your provocation strategy?"

"What else can I do? Stay in Snowy Bank with you, Tor, and Irikhos? Draw this daemonic being to you all and facilitate the death of Moonstone's future?"

"You— you don't need to head towards the castle to keep that thing away from us."

"I'm not leaving General Kareon permanently on standby. Somebody needs to keep an eye on Razarkha," Rakh said, and with that, he projected a red, flickering light above the city. "Once I leave you in Snowy Bank, promise you'll be the best wisdom Lady Torawyn can have. Until Rarakhi comes of age, she's likely to be down one advisor."

"You deserve to be part of Moonstone's future too," Erwyn protested.

"Deserving has nothing to do with this. Come, let's find Torawyn."

\* \* \*

Irikhos and Torawyn were a pair of hooded people amidst the sea that poured from the Moonstone catacombs into Snowy Bank. It lacked walls, and the relative lack of tall buildings rendered its ruling city visible over the horizon, standing behind the sparse pines beyond the village. The largest building in the village was the train station, which was already overrun by refugees who'd reached it long before Irikhos.

A thick layer of snow covered the ground, so sitting wasn't an option for those who'd fled Moonstone. While a cart full of long-keeping foods had been wheeled along with the people, there were far too many refugees for the village to sustain beyond a month. The sights from afar weren't encouraging; Irikhos and Torawyn had watched Yarawyn's wyvern burn the southern battlements. The view was occasionally confusing, as though the wyvern was hidden but its flames weren't, but the message was clear to the lowborn refugees. Some had already given up on waiting and took a train to anywhere else in the Kingdom. Others wept for their lost lives, bitterly claiming Rakh Fel'thuz had forced them into homelessness.

Irikhos looked to Torawyn, whose eyes had run out of tears. "It looks like Yarawyn got what she wanted."

"Rakh always intended to give her that, but it should be temporary," Tor mumbled. "We can't stay here, huddling strangers in tents forever. What if Yar wins *permanently?* When do we stop waiting?"

"I'm not sure," Irikhos admitted. "But when this is over, you're going to be lady, and hopefully you'll be willing to take me as a lord consort. It'll be our duty to tell the people when they should give up."

"Hope is a valuable resource, yet I've lived without it for so long. Yarawyn spent her life determined that she'd return to Arkhera, yet I settled for Elarond. I'm not sure I'm the lady Moonstone needs."

Irikhos glanced at Moonstone's distant battlements. "After a crisis like this, what lady do you think the people will need?"

"One who can assure them this strife was worthwhile. Someone that knows they'll rebuild stronger than before. If both Fel'thuz siblings die, with Rakh as the hero, then his ghost will overlook my entire ladyship. He'll be a martyr, and I'll be some foreigner who stepped in from Elarond like my wyvern-wielding sister before me."

"At least you have an idea of what you want to be," Irikhos said with a smile. "If Kag were in your situation, she'd just assume the people would accept her words and move on."

"I envy that blithe confidence," Torawyn said, then shot her gaze towards the train station. "Iri, did you see that?"

Irikhos checked where Tor looked, finding nothing but a train station guarded by tired orcish soldiers. "What am I supposed to be looking at?"

"I'm sure I saw a glimmer, something golden, travelling along at around hip height," Torawyn insisted, moving towards the station and pointing. "It's around here, I'm sure of it."

After swallowing of his scepticism, Irikhos squinted, yet no such glittering object could be seen. He did notice, however, two sets of recent footprints whose trail led nowhere.

"What in the world?"

"Did you see it too, Iri?" Tor asked.

"Not quite, but there's some orphaned footprints," Irikhos explained, walking along the trail. "Razarkha and Rakh are in Moonstone, while the bastard boy is somewhere else, at least from what I know. If they don't belong to illusionists, who do they belong to?"

Torawyn joined Irikhos in following the prints. "The bastard boy?"

"You know, Rarakhi Fel'thuz. Oh, wait, you never met him. Count Fel'thuz is quiet about who his mother is, but I met him when they visited Ashglass," Irikhos said, keeping his eyes on the tracks. "I didn't really speak to him, he seemed like a bit of a thug, but come to think of it, he's the only one they could belong to. Unless that third Fel'thuz sibling, Tau or something, headed to Snowy Bank—"

Irikhos's speech was halted when he bumped into a thick-furred orc, who puffed his chest and shoved him back.

"You blind, or just stupid?"

"My apologies," Irikhos stammered, feeling Torawyn bump into his back. "Did you see a black-haired spellbinder moving past…"

Irikhos trailed off as he noticed the crowd beyond him. If the mysterious set of tracks came from an illusionist, they'd made up for their blunder. There was no picking out which set of footprints were orphaned past the sea of men, and it appeared the illusionist knew this.

"…never mind," Irikhos finished.

"Just watch where you're going. You'd think with such a posh mouth you'd at least have manners," the orc snapped.

Irikhos lowered his head, then turned to Tor. "We've lost them."

Torawyn played with her hair. "So the only suspects are Tei Fel'thuz or this bastard?"

"Yes."

"The bastard is on his father's side, isn't he?"

Irikhos chuckled. "He looked ready to die whenever his father spoke, but yes, he's on his side. As for that third Fel'thuz, you probably know more about her than I do."

"All I remember is she started getting fat and tried to hide it with illusionism, something I envied her for. Then she vanished without a trace."

Irikhos looked back to Moonstone. "I hope I haven't let an enemy through."

"If it *is* Tei, I can't imagine she's on Razarkha's side. Razarkha bullied her for her height her entire life. Not to mention, her and Rakh were sometimes uncomfortably nice to one another. I say we let her through. She's probably a friend," Tor concluded.

"If you say," Irikhos said in a flat tone.

"Say, how old is that bastard?"

Irikhos frowned. "I think he's around thirteen. Why?"

Torawyn rubbed her chin. "No reason. I'm hungry, let's get some pickled vegetables."

Though it was hard to dismiss the idea that he'd let an anonymous Fel'thuz saboteur get away, Irikhos was glad Tor was eager to eat. He took her hand and approached the food wagon.

# Trails

"Well? What can you trace? I hope you're not going to treat this like another one of your mountain beasts, because my brother is an *illusionist,*" Razarkha ranted while her half-daemonic lackey sniffed Rakh's letter.

Naas'khar's tentacles twisted along with his expression. "There's an overpowering scent of ink, but there's definitely sweat beneath it. I think I can trace— ah, yes, that way."

Though his arms remained limp, his tentacles jabbed in the direction of the nearest staircase, an overly smooth, grey case heading downwards. Razarkha folded her arms.

"Do you think he followed me down to the foyer?"

"Possibly," Naas'khar said, dragging himself along what appeared to be the trail.

Between the slippery floors, his lack of functional arms, and the bony nature of his legs, the nephil looked like he'd collapse at any moment. Razarkha could hardly pity him; without a friendly necromancer on hand, her physical decay was inevitable, even if she consumed all the souls in the world. As Naas'khar led her to the ground floor, the Sovereign started wittering.

*"What's wrong, Razarkha? You seem perturbed."*

"Rakh's *missing,* that's what's wrong. Every passing day reminds me this time is borrowed, and if I'm wasting it searching Castle Selenia for my brother, what's the point?"

*"Indeed, evading death is futile. Admittedly, if I let you die in Ante Tertia, your soul would likely never reach the Underworld. It'd linger in the Soulstealer of Craving for eternity. Who would claim it in a place as unpopulated as Sula's dead megalopolis? The Prospector? I'm glad you were as short-sighted as I hoped you'd be."*

"So you tricked me into accepting this form of undeath? You made it appear as though you were making a concession!"

*"Are you honestly shocked that I, ruler of the Underworld and curator of sin, free will, and selfishness deceived you?"*

Razarkha squeezed her soulstealer as her abdomen sizzled. Naas'khar cocked his head and slipped his tentacles back into his body, evening out his gait.

"What language were you speaking? Some new dark tongue?"

"It doesn't matter," Razarkha muttered. "Where are we—"

Naas'khar had led her back to the foyer, where Yarawyn was nestled against her sleeping wyvern. Upon seeing Razarkha, the elf stood, startling the beast awake.

"Ah, Countess Razarkha, you'll be pleased to know all pigeons have been eaten. There'll be no surreptitious communication from—"

"Did you spot any signs of an illusionist moving past you?" Razarkha quizzed.

Yarawyn's tone lowered. "Signs? What signs do you expect me to notice? Isn't the whole point of illusionism that it's unseen?"

"Oh, you're *useless!* Naas'khar, where does the trail lead from here?"

The nephil wrinkled his nose, ejected his tentacles, then leaned towards the castle exit, staggering where his body's weight took him. Razarkha waited for the daemonic bodyguard to leave the building, then shot Yarawyn a sharp glance.

"The next time you question my expectations is the last time you'll question anything. Am I clear?"

The high elf shuddered. "I'm sorry."

"I fully intend to let you enjoy your ladyship long after I'm gone," Razarkha claimed. "Don't interrupt my plans by being insufferable."

Yarawyn averted her eyes. "You think I'm insufferable?"

"Everybody does," Razarkha spat, and with that, she rushed towards the courtyard.

Snowfall had partially covered them, but Razarkha could still see two sets of footprints, along with the dragging tracks left by her half-mortal henchman. Eventually, the nephil stopped by a greenhouse, picking up a familiar black-and-purple item of clothing. Seeing the feathers at the shoulders was enough to force her illusionism to falsely fill it.

Razarkha charged towards Naas'khar and snatched it from his tentacles. "You tracked down a *coat,* imbecile."

"There's also a trace of ink," Naas'khar added.

"I don't think you understand the problem," Razarkha began. "I know you haven't met Rakh before, but you're aware siblings tend to be similar to one another, yes?"

The half-daemon raised an eyebrow. "What are you trying to say?"

"Well, it's just that I'm mostly made of flesh and blood, wouldn't you agree?"

*"Cold* flesh, but yes, you're correct."

"Then why are you acting *as though my brother is a coat?"* Razarkha screamed, her soulstealer unleashing a blast that set a nearby hedge on fire.

"I never said I was satisfied with the search," Naas'khar replied. "There's many bodily aromas on this, so I can track him down. He doesn't seem to have doubled back. He's somewhere beyond this building."

Razarkha stared past the courtyard's gates, into the abandoned city of Moonstone. Flags upon the battlements were still burning, but the buildings were mostly unmolested. A citywide search would be inefficient and leave the castle unoccupied for longer than she preferred. She turned back to Castle Selenia.

"I task you with finding Rakh, wherever he may be. Once you do, incapacitate him, but make sure he's alive. If you eat him, you'll wish you could die like a regular mortal."

Naas'khar's eyelids slid over his wide-pupiled eyes. "I already wish for that."

"I'll find another way to punish you," Razarkha promised. "Come with me. You have an advantage over my brother, but he's not to be underestimated. I wouldn't want Yarawyn blaming me for denying you a farewell, so please, do what you must before you leave."

Together, the pair returned to the castle, letting the sparse snowfall fill the air in lieu of speech. The daemonic hybrid stretched a tentacle, then attempted to cut through the silence.

"Your courtesy is appreciated—"

"Don't pretend you're civilised like Yarawyn and I. Daemons are monstrous at worst and tone-deaf fools at best," Razarkha snapped. "You don't need to thank me, just shut up and be happy I didn't send you without an opportunity to bid farewell."

Naas'khar paused. "What makes a person civilised? If it's living with lots of people, it appears Alaterra is more civilised than Moonstone. Did all the mortals flee?"

Razarkha hacked out another glob of blackened blood. "No, we Moonstone folk like to construct empty terraces and estates for their own sake."

"Oh. That must be an Arkheran tradition. I'm sure Yarawyn will explain things to me in a way that makes sense."

There was no insulting this uplifted animal. Razarkha didn't deign to respond to the moronic half-breed, and once they'd returned to Castle Selenia's foyer, she was gratefully separated from him. Naas'khar rushed to Yarawyn and took her into his many tentacles, and together, they whispered something to each other.

The small, secret remarks caused Razarkha's illusionism to act out. Wavering over Yarawyn was Praetor Erre, tall and proud, with a beautifully intact stomach behind a full, elaborate outfit. In Naas'khar's place was Weil, chubby-faced and foolish, his long tail extending beyond his cloak. Something oozed from Razarkha's eyes, and just as she made to break up their traitorous conspiracies, she broke into the longest coughing fit of her life.

Her telekinesis lifted trinkets at random, gore leapt from her mouth in flecks, and her eyes refused to stop leaking. Though her vision was blurred, her illusory projections were unnervingly clear. Crouching by her was an immaterial Rakh, staring dispassionately at his corporeal sister. A distorted echo aided by her recollection slipped from his mouth.

*"I know you're angry, but I'm grieving too. I'm not going to waste time listening to your poison."*

"Don't leave me," Razarkha begged, clutching the crystal that had long replaced her womb. "Please don't leave me."

The vision stopped, and looming over her was Yarawyn Selenia, offering a hand.

"Are you all right, Fel'thuz?"

Razarkha slapped her hand away and struggled to her feet. Naas'khar was nowhere to be seen. She shook her head, then turned to climb the stairs.

"I'm going to see what other records Erwyn has kept. Perhaps I can find out more about my bastard nephew," she mumbled in a poor approximation of a neutral tone.

\* \* \*

Arkheran trains were much like their Ilazari equivalents; steam chugged from the engine at the front, while the carriages clattered at the back. Weil was sat at a table, across from a spellbinder half his height and between a gaggle of friendly daemons. The scenery beyond his carriage had shifted from temperate to grey-skied and miserable in a matter of hours. According to the forgotten Fel'thuz, he was an Arkheran citizen. There was nothing left for him in Zemelnya, and knowing that Anya Kasparov ruled the city, it was best to devote himself to learning fluent Common, lest he remain a jobless Ilazari-Arkheran forever.

"I hear train announcement say this is 'Raining Bow Fort' line. Is this ultimate destination?" Weil asked, adjusting his tight, somewhat itchy woollen coat.

Tei nodded. "Yes. The Rainbow Fort is the northernmost city in Arkhera, deep within the Frostbitten Forest. Normally, Moonstone would be a stop along the way, but it seems Rakh has done a good enough job that the train operators know to pass it by. Instead, we're going to stop at the nearby village of Snowy Bank, then walk the rest of the way."

"How long shall walk take?"

Tei pondered. "I'm not sure. Intelligence suggests the Moonstone catacombs extend far beyond the city walls and are often used as smuggling routes. If there's catacombs entrance in Snowy Bank, it may take less than a day. Otherwise, we'll need to brave the forests."

The Riversong sister with blue, tentacular hair, who Luna called Meredith, spoke up. "No, no, absolutely not. You are not taking us to those catacombs! All these northern cities are infested with Yukishiman knotweed hosts, but beneath Moonstone a great tragedy occurred."

"It's true," the brown-haired, husky voiced Riversong named Lyra muttered. "A centuries-long experience was terminated by a foolhardy mortal wielding the knotweed."

Luna put her hand on Weil's face. "I consider it a blessing from the Rakh'vash itself that Weil lost his own knotweed weapon. We wouldn't follow him if he still possessed it."

Across the table, Tei's face grew peculiarly still. There were minor distortions around her eyes, and so Weil whispered to the daemons in Chaostongue.

*"You have upset Tei Fel'thuz."*

*"Really? How so?"* Luna asked.

*"The blade is abominable, but its disappearance was linked to her son going missing. By expressing joy at the knife's loss, you're implying that you're glad her son ran away."*

Without a trace of subtlety, Luna's expression morphed into gratuitous contrition. "My apologies, Tei Fel'thuz. It was not my intent to celebrate your son's disappearance."

"I know you daemons aren't equipped for mortal conversation," Tei said. "Don't worry yourself with such nuance."

"Ah, thank you for forgiving us!" the Riversongs said in unison.

Weil wondered how daemons who'd spoken the Common Tongue far longer than he could miss Tei's cues. It occurred to him that perhaps Tei shared more with her sister than her looks suggested, and that his reading of her was just an echo of his days reading Razarkha.

"If the Riversongs refuse to walk through Snowy Bank's catacombs, catching up to Rarakhi will depend on your portal magic," Tei said. "I'll admit, the thought of travelling through the Chaotic Realm terrifies me."

"Razarkha is dangerous woman," Weil brought up. "She turns region into warfare. Little Fel'thuz is not equipped. Stay in Snowing Bank."

Tei narrowed her eyes. "Spellbinders aren't known for their physical strength. Magic is what counts, and unless you know something I don't, magic doesn't care about how tall its caster is. I'm a smaller target if anything."

"If little Fel'thuz says."

"Please call me by my name," Tei commanded.

"If Tei Fel'thuz says."

A smile reached the youngest Fel'thuz's eyes. "I can see why Razarkha got along with you. You're quite the submissive fellow. Razarkha wanted to bend Rakh to her will from their wedding day, but my brother was never the sort to back down from a challenge."

Weil shifted in place, causing Luna Riversong to reshape herself as though a living cushion. "Razarkha tell me Rakh is great evil man. He mocked her for dead baby birth."

"I don't know the full story regarding Razander's birth," Tei said. "Razarkha told me Rakh abandoned her, Rakh claims she was spouting nonsense about killing Wisdom Waldon. Razarkha may be mad, but I think that the truth is somewhere between their accounts."

"Who is Wiss Dumb Waldon?"

"The term 'wisdom' refers to a noble's scholarly assistant, responsible for handling letters, academic matters and the like," Tei explained. "An expert opinion to consult. Waldon was Moonstone's wisdom before he fell out of his spire."

Weil's chest tightened. "Razarkha favoured dropping people from high place."

Tei nodded. "Rakh and I both suspect her involvement in Waldon's death. While Razarkha's telling no doubt contains truths Rakh would hide, she's ultimately a biased source. She would—"

The train came to a stop, and an orcish announcer blew a whistle while striding through the carriage. "Get off here for Snowy Bank! I repeat, Snowy Bank's the current stop!"

Tei was quick to stand, scurrying to the carriage doors, while Weil untangled himself from the Riversongs' comforting touch. Once he and his immortal compatriots joined the little Fel'thuz within the oversized shack Snowy

Bank apparently called a train station, the Royal Looking Glass clapped her hands.

"All right. Let's head north. Hopefully Rarakhi isn't too far ahead," Tei said, before her voice faltered. "Rakh trusted me to keep him safe. I'm a terrible mother, aren't I?"

"Answering impossible question does not bring child to us," Weil said, following the diminutive illusionist towards the station's doors.

Tei laughed weakly. "I imagine Razarkha didn't like it when you spoke candidly."

"Razarkha was great lover of truth, but only her own."

"It's a shame," Tei remarked as she handed her tickets to a checker. "It seems like you truly befriended her. I'm sorry she rewarded your kindness with murder."

Weil shook his head. "I am no innocent. I kill countless alongside her. I only anger over my father. I am selfish."

"As are all of us," Tei concluded as they stepped into the crowded streets of Snowy Bank. "I won't condone the atrocities you helped Razarkha perform, but here, now, you're putting an end to it."

"I suppose," Weil said, glancing at the various tents and shivering people.

While they weren't as varied as Deathsport's masses, the sheer diversity of Arkhera still took Weil by surprise. Tailless folks with thick body hair and tusks loomed alongside short, bulky humans, pointy-eared, youthful elves, and short, monkey-like goblins. The village didn't appear capable of sustaining the crowds, a fact Luna Riversong was delighted to notice.

"Imagine how frustrated these mortals are!" she said. "Crowding causes tension, it's why Deathsport is so wonderful. Much like a packed, high-temperature body, this chaotic system is capable of great change if left unchecked.

Mortals, like matter, when faced with impossible maintenance, eventually embrace change."

Weil briefly considered what linguistic barriers needed to be vaulted to understand the daemon's chatter, only for Tei's expression to confirm that she was equally confusing to people who spoke Common. He mused over a possible remark, only for Tei to rush ahead. The Riversongs squealed with unified glee, turning to Weil.

"It appears even our overly controlled Royal Looking Glass can prove unpredictable," Luna remarked. "See, Meredith, this is why killing mortals is lowbrow; yes, you can invoke terror in other mortals, but they're much more interesting when left to their devices."

Meredith frowned. "I still think we should hunt a little more often. A fourth member of the band would be helpful."

Luna eyed Weil, then stroked along his neck, causing him to pull away.

"What are you doing?" he asked.

"Evaluating your vocal cords. It appears you sing regularly. Quite interesting. Come, let's see what Tei Fel'thuz has spotted."

When the chaos-speaker and his chaos-invokers caught up to Tei, she'd stopped in front of a pair of elves. One of them had dark skin, golden eyes, and tied-back ashen hair. The other was a woman that lacked the usual elven rounded face, instead reminding Weil of Razarkha. She was quietly trembling in the cold while Tei and the dark elf chatted with one another.

"Look, I'm as annoyed with Rakh Fel'thuz as the next man, but this situation is almost unavoidable," the dark elf claimed. "At least they aren't still in Moonstone."

"It's good to know civilians are evacuated, but does Rakh honestly think this will work? Doesn't he know how slow Landon is to deploy royal troops? It could take *months* for Moonstone to be liberated without Weil!" Tei ranted. "Oh, it doesn't matter. Have you seen an illusionist at all?"

"An illusionist?" the dark elf echoed. "Come to think of it, there *was* something suspicious. A glint and some orphaned footprints."

Tei's already frenzied tone grew feverish. "Tell me everything you know about it! Weil, don't just stand there, find whatever soup kitchen is here and get us some food while I gather information."

Weil almost let himself laugh. Razarkha's bossiness was once something he'd loved; seeing it in a small, harmless container was enough to make him misty-eyed.

"As you wish, Tei Fel'thuz."

The high elven woman spoke. "Who is that fellow, Tei? I know who those daemons are, they haven't changed since I was little, but that spellbinder seems foreign."

"He's the man who'll kill Razarkha, but for now, he's a waiter. Go on, get enough for four," Tei said, pointing into the crowd at large.

Weil shrugged, gave the Riversongs a nod, and left Tei to shout at the elves. While there wasn't a whiff of hot food, pushing through the most crowded parts of the village led him to a wagon full of mostly depleted supplies of food. He took eight hardtack crackers and a jar of offal paste, then turned around only to bump into thin air.

"An illusionist!" Weil called towards where he hoped Tei still was. "It is Kin-keeper— er, Rarakhi!"

The mage revealed himself, proving much taller than any thirteen-year-old spellbinder. He was somehow braving the cold without a coat, and beside him was a high elven man in a red-and-blue coat. The illusionist's eyes were red, but otherwise, he was feature-for-feature copy of Razarkha, down to his dyed hair and high cheekbones. The two spellbinders stared at each other, until the man's expression twisted into a breed of murderousness he'd seen on Razarkha's face countless times. He took Weil by the collar and held him up with surprising physical strength given he was using his left hand.

*"Who are you? Why are you wearing Rarakhi's coat?"* he demanded.

"I am foreign friend of Tei's, she is—"

"What kind of person steals a friend's son's clothes? What have you done with him?"

Weil whispered in Chaostongue, opening a portal beneath the pair, then re-entered the mortal realm with their orientations rotated. The result was the man landed face-up with Weil on top of him. Weil kneed his groin and broke free, then noticed the crowd had parted over the disturbance. The high elven man was panicking, but Weil had no quarrel with him. He picked up his food, then spotted Tei charging towards him with the elves and daemons in tow.

*"What are you doing?* I sent you to retrieve food, and now you're starting fights? I trusted you to— Rakh?"

The high elven fellow in the coat helped the illusionist up, before turning to Tei. "What are you doing here? Why aren't you looking after Rarakhi?"

The illusionist man brushed some snow off his shirt. "Furthermore, how do you know this man? He's stolen Rara's clothes, it's plain as day!"

"I let him borrow them myself!" Tei shouted. "Don't tell me you started this fight."

The spellbinder tugged on his collar. "I— I misjudged him, that's all. I didn't know how he'd got a hold of that coat."

The dark elf from before rubbed his head. "Why isn't Rakh in Castle Selenia? Who, exactly, is running the castle, if not you two?"

Rakh swallowed. "It's fallen to Razarkha, but don't worry, I have every intention of heading back."

Weil looked to him. "I shall accompany you! You are Razarkha's brother, yes? Then we are both here to end her. I am her former friend, Weil of Zemelnya. I showed her hospitality, then she—"

"That's good, I need all the help I can get," Rakh said. "Erwyn is to stay here; when I last saw her, Razarkha intended to kill the carrier pigeons, so his role in the castle is over."

Erwyn frowned. "Tei, you never answered my question. Yes, this Ilazari is our ally, but why have you and the Riversongs travelled north?"

Tei folded her arms and looked away from Rakh. "I'm sorry. I— I lost our son."

*"You did what?"* Rakh exploded.

"I was working, then I came home to find their orcish bodyguards dead— well, more dead— anyway, it was as though Plutyn Khanas had died, and Plutera must have convinced Rarakhi to head to Moonstone, because neither were in the house."

Rakh froze, as did the dark elven man. The high elven woman attempted to interject.

"I'm sure I saw an illusionist head out from this village's train station, but I couldn't track him down. We thought that it was perhaps—"

Rakh stopped listening and charged away from the situation. Weil reached out, but he couldn't find the correct Common words in time. The dark elf bit his lips, then spoke.

"If he's headed the same way Plutyn led us, he's likely going into the catacombs."

Weil glanced at the Riversongs. "But we do not travel that way. There are dangers to daemons. He is headed to Moonstone, yes?"

Tei nodded and pointed to a grey settlement covering the grey sky. "Yes. Go ahead of us, Weil, there's no time. See that city? That's Moonstone. Take yourself and the Riversongs there by any means necessary, deal with Razarkha, and most importantly, *save my son's life."*

Weil swallowed. "You trust me to do this?"

"I do. Go on, don't let yourself be slowed down by me."

With a nod, Weil opened a portal, then waved the Riversongs over. "This way."

He dived into the portal, and once the Riversongs joined him, he transported them a small distance beyond the crowds in Snowy Bank. In an unfamiliar land, his teleportation would be about as effective as running, but given that was all Rakh was doing, there was every hope he'd reunite with the bane of Razarkha's existence on the other side of Moonstone's walls.

# Murmurings

Moonstone's streets weren't the same without the bustling crowds Rarakhi would normally evade. He still needed to cloak, however; soaring through the dim sky was a great purple-and-red lizard with the beak and scutes of a bird. Upon it was an elf, though he couldn't make out much beyond that. He and Plutera hadn't spotted any of the Boss's forces manning the southern battlements, and the city walls had chunks missing, as though some great hand had gouged them out. It appeared that neither the wyvern nor its rider had spotted them through their long walk, and after hours, Plutyn Khanas's estate was finally in sight.

"Father kept his fallen kin in a mausoleum behind the manor," Plutera mumbled. "I hope we can kill your aunt quickly enough that we can bring father back too."

Rarakhi checked his thread blade. "Don't worry, Petal. She won't see me coming."

"Your father was able to see through your illusionism and remove it," Plutera pointed out. "Don't underestimate her. I want to see her dead but remember that we're betrothed. If you don't return, I'm following you to the grave."

Rarakhi's throat stung. "Don't say that. You could move on, marry some handsome necromancer or something. If I'm going to die, I want tp die in your place, not drag you down with me."

"Would you find another girl if I died?" Plutera asked.

"I'd probably want to die too," he admitted.

"Then we're in agreement. Kill your aunt, then come back safely."

Rarakhi nodded, then continued his escort in silence. Throughout the estate, formerly undead gardeners lay face-down, sometimes amidst the flower beds they once tended.

One sat motionless by a lilac bush, his pruning shears dropped and his stench fittingly masked. Every fallen zombie Plutera passed twisted her expression until she no longer resembled the gentle healer Rarakhi fell for. By the time she reached the Boss's manor, her movements were stiff.

She pounded at the door and turned to Rarakhi. "Reveal us."

He did as commanded, and after a short wait, a throaty voice spoke from the other side.

"You with that wyvern riding bitch or Countess Cuntface?"

Plutera spoke softly. "It's me, Varyx. I have reason to believe my father's— he's—"

"Little Lady Plutera?" the voice spluttered, and the door opened, revealing a dark elf with laughter lines around his crimson eyes. "What in the world are you doing here? Weren't you s'posed to be evacuated?"

"We were, but when Bloodmetal and Notongue's revenancy faded, I knew that my father was— was gone," Plutera said, her verdant eyes dashing about. "Surely you noticed the same from his gardeners."

"Come in, you two," Varyx said, moving to the side. "It's worse than just the Boss dying. All the gunners across the battlements are dead or deserted. A wyvern flew up, then vanished. From there, a stream of fire took the entire perimeter of the city. After that, the count sent a signal for us and that bloody high elven general."

The pair entered without a word. Once the door was locked, Plutera spoke again.

"What did the signal mean?"

"It said not to retake the castle. Surviving soldiers only reported three invaders; the wyvern rider, Countess Cuntface herself, and some tentacled person. Seems like the Beast of the Catacombs ain't the last daemon Moonstone's seeing," the dark elf reported, before putting a hand on Plutera's shoulder. "I'm sorry you've lost 'im, lass."

Plutera's silhouette shrank. "It would happen eventually. I didn't expect to take over the family business so soon, nor deal with his loss, but this is the duty of every old system ruler. Profiting from your loved ones' death is natural."

"It don't make it hurt any less," Varyx said. "My squad ain't had a finer boss than your father. More'n you will miss him."

"Thank you," Plutera said, then turned to Rarakhi. "Put your knife away."

Rarakhi hesitated, then obeyed. Before he could prepare, his love ambushed him with a kiss deeper than any he'd experienced before. His hands hovered at her sides, then found their places around the base of her tail. Once it was over, he rested his forehead against hers.

"It's almost time for me to find my aunt," he whispered.

"It is," Plutera said, giving him one more peck on the lips before slipping out of his grip. "Varyx, gather men who want to honour my father's memory, and ask them if they know of any opportunists within our ranks. Once all is ascertained, a purge is forthcoming."

Varyx swallowed. "At once, Little Lady."

"That's Lady Plutera to you," she affirmed. "When you're done, find me in my office. I assure you father left it to me in his will."

The dark elf bowed. "I'm sure he did, m'lady. See you soon."

Once Varyx left, Plutera kissed Rarakhi another dozen times, stroked his hair, and snared him with her eyes. Despite the murder he was about to commit and the grief swimming in Petal's stare, Rarakhi couldn't help but smile.

"I'll always love you," he finally said.

"You'll have plenty of time to tell me that once this is over," Plutera promised. "Once your aunt is dealt with, find my father's body. Bring him to his rightful resting place."

"Of course. I know I'm not supposed to do anything stupid, but just in case something bad happens, should we do something to remember each other by?"

Plutera squeezed her betrothed with all her might. "After Ashglass, I was starting to worry you'd lost interest."

"I didn't know if you wanted anything like that after— well, you know."

"I've needed something happy since getting on that train," Plutera said, releasing Rarakhi's body and taking his hand. "Let's do this, then."

"Yeah. Let's do this."

\* \* \*

Razarkha had long since thrown Plutyn Khanas out of the study window, and was digging through Erwyn's desk, pulling out every note on the bastard child Rakh had hidden from her. The boy had been kept in some pretentiously named orphanage, and the mother, of all people, was Tei. Behind her, apparitions of her siblings lay together nude, kissing and exchanging nothings she'd not once received from her brother-husband.

There was no record on where he'd been sent, however. There was a similar lack of information on where Tei had hidden herself, but both would face their reckoning once Rakh was dealt with. She turned, pointed her soulstealer at the two illusory lovers, and made shallow, laboured breaths.

"Why, Rakh? I knew you had a taste for short, fat women with lacking tails, but I didn't think you'd started with Tei. What did she have that I didn't? Well?"

*"What information do you hope to receive?"* the false Rakh asked, conjuring his own clothes while Tei collapsed into dust. *"You know this is all in your head."*

"I don't care. The real you would never explain himself. He'd just mock me for being unattractive or tell me that I shouldn't be angry that every child we had died," Razarkha replied, keeping her soulstealer pointed. "How is it fair that the deformed, twisted, irrelevant child got a healthy womb? I was *perfect!* I was beautiful, ambitious, tall, what more could you desire?"

*"An intact mind,"* Rakh's shadow answered.

Razarkha shot a beam through the fake's chest, yet he remained standing, the burning hole in his chest not so much as slowing his response.

*"See? All you know how to do is kill. Even when you helped the people of Nortez, you only did so by killing the Sons of Sula,"* Rakh claimed. *"You brought nothing but death to Weil, and your insurrectionists. It was a simple continuation of the pattern that started with every child that rotted within you."*

"Stop it," Razarkha choked out, her eyes oozing once more. "Stop talking."

*"I'm a figment of your imagination,"* the Rakh reminded her. *"The only way I stop talking is if you make me. Perhaps you needed to hear this."*

"I don't need to hear these lies," Razarkha insisted.

*"Then make me disappear."*

Razarkha shot ray after ray through her illusory brother until he was naught but ash and bones. She limped to the grey pile in front of her, stepped on it, and thankfully it let her foot through. Beyond the study doorway was the spot where her beams hit the walls; the ilmenite wasn't shattered, but red from the heat. Her body slackened against her volition, and on her way out of the study, she almost collapsed down the stairs. The souls that powered her were depleting with every wasted beam, yet she couldn't stop unleashing them.

"This isn't how it should be," she mumbled as she descended the spire and strode through Castle Selenia's halls. "I did everything right, mother. I made our life a competition. I made him insecure in his standing. Why did he look to *Tei?* She's an *imp!*"

Terreza Fel'thuz walked beside her in a bedgown soaked from the waist down. *"Tei had an edge. She was a killer from birth. She was always stronger than you. You couldn't successfully hurt a toddler, and you cowered in the shadow of my worthless husband."*

"Father hated me."

*"Rani hated your weakness."*

"If he hated weakness, why did he love Rakh and Tei? Why was *I* the failure?"

*"You've always known, Razarkha."*

Terreza vanished, leaving her corporeal daughter to speak to the air. "I was even weaker than Rakh. But not anymore. This time, he'll fall by my hand. My perseverance outperforms any innate skill my worthless siblings have."

A glimmer in Razarkha's peripheral vision disrupted her soliloquy, causing her to swivel on her feet and make a lumomantic incantation. Before her spellwork came into effect, however, her balance forsook her, and she fell onto the floor face-first while a beam shot into the ceiling, causing a brick to thud upon her crystalline leg.

She screamed, scrambled towards her soulstealer even as the lower nub of her false leg shattered, and instinctively swept the space in front of her. Her arm hit what were likely two legs, and a slamming sound was quick to follow. Razarkha grinned and lifted herself with telekinesis, then pointed her soulstealer downwards. As she loomed over the cloaked illusionist, she noticed a golden, shimmering knife, which swiftly disappeared.

"Why not show yourself, Rakh? If I hear you move, I'll shoot your face off. Don't think I'll show you mercy just because we're kin—"

Chest pain assaulted Razarkha from outside for once, disrupting her telekinesis and knocking her soulstealer out of her hand. Something that had spent days lodged in her trachea came loose, causing a coughing fit followed by feverish retrieval of her artefact, yet there was no wound, only aching. When her vision finally cleared amidst the tears and hacking, she couldn't find a trace of Rakh, his illusionism, nor the peculiar knife he'd dropped.

Telekinetically floating through the halls, she called to her invisible aggressor. "What's the matter, Rakh? Did you realise that you'd rushed in prematurely? It's unlike you to let your steps be heard. It seems even you can let your excitement get the best of you. Come out, dear brother. You were eager to fight moments ago. Why not try again? I'll give you a free hit."

There was no response. Razarkha increased her speed through the halls until her abdomen abruptly cooled, deactivating her spellwork and forcing her to limp on her ruined crystalline leg. After hobbling down Castle Selenia's many floors, she noticed that Yarawyn and her pet had returned to the foyer. While the idiotic beast had snow in her hair, the wyvern was slick with its melted remains.

"Good news, Countess Razarkha. There are no new threats since I last checked. If there are any soldiers remaining, they're too afraid to leave shelter."

Razarkha gritted her teeth, then lifted Yarawyn for but a moment before her magic failed again.

"That's brilliant, Yarawyn, no new threats, only *an old one your idiot daemonspawn failed to track down!*"

The high elf backed towards her wyvern, who fanned his neck scutes. "What are you talking about *now?*"

"*Rakh, Rakh,* it's always *Rakh!*" Razarkha screamed. "He's not doubled back, that's what Naas'khar told me, yet there's an illusionist here, equipped with some strange knife, skulking through the castle waiting to assassinate me. *How did Naas'khar let him through?"*

"I don't know, why are you asking? Some invisible snake with a knife is nothing compared to your abilities anyway. You've thrown me off Moonrazer more times than I can count and that lumomancy trick you're so fond of can kill anyone. Just calm down and—"

*"Calm down?* You're telling me to calm down, when you do nothing but obsess over some dark elven imbecile who only loved you for your body!" Razarkha screeched, a thousand raucously laughing Rakhs populating the foyer. "There's a dangerous illusionist in this castle. You can't sleep here. I'll search the halls, you check beyond the walls for liberation efforts. Check the south for royals and the north for Foenaxases and Gemfires."

Yarawyn sighed. "I've just got back from patrolling."

"And you only mentioned what's going on within these walls. Do a more thorough search and sleep away from my mad brother."

The elf slowly mounted her wyvern, then pointed towards the castle exit. "All right, let's go look for food, Moonrazer, there's a good boy."

Moonrazer made a few croaks and rattles, but obeyed his mistress nonetheless. Once alone with the jeering crowd of Rakhs, Razarkha roared and flailed her arms at every illusory copy in punching distance until she was on the floor, surrounded by the smoky remnants of vanquished mirages.

"I'll find you," she promised. "I'll find you and kill you in front of everyone you love. Tei, your bastard, Erwyn. They'll all watch as you bleed out. You thought that you could bully me to your heart's content, but I *grew,* Rakh. I'll show everyone how much I've grown."

A bizarrely accented Isleborn-speaking voice echoed in the back of her ringing ears. *"To summarise, you haven't grown at all."*

\* \* \*

A waning moon illuminated Weil's journey through the Forests of Winter, and though he'd begun his journey from Snowy Bank with purpose, his body proved susceptible to mortal needs. The Riversongs walked beside him without a hint of fatigue, practically dancing with their steps. Weil, meanwhile, battled to keep his eyes open until he tripped over a gnarled, frost-covered tree root.

His body was certainly capable of motion, as he'd successfully rolled onto his back, but the prospect of standing killed itself the moment it travelled beyond his brain. The two younger Riversongs kept moving, but Luna crouched by her pet mortal, stroking his hair while she spoke an oddly gentle rendition of Chaostongue.

*"Are you struggling to move in the dark? It is odd how humanoids tend to function as though they are trees. We have consumed enough of them to know they don't have means to store the sun's energy, yet almost all become still at night. Sleeping mortals are adorable."*

Weil's mouth moved slowly and imprecisely. *"There is snow beneath my head. This is no place to sleep, yet my body wishes to sleep. Please can you carry me?"*

*"Your chaos-speech makes you innately convincing, but I'll admit I've wanted to carry you for a while. In a non-predatory way,"* Luna claimed.

*"Then please do so. In a non-predatory way."*

Soon enough, Weil was cradled in the arms of the friendliest daemon he'd ever met. He expected her grip to be indistinguishable from any of his summoned tentacles, but it seemed Luna Riversong took her simulated form seriously;

it felt like true bones existed within her limbs. Weil glanced at the moon, then its reflection in Luna's eyes.

"*What do you think of the moon?*"

"What do you mean? Are you asking if I attribute importance to it?"

Weil reorganised his shuffled-together thoughts before he replied. "*I have heard that in Arkhera, tribal peoples see the moon as a god, while others see it as an afterlife. In Ilazar, the moon is simply a source of redstone. See the red veins? Rocks from those veins come to our world when the moon bleeds. There is revelry every full moon in Ilazar. It usually results in at least one death, so I never partook.*"

Luna laughed. "*I find it amusing how mortal minds connect their experiences with stories. The veins of the moon are indeed redstone, but several cosmic rocks contain arcane ores. The moon is not unique. It is, however, the only rock beholden to our own little rock, and for that, we must be grateful.*"

"Beholden? How can rocks be beholden to anything?"

The daemon's expression hardened for a moment. "*The Rakh'norv in its infinite idiocy believes that it is an expression of the innate order the cosmos has, but the Rakh'vash knows the truth of it. Cosmic masses ensnare cosmic masses due to mindless attraction.*"

"*You speak of our world as though it is a fellow cosmic mass,*" Weil remarked.

"*Why wouldn't it be?*" Luna asked.

Weil slumped his weight a little. "*Before you, the only chaotic force who bothered to communicate with me was the Rakh'vash itself, and they considered me unworthy of polite discourse. I could learn a lot from you.*"

"*And I hope you shall. I've decided to adopt you.*"

"Did you ever consider I may refuse?"

Luna gave him a glassy-eyed smile. "*Not once.*"

*"You have much to learn from me too, it appears,"* Weil said with a weak laugh.

He took a half-hearted glance at the two Riversong sisters ahead and yawned. Just as slumber snaked over to consume him, a distant screech woke him up. Barely illuminated by the moon was a great, membranous-winged creature with a pointy-eared humanoid atop it.

*"I remember that dark-skinned man speaking of a wyvern rider laying waste to Moonstone. The rider's name was 'Yar', yes?"*

*"Short for Yarawyn,"* Luna explained. *"The last time I saw Yarawyn Selenia she was an adolescent. She and Torawyn were exiled to Elarond by their older sister, but I cannot remember why. At least Razarkha Fel'thuz earned her exile through dishonourable duel conduct."*

Weil frowned. *"Razarkha told me Rakh framed her and used it as pretext to exile her."*

*"It didn't look that way when we were watching,"* Luna insisted. *"Still, it is odd that humanoids, who are allegedly cooperative creatures, can so easily betray their kin."*

*"It appears that every Arkheran noble house fosters discord and idiocy. Are there any noblemen in this kingdom worth swearing loyalty to?"* Weil asked.

Luna chuckled. *"We have attached ourselves to Quira Abraxas because of personal fondness, but we don't swear ourselves to factions. I imagine it's much the same in Ilazar; mortals that turn kinship into a power retention scheme inevitably decay from the gangrene they gave their filial bonds."*

*"The Gavrilovs collapsed from angering the Kasparovs, the Kasparovs collapsed from angering me and the War'mal Group, and now it seems that the War'mal Group will collapse from an angered surviving Kasparov,"* Weil rambled. *"If it is all the same in Arkhera, then I shall be beholden to nobody."*

*"Becoming nobody's satellite is an admirable goal. You wish to drift through the small piece of the cosmos gifted to you until you decay?"*

Weil yawned once more, trusting the daemon to hold him steady. *"I've tethered myself to others for too long."*

Something stroked Weil's face, and given Luna's arms were occupied, it was likely a tentacle. Once she was done probing him, she adjusted her grip.

*"If you don't want to be beholden to anybody, am I allowed to be beholden to you?"*

Weil closed his eyes. *"If you make the choice freely, then you do what you want. You can follow me, you can leave me, it's up to you."*

*"You're an exceptional young man. Most mortals gifted with control over entropy attempt to redefine it to fit their whims. You understand us, however. I won't betray your trust."*

Though Weil was unsure why she sounded so earnest about his sleep-deprived ramblings, but knowing this daemon looked at him the same way he used to look at Razarkha liberated him from his worries, if only for the night.

# Confrontations

Rakh hadn't slept, even as the dimness of the catacombs tugged at his drowsiness. His illusionism acted in place of dreams, and along his subterranean journey to Moonstone, he'd conjured up some terrified mixture of elf and daemon, screaming at every flickering light along the way. Once he exited the tunnels, morning light and the knowledge that Rarakhi was charging towards a young death propped his eyelids up. An Old Orcish proverb said that a mother's job was to keep her sons out of the grave, while the son's job was to yearn for it. If Plutyn was a reliable source, Rarakhi was always good at his job.

Perched atop the city walls was Yarawyn Selenia's wyvern, its wings folded and its scutes flattened. No doubt the elven usurper was nearby, but Rarakhi wouldn't have been foolish enough to assassinate a woman guarded by such a beast. If the boy considered anyone a viable target, it was his aunt. Though Rakh's illusionism was waning from his perpetual cloaking, he pushed on to Castle Selenia, the thought of his son being bisected by a lance of light keeping his legs in motion. When he entered the castle, he pushed the door too hard, causing it to swing swiftly and slam against a nearby wall. His frenetic attempts to mute the noise proved futile, and like gnomish clockwork, a roar of seething rage echoed from upstairs.

"I searched for you *all night,* Rakh, and now you think you can just open the door and not be noticed? Don't you *dare* run from me again!"

Rakh maintained a shaky cloak and moved towards his sister. If she was still searching, that meant that any scuffles Rarakhi had were inconclusive. In addition, it appeared that she was unaware that there was another illusionist she needed to watch for. As such, he climbed the stairs and caught sight of Razarkha stalking the halls where the Fel'thuz bedrooms resided.

It was as though his older sister had lost access to her illusionism. Tei covered her lower face to project a more pleasing façade over her deformities, yet Razarkha openly limped about as a partially clothed, pallid abomination. Rakh wondered how he'd cope with being such a degraded revenant; perhaps his sister was past the point of caring. His thoughts were interrupted by the sight of a golden glint on the opposite side of the hallway. The rippling, hasty projections were obviously the work of Rarakhi. Unfortunately for Rakh, his sister had noticed too.

*"There you are!"* Razarkha called, turning her back on Rakh to point her weapon towards his son. "You thought you could run me around, slip in and out all night. Well, I knew you'd slip eventually. You need to sleep, I don't. Reveal yourself, or I'll shoot. If you're invisible I can't guarantee I'll make your death quick."

Rakh's body drew energy from a well that had no bottom. He came out of cloaking, rushed towards his exiled wife, and grappled her from behind, screaming to Rarakhi.

"Erwyn, *run!*"

Razarkha struggled against Rakh's grip. *"What?* That was— Erwyn's been sneaking around too? How did you—"

"That's a mystery you'll never solve—"

Rakh felt his arms forcibly straighten, and he was soon pushed against a wall with the force of a dozen orcish arms. Razarkha lifted herself telekinetically, rotated without a single bodily motion, and stared into her brother's eyes.

"You don't know how wonderful it is to see you again," Razarkha said, her voice soft, yet ragged. "I see you still keep your hair grown on one side."

Rakh looked over her shoulder and confirmed that Rarakhi was gone. With that knowledge, he closed his eyes and smiled.

"It looks like you had a hard time finding dye during your adventures."

Razarkha chuckled. "You're surprisingly tactful. Go on, talk about my stomach. I know you want to."

Rakh sighed. "You look awful, Razarkha. Would you like to talk about it?"

"I'd like to kill you, right here, right now," she claimed with a dry wheeze.

"Yet you're wasting time chatting with me. Why?"

"I'm saving your death for a better audience. I know about your little love affair," Razarkha began, her grin so gritted that Rakh feared her teeth would shatter.

"Which one?" Rakh shakily asked.

*"Don't play the fool!"* Razarkha screamed. "Tei! What was it you feared so much about me? Was it that I was your equal? You just *love* fucking crippled little sisters and peasants who couldn't possibly look past your title, but me, your spouse? I'm just not good enough, am I? *People loved me, Rakh! I'm not unlovable!"*

Rakh let himself go limp in her telekinetic grip. "I'm sure that's true. I met someone recently, a man with an Ilazari accent. His name was Weil, he said he was a former friend—"

*"Don't you dare mention him!* You couldn't have met him, he's probably in Zemelnya or happily wasting time with the Prospector or— he's not here, he's happy, he's free, he's *away from me...*"

Razarkha's eyes had started to fade, and oozing from their lower edges was a strange, milky substance with speckles of black. Even though it sounded like her lungs were incapable of retaining air, she kept gasping anyway, her levitating body trembling with rage.

"I know what I saw, Razarkha," Rakh said, his tone draining of enthusiasm. "Listen, I'm ready to die if that's what you want. I could listen to you, explain everything I did to you over the years, just tell me what you need."

"You're tricking me," Razarkha seethed. "Why are you being cooperative? You spent days leaving me notes and breaking my mind. This is part of a plan. What do you *really* want?"

Rakh beheld the shambled together remains of his wife and failed to summon the necessary hatred. He looked away, then focused his efforts on projecting his voice to the city.

"Do you remember how you got exiled, Razarkha?"

"You provoked me," Razarkha snapped. "You dangled an opportunity to kill you in front of me, just so you had an excuse to send me away."

"You're stupid, even now," Rakh snapped. "After what you attempted, any lawful, fair person would have had you executed. I was merciful, moronically so. I shouldn't have let you live, yet you have the gall to claim I manufactured an excuse to exile you."

"Why are you talking about this?"

"Because there are troops I've kept hidden throughout Moonstone. Common men and criminals who respect me. People you would have fun killing me in front of. I propose we have another duel. Don't worry, this time if you kill me, it's not breaking the rules."

Razarkha's voice became so quiet that Rakh needed to up the amplification. "You want an Ilazari honour duel? A proper one, to the death?"

"Yes. Unless you're afraid I'll win."

Razarkha tightened her telekinetic grip upon Rakh. "I fear no such thing. If another duel is what you're after, so be it. I'll invite more than just some stupid soldiers. Bring Tei from whichever rock she's hiding under, bring your bastard, everyone can behold the fate of those who oppose me."

"Our first duel pokes a hole in that rhetoric," Rakh remarked.

Razarkha responded without missing a beat. "It's been good to speak to you again, dear brother. But for now, you're going to the dungeons. I'm sure you could do with a rest. I'm not going to duel some half-awake crippled shadow of my brother. You'll have to tell me how you got that wooden hand before you die."

Rakh smirked. "I lost it killing a daemon."

Razarkha's expression flattened. "Is that so? I suppose I know what happened to Naas'khar, then."

"Who?"

"No-one."

With that, she pulled Rakh towards herself, then pushed him back, knocking his head against the wall until his vision blacked out.

* * *

Sitting by the catacombs entrance at the northern outskirts of Snowy Bank, Irikhos bit into some hardtack while listening to Tei Fel'thuz weeping and Erwyn Yagaska murmuring words of comfort. Tor was beside him, equally silent while the two intellectuals shared in each other's misery.

"I should have followed Rakh," Tei said through her tears. "I should be in Moonstone, saving my son."

"Tei, I mean no offence, but your legs are half the length of Rakh's," Erwyn pointed out. "You'd have never caught up."

"I could have called to him. I could have made him wait."

Erwyn shook his head. "You know Rakh. If he's decided he's going to throw himself into danger, he's not going to pull out willingly. It feels like a lifetime ago, but I remember the day before the duel that started it all. He wouldn't even back down on the Eternalist Church calling in their debts."

"I'm his sister. The woman he loved. He would have listened to me."

"Perhaps," Erwyn said, and with that, the conversation trailed into uncomfortable quiet.

Irikhos stewed on the situation, and despite seeing Count Fel'thuz as the man who forced visions of monsters devouring his nephews upon him, he couldn't help but speak up.

"He would be right to leave you behind even if he thought it over," Irikhos said.

Tei looked at Irikhos, her mismatched eyes filled with tears. "How can you say that?"

"If the illusionist that passed me and Tor was your son, then he has a head start. Rakh slowing down so you can follow him, or carrying you to maintain his running pace, could be the difference between Razarkha killing him and Rakh saving him. I'm sure you've done well for yourself, but here, putting long legs to waste could cost the kid's life."

Tei stared at a snow-covered tree stump and hid her hands in her sleeves. "It's funny, that Ilazari treated me as some crippled liability too."

Irikhos repeatedly failed to form a coherent sentence, causing Tor to verbally step in.

"There was no offence meant," she insisted. "It's not that you're weaker as a person because of your height, it's just that in this case—"

"This case involves the life of my son, forgive me for feeling like my nature's failed him!" Tei yelled. "It's not just my height, if I'd have spent more time looking after him and less time in the Palace, Rara wouldn't have come north at all! I'm a failed mother."

Erwyn shakily interjected. "Rarakhi's a strong, resourceful boy. There's every chance he's alive."

"If he is, it proves his greatness. It doesn't erase my failure," Tei concluded.

Before Tor or Erwyn began another doomed attempt at consolation, Irikhos spoke. "Perhaps it's best we let her feel bad. I know if anything happened to one of Strakha's kids, even if there was no way I could have helped, I'd blame myself until I died."

This immolated the last scraps of composure Tei had, and she began wailing into her hands. Passers-by eyed the four pitilessly, and while Yagaska took the spellbinder into his arms, Tor lowered her voice to a mutter and addressed Irikhos.

"That was tone-deaf. I expected better of you."

"She wasn't about to accept any assurances that she wasn't at fault," Irikhos whispered. "She wanted permission to be upset over feeling powerless, and I gave it to her."

"I understand what you mean, but you could have phrased things in a way that didn't completely crush her," Torawyn pointed out.

"Would you consider me wrong to be crushed by the death of Morganix?" Irikhos asked. "Sometimes, it's right to be miserable. You're a doctor, surely you know of cases where pain needs to be endured for healing to begin."

Tor paused. "Like a broken bone held in place by casts and splints. I'm sorry for questioning you."

Irikhos sighed. "Don't apologise. I'm not Yarawyn. I'm glad you found the strength to disagree with me. I know you've been trying hard to play the ideal wife, but once we're lord and lady, we're not going to agree on everything. You forget that I've lived with a married couple most of my adult life."

"It must have been unusual, seeing your sister kissing someone."

"I'm happy for her. Being honest, Strakha was always awkward about men before Solyx came along. Too caught up in religious talk, too focused on marriage as a way to 'continue the cycle'. Something changed after her wedding day. I don't know the details, but I do know those two have shared their bed more than the five times Mor'kha's had a child."

"It's a rarity, an arranged marriage with affection," Torawyn remarked.

Irikhos paused. "Indeed."

Tei's whimpers filled the audial void, backed by a hollow wind. Then, in the corner of Irikhos's eye, a silhouette rose from, of all places, the catacombs entrance. It wasn't some late group of evacuees; there was no sign of a food wagon or multiple people in tow. It was a solitary humanoid, hunchbacked and pointy-eared. His matted black hair covered his eyes, and his arms hung slack, dragging his entire posture down. Torawyn was quick to get up and approach the unusual individual. Irikhos stood and kept his hand on his sword's pommel.

"By God, what happened to you?" Torawyn asked. "No minor injury can cause fractures like these."

Tor felt over the elven lookalike's arms, then backed off, her skin growing pale. Irikhos drew his sword and moved closer.

"What's wrong?"

"Everyone, run, it's with Yarawyn!" she screamed.

Irikhos refused to heed the command. Octopoid tendrils erupted from the monster's back, so Iri lunged forward, shoved Tor out of harm's way and severed one of its tentacles before it could strike. The creature grunted, then tackled him, ignoring the sword he attempted to guard himself with. Irikhos had his back to the floor, and the daemonic beast loomed over him, oozing black-and-crimson ichor from a chest-wide gash that nestled his sword. Iri glanced at its wide-pupiled, scarlet eyes, then spluttered a few words.

"You're the cave-person, aren't you? Yarawyn's friend? You don't need to do this, you can be your own person!"

The creature lifted itself off the sword with the help of its remaining three tentacles, then revealed it could speak. "You're Irikhos Foenaxas. The man who Yarawyn loved, despite everything. I was after Rakh Fel'thuz, but I'm sure Razarkha will forgive a little selfishness."

Irikhos glanced beyond his predicament. Erwyn had already backed off, Tei had vanished and Tor was trembling on the floor, while countless peasants gawked at the spectacle.

"Tor, usher the commoners away! I'll deal with this beast," Irikhos commanded.

Once Torawyn was up and shouting, Irikhos wrangled the last tentacle on the creature's right side, causing it to fall onto his sword once again. The beast howled, then took its remaining tentacles and wrapped them around Irikhos's face.

He could feel his skull straining, and his lungs started begging for air. As sucker pads pulled on his eyelids, a vision of him listening to his big sister playing the lute replaced the unrelenting darkness. Even as pain subsumed all beyond his head, within, Morganix's promise that one day, he'd beat him in a sparring match echoed. Somehow, even in complete darkness, he knew his left eye was gone. It was only a matter of time before the rest of his face followed.

Abruptly, light returned to his remaining eye, and his skull no longer ached. Rearing over him was a writhing, screaming rendition of Yarawyn's daemonic friend, with a dagger jabbed into its side. Soon, it was shoved off Irikhos entirely by some invisible force, allowing him to get up and pull his sword out of it.

Irikhos grinned through the pain; with a high strike, he'd miss his illusionary ally. In one quick motion, he beheaded the daemonic hybrid, causing its body to collapse into a pile of inky mush and orphaned bones. Despite this, its head remained intact, and some of the slime moved on its own, reforming a part of his ravaged neck. As though a centipede, numerous tiny tendrils formed at the base, creating legs for a form no man would envy.

Tei revealed herself by the ruined pile of daemonic goo, her eyes still red from weeping. "Sometimes, being a smaller target helps."

"Thank you for saving me," Irikhos said, wincing when he attempted to blink. "I need to see Tor or Erwyn as quickly as—"

"Why did I do it?" a voice mumbled from the floor.

Irikhos froze, then brought what remained of his gaze towards the disembodied head of Yarawyn's pet monster. Its eyes moved, and though its voice was barely a croak, it was comprehensible. As his eye socket blazed against the air, Irikhos crouched by his fallen foe.

"Why did you do what?"

"Yarawyn already gave me a description of you. I tried to become you once," the hybrid mumbled. "I knew who you were, and even if you didn't have your blade, I'd have attacked you. If I returned to Yarawyn saying you were accidentally killed, then perhaps… perhaps…"

"Yarawyn wouldn't have loved you," Irikhos said. "No matter what she thinks, she doesn't love me either, just the boy I used to be. If she put you up to this, getting yourself killed just to follow an enemy you don't care about, perhaps she isn't worth the love you bear her."

"She is," the creature insisted. "She's the only one who didn't shun me. My daemonic mother saw me as some fun trial to leave in the mountains, the people of Alaterra would have hunted me down if I ventured too close. Yarawyn was different. Who else should I love, if not the person to see me as more than a monster?"

Tei picked up the head, allowing its tiny legs to dangle. "You're pitiful, but I was once like you. I thought only Rakh could love me, so we took solace in each other. Now I have my own purpose. Are you dying?"

"I don't know. It looks like my body's unable to move on its own," the head replied. "It's not as though I have anything to live for. How can I return to Yarawyn like this, after she finds out I attacked her true love?"

Tei offered Naas'khar to Irikhos. "Hold him for a moment."

Before Irikhos could properly respond, the daemonspawn's talkative remains were in his hands. Tei rummaged through her inner pocket and produced a map of Arkhera. She pointed to the north-east, then to a spot near the western coast.

"You're currently up here, near Moonstone. Down here, there's a place called the City of False Faces. It's full of daemons, and probably nephilim like yourself. I found purpose away from the person I thought I could never function without. If you have any life left, I'd use it to find this city. There, you'll find purpose, I assure you."

Naas'khar made a small, rumbling noise, then pushed his tendrils against Irikhos's hand, forcing him to let go. Once on the floor, the nephil crawled in an insectoid manner towards Tei's dagger, took the handle within his mouth, and strained to pull it from his melted body. He tugged and tugged, but what little motile matter he had couldn't grant him the strength. Eventually, he let go, falling onto the snow and whimpering.

"I can't," he croaked. "I can't find purpose."

Tei sighed and took the dagger out for him, then crouched so she could point it in front of him. "As you wish. Here, fall onto it. I won't stab you, but if you want to die, I can't stop you either."

Naas'khar righted himself, then backed away from Tei, preparing for a run-up. After the disembodied head lingered as long as a regular mortal might have, Irikhos interjected.

"Well? What's keeping you?"

Without a word, the crawling head turned and fled towards the gates of Snowy Bank. Irikhos tore a rag off his cloak and wiped his sword down, then looked to Tei.

"Should I follow him?"

"No. He's not going to be a threat any time soon," Tei remarked, prodding the decaying mass of organs he'd left behind.

Irikhos instinctively brought his hand to his eye, before pulling it away. "Thank you."

"I wish I saved you sooner."

Irikhos's eye socket finally revealed its true agony, and as he grimaced through the pain, all he could do was consider it the God of Renewal's karmic justice. Even after Tor fixed him, he'd see as well as Tei could run.

\* \* \*

The Moonstone dungeons had long since been abandoned in favour of above-ground prisons that some former Selenia overlord considered more 'ethical', as though prisoners cared about what room they spent their captivity in. Razarkha limped through the dungeon halls with the help of illusionism-powered light, her actions the result of mental captivity.

If she was independent enough, if she was truly strong, she could have left Rakh alone until the duel, but her mind was restless. Rakhs had stopped appearing throughout Castle Selenia, but in their place, Tei and the likely deformed youngster that she'd spawned appeared in droves. Rakh would die in a day, as would his secrets. This was her only chance. When she reached her brother's cell, she was disappointed. The fire in his crimson eyes had dimmed to an ember, and he'd folded his legs as though content with his imminent demise. When she walked into his view, he was quick to fill the air with blether.

"Hello again."

"You just can't help but speak first, can you?" Razarkha snapped.

"It's a shared weakness of ours," Rakh said. "We love to hear our own voices. I can't imagine what happened in Ilazar and Galdus were quiet affairs. Seeing as one of us is going to die tomorrow, why not tell me about your adventures?"

Razarkha laughed. "You were always terrible at manipulation, but this is pathetic even by your standards. Did you think you could wrangle my weaknesses from me so easily?"

Rakh's voice remained level. "Even now, I'm still your brother. I've failed you as a husband, nobody can deny that, but I want to listen to you as my sister before the end. Is that really so hard to believe?"

"It is when you're my opponent," Razarkha pointed out. "Speaking of your failures as a husband, I want an explanation. Why Tei? Why ugly, short, deformed, worthless, spare Tei?"

"Living with you was miserable, especially after father died," Rakh said, meeting his sister's height. "Tei believed your every word. She believed she was ugly, worthless—"

"She *is* ugly and worthless!"

Rakh's voice peaked. "And you're a rotting, foul-smelling wretch. I don't see you taking that to heart."

Razarkha's words began to quaver. "That's because I'm stronger than her."

Rakh lingered on these words, then lowered his volume. "I don't know what's wrong with you, why you were born with the mind you have, but there's a sickness in you. My words hurt, don't they?"

"You're not affecting me, your words are hollow—"

"My question was rhetorical," Rakh snapped. "You know how words, even if they're true, can cause undue suffering. I just hurt you, yet you don't feel a shred of remorse for hurting Tei. Whenever I look back on my affair with her, promising her a love I couldn't possibly provide, crying as she cried, I become consumed with regret. But you, despite knowing the pain words carry, don't regret hurting her, do you?"

"If I'd have known it'd lead to a pure-blooded Fel'thuz bastard, I'd have—"

"That's what it's all about to you," Rakh began to rant. "Pragmatism. You don't see people as people, you see them as objects. You did so with me, you did so with Tei, and when you killed Waldon, you likely felt the same remorse one might feel for throwing a scrap of paper away."

*"Waldon murdered Razander!"* Razarkha yelled, her peripheral vision plaguing itself with Teis. "I assure you, I felt a great abundance when I shoved him out the window. I felt *joy*. I also remember what he was doing when I found him. He'd already opened his window. He *wanted to die,* but couldn't make the leap. I *helped him."*

Rakh sat down again. "This is why I blurred you out. Saw you as nothing more than a monster. You don't appear to regret anything for personal reasons. It's never about ethics, and *always* about consequences. That's why, though I hadn't thought much of it at the time, Weil of Zemelnya perplexes me."

"No. Stop. You're not talking about him."

"Why not?" Rakh asked. "I'm not mocking you for your association with him. Aside from the scuffle we had, he seems like a decent man. He offered you hospitality, didn't he?"

Razarkha sat as well as her crystalline leg allowed her to. "Fine. I'll admit it. You must have met Weil if you know this much. Why is he in Arkhera?"

"He claims to be Tei's ally now, and your former friend—"

*"Again!"* Razarkha snapped, shooting a stray beam from her soulstealer while her stomach blazed. "Why does Tei steal *everyone* from me? She's *ugly!"*

"I don't know how he and Tei became associated. I didn't have time to ask," Rakh claimed. "Still, he called you his friend. Did you feel the same way, or was he another Tei? Another Waldon?"

Razarkha forced her eyes shut and scratched the ground, snapping most of her left hand's nails. She shook her head, and her foolish Ilazari compatriot's face lined her eyelids.

"Stop using him. Stop trying to leverage a weakness. We're separated now, what does it matter to you?"

"If he's proof that somebody like you can love, he means everything," Rakh replied.

"You're going to use him as an illusion in the duel tomorrow, aren't you?" Razarkha said, her lungs failing to give her voice the punch she'd hoped for. "Admit it."

"I'd be a fool not to," Rakh said with a bitter edge. "Still, if you can love, then part of me wishes you could have loved me. Perhaps I had the means to be lovable in your eyes. There's one event that's haunted me lately. While we're both here, I should apologise for it."

"I'm not going to listen to your lies."

"Yet you haven't left," Rakh stated. "When Razander died, and you were recovering, spewing angry remarks about Waldon, I should have tolerated it. Any woman in your position would be upset, and we were both grieving. I didn't want any more strife, so I ran from you. I was cowardly. I was wrong. I abandoned you when you needed me most."

"You're trying to make me hesitate," Razarkha said, her words catching in her throat. "You're assuming I'll befriend you like Weil. You aren't half the man he is."

"That may be so," Rakh admitted. "Regardless of what you think of me, I've said it. I apologise for abandoning you. No doubt it drove you to kill Waldon. I should have talked to you like this back then. I should have tried to find meaning in your madness. Knowing that you made a friend makes me grieve for you, more than you could possibly know."

"Why grieve for me? Weil isn't dead. If he'd have stayed away from Arkhera, he could have been happy," Razarkha said, glaring at Rakh. "What possible reason could you have to grieve for me?"

"Isn't it obvious?" Rakh asked. "You lost his friendship. If Erwyn stopped believing in me, if Lady Kag stopped looking up to me, I'd be devastated. I recently realised that I couldn't relate to the common man as I'd believed I had all these years, and it tore me apart. I still can't see any redemption beyond death for such failure.

"Weil was your only friend, from what I can gather. Even if you choose to ignore others' pain, I can feel yours pulsing through me. It's part of an illusionist's skillset to delve into imagery that means something to others. You're overcome with anguish, I can feel it in the air. You loved Weil, and he loved you. Now that part of you is gone, and I'm sorry that happened. If you'd have settled and stayed with an overseas friend forever, I'd have rested easy knowing that letting you live was a good thing. Instead, I grieve for the path that could have been."

Razarkha couldn't feed the monster any more information. She struggled to her feet, wiped away her leakages, and turned away. "You can't stop me anymore. This is my purpose."

"It seems both our purposes amounted to little. I hope you remember I was your little brother. I'm trying my hardest to see you as my big sister."

"A pity," Razarkha said, leaving before Rakh could lure her in with another response.

# Severances

With the Riversongs' help, Weil had passed the dark forests of Northern Arkhera into a clearing where Moonstone stood amidst a near crater-like slope. The provincial capital's walls loomed over him and his daemonic compatriots, and while the southern gate was closed, it was no obstacle to the chaos-speaker who'd once flung himself across the skylines of Galdusian megalopolises. He looked to the Riversongs and pointed to the closest battlements.

"*Arkheran cities have a lining along their city walls that can be stood upon, correct?*"

"*Yes,*" Lyra Riversong replied. "*We've occasionally seen that wyvern perching upon them.*"

Meredith's tentacular hair writhed and pulsed. "*It looks delicious. There's probably enough meat on it to form a fourth Riversong.*"

Weil spoke to the Rakh'vash. "*This shall be easy. Form two linked portals, one down here, one above the walls. Don't bother with any trickery. You admonished me in Ilazar for trying to delay my father's inevitable decay, and Razarkha's doing the same for herself if the Imperial Engineer is correct. She must be stopped.*"

"**As you say,**" the Living Entropy said.

When the portals opened, Luna Riversong dove towards Weil, knocking him to the floor as a stream of fire left a charred path where he once stood. Aerially veering from its charge was the wyvern Lyra mentioned, its elven rider easily spotted. Weil had put down wyvern-like ascendants before; the act would be easy to perform, but difficult to reconcile.

Ascendants were cowards who'd fled their very bodies just to avoid mortality. Fate had punished Weil for making the same cowardly decision on behalf of his father; the ascended had earned their downfall. All Weil knew about this wyvern and its rider was that they were Razarkha's allies, like he once was.

"*What are you doing?*" Luna shouted, picking Weil up and evading another fire-spewing dive. "*Don't just lie around thinking, we're under attack!*"

Weil wriggled out of Luna's grip and refocused while the wyvern righted itself. Meredith and Lyra had scattered in a deliberate ploy of unpredictability.

"*Thank you for saving me,*" Weil said with a nod. "*How high can you jump?*"

"*About three times the height a regular mortal would achieve,*" Luna said, ejecting a set of tentacles. "*Are you suggesting we knock the beast out of the air?*"

Weil checked the wyvern, expecting yet another dive, yet instead, it circled. The elven rider called from her vantage point, revealing a surprisingly high pitched, somewhat accented rendition of the Common Tongue.

"You four, stay out of Moonstone! Countess Razarkha Fel'thuz has arranged a special event, and interlopers aren't invited! Turn back, and I promise you won't be killed!"

Weil called back. "You try to kill us twice. Your offer is meaningless. I am here for Razarkha Fel'thuz; fly away, and you shall not be hurt."

"Oh, you're bold, hoping to threaten a wyvern rider. All right, Moonrazer, take your pick, then *cook your dinner!*"

The flying lizard made a loud, excited warble, then screamed as it swooped downwards, straight towards Lyra. While the youngest Riversong had her combat tentacles ejected, the fire would hit her before she could conceivably land a hit. Weil pointed towards her, muttered a quick incantation of Chaostongue, and opened a portal beneath the daemon. She re-entered the mortal realm by his side, leaving only Meredith on her own.

The wyvern nearly scratched the ground as it passed where Lyra once stood, and was quick to rise, tilt, then flap towards Meredith, its beak still spewing flames. Weil raised his arms and summoned a tentacle between the wyvern and the middle Riversong, forcing the beast to slow down with hurried, desperate flaps.

"Whoa now, Moonrazer, we're going to hit, we're going to hit!" the rider began, only to stop when she slowed just in time. "Oh. Good boy—"

*"Seize it while it's still,"* Weil said, pointing at the relatively immobile threat.

**"We didn't need the command,"** the Rakh'vash said.

The protective tentacle went on the attack, wrapping around the wyvern and slamming it downwards. The beast unleashed a piercing howl, spewing fireball after fireball into the snowy surroundings while the Rakh'vash's tentacle bashed it against the ground again and again. Weil tried to find its rider amidst the wrapped-up mess of wing and sucker pad, but it was too far away to properly discern.

Eventually, the tentacle took enough bites and fire to retreat into the Chaotic Realm, leaving a trembling, grounded wyvern behind. Weil approached the creature, beckoning for the Riversongs to do the same, but oddly, it didn't seem concerned with the approaching enemies. It probed the area, slowly swaying its serpentine neck, limping with folded, shredded wings. It eventually found what it was looking for, and Weil signalled for the Riversongs to stop.

*"Allow it a moment."*

*"What are you talking about?"* Meredith asked. *"It just tried to kill us."*

*"It's a trained animal,"* Weil said. *"It's looking for its mistress. It isn't a threat anymore. At least, I hope it isn't."*

Luna frowned. *"I have presumed a mortal beaten many times. It's always when they're cornered that they reveal their true persistence."*

***"Then we shall not corner them,"*** Weil said. ***"Not yet."***

The wyvern had limped over to a broken boned, vaguely humanoid mess whose final actions were dyeing the snow around her pink. Weil moved close enough to tell that her hair was once blonde, and that she'd landed head-first. The beast still recognised its rider and nudged her unmoving body with it beak. It made a quiet rattle, then lowered its body, curling around the fallen elf.

*"It's dormant,"* Lyra said. *"Let us consume it."*

Weil swallowed. *"I'll make sure its passing is quick. Living Entropy, lance a tentacle through its upper neck from above."*

***"May its decay be forever celebrated,"*** the Rakh'vash said.

A portal opened above the dying beast, and swift as a dagger, a hardened tentacle shot out of it, shredding through Moonrazer's spine. The deed was done, as was the wyvern's suffering. Weil moved towards the corpses and grimaced. When he fought in Galdus, it was easy to grow lost in the madness, to forget the horrors of conquest. There were no bodies left behind, no pathetic final struggles to witness. Luna Riversong put a hand on his shoulder.

*"You're a gentle person,"* she remarked. *"Will you be able to end your Razarkha?"*

*"With Razarkha, I know what must be done,"* Weil claimed. *"This elf and her loyal pet were nothing to me. If we'd have met in any other circumstance, we'd likely pass each other by and live the rest of our lives. I've helped Razarkha kill so many and dropped daemons upon ship after ship. Going without conflict has made me lose my stomach for it."*

Luna hugged him from behind. *"If you don't enjoy it, that's for the best. Mortals aren't daemons, and that's a good thing. If we were the same, I'd have nothing to learn."*

Just as Weil allowed himself to take comfort in the well-meaning immortal's touch, a rasping voice echoed within Moonstone's walls. It rang out far beyond what an ordinary shout could, and despite him not recalling her manipulating sound, he knew the voice's owner; her tones were etched into his very being.

"All craven soldiers cowering in your buildings, listen closely! If you have a modicum of bravery, come to the city square. As you can tell by this amplification, your beloved Count Fel'thuz is alive and well, assisting me in this announcement," Razarkha blared out. "Soon, he and I will duel, and no doubt you've heard his challenge yesterday; this time, there are no absurd limitations. It'll be a fight to the death. Be thankful for this opportunity; if you arrive at the square, no harm will come to you, though after my inevitable victory, you must swear your loyalty to Lady Yarawyn Selenia. Be there or be a coward. That is all."

Weil took a sharp breath through his teeth. *"Riversongs, do what you must with the wyvern and its rider. I'll put an end to Razarkha here and now."*

Luna nodded. *"As you say, Weil. Meredith, Lyra, it's time to eat!"*

All three daemons' eyes shifted from a pleasing glassiness to a wide-pupiled, squid-like appearance. Their humanoid bodies degraded into a black, formless ooze that merged and smothered the pile of broken mortal matter. Weil averted his eyes and opened a portal above Moonstone's battlements, then hopped into a linked portal in front of him.

\* \* \*

Razarkha had cobbled together a stage from pulled-apart buildings that once surrounded the city square. Her brother was tied to a post beside her, and together the siblings watched as people left their hiding spots. Gradually, a crowd formed, but by the time it stopped growing, she was left wanting. There weren't even fifty attendees from what she could see, and save one nicely dressed necromancer girl, there was nobody noteworthy. Of course, Tei and her son wouldn't have been foolish enough to watch without staying hidden, but this knowledge didn't hold off the encroaching emptiness.

"Shall we start, then?" Rakh asked.

"Allow a moment for the crowd to gather," Razarkha stammered.

"Do you honestly think more people will arrive? You're not a complete idiot. Surely you understand why soldiers may not wish to gather at a hostile party's behest."

Razarkha walked up to her restrained brother and jabbed a finger in his face. "I'm not starting until Yarawyn arrives. She's just finishing her southern patrol, she'll be back soon."

"And if she isn't?" Rakh asked.

"Just shut up and wait," Razarkha scoffed. "I've never seen someone so eager to die."

Rakh smirked. "Given I'm the one who controls the reach of your announcements, I'd be a little kinder. How about this? Another five minutes, and from there, even if Yarawyn hasn't arrived, we start."

"Fine," Razarkha muttered as the eyes of Moonstone's ineffectual protectors blazed against her. "I'm only allowing this concession because you're about to die."

"So generous," Rakh replied.

The ensuing wait was almost as intolerable as Rakh's voice. One or two soldiers arrived from who-knows-where, yet Yarawyn and her wyvern refused to appear. Instead, Razarkha's illusionism malfunctioned. This time, a great tentacle akin to those Weil once summoned sprouted from the southern battlements, flinging a humanoid shape through the grey skies.

"Are you doing that?" Razarkha asked.

"Doing what?" Rakh replied, his tone exaggeratedly quizzical.

"You're a vile cheat," Razarkha muttered. "Play the fool all you like, but once I'm free to kill you, you'll suffer for every game you've played at my expense."

"The only person stopping you is yourself. I'm ready to start when you are."

"I hate you so much," Razarkha snapped, then tapped her crystalline foot against the stage. "What's taking Yarawyn so *long?* That worthless elven wretch would be dead if not for me, the least I expect is some consideration for my only desire in exchange for Moonstone."

"Everyone is worthless to you," Rakh remarked. "Are you worthless to yourself too?"

*"Shut up!"* Razarkha screamed, telekinetically untying Rakh. "Go on, amplify my voice. You've done it, you've got me to start early, are you happy?"

"Overjoyed," Rakh said in a soulless drone. "All right, make your announcement."

"People of Moonstone! On my say-so, the duel shall begin. As promised, all in attendance shall be given the opportunity to swear themselves to their new lady, Yarawyn Selenia. Worry not, brave onlookers; those who failed to arrive will be hunted down to receive the wage treachery pays. Now, to establish expectations; this is a duel to the *death.* I don't want to hear your feigned moral qualms or shock when Rakh dies in front of you. When he does, you'll accept me as your countess and share in my joy. Am I understood?"

The crowd's silence burnt her from within, and the Bold Individualist offered his salient divine commentary.

*"What is your goal? Why are you so taken with securing these people's loyalty? You're an individualist, are you not? A single influential woman, the slayer of my longest-lived child, the toppler of the Kasparov Family. Why do you care about their disapproval?"*

"*Shut up!*" Razarkha screamed, the amplification rendering the outburst outright concussive. She regained her composure, and falteringly continued her address. "That is— the— the fact you've all shut up means you understand the ease with which I can erase you. That's good. When Lady Yarawyn returns, you shall all kneel to her, but for now, watch as your last bastion of hope dies. Rakh, to your starting position!"

Rakh walked to his end of the stage and offered one last remark. "Are you sure you want to face me? I won't hold back."

Razarkha laughed and moved to her end. "You're in no position to intimidate me. Make peace with whatever matters you left unresolved. This is it. *The duel has commenced!*"

Before she could even point her soulstealer, the city of Moonstone dissolved around her. Abruptly, she was flung to a floor that rippled upon contact. Images of Weil wearing a coat she'd never seen before surrounded her, dancing in unison and singing to a distorted, jazzy tune. The lyrics were arrhythmic and in the Common Tongue, yet every Weil's face was unnervingly accurate.

"Why did you betray me? Why did you cast aside your only friend?"

Razarkha got up and shot through the false Weil. "It won't work, Rakh. If you think I'll hesitate just because you're wearing his face, think again."

"You aren't the monster you think you are," the poorly accented Weil claimed. "You could shoot through as many fakes as I could conjure, but what if one of these Weils is real? Would you shoot then?"

"I'll never need to find out—"

She was once again thrown to the floor, then took a blow between the legs. Her wrists were pushed down, and her invisible foe attempted to pry her soulstealer from her fingers. Thankfully, that meant his unoccupied hand was incapable of grip. She overcame the illusory futility, kicked him off her with her crystal leg, and watched the void jitter while her brother's agonised wails filled the air.

"*My fucking stones!*"

Razarkha got up with the help of her telekinesis, then pointed her soulstealer at where she assumed Rakh had stumbled. Just as she prepared to cast her lumomancy, the Bold Individualist broke in.

**"This might be a bad time, but with your liberal use of telekinesis and lumomancy, the souls within you are unlikely to sustain anything beyond four or so beams, less if float around flippantly. I wouldn't want to lose my source of entertainment so anticlimactically."**

"Oh, *now* you tell me!"

**"Make those beams count, Razarkha! Or rather, make those beams hit the count."**

She grunted in the hopes it would shut her aggravating god up, but it was no good; even though his life revolved around his stones, Rakh would have ceased his writhing by now. He hadn't conceived any new illusions, however, instead leaving her in a void that occasionally flashed into colour in time with the fuzzy jazz music he'd insisted on illusorily playing.

"Well? Show yourself, Rakh. Your big ploy to use Weil failed. Unless you have something more impactful to show me, you may as well stand before me and surrender—"

Out from the dubiously liquid floor rose five mirrors, each one's shiny face pointing towards her. Razarkha saw, from every angle, the sack of flesh she'd become. Her makeup had long since merged into her pallid skin, all purples had faded from her hair, and at the back, patches had fallen out. Abruptly, the mirror images shifted to five separate angles of her being ran through by a set of tentacles, and Rakh's voice echoed through the void.

"Ah, I finally understand. Weil seemed so mellow about you, so I didn't realise he was your killer," Rakh said. "No wonder reconciliation isn't an option. How could you go back from that? It's a shame, because that tentacle you saw in the distance? It was real."

*"You're bluffing!"* Razarkha screamed, staggering towards any ripple resembling her brother's cloaked form. "You just dug through my memories and placed that tentacle there! Weil wouldn't track me down, he'd probably just settle for Tei. She's obviously uglier than me, but he was always a desperate sort."

"Putting his standards down just to escape the thought that you could have been loved," Rakh continued. "That's the saddest thing I've heard in my life."

*"Shut up!"* Razarkha screamed, shooting a beam through a mirror, achieving precisely nothing.

***"Careful now."***

"Oh, be quiet, you worthless god!"

"Worthless, worthless, you're so fond of that word," Rakh mocked, before a force swept Razarkha's balance out from under her. "You always loved reading. I hoped by your fortieth year you'd have a wider vocabulary."

Razarkha knew he was above and behind her. She rolled over, pointed her soulstealer, then squinted; somehow, there was a cloaking distortion much further than she expected. Had he run that far back already? She made a sweeping motion in front of her as she got up, and once she confirmed Rakh wasn't close, pointed to the man-sized ripple.

Just as she shot another beam, her aim was wrested rightwards, and the illusory void vanished altogether. Rakh was gripping her wrist, staring intensely while he attempted to wrest the artefact from her hand. She overcame her confusion and kept her grip steady; his wooden hand was hardly going to assist in any grappling endeavours. Her triumph evaporated as Rakh kneed her groin, clubbed her face with his prosthetic, and knocked her to the ground, pouncing onto her to continue the beatdown. Something about him had changed; his crimson eyes were wild and fearful, and he seemed incapable of conjuring a single illusion.

Razarkha's vision worsened with every strike she took, and Rakh's wooden hand was increasingly growing black with what she assumed were the remainders of her face. Her soulstealer stayed firm within her hand, however, and now that his illusions were vanquished, the fight was over. With the last vestiges of her focus, she telekinetically lifted her husband off her, held him above her, then pointed her soulstealer. Rakh's eyes widened with primal terror, and Razarkha grinned.

"Goodbye, dear brother."

A lumomantic lance shot upwards, piercing Rakh's chest and the sky beyond. Razarkha slung his limp remains onto the stage floor and got up, wheezing as her very posture betrayed her. Her soulstealer and abdomen were peculiarly cold, but after a pause, the former glimmered in a comforting process she'd come to miss.

"That was him. That was Rakh," she said, glancing at the crowd before limping towards her brother's corpse.

She bumped the body with her foot, and while she expected its solidness to make her smile, all she could do was stare. It was finally over. Rakh had finally paid for his neglect and hatred of her. He wouldn't exploit her weaknesses or mock her anymore. He was naught but fuel for whatever remained of her unlife. She turned to the crowd, hoping to address them, only to see that beyond them was a tentacle, looming over the people while a spellbinder slid down its length, leaping towards the stage. Razarkha's gaze was unbreakably fixated.

"Weil?"

Just as she said his name, a pain shot through her back. She gasped, twitched, then looked over her shoulder to see a youthful-faced, Fel'thuz-looking man, tall as his father, with eyes that resembled Tei's teal side. Weil landed on the stage, and Razarkha staggered forward, forcing the illusion to catch her.

"*I wish you were real, Weil,*" Razarkha croaked in Isleborn while motionlessness spread through her body. "*You're just some trick, I was tricked until the very end. I wish you were here. I had so much I wanted to say.*"

"*I'm here,*" the illusion promised. "*Tell me what you need to tell me.*"

The Soulstealer of Craving slipped from her numb hand, and the sound of flesh detaching from her abdomen crystal was heard beneath her. None of it mattered. She could still look upwards; she could still meet Weil's eyes.

"*Rakh's Weils didn't speak Isleborn. Illusions can't hold anything.*"

"*That's right. I wanted to kill you again, but somebody else had more of a stomach for it,*" he said, looking to her boyish slayer.

"*I don't blame you,*" Razarkha mumbled. "*I'm sorry for everything I did to you. Everything I ruined. Weil?*"

"*What is it, Razarkha?*"

"*Don't let me go. Please don't let me go.*"

"*I won't.*"

As feeling fled everything below her neck, Razarkha accepted the sensation of Weil's chest against her hair. She wondered why she'd never asked to be held like this in life.

"*Weil.*"

Her mouth stopped moving, and her body voided itself of feeling, thought, and soul. Beyond her broken body, time slowed, and a familiar voice echoed through a monochromatic rendition of Moonstone.

"**Well, you've delayed it long enough. It's time to let Elki Kasparov move on while you take his place powering the Soulstealer of Craving.**"

"*No, I'm not done, I have so much more to say!*" Razarkha's soul begged.

**"*Don't worry, I have a special arrangement in mind. You'll never be alone.*"**

# Farewells

Razarkha's upper half stopped moving shortly after she stopped talking. She was already cold, and without the person inhabiting the flesh, holding her was futile. Weil's grip loosened, and his former friend's torso joined her legs, tail, and soulstealer on the floor. In front of him, some necromantic girl clambered onto the stage and approached the boy assassin. The knife lodged within her back, along with the woollen coat that matched his own, made her killer's identity obvious. Between himself, her brother, and her nephew, Razarkha was doomed.

The Fel'thuz boy lingered over his father's corpse, held by the necromancer until eventually, he held her in return. Razarkha never needed comfort following her killings, and until lately, neither did Weil. He gazed towards Moonstone's southern wall, then closed his eyes, remembering the harsh, fading pain of a cigarette stubbed out against his chest. Comfort wasn't what he craved; punishment was what he needed.

The Soulstealer of Craving glittered amidst the pile of flesh that Razarkha once was, and against every healthy aversion mortals had, Weil picked it up in the hopes of hearing her voice again. Whispers teased the edges of his ears, but it wasn't the same. It resembled the bickering one expected from participants of a relationship long since soured, abstracted and reduced to vague murmurings. A louder, coherent voice overtook the chatter, its tone bleeding a familiar godly darkness.

*"Weil of Zemelnya,"* the Bold Individualist said. *"It's good to speak to you directly. You've come a long way from the frightened, indebted boy with a dying father. It seems you've even got your personal face of the Rakh'vash under control. You killed Razarkha initially, and now you've picked up her soulstealer. I'm sure adding another*

*dark god's power to your repertoire would be something your father would be proud of."*

"Not if I become what Razarkha did."

*"What's changed? You supported Razarkha through what most mortals would consider to be her worst crimes. Even if you don't use the soulstealer as a weapon of conquest, what's the harm in keeping it as a memento?"*

"What treasured memories are associated with this rock?" Weil asked.

*"The joy of bringing an orderly, delusional shadow empire to its knees, your closest friendship blossoming and fading, even the tale of its acquisition is something to tell whatever nephil children you create."*

Weil furrowed his brow, then turned to Tei's weeping son. "You, Fel'thuz child."

"What?" the boy asked, his voice strained.

"Catch," Weil replied, giving the Soulstealer of Craving an underarm toss. Once the boy caught it, he attempted to explain himself. "You kill her, you earn this."

"Thanks, I guess," Rarakhi muttered. "Who are you? Why are you wearing one of my coats?"

"I was your mother's prisoner, once," Weil said as he opened a chaotic portal. "Razarkha was my friend, but no-one in Kingdom of Arkhera loves her. You shall keep her dreaded stone, but I shall take her body."

"There's a voice going on about the power I could wield if I 'claim' this rock. Aunt Razarkha used it to shoot beams," Rarakhi noted. "Anything worth listening to?"

"Ignore it, and any god claiming knowledge," Weil said, picking up Razarkha's remains, but not before yanking the thread blade out and casting it to the floor. "There are three daemons who resemble human beyond wall. Do not attack them, they are friend."

"It's fine, I don't think I'm gonna attack anyone for a long time after this," the boy said, moving to pick up the thread blade. "You were the one who brought this thing here, weren't you? You sure you don't want it? It's apparently priceless."

Weil looked at his portal and shook his head. "I cannot travel where I need to with it."

***"Go through,"*** the Rakh'vash said. ***"Though that blade is still abominable, it appears its victim experienced arcane severance rather than knotweed infestation."***

*"I presumed so when you allowed me to open the portal,"* Weil said in Chaostongue, before turning back to Rarakhi. "Good fortune, Fel'thuz boy."

Weil stepped into the Chaotic Realm, quickly opening a connection to the top of the Sudovykly Cliffs. He dropped out of the lawless void and into the outskirts of his lawless motherland, standing against the screaming coastal winds with Razarkha's remains secure in his grasp. He walked towards the precipice he'd once led her down, and for a moment, a ruined ship appeared across the sea.

*"You once told me that I needed to stop denying the evils I'd committed. You thought it was better to embrace the carnage, and I believed you,"* Weil said to the stinking pile of meat. *"You were right about one thing; there weren't any excuses. I did terrible things to save doomed man and serve a doomed revolutionary. Would you be happy knowing that I shall only serve myself from now on?"*

Weil expected silence to be his only answer, yet a man's voice was heard behind him, speaking Isleborn in an obnoxious Arkheran accent.

*"Is that Razarkha in your arms? I'm surprised you did it, speaking honestly."*

The intruder upon his introspection was Rowyn Khanas, of all people. Weil glanced at the necromancer, noting a resemblance between him and the girl he'd spotted in Moonstone.

*"I didn't kill her,"* Weil said. *"I'm dealing with her body, though. Here, at the Sudovykly Cliffs, she shall feed the waters."*

"*Do you still hate her?*"

"*Nobody can hate a corpse,*" Weil said, tossing the body over the edge.

Instead of watching it fall, he stared into the horizon, grim and grey as it was. Rowyn Khanas put a hand on Weil's shoulder and continued to botch his mother tongue.

"*We shall live, we shall survive.*"

Weil bitterly chuckled. "*The proverb is 'we will be alive, we won't die'. The feeling is the same, at least. Before you left Arkhera, did you have a daughter or niece?*"

"*A cousin once removed named Plutera. Why?*"

"*I believe I saw her. You must have your reasons for staying in Ilazar, but would you like me to tell her anything?*" Weil asked, opening another chaotic portal.

"*Tell her that I'm alive, but hiding from the Yukishimans,*" he said. "*She's a smart girl, she'll know to keep it secret. Also, tell her she has a second cousin on the way.*"

"*You're a father?*"

"*Once I started laying with Vi'kara, I couldn't stop,*" Rowyn admitted with a laugh.

"*I'm happy for you. I wish you good fortune in your coming life, Rowyn Khanas,*" Weil said, and with Razarkha feeding the crabs, he stepped into his path back to Moonstone.

\* \* \*

Though spring had allegedly arrived, Moonstone's air felt colder than ever. Commoners had begun their return to the city, with Rarakhi's Khanas comrades being amongst the first. The Boss's body was found in Castle Selenia's courtyard, broken from a fall, and had been swiftly returned to his family home in a closed casket.

Rakh's relatively intact corpse lay encased in a pine box, suspended above an as-yet-unlit pyre beyond the castle gates while an Eternalist priest rambled about the importance of virtue in life in service of a second, everlasting life. Gathered for the occasion were Erwyn, Tei, Irikhos Foenaxas, his Selenia lover, and surprisingly, the former lady, Kagura Selenia.

The Boss had already been given a necromantic funeral, with Plutera's only comfort coming in the form of Tei's Ilazari acquaintance informing her of Rowyn's survival. As Rarakhi's hand squeezed his love's, he couldn't help but think he didn't deserve consolation. Plutera and the Boss loved each other so much that even the undead gardeners envied them, yet all Rarakhi could offer were mild words and embraces.

Meanwhile, he'd done nothing but complain about his own father. What right did he have to Plutera's kindness, or every passing Khanas man's commiserations? For all they knew, he hated his father, and as much as Rarakhi didn't want to admit it, if his father was alive, he'd have acted as distant as always. The Eternalist priest finished droning and gestured towards the crowd, making one last announcement.

"Wisdom Erwyn Yagaska has agreed to light the pyre for his dear friend and wishes to say some words regarding the late Count Fel'thuz."

"Thank you," Erwyn Yagaska said, clinging to a set of papers in one hand while he fretted over his monocle with his other. Once he took his position by the pyre, he continued. "I won't claim that Rakh was a perfect man. He always made decisions that he hoped would benefit those less fortunate than him, but he was regularly mistaken.

"He wrongly took pity on his sister-wife, leading to a crisis we're still recovering from. He regularly antagonised key allies such as the Church of Eternity in the hopes of protecting those he deemed more worthy of his aid. His path was fraught with crises, but he never hid from the consequences of his actions. He fought to repair his relationship with his son, he fought for Moonstone's assistance regarding the Ashglass rapeworm epidemic, and he fought to ensure the safe evacuation of the common man in Moonstone.

"His sister's return was a crisis caused by his misguided mercy, but he made sure that if anyone was put at risk, it was himself most of all. He died at his sister's hand to buy the time Moonstone needed to be liberated, and while the vanquishing of his older sister ultimately fell to his brave son, he fought to the death to us all from her madness. If only he'd put an end to it sooner. I'll miss you, Rakh. I'm sorry I couldn't prevent your stubbornness."

The high elven wisdom folded his papers and hid them in his waistcoat pocket, before turning to one of the many priests milling about the area. The holy man lit a torch on a nearby brazier, then handed it to Erwyn, who took a deep breath before lighting the pyre. The oil-covered pile steadily but unquenchably consumed itself, its growing flames licking Rakh's casket until it, too, started to blaze. Rarakhi at the strange artefact the Ilazari had thrown his way. Despite the incomprehensible mutters from the crystal containing a marked tension, something about it felt familiar, and so he'd held it over the days following his father's death. Even as his father's body immolated, the soulstealer's mutters kept him from weeping.

"It's all right if you want to cry," Plutera whispered. "You'll always be my strong ghost."

"It's fine," Rarakhi mumbled. "It's as though my dad's here, letting me know the future's safe. Telling his bitch of a sister to shut up."

Plutera released his hand. "I'm sure that's the case."

Rarakhi's mother was beside him, her face hidden, but her tears visible. Even the retired idiot lady was sniffling, going on about the moon for reasons unknown. Erwyn stayed as close to the pyre as the priests allowed him, before returning to the crowd, his resolute expression wavering. He approached Rarakhi and Tei, then handed them a piece of paper each.

"Rakh wrote these," Erwyn said. "In case he died."

Tei spoke first, despite the sobs distorting her words. "He wrote me a letter, even though his writing hand was gone? I'll— I'll always treasure it, as I should have treasured him before he— he— I'm a terrible sister."

With those words, Tei vanished, leaving Rarakhi to unfold his own letter. Its hand was jagged and scrambled, but just about legible.

*Dear Rarakhi,*

*If you're reading this, then I died before I was able to see you mature into a man grown. I'm sorry for everything I've put you through. If I never entered your life, you'd be free of the conflicted feelings you are no doubt experiencing. I want you to know that it's all right to be confused about how you feel about me. I wasn't your father for most of your life, and I know I wasn't always effective at connecting with you.*

*I'm sorry I argued with you before sending you off. I'm sorry I hid myself as I watched your train leave. I didn't want you to think I was giving you a farewell you didn't want from me, but looking back, I was a fool. Life is too short to leave love, even unrequited love, unshared. Know this, Rarakhi; while I cannot force you to look upon me fondly, I will always be proud of you.*

*If you choose to accept the Fel'thuz name despite my passing, then I wish you every success advising Lady Selenia. If you abandon it, then I wish you success in your continued forging of an independent path free of my baggage. Whichever choice you make, know that you were beloved to me. I'm sorry I wasn't here for more of your life.*

*With love,*
*Your father.*

Once Rarakhi's eyes were done scanning the page, they failed completely, clouded by waters that refused to be dammed. He folded the paper carefully, then hid it in his inner pocket. He kissed Plutera's forehead, then ran beyond the crowd, calling to the air itself.

"*Mum!* Show yourself, I don't want to cry alone."

Abruptly, something took hold of his legs. Tei revealed itself, and though she only came up to his waist, he squeezed her as though she was the size of Bloodmetal.

"I'm sorry I fled," Tei mumbled.

"I fled from you too," Rarakhi said with a broken laugh. "Guess I got my running skills from my mum's side."

"Your father always ran *into* danger. I just avoided everything until it was too late. I don't want to be alone while I'm like this, Rara."

"Neither do I," Rarakhi admitted. "If you'll have us, me an' Plutera could live with you for a while."

Tei paused. "I'd like that."

\* \* \*

Irikhos still wasn't used to his eyepatch, and he was clad in striking black-and-red finery, there was no hiding the fact he was an eye short. He fixed his gold-and-red cravat and turned to Torawyn, who he'd been sharing a room with throughout the return of Moonstone's peasants. She was fixing a long, Elarondian-styled dress in the blues and silvers of the Selenias, complete with a corset that pushed up what little bust she had. She had a tricorn hat made ahead of time and had spent half her time in front of the mirror putting it on, then removing it.

"I think a hat would look good, but what if it comes off as too Elarondian? I know I've got an accent, and the people may pick up on it if I go with the hat," she muttered to herself.

"My brother-in-law wears a tricorn as a *man,* and he's accepted as the lord consort of Ashglass. Appearing 'too Elarondian' isn't anything to fear."

"It is when I've appeared from nowhere," Torawyn said. "How can I lay claim to these people if I don't come off as authentically Arkheran?"

Irikhos moved over to Torawyn and massaged her bare shoulders. "Just stay calm, look at Erwyn's notes if you need to, and speak with sincerity."

Torawyn's face reddened, and she smiled. "If you were the lord in your own right, you'd succeed easily. It's a shame this falls to me."

"If I were in your position I'd be just as nervous," Irikhos assured her. "The only reason I'm calm is 'cause I'm not giving the speech."

"Are you looking forward to seeing your family again?"

"More than anything," Irikhos admitted. "Speaking of which, I should probably head out to join them in the stands before you leave the castle."

Just as Irikhos made to leave their room, Tor took hold of his sleeve.

"Remember your part in this."

"Of course," Irikhos replied with a smile. "All I need to do is say 'yes'."

"It's a little more than that, but— oh, go on, I won't keep you from your sister."

With a nod, Irikhos headed into Castle Selenia's halls, down what felt like a thousand staircases, and beyond the castle grounds. The streets weren't quite bustling, but seeing peasants going about their affairs was a pleasant change from the aggressive overcrowding of Snowy Bank and the terror-stricken streets of Ashglass. A podium had been set up in the city square, with much of the space being reserved for commoners. Two stands lay beyond the crowds; one contained the blonde, olive-skinned human nobility of the Rainbow Fort and other minor vassals, and the other contained the Foenaxases and their guardsmen alone.

Even from afar, the children warmed Irikhos's heart. He shoved through the crowds, shimmied past the guards, and climbed up, expecting to call to his kin. Instead, the moment he neared the stand's lowest seats, he was leapt at by Darkhal and Irigax, his two youngest nephews. While they held him in place, Lexana waved from her seat, revealing Moryx and Morganix sitting either side of her.

"Uncle Iri, Uncle Iri, we saved you a seat. Morganix said that as the oldest he should sit next to you."

Morganix grinned. "I've been practising my swordplay. I think I can beat you now."

"Is that so?" Irikhos asked. "Once we're done listening to this speech, we'll have to buy some sparring swords and put those words to the test."

Mor'kha was behind her three eldest children, weeping with joy while her dandy husband whispered something to her. Whatever Solyx said forced her out of her seat to meet him. Even with her two youngest clinging to him, she brought Irikhos into an embrace that he readily returned.

"I heard about your fight with the half-daemon," she said, keeping her grip tight. "I prayed night and day to prevent your wounds from festering, and the God of Renewal is good."

Despite knowing that Erwyn Yagaska was the one who truly deserved thanks for his recovery, Irikhos was glad his sister was back to her steadfast, faithful self.

"The God of Renewal would never refuse His most dedicated servant."

Mor'kha chuckled. "Claiming such a title is a mite blasphemous, but I accept the compliment. You're here, and that's what's important. Magaral drew a picture for you, I've kept it safe in Ashglass."

"I can't wait to see it," Irikhos said.

Before the conversation could continue, a blaring fanfare deafened the city square's residents, expectation alone forcing Irikhos into his seat. Wisdom Erwyn's voice rang out shortly after, his tone surprisingly level given he'd done nothing but work and weep since Count Rakh's funeral.

"All remain silent for Overlady Torawyn Selenia!"

A second fanfare followed, during which Tor walked towards the podium, flanked by a squad of armoured guardsmen. While her willowy nature was evident even from a distance, her clothes and hat had done wonders for her form. She wasn't exactly intimidating, but she lacked the fragility she often conveyed.

"People of Moonstone, and nobility of the Forests of Winter, let me be the first to thank you for coming all this way just to hear me speak. While I've been acting as Moonstone's lady for a while, this is the first time I've addressed the public as a ruling noblewoman.

"The Forests of Winter have been struck by crisis after crisis, some inevitable, some avoidable. The rapeworm epidemic of Ashglass, the flight of Amerei Gemcutter, and of course, the return of Rakh Fel'thuz's older sister, along with my— my younger sister. I can understand why, in such a situation, you may have doubts about me, another Selenia, ruling over you, and have even more scepticism regarding Fel'thuz influence.

"I shall not appeal to tradition, nor birthright, as I am representative of neither. My older sister, Kagura, would be the ruler if all were according to birthright, and I would be seeking a high elf of similar standing if I clung to tradition. Even Rakh's legitimised son, Rarakhi, has turned his back on his family's inherited position as advisors to the Selenia family. My rule will not be more of the same.

"I was once a doctor, working in a Soltelle-led nation that didn't care about my upbringing. I cannot promise that I was born to rule, but I can assure you I'll listen to the educated opinions of Wisdom Erwyn and my council members. In addition, I would like to show, in the eyes of all, my disregard for the laughable notions of purity and tradition that have plagued Fel'thuz and Selenia alike for so long. Irikhos Foenaxas, are you in this audience?"

This was Irikhos's moment. He stood and projected his voice as much as elvenly possible.

"I am here, and happy to serve my overlady."

"Our fathers shared a controversial notion for what constituted a good political match. They didn't care about our racial differences and were happy to match you with my younger sister. Though she proved to be tyrannical, I will not let our fathers' progressive hopes to be dashed. If you'll have me, I would like to arrange a betrothal between you and me. Do you accept?"

Irikhos stuck to his script. "For the stability of the province, I accept."

Torawyn stammered before continuing. "One day, Arkhera will lose the need for notions such as nobility, purity, and inheritance. I cannot guarantee I'll live to see that day, I hope to die knowing that I helped it arrive. Today, we bid farewell to the crises of the past, and warmly greet a tomorrow with no bounds!"

While the crowd was slow to start, the city square became overtaken with roaring applause. Irikhos's lady sister mussed his hair, Solyx mockingly welcomed him to married life, and Morganix was already asking him for a little cousin. Despite everything he'd gone through, self-inflicted or otherwise, Irikhos wanted to believe in Tor's speech. Its topics may have been vague, its 'surprise' betrothal may have been staged, but the Forests of Winter finally seemed ready to thaw from its permafrost of despair.

# Epilogue

Parakos was the same as ever; gargoyles perched upon flat-roofed buildings, their features blunted by winds and millennia. Dust shifted with every step Antique took, and as a flare skink set itself alight and skittered away, he smiled, grateful for his home. The orcish adventurer would never be content to stay in one place, but there was something about having a place to regularly return to that he couldn't fully detach from.

Night was falling upon Arkhera's oldest city, and his backpack grew heavy. His thick, hairy legs pushed him through Parakos's mean streets, then south towards his manor, lying just beyond the Yookietown. It was a relatively small brick-and-mortar affair, its only exceptional feature being a vault containing the treasures he was unwilling to sell. Still, the property's size combined with his frequent adventures had forced him to hire a maid and a couple of guards, along with an accountant to ensure the former three were properly paid.

Antique knocked on his own door and, after a short wait, removed his backpack. Just as he retrieved his key, the door opened, revealing an orcish woman in a simple, black dress that let her fur flow mostly free. Her large, dark eyes glinted as she saw Antique, and she backed from the doorway.

"Mr Antique, I didn't expect you to be back so soon!" Vaultduster said.

"Yeah, exploring the Yukishiman wilds didn't go as planned. Had to help find some runaway I enabled," Antique said, removing his khaki shirt and handing it to his maid. "I helped this little girl run away to Midori Sora, then it turns out she was a bloody noblewoman's daughter. Long story short, the guy looking for her roped me into his adventure."

"Ah, so no new treasures?" the maid asked. "That's a shame."

Antique took a jar of Oukinese candied plums from his backpack. "Don't worry, I didn't forget you and the boys. The forest elves of Oukina Mori are frightening, but their confectionary is some of the finest in the world. I s'pose the secret to their unity is sweets."

Vaultduster hung his shirt on a coat-hanger, then gingerly brought her hand towards the jar. "May I?"

"No, I brought these plums back just so I could talk about them in front of you while you cry. Go on, silly, they won't bite."

The maid unscrewed the lid, took a plum out, then devoured the entire fruit. Antique frowned, shut the door, and changed his tone.

"You've been eating properly, haven't you?"

"Well— father's been particularly demanding lately, and—"

"Me and your father are going to have words if this keeps up. Your salary is for *you,* am I understood?" Antique said.

"It's not his fault his back's crooked," Vaultduster began.

"Plenty of folks with crooked backs get by without stealing their children's salaries. Stand up for yourself or I'll stand up for you, and for your father's sake, I hope it doesn't come to that," Antique said. "Keep the jar to yourself, there's more stuff for the boys in the bag. Speaking of which, go ahead and unpack it. If you don't know where to put something, just leave it on the coffee table. I'm going to say hello to my babies."

"Of course," Vaultduster said, curtseying and allowing him to move on.

Shirtless and free of the burden he carried everywhere, Antique was able to slow his pace for once, practically moseying through his orc-sized halls until he reached a vault door guarded by two Yukishiman humans, one the typical blonde and freckly sort, the other possessing the black hair, pale skin and folded eyes of an Ikinamese expatriate. Both wielded the most advanced Soltelle firearms legally distributed to non-Soltelle military, and always wore masks of professional neutrality.

"Hey, boys," Antique said. "Bought some Elarondian vintage, they're selling it by the bottle in Wrenfall these days. Figured you might want some."

"We'd never drink on the job, sir," Asahi, the blonde one, said.

"Indeed, our resolve has not wavered in your absence," Shou-Wan, the black-haired one said.

"Then drink off the job," Antique said, pointing his thumb over his shoulder. "Go on, I'm home, get some rest."

Asahi gave Antique a respectful bow, and Shou-Wan charged from his post, rushing upstairs and making a loud groan of relief from an echoing room. The orc shrugged and turned to the Yookie human.

"All right, Asahi, off with you. I got to spend some time with my babies."

"Yessir."

Once he was gone, Antique rolled the vault's numeric locking mechanism to the correct combination; the year of his first quest for the Na'liman crystal skulls. The door opened, revealing a set of shelves and glass cases, all for the beauties he couldn't part with no matter how much he was offered.

Upon stands were various Galdusian staffs, framed upon the wall was a coloured photograph of Empress Marya Soltelle shortly after she'd bought a dragon horn cup he'd found in Nandani, and along the shelves were everything from long-disused Nuish spittoons to Madaki scrolls from before their mass conversion to monotheism. Most treasured of all were seven small pedestals, three of which had been filled.

The leftmost pedestal bore the Soulstealer of Obsession, a pink-and-red crystalline ladle, the middle one had the Soulstealer of Emptiness, a similar, yellow-and-blue structure, and rightmost had the Soulstealer of Vanity, whose colours were purple and blue. Antique sighed and shook his head. It was foolish of him to think that he'd acquire all seven, but given he'd found three before he was thirty, he'd done all right. A knock echoed through his house, snapping him from his adoration, and he swiftly left his vault, slamming the door behind him.

"Vaultduster, go ahead an' open the door," Antique commanded as he approached.

When he reached the door, he found a spellbinder boy, a necromantic girl, and some strange being that resembled a gnome-spellbinder hybrid. Antique briefly shuddered at the thought of the woman's conception, before taking over for Vaultduster.

"Hey there, friends, what's this visit in aid of? If you're after artefacts, sorry, none around for sale right now," Antique said. "Hold on, you're that Fel'thuz guy, aren't you? I thought he died. Sorry, didn't get to follow the Moonstone crises all that closely."

"I'm his son," the boy said, then stuck his hand in his coat's inner pockets. He pulled out a crystalline ladle of familiar design, coloured aqua, blue, and red. "I was the one to kill my aunt, and she was wielding this—"

"A *soulstealer?*" Antique blurted, pushing past Vaultduster before turning back to her. "Sorry, 'duster, I didn't mean to— still, that's genuine, isn't it?"

"I think so. My aunt was shooting light from it," the young man said. "And when I hold it, it's as though my father's whispering to me, along with something extremely angry."

"By your aunt, you mean Razarkha Fel'thuz, right?" Antique said, resting his back on the doorway. "I suppose the short woman with you is Tei. As for the necromancer, sorry, haven't a clue."

The necromantic girl curtsied. "Plutera Khanas, keeper of the old ways."

"Antique, keeper of old things," he replied. "I remember meeting Razarkha once, before she was exiled. She wanted to buy a soulstealer, and I told 'er it wasn't for sale. Funny that she ended up bringing one to me in the end. May I hold it?"

"Sure, you can have it," Rarakhi Fel'thuz said, handing it over. "It's as though my dad's telling me it's time to let go."

Antique smothered the artefact with his massive hand, closing his eyes to hear the voice of its former owner. Instead of a simple, resentful wind, there was an outright maelstrom of bickering exuding from the magical device.

"Sounds parental, all right."

"Is that a good thing?" Rarakhi asked.

"Fuck no, there's a reason I ran away and became an adventurer! Seems like something special's happening in this soulstealer. Most former wielders eventually figure out people can't properly understand 'em, but this one's very talkative."

"Is it possible there could be two souls sharing it?" Tei Fel'thuz asked.

"I mean, it's Sovereign tech. That god isn't known for rigid rules. He takes matters case by case," Antique explained. "All right, how much you want for it?"

"You can have it," Rarakhi insisted. "No price."

"But this is— look, a shrewd buyer is supposed to downplay these sorts of things, but once I own this soulstealer I'll have most of 'em. Four out of seven. I can't accept it for free."

"Fine, how about a gold, then?" Rarakhi said, before crouching to listen to something Tei was whispering. "Actually, fifty gold."

Antique barely concealed his smirk. "Done. Let me write you a cheque, I'm with the Bank of Parakos, they'll know my signature when they see it. Vaultduster, get me my chequebook and pen!"

"At once," the maid said, rushing off.

"Now, how'd you spell your name? Rarakhi with a 'kh', yeah?" Antique clarified.

"Yeah, I think so, though everyone but my family pronounces it with a hard 'k'. Just what it is, I guess," the boy said with a shrug.

"And your noble name's Fel'thuz, same as your dad?"

This caused the young man to hesitate. "Yeah."

Silence lingered until Vaultduster returned with the requested items. Antique was quick to write a cheque up, signed his name, and numbered fifty gold as the amount given. He passed the paper to the boy, then grinned.

"Don't drop that, now, it's enough to buy you a small house. Perhaps. I'm not sure how Arkheran property prices have changed since I last bought a home," Antique said.

"Fifty isn't enough for anything decent these days, and the prices appear to be forever increasing," Plutera broke in. "I hope to take advantage of that sometime soon."

"A businesswoman from a young age," Antique remarked, mussing Rarakhi's hair. "Don't let her get away, you hear? Marriage ain't for everyone, but if you're not an adventurer like me, you have no excuse."

"Thanks, but we're betrothed already. Enjoy your rock," Rarakhi said with a shrug.

Antique watched the trio of serpentine humanoids leave, and once his door was safely shut, roared loudly enough that Vaultduster backed away from him.

"*Yes!* Only fifty gold, did you see that, 'duster? Only fifty!"

"Not to trample on your triumph, Mr Antique, but that youth was going to give it away for free."

"Like I was going to risk them coming back later claiming I stiffed them," Antique said with a laugh. "Time to add this baby to the family."

Before Vaultduster could respond, Antique bounded towards his vault, hurriedly rolled in the combination, and slowed his movements by the time he'd opened the door. Just as he made to place the soulstealer down, he heard an all-too-familiar voice.

**"Should I bother asking?"**

"Still not interested, Sovvy."

**"Suit yourself."**

With that, he pondered over the device, then deduced it was likely the Soulstealer of Craving. He placed it left of the Soulstealer of Emptiness, giving it a pat before he let go.

"I'll have to find the Soulstealer of Ruination to keep things symmetrical," he remarked, then turned away from his collection. "See you around, babies."

\* \* \*

In the darkness of Antique's vault, the Soulstealer of Craving lay beside its three siblings. Within, two disembodied voices began to chatter. The feminine, ever the instigator, struck first.

*"Why didn't you try to stop him? You were getting through to that idiotic brat, why didn't you persuade him to become a wielder?"*

*"That 'idiotic brat' is my son,"* a masculine voice responded. *"All I could do was comfort him—"*

*"Because you never tried anything else! Now we're going to rot in this imbecilic orc's vault for the rest of time!"*

*"Oh, I'm sorry, was I supposed to turn my son into what you wound up as before your death? Frankly, I'd rather rot in a vault until this orc dies than prevent my son from living his best life."*

The feminine voice strained itself. *"No, no, this can't be happening. I'm going to be stuck here for centuries with you!"*

*"If it's any consolation, I'll be suffering too. I'm sure you don't need a reminder that you were, perhaps, the worst sister of all time."*

*"Oh, go die a second time."*

For a moment, the masculine voice allowed silence to mature within the soulstealer's gemlike confines. *"Seeing as we're going to be stuck here for a while, why don't we use this time constructively?"*

"Constructively? *What constructive endeavours are there for entrapped souls?"*

*"Well, by some twist of fate or dark divine humour, we have each other. Why don't we talk about what happened, and make sense of it together before a new wielder finds us?"*

The feminine voice hesitated. *"Fine, I'll go first. I'll tell you everything from my perspective. No interruptions, you'll shut up and let me talk, am I understood?"*

*"You are. Start from the beginning."*

# Afterword from the Sovereign

It appears you've read all the way through this three-part account of Razarkha Fel'thuz's journey, as well as her less notable brother's drama. While I cannot tell you the source of these tales, save that they appear to be some extra-cosmic being able to latch itself onto the thoughts and feelings of any given person, I'm glad that the story has been preserved. Alas, it appears their endeavours have come to an end, and it falls to me, the Sovereign, to let the readers of these accounts know what happened to the various interesting mortals that caught the narrative's eye over the course of Razarkha's extended tantrum.

Rowyn Khanas has found a new home in Ilazar; even as Anya Kasparov attempts to control the Isle of Dreams' capital, there are always street fights, which means, as a medic, Khanas is never wanting for work. Between him performing genuine healing and his lover, Vi'kara, hawking false remedies, they have bought a house, which is just as well, given they have a child on the way. I shall assign it a new soul shortly.

Speaking of Ilazar, it appears Anya Kasparov has continued to evade death. Her abominable practice shall not go unpunished; it's simple godly knowledge that all souls, given enough time, will be sapped of desire, individuality, and hope. For now, she continues to puppeteer War'mal in a sick mockery of leadership, but a time will come where she wishes she rejected Baron Oswyk's ascension stone.

Erwyn Yagaska has continued his work as a wisdom, serving Torawyn Selenia to the best of his ability. Due to Torawyn not requiring the same level of hand-holding her older sister did, Erwyn has been freer to visit Starfall to meet up with his niece, Strakha Safiros. He's even taken on a novice, a bright high elven fellow named Jarvos who is quickly picking up skills in biology, though his diplomatic restraint still needs work.

Speaking of Torawyn, she and Irikhos married to little fanfare by Arkheran overlord standards. They're not eager to have children, despite young Morganix Foenaxas's urgings, and are mostly focused on rebuilding the Forests of Winter following the repeated crises the province has suffered. Though Yarawyn Selenia's body was never recovered, the two have privately set up a grave beyond Moonstone's walls. Both have accepted that while they cannot grieve the monster Yarawyn became, they can grieve the girl who'd vanished over her exile in Elarond. It's an amusing abstraction, but that's what mortals excel at.

The stupid sister, former Lady Kagura Selenia, has been living a carefree life in the Great Vale ever since attending her sister's wedding. She's the favourite model of impressionist painter Eiji Hibari, and despite the artist having plainly fallen for her, she has remained amusingly oblivious to his advances. Once the fool figures out she prefers women, it's likely her prominence in his works will decrease, but for the time being, she is Hibari's muse, her pretty face likely to infest local galleries for years to come.

Meanwhile, Ashglass has been growing more religiously diverse than Lady Mor'kha Foenaxas would like. However, seeing as the faith-polluting Eternalists were also the men who helped rebuild her city, she's grown to begrudgingly tolerate them, same as she tolerates her lord consort. The Foenaxas children are regular visitors of Moonstone now that their uncle is the overlady's husband, and though she fears their drifting from Renewalism, Morganix, at the very least, has been quick to assure his mother that his faith is strong.

Melancholy left copies of her notes on the cure to rapeworm in the hands of Wisdom Khalver Veritas, and following that, she left Ashglass, presumably to move onto the next settlement affected by an epidemic. She has recently received a summons from the Royal Court, supposedly to reward her for her hard work in Ashglass, but she's proven too paranoid to accept the invitation, especially when there are people to cure.

Duncan Godswater was temporarily arrested by the Royal Electorate's forces when they finally got around to addressing the crises in the south. Petyr Godswater was also put into royal custody, and so Shiloh Godspawn was placed as interim Lord of Godswater while the other Godswaters were interrogated. With the testimony of Duncan, Rosaline, Shiloh, and Gerold, along with countless curiously free-minded women who'd once lay in the apostle's thrall, Petyr Godswater was publicly convicted of numerous counts of rape, corruption, and conspiracy to commit murder.

My dear child of wrath, Sarcet, better known by mortals as Prince Komekk Axol, personally severed the head of Petyr Godswater. While Sarcet will receive his soul once he dies and becomes a warden, in the meantime, he's in my hands, and with the conspicuous lack of lust wardens in the Underworld, I took the liberty of forcibly converting Petyr's soul into a nymph. When the lusty souls of the Underworld desire a prostitute, Petyr's soul will transform into a mate of their choice. Despite how much he disregarded the consent of the women he ensnared, he appears to be quite miserable being a voiceless, helpless sex object.

Duncan, meanwhile, has had his exile pardoned by King Landon Shearwater, and while he has been disinherited from Godswater on account of his immortality disrupting succession law, he floats resolute as an advisor to Shiloh Godspawn. Rosaline, meanwhile, has left the city that brought her so much misery, along with Pleura, who stepped down from her position as High Ascetic of the Moon Man. She parted from her family with a generous inheritance and has bought a small plot of land by the Sunfort, a much more tolerant city. Together, they hope to become farmers, though it's likely Rosaline will need to get her electromancy under control before they start in earnest.

Darvith, my eldest and most despicable son, has been spending some quality time with me in the Underworld. He still hasn't found the humility to thank me for preserving a fraction of the souls Razarkha intended to annihilate; he's lucky to be a warden at all, yet he appears too affected by his own abilities even beyond death. As such, I regularly ensure he's humiliated in front of his assigned souls.

Another amusing game I've been playing in the Underworld pertains to the ever-lustful Consigliere Lesteris. He's been wandering about the lust-based regions for a while, without a warden to guide him. I have my plans, however. I shall send a beautiful, feminine envy warden his way, and let him experience true love. After that, I'll send another, dominant, masculine envy warden to show him what it's like to have it all taken away. I'm sure seeing as he spent his life doing the same, he won't mind my little prank.

Elki Kasparov's soul, meanwhile, is attempting to play the crime lord, but is having trouble competing with his fellow deceased mobsters. So many Ilazari die young and motivated; living long enough to grow complacent has left the fool ill-equipped for the anarchy my Underworld presents. Perhaps one day he can shed enough pride to become a subordinate to his far superior great-grandfather, Aleksei Kasparov, but for now, he's trying and failing to rally his late sons and grandsons for a gang war he'll never win. Not that I let *any* faction win permanently.

Ariel of Demidium, despite her shattering at the hands of Razarkha, brought herself back together. With the assistance of Ferrus and her devotees, she has resumed her role as a bringer of hope to the coastal city of Ma-Hith. It's enough to make me sick to my non-existent stomach, but I'm sure when somebody finally finds a way to kill her, the Mother will enjoy having her soul. She isn't welcome in the Underworld.

The Sons of Sula have mostly receded as a political group due to Darvith's fatal bout of arrogance, being fully driven from Nortez and steadily becoming an irrelevant conservative group even by Sulari standards. Imperial Engineer Hildegard Swan, content with the progress of the Soltelle Empire's Galdusian campaign, has returned to the Soltelle capital, Wrenfall, and has continued work on an abominable, terrifying weapon: The threadbomb.

Naas'khar managed to, through steady absorption of rabbits, shadowcats, and wolves, return to a regular humanoid size. Unable to face his former love, he instead took Tei Fel'thuz's advice, and reached the daemonic settlement known as the City of False Faces. His mostly daemon-like form has allowed him to be accepted amongst its denizens, and while he shall no doubt grieve for years, there is still hope for the wretch.

Speaking of daemons, Weil of Zemelnya, following his rejection of my kind offer, retreated to Deathsport with the Riversongs. He is learning the Common Tongue and is a regular guest singer at the Carminium Music Hall, starring alongside his daemonic friends. It appears Luna Riversong has roped him into being the next in her long line of mortal lovers. Along with earning money through performance, he appears to be working on numerous Ilazari-style gravestones, carving them, then transporting them to the Sudovykly Cliffs. While his notion of penance is absurd, absurdity is what makes mortals amusing.

Speaking of rejections, I've not forgotten about Rarakhi Fel'thuz. While his love, Plutera, has expressed interest in continuing her father's criminal empire, both she and him have taken a break, staying with Tei Fel'thuz out of choice. Naturally, the Royal Looking Glass has a few things to say on being related to an organised criminal, so it's uncertain whether Plutera will stay true to her father's nature or take a different path.

Rarakhi, meanwhile, has chosen to set aside the baggage his father wished to burden him with, happy to follow his betrothed no matter which path she takes. All he knows for sure is that he doesn't want to be an adviser to a woman twice his age. It appears that while he had enough individuality to reject my offer of soulstealer ownership, he's willing to let his lover rule his life.

As for the Soulstealer of Craving, it's gathering dust in Antique of Parakos's vault, with a certain pair of souls roiling about within. Orcs don't live forever, of course, and one day, his accumulated soulstealers will find new wielders. When the Soulstealer of Craving's next wielder dies, I look forward to welcoming Razarkha and Rakh to the Underworld. Even I don't know what state their souls will be in after spending so much time together.

Well, this mortal drama has been interesting to me, and I hope it was for you too, reader of this afterword. May you, through your powerful individualism, bend whichever world you reside in to your will.

With divine providence,
The Sovereign

# Appendices

# Appendix I: Map of the World

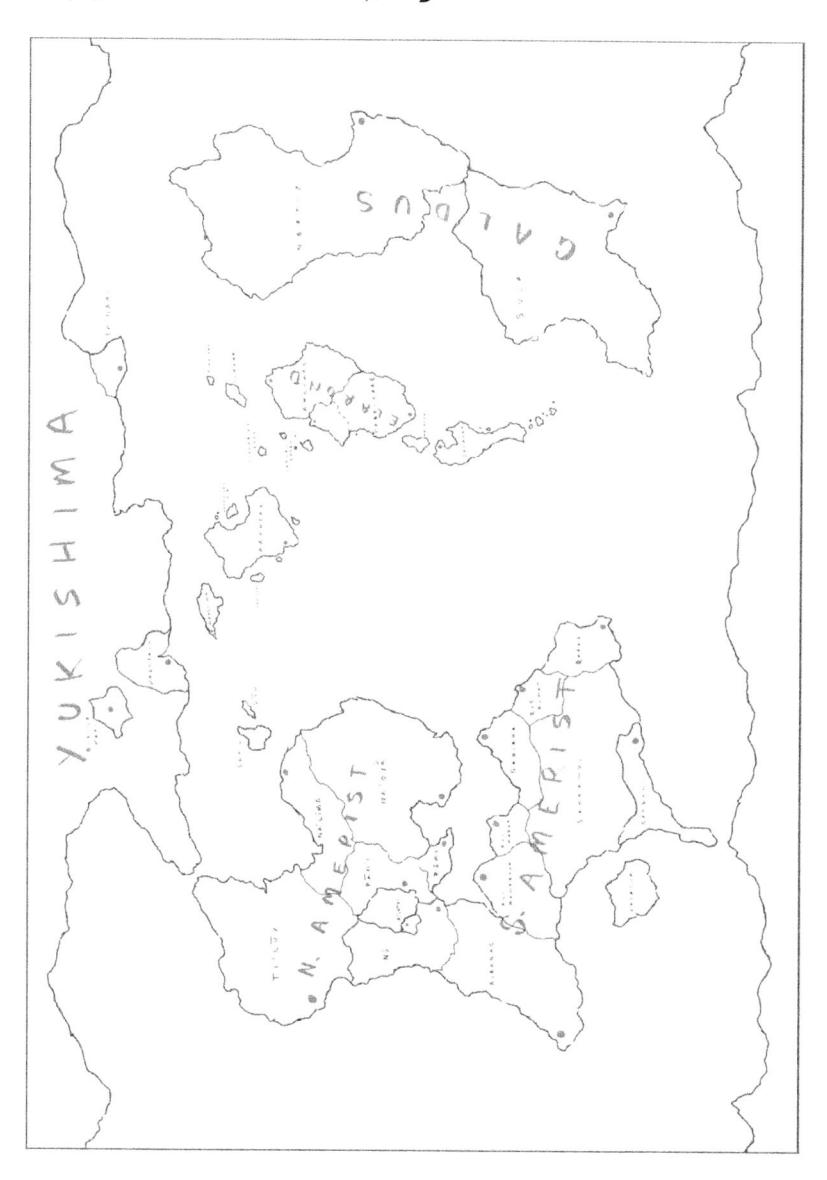

# Appendix II: Races of the World

**Humans:** Humanoids much like the reader of this novel. Capable of magic in semi-rare cases, tend to be hairier than most other races save orcs. Populate most of the world and come in a variety of colours and cultures.

**Elves:** Beautiful, tall, dextrous humanoids who have long, pointed ears, youthful looks, and tend towards being non-magical. They have multiple subraces and cultures, such as pale-skinned high elves, charcoal-skinned dark elves, diminutive and red-haired forest elves, and the highly magical, mostly identical Kakajuan elves. Like humans, their presence is widespread.

**Spellbinders:** Willowy, pale, small-nosed humanoids who, while fragile, perform their natural magic with the same ease as breathing. They have long, rat-like tails and two primary cultures: The conservative, disciplined Galdusians and the bold, expressive Ilazari, both of which also populate Arkhera.

**Necromancers:** Cousins to the spellbinders, they are slightly shorter in both stature and tail length. Their magic, as their moniker implies, largely centres around control of the dead. An endangered race that is largely endemic to Galdus and Arkhera.

**Orcs:** Non-magical, apelike humanoids whose body hair makes them resemble sentient yetis. They are the dominant natives of Arkhera; the land is named for the Old Orcish for 'Orc Home'. Despite their lack of magic, they are tall, strong, and surprisingly quick.

**Goblins:** Green-skinned, scaly, and short beings who have more in common with monkeys than the apes most humanoids resemble. Bearing protractible claws, they are gifted climbers with large eyes they use to see distances other races cannot. Native to Malassai, though a healthy population exists in Arkhera.

**Gnomes:** Short humanoids with highly light-sensitive, myopic eyes and a sense of hearing that enables them to hear infrasound, gnomes are well-adapted to life underground. Modern gnomes that work in above-ground cities tend to wear goggles or sunglasses to avoid retinal damage.

**Seers:** Diminutive, waifish people native to Sanguinas Isle named for their race's limited prescience. Their abilities usually manifest as visions, but others experience their abilities the same way other humanoids anticipate events. Though they've spread to mainland Arkhera, they are relatively endangered after enduring multiple genocides.

**Beastmasters:** An endangered humanoid race endemic to the Arkheran Isles. They can bond with animals and share minds with them, enabling a unique, collaborative approach to animal husbandry other humanoids can't achieve. Most exist in the Iron Hills of Arkhera and as tribal communities on the Isle of Wor'ghan.

Printed in Great Britain
by Amazon